CONSORT

OF THE

FEMALE PHARAOH

Hat-Shep-Sut, Senen-Mut

&

Egypt's 18th Dynasty

A Novel By

Eugene Stovall

Other Books By Eugene Stovall

Fiction
Frank Yerby: A Victim's Guilt
Blood And Brotherhood: A Novel Of Love In A Time Of Hate
The Idumean Covenant: A Novel Of The Fall Of Jerusalem
Cassandra's Curse: A Black Life In A Police State

Non-Fiction
Stovall's Guide To Media Pins
Stovall's Guide To Disney Pins Of The Twentieth Century

ISBN 978-0-9716691-5-4

Book design: Jim Bisakowski, bookdesign.ca

To Jennifer.
Who translated the first hieroglyphic centograph
From Dad

"The Sage, Senen-Mut, designed Hat-Shep-Sut's symbol to reveal the secrets of her reign. Senen-Mut's symbol appears on all Hat-Shep-Sut's statues, steles, monuments and temples. What Senen-Mut and Hat-Shep-Sut create together has never been seen before and has never been seen since."

"But Master, is not Senen-Mut's symbol merely a pun of Hat-Shep-Sut's name?"

"You should know, Initiate, that mysteries are hidden in many ways."

"I know that a mystery is a riddle."

"Then you must need no further instruction and already know the mystery of Senen-Mut's symbol."

"I *do* know the mystery of Senen-Mut's symbol, Master."

"Then tell it to me, Oh Initiate of the Outer Temple."

"*Who desecrated Hat-Shep-Sut's monuments, cartouches and even her sarcophagus and why?* is the mystery, Oh wise Master."

"Well, my young friend, you have outdone yourself."

"How so?"

"You promised me one mystery and have given me two."

Everything in the universe has a beginning and an end. Everyone who is born must die. Yet, human beings seem unaware of this simple truth and try to stand apart from the rest of universe.

Why do humans fear death so!

Is this not a mystery?

The ancient Egyptians were very clever. They lived in a *Garden of Eden*, but fashioned their society based upon a primordial fear of death. Their social classes, rituals and symbols of ancient Egypt had but one purpose: *cheating death.*

The world is not mysterious for modern man. He is far too civilized to turn his fear of death into a religion. Though modern man has overcome his own *fear of death,* his society is meant to inspire the fear of death in others. Modern civilization is so well organized around death that war has become a religion of *the new world order,* politics the art of getting the population to support the new religion and its practice is the extermination of the uncivilized. Amazingly, ancient Egypt, in the time of the *female* Pharaoh, Maat-Ka-Re Hat-Shep-Sut, was exactly the same.

Pharaoh Nefer-Kheperu-Ra Aa-Khuen-Aten, also known as Akhen-Aten, attempted to overthrow Egypt's ancient gods and establish the Aten as the one god who ruled over all the other gods. Many believe Akhen-Aten's revolt against the gods ended the period of the *lunar cult epoch* and inspired a new period of the *solar cult* epoch. But, of course, this is not true. After Pharaoh Akhen-Aten's death, Amen, as well as Ptah, Thoth, Isis, Hathor and all the other gods were reinstated. The Two-Lands had already entered the *epoch* of the *solar cult* and continues so until this day. Ancient Egypt entered the epoch of the *solar cult* hundred years earlier under the female Pharaoh Maat-Ka-Re Hat-Shep-Sut and her consort, Senen-Mut. It was they who began the war of *The Gods Against A God* and decided the destiny of the Eighteenth Dynasty.

Eugene Stovall

PROLOGUE

"**I** should like to know," asks Pharaoh Ka-Moses, "where is my strength when a bandit chief rules in Avaris and an African chief rules in Kush? Must I be hemmed in by an Asiatic in the north and a Nubian in the south?"

To the east and west, *Hapi* creates a majestic valley out of herself. *Hapi*, the god of the Nile, creates the black, fertile land that holds back Seth's burning deserts.

In the south, great cataracts divide the Nile River establishing the centuries-old boundary between Egypt and Nubia. The Nile flows *north* in a serpentine fashion from the cataracts of Upper Egypt where the land is narrow on the river, resembling the stem of a lotus plant. From the south the Nile flows north down to the Great Green Sea, feeding fertile lands and spreading out in the north like the beautiful bloom of a lotus flower. The great river delta of Lower Egypt broadens out into bountiful grasses, rich farmlands and reedy marshes. Hundreds of thousands of cubits of fertile soil in the Nile Delta produce a great abundance of everything good and bountiful and attract not only the Egyptian people, but also tribes of nomads from across the northern desert as well. Nomadic tribesmen migrate into the Nile delta from Palestine, Persia, Lebanon and Syria. Victims in their own land, these tribes of nomads settle into the lush Egyptian land and claim it as their own. The Egyptians call all those tribes crossing into Lower Egypt from the Sinai Desert to claim the land that *Hapi* has reserved for her people, *asiatics*.

Along the banks of the Nile, naked men toil at their *shadoofs* scooping up water from the river and pouring it into great canals. *Shadoofs* are great containers, balanced on long poles that swivel back and forth. These containers hold large amounts of water. The *shadoof* workers sing sad songs and chant in rhythm. Like all the gods, Hapi loves music. She allows their songs to ease their labor.

The *shadoof* workers do not complain about their miserable lives and arduous labor. They are happy to serve Pharaoh, to whom *Ra* gives power and *Hapi* gives riches. The priests teach the *shadoof* workers and everyone else in the Two-Lands that the sole purpose for their existence is to serve Pharaoh. As a reward to all who are obedient and serve Pharaoh the priests promise an afterlife where they may continue to be obedient and serve Pharaoh.

Pharaoh is personality, *par excellence*, and power in action. If Pharaoh runs, he is the perfect symbol of human movement. If Pharaoh shoots an arrow, he personifies the principle of force. At the helm of his royal barge, Pharaoh is the principle of control. When he uses his enemy as a footstool, Pharaoh shows his power to control hostile forces. Pharaoh is the everlasting idea incarnate in action; he personifies human existence.

Pharaoh owns the Two-Lands of Upper and Lower Egypt. He owns everything on, over and in the land. Every person living in the Two-Lands of Upper and Lower Egypt belongs to Pharaoh. Pharaoh is the Supreme Ruler; he is the Chief Priest; he is the Civil Administrator; he is the Chief Justice and he is the Army's Supreme Commander.

The Two Lands are divided into forty-two nomes and ruled over by nomarchs, responsible for collecting Pharaoh's revenues and administering Pharaoh's justice. Nomarchs exercise absolute

Eugene Stovall

power and administrative authority over their lands, villages and towns in the name of Pharaoh. Only the priests claim independence from Pharaoh's will. The priests answer to the gods. The Supreme God in Egypt is Amen-Ra, the invisible manifestation of the raw absolute power of the universe over which, the Aten, the Sun, reigns in the absolute.

The Thirteenth Dynasty is swollen with riches and wealth. Thebes, its capital, is located *seventy iteru* south of the Great Green Sea, too far to hinder nomadic tribes wandering into Lower Egypt and seizing Hapi's fertile lands as their *own*. Not only is Pharaoh too far away, he is too weak and too comfortable to stop the flow of asiatic invaders bringing to Lower Egypt a foreign language, strange gods and an advanced military. Despite its wealth, the Thirteenth Dynasty collapses when the Hyksos colonize all the nomes of Lower Egypt. The Hyksos army possesses lightening quick chariots and superior bronze weapons. Hyksos fighters easily outmatch and slaughter each Egyptian soldier that Pharaoh sends against them. The Hyksos burn Pharaoh's cities, raze his temples, and enslave his women and children. Pharaoh's nomarchs in the north either 'kiss the ground' before their Hyksos masters or decorate Hyksos pikes with their heads. In Sais, Bubastis and especially Avaris, Hyksos warlords employ Egyptian scribes and administrators to insure that the bounty of Egypt is sent back to their king. The Hyksos build temples in each of the Egyptian cities to honor Astarte, the Hyksos goddess of war. The Hyksos force the people of Lower Egypt to worship Astarte and her consort, Seth. No longer does Amen-Ra rule the people of Lower Egypt.

For two hundred years the Hyksos rule Lower Egypt and allow a weak Pharaoh to remain in Thebes, ruling over a smaller and more humbled Upper Egypt. Then Apophis, the Hyksos king, sends a message to the Seventeenth Dynasty Pharaoh, Seqenen-Re Tau-aa.

"The hippopotamuses of the Nile, with their constant bellowing, disturb the sleep of my master, King Apophis," the messenger complains. "My master orders that Pharaoh deliver all the hippopotamuses of the Nile to the capital of my master. Furthermore, he desires that Pharaoh deliver the hippopotamuses to him personally and kiss the ground at his feet."

The gods rouse the Two-Lands to war. Pharaoh gathers his army and engages the asiatic invader in a titanic *War of Liberation*. Not only does Pharaoh Seqenen-Re Tau-aa lose his life on the battlefield but the next three pharaohs die in battle as well.

Pharaoh Ka-Moses stares at his military advisors, who remain silent.

"What serves this strength of mine when a Hyksos bandit resides in Avaris and a tribal chief occupies the Nubian Kush?" Pharaoh shouts at his Inner Council. "I can tolerate the pollution of these foreigners no longer."

Ka-Moses sends an army south to crush a Hyksos-inspired Nubian insurrection while he leads another army to blockade the Nile at Memphis, choking off Hyksos' access to Lake Moeris and fresh drinking water. When the Hyksos take refuge in the cities, Ka-Moses attacks their strongholds, one at a time. But in the terrible battle for Sais, Pharaoh Ka-Moses is pierced by a Hyksos arrow and falls mortally wounded.

Pharaoh's brother, Ah-Moses presses Egypt's *War of Liberation* for another six years. He attacks and captures numerous Hyksos' strongholds. Finally, only the great city of Avaris remains under Hyksos control. Rather than attacking this mighty stronghold directly, Ah-Moses crosses the Sinai desert and attacks the Hyksos fortress of *Sharuhen* in southwest Palestine. After annihilating the Hyksos garrison, Pharaoh captures the town of Gaza, seizing control of all military and trade routes into Egypt from Palestine. Pharaoh cuts off the Hyksos supply line to Avaris and mounts a siege. Within six months, the Hyksos lose control and Avaris collapses. Thus ends two centuries of asiatic domination over the fertile Egyptian delta. Out of the *War of National Liberation*, Ancient Egypt's Eighteenth Dynasty emerges as the world's military and economic superpower.

BOOK ONE

CHAPTER ONE

Senen-Mut pretends that he doesn't hear Amen-Nen-Het calling for him to return back to work. He hides in the tall reeds until his older brother wearies of searching for him and returns to the huts where the other workers prepare flax for the looms. Once his brother is gone, Senen-Mut slips out of his hiding place and returns to the pond to watch the fish swim from the canal to his feeder. Senen-Mut installed a wonderful feeding device that attracts fish into his pond and Ra-Moses' youngest son enjoys watching it work. Since the feeding device began attracting them into his pond, Senen-Mut's mother has never had so many fresh fish for her family's meals. Hat-Nofer is proud of her youngest son and it makes Amen-Nen-Het jealous.

None of Hat-Nofer's other children resent the special bond between her and her youngest son and neither should Amen-Nen-Het. He will inherit his father's entire estate, including the flax plantation that Ra-Moses operates for Amen-Nati, Nomarch of Wast. Ra-Moses, a veteran of Pharaoh Amen-Hotep's War of the Northern Nomes, has two hundred workers and an equal number of slaves growing and harvesting the flax that produces the finest linen in the Two-Lands. Amen-Nen-Het oversees the plantation and Senen-Mut's other two brothers and two sisters jump whenever Amen-Nen-Het barks. But not Senen-Mut.

Few commoners in Wast are as wealthy and important as Senen-Mut's father. And Ra-Moses believes Senen-Mut has great potential and hopes that one day his youngest son might become a scribe or even a priest. Ra-Moses is the *Confidant and Friend* of

Lord Amen-Nati, *Nomarch of Wast*. The Lord Amen-Nati agrees that Senen-Mut is *Wast's* smartest student.

Senen-Mut's family lives in Armant, a town in the southern part of the Nome of Wast, barely fifteen iteru south of Pharaoh's great capital of Thebes. Today Senen-Mut promised to bring his mother fish that she can trade in Armant's marketplace. Hat-Nofer has so often boasted of the fish that her son's pond produces that Armant's fishmongers challenge her to bring these 'wondrous' fish to the market so they can judge for themselves. Senen-Mut selects four fat cat fish, the kind that Egyptians love to bake, and two Nile perch that are rarely available. Egyptians prize Nile perch highly for their taste and the fishmongers would trade anything for them. Pleased with himself for having avoided his overbearing brother, Senen-Mut strings his fish on a line and races home to his mother.

Ra-Moses's family lives in a charming country home that sits off to the side of the great expanse of marsh where workers labor in fields of flax grown in patchwork sections. The workers harvest the flax, pulling the stalks up by the root from the marshy soil before the blue flowers have wilted. The work is difficult. Other workers gather the flax and tear the flowers from the stems by holding a wooden comb on the ground with one foot and pulling a flax bundle through the comb with both hands. The combed stalks are bundled and stored in huts to dry. Once the flax has dried, it is *rippled* to remove the seeds and *retted* with water to expose the inner fibers. Laborers remove the *tow* and *strick* from the flax stalk, cut it into equal lengths and prepare it to be spun into linen. Sitting some distance away from the flax fields, the family home is actually a compound fronted by a courtyard and bordered on three sides by gardens and orchards lined with sycamores and date palms. The main structure is a rectangular building with a second floor rising in the rear. This two-story building joins three additional buildings by a covered walkway. All the structures are plastered over to resemble the limestone exteriors that are found on their mansions and palaces of the nobility.

Inside Ra-Moses' home, the high walls are covered with *strick* and *tow* weaved in a wicker-basket pattern. Small windows high up on weaved walls are supported by brightly colored cornices. The great double doors that open inward from the courtyard are cut from a rare ebony tree of the type found only in Persia.

Senen-Mut enters his courtyard and sees his mother hovering over the cooking mound, overseeing the cooks who prepare the noonday meal. He smiles. But before he can run over and deliver the fish to his mother, his father appears from nowhere.

"What fish have you caught today, my son?"

"I have caught many fish for your wife and my mother, my father," Senen-Mut replies, keeping the fish from his father's sight.

"Have you caught any perch?" Ra-Moses asks.

"Yes father," Senen-Mut confesses. "I have caught two perch and several of the cat fish that you love, so well." Senen-Mut glances at his father's round belly.

"My son, take the perch and present them to our lord Amen-Nati's cook," Ra-Moses instructs.

"May the Lord Amen-Nati continue to bless us and keep us prosperous," the youngster mumbles, turning away before his father can see his disappointment. Slowly he walks over to his mother and her cooks. He passes Hat-Nofer the catfish.

"Oh! Senen-Mut!" Hat-Nofer exclaims. "These are the fattest catfish yet."

Then she gives her son a big hug and a kiss on his cheek.

"I have two perch, but Ra-Moses, your husband, directs me to give *your* perch to Lord Amen-Nati," Senen-Mut says, half expecting to see disappointment on his mother's face. But instead, Hat-Nofer gives a little laugh.

"My husband and your father wants the *Nomarch of Wast* to continue to favor us with his blessings," Hat-Nofer says, smiling.

Hat-Nofer understands her son's disappointment. Since he was a small child, Senen-Mut has always wanted to please her. His father always seemed so stern, so distant. It was like Ra-Moses' didn't love his wife, Senen-Mut's mother.

Eugene Stovall

And so Senen-Mut always does every thing he can to show his mother how much he loves her. It hurt Senen-Mut to give the coveted perch to Lord Amen-Nati's cook. What Senen-Mut does not realize is that his mother knows how much he loves her and she loves him as well. Hat-Nofer loves all six of her children, each in her own unique way. She even loves Amen-Nen-Het. Hat-Nofer's love is dispensed to her children not on the basis of merit but upon the basis of need. Many on Ra-Moses plantation hate Amen-Nen-Het for being the cruel taskmaster of *Wast's* largest and most important flax plantation. Thus of all of her children, Amen-Nen-Het needs Hat-Nofer most.

"I thought that you wanted to go to the marketplace today," Senen-Mut says. "You could have traded my perch for the image of Sekhmet that you've been wanting."

"My son," Hat-Nofer laughs, "those perch are more valuable to this household than an image of Sekhmet."

"But you told me that Sekhmet's image could overcome any affliction of the body caused by Seth," Senen-Mut persists. "Who knows when Seth will strike and we will need Sekhmet's assistance."

Senen-Mut worries that Hat-Nofer grows older and weaker. He believes that Sekhmet's image will protect his mother in her old age.

"My husband and your father say that these fish are to go to the Lord Amen-Nati," Hat-Nofer chides her son. "Your father is fortunate to have the *Nomarch of Wast* as his patron and friend. Soon you will learn that to be successful, you must always consider your master's will above your own."

"Then I will take these fish to the Lord Amen-Nati's cook," Senen-Mut replies. Now that he no longer has a reason to be sad, he changes his mood, happy that his mother is not disappointed. "I will tell the cook that my father and Hat-Nofer's husband, Ra-Moses, presents these fish for the nomarch's table with fond esteem and in continued friendship."

During a battle in *Pharaoh's War Against the Northern Nomes*, a contingent of soldiers directed by their rebellious nomarch attacked Pharaoh's army. In a desperate gamble they attempted to kill Pharaoh's captain of captains, the general of the army, In the ensuing fight, Ra-Moses defended Amen-Nati by killing several rebel soldiers. After the war, Pharaoh appointed Amen-Nati *Nomarch of Wast*. In turn, Amen-Nati rewarded Ra-Moses by settling his family in Armant. Through the years the two men remained friends. And one thing that Ra-Moses knows is Amen-Nati loves nothing more than a meal of delicious Nile perch.

Pharaoh Amen-Hotep set the founding principle of the Eighteenth Dynasty as perpetual hostility against the asiatics remaining in Lower Egypt and enmity for those nomarchs who support them. The battles are many and bloody. Hand-to-hand encounters pit Egyptian against Egyptian. Amen-Hotep's war is a merciless campaign to exterminate disloyal nomarchs, their families and their soldiers. Pharaoh's army improves its killing efficiency by adopting the bronze Hyksos battle-ax and developing their own unique sword known as the *kapesh*. The razor-sharp kapesh not only hacks and punctures its victims but rips and tears through their shields, as well. Pharaoh protects his soldiers with battle armor. But the most important innovation adopted by Pharaoh's army is the Hyksos-style war chariots.

In battle, Ra-Moses never flinched nor fled; neither did he question or doubt. Ra-Moses did what so many other Egyptian soldiers failed to do in Pharaoh's war; he stays alive. By staying alive, Ra-Moses rose through the ranks. When he retired, not only was Ra-Moses an officer but also he wore the insignia of Pharaoh's highest military honor, the *Order of the Golden Fly*. So it is that Ra-Moses owes his country estate and his lucrative flax plantation to Pharaoh's generosity and his nomarch's patronage.

"Bow down to his lordship, *Vizier of Wast*, my sons," Ra-Moses orders as he escorts Amen-Nati's grim-faced vizier, Menkh,

Eugene Stovall

through the great ebony doors into the central room of his house. "Pray to Amen that you have brought no shame upon my house this day."

Senen-Mut immediately falls to his knees with his head resting on the matted floors. His other brothers fall down besides him.

"Rise!" Menkh orders. He surveys each of Ra-Moses' sons with an imperious look, but when his gaze falls upon, Senen-Mut, it changes from imperiousness to curiosity and *disapproval*. The vizier of *Wast* is a tall man, with a slightly gaunt look. His bald head is covered with a skullcap. He wears a white linen cloak over his kilt and around his wrinkled neck hangs a golden chain holding his insignia of office, *an ankh over a golden scepter*.

"We have heard of your behavior from your school-master, young man," the vizier says addressing Senen-Mut.

"My son," Ra-Moses asks, "can you explain your behavior to his lordship?"

"I might explain my behavior better, Father," Senen-Mut replies, keeping his eyes fixed upon the aged priest, "if I knew what behavior most concerns his lordship."

The boy has a contemptuous manner, Menkh notes. *In this one, Amen-Nati may have mistaken the slyness of Seth for the wisdom of Thoth.*

"Did you learn your insolent manner from your teachers at the temple or here in your home?" The vizier's eyes narrow and his lips curl.

"Master?" Senen-Mut responds wearing a look of wide-eyed innocence prompting the vizier's disapproval, even further.

"Heretics have begun freely criticizing the will of the gods, lately," Menkh announces. "It has been reported to the high priest of Amen that you are one of those heretics."

Menkh's eyes remind Senen-Mut of the eyes of a cobra preparing to strike.

"I am no heretic, master," Senen-Mut replies.

"Why, then, do your teachers report you as such?"

"I only seek answers to the questions that occur to me."

"You may leave," Ra-Moses tells his other three sons. "This is between the Lord Menkh and Senen-Mut."

At the door, Amen-Nen-Het turns and gives Senen-Mut a smirk. After Ra-Moses older three sons depart, Menkh continues. "The heretics say '*the priests have become too powerful*' and '*blind obedience led to the fall of the Thirteenth Dynasty.*' Is that what you believe, son of Ra-Moses?"

"Master!" Ra-Moses addresses Menkh. "Does his lordship believe that my fifteen-year-old son really understands these matters?" Ra-Moses gazes steadily at the vizier. "Neither children nor commoners could possibly know what is being discussed in Thebes."

Menkh studies the flax farmer who wears his prosperity about his middle.

"You and your youngest son may join me." Menkh turns on his heel and strides through the ebony doors, into the courtyard. "I wish a tour of your lands," the priest orders.

Ra-Moses leads the vizier of *Wast* through the courtyard and onto a path that leads through the vegetable garden. They walk for some distance in silence before coming to the center where an orchard of date palms and doum-nut trees encloses a circular resting area.

"How beautiful," Menkh comments. He is surprised at the commoner's ability to mate the universal principles so well within his gardens and orchards. "Colors glow in your garden and rejoice the eye," he observes. "Birds sing and delight the ear; perfumes burst from every flower and delight the nostrils. And what a beautiful pool!"

Too idyllic an estate for a commoner, the vizier thinks. *Many a noble would consider this residence above Ra-Moses' station.*

Ra-Moses doesn't know whether Menkh's comments are genuine or cynical. "Thank you, Your Excellency." Ra-Moses bows his head in respect. "Know that my wife designed the pool and planned the entire garden. She has worked tirelessly since we moved here some years ago."

Menkh pauses in front of a bench sheltered by a trellis. He can delay discussing the purpose of his visit.

"The Lord Amen-Nati wants to know if your son is fit to be sent to the royal school," Menkh confides in Ra-Moses.

"Ask the questions the Lord of *Wast* wants to know," Ra-Moses replies.

Amen-Nati already warned Ra-Moses that Menkh believes his youngest son to be a heretic and the eyes and ears of the high priest of Amen intends to thwart their plans for the boy's education. Menkh is an initiate of the outer temple. So, even though he is a professional administrator, Menkh is also a priest and a member of the *Seeing Waters*, the secret group that reports heresies and other acts of disobedience to Amen's high priest at Karnak.

"Know you, young man, how your father found himself enrolled among heroes of the *Living God* in the *Order of the Golden Fly?*"

"Yes, my lord," Senen-Mut replies without hesitation. "My father fought bravely in several battles against Pharaoh's enemies. He has taken many hands of Pharaoh's enemies and has taken other of Pharaoh's enemies captive."

"Yet, on more than one occasion, you have questioned your teachers about why nomarchs of the north are called enemies of Pharaoh. Is this correct?"

"I asked how can Egyptians be Pharaoh's enemies when they worship Amen?" Senen-Mut replies. "Are not Amen, Ra and Ptah worshipped by all who serve the *Living God?*" Senen-Mut isn't afraid of Menkh. This fact alone makes Ra-Moses' youngest son a heretic in Menkh's eyes. Priests demand blind obedience from commoners, *else how could the priests, themselves, withstand Pharaoh's awesome powers?* Menkh cannot imagine a greater heresy than a student questioning a priest.

"How dare you question the will of Pharaoh?" Menkh roars out. "You see, Ra-Moses! Your son utters the same heresy that is rampant in Thebes. This heresy is worse than those plagues that Seth sends to wipe out you commoners, every so often."

"I do not question Pharaoh," Senen-Mut replies. His voice is quiet and mature. "I question my own ability to understand what others seem to understand, without difficulty."

"What is there for you to understand, foolish boy?" Menkh asks. "Pharaoh is the *Living God*. He is the human personality; he is wisdom and power in action. His gestures symbolize the meaning for nature's movement. If Pharaoh declares the birds of the air and the fish in the river his enemies, who are you to question the *Living God*?" Menkh glares at Senen-Mut before continuing. "The divine Pharaoh owns the land and everyone on it. He is ruler, chief priest of every cult, head of the civil administration, lord chief justice and supreme commander of the army."

"I'm certain the boy means nothing by his words, your lordship," Ra-Moses intervenes, "sometimes young boys become confused by all that they learn in school. Senen-Mut is just a bit slower than the other lads at understanding the existence of the *Living God*.

"Well your son had better speed up his learning a bit hadn't he?" Menkh snarls.

As a member of the *Order of the Golden Fly*, Ra-Moses is also called upon to provide army intelligence. He knows that the vizier of *Wast* is a member of the *Seeing Waters* and an informant. Amen-Nati even warned Ra-Moses that Menkh suspects Ra-Moses, himself, of heresy.

Ra-Moses continually relives the war. Not a day passes when he does not pray for the *KA*s of the men he slaughtered. They were good Egyptian soldiers who prayed to Amen, Ra and Ptah, just as he and Amen-Nati. Ra-Moses and his family live magnificently because he killed many Egyptians who were not even given proper burials. Sadly, their *KA*s wander about, unable to enter the afterlife. When Ra-Moses first started discussing these things with his youngest son, the troubled war veteran believed that Senen-Mut was too young to understand his words. Now Ra-Moses realizes that it was foolish to introduce Senen-Mut to his own doubts about the slaughter he witnessed.

Please Amen, Most Merciful, do not force my son to suffer for my sins, Ra-Moses prays.

"When our Lord, Amen-Nati, the Ruler of *Wast*, asked my opinion about the fitness of your son to enter the Royal School," Menkh says. "I confess that I did not believe Senen-Mut could represent *Wast* suitably."

"*Praise be to Amen,*" Ra-Moses offers a prayer. "I am certain that his Excellency will search the wisdom of his heart and make the proper recommendation."

Menkh smiles outwardly, but vows to himself, *Before the son of this flax farmer gets access to the secrets of the outer Temple, I will see him in the army, in the front ranks. Let this heretic face Pharaoh's enemies in person. Blasphemers such as he will learn of their errors in the afterlife.*

Even before Menkh reports his observations to Amen-Nati, Senen-Mut's youngest sister is all over her brother. She had been listening to the entire conversation from their secret place in the garden. Senen-Mut knew she was there, listening. When Menkh takes his leave and returns to the *Palace of Wast*, escorted part of the way by Ra-Moses, Nof-Ret-Hor leaps from her hiding place to confront her brother. Senen-Mut and Nof-Ret-Hor share a bond; they have entered each other's dreams since they were small children.

"Your mother will be sad if you leave her now," Nof-Ret-Hor blurts out. "Even when you attended temple school, your mother worried. I know she will not want you to leave Armant and go to Thebes."

"Every day I attended temple school," Senen-Mut tells his sister, "my mother sent you or Ah-Hotep to bring me bread and beer, as well as onions and lettuces. And she made certain that you brought the fish and fowl that I love to eat. My mother wants me to get an education and so does my father. My mother wants me to become a scribe or even a priest."

Tears flow from his sister's eyes. Nof-Ret-Hor does not want him to leave. Senen-Mut stares at the ground.

"If given the chance, I must accept the nomarch's command to represent *Wast* at the royal school. My mother will understand."

"Mother loves you and condemns nothing you do," Nof-Ret-Hor retorts. "But see how happy she is since you designed that fish pond. Everyone at the marketplace treats your mother as if she were a member of the nomarch's own family. Even we, your sisters, receive great respect."

"That must mean that the eligible young men are paying more attention to my sisters than usual," Senen-Mut teases. Nof-Ret-Hor and Ah-Hotep continually scheme to get some young man to marry them. Now that Senen-Mut's magical fishpond is attracting attention, both sisters are receiving the attention of every eligible bachelor in Armant.

"You just wait until I tell your mother what terrible things you said when I insisted that she would miss you."

Nof-Ret-Hor turns her back so that Senen-Mut cannot see her tears. Both remain silent. Finally she confesses.

"You are right, my brother; it is I who doesn't want you to go to the Royal School. But it is not because I want to catch a husband." Nof-Ret-Hor sits down near the base of a doum-nut tree. "I will miss you terribly, if you go." She starts to cry, again. "I will miss you because I know I will never see you again."

"I will miss you, as well, Nof-Ret-Hor," Senen-Mut replies taking her hand. He tries to say something comforting, but there is nothing to say. Both have shared the same dream and both know what she says is true. "Are you still having your dreams?" he asks. He knows the question is unnecessary.

"Uh-huh," Nof-Ret-Hor shakes her head positively.

"I will miss you telling me about them."

"Do you want to hear about the one that I had last night?" Nof-Ret-Hor climbs up onto the bench facing the pool where Senen-Mut is lounging.

"Yes, please tell me," Senen-Mut says. He hopes her story will ease the pain of his leaving. When they were very young, Senen-Mut and Nof-Ret-Hor entered each other's dreams and remembered them afterwards. As they grew older, they could no longer dream together. Now they can only tell each other about their nocturnal adventures. Lately, both Senen-Mut and Nof-Ret-Hor have had the same dream. Senen-Mut prays that it is not an evil omen. And he hopes that attending the royal school does not cause his mother too much pain.

Striding between the pylons, Menkh crosses the courtyard, climbs the marble stairs and enters Amen-Nati's palace. Inside a long hall with a high roof, supported by a double row of pillars, leads to where an alcove dips inwards. Here a soldier guards the double door that opens into the nomarch's study. The walls are lined with shelves containing all manner of scrolls, shards and tablets. The Lord Amen-Nati, Pharaoh's scarred veteran, sits in a high-backed, leather-lined chair at a wooden table with legs carved into lion paws.

"Lord," Menkh says after bowing low before the *Nomarch of Wast*. "I do not believe the youngest son of Ra-Moses will suitably represent *Wast* at the Royal School."

"Why not?" Amen-Nati asks, reluctantly raising his eyes from the scroll he is studying.

"Ra-Moses' son is insolent," Menkh replies. "He does not understand a commoner's place."

"In addition to his mannerisms, did you examine his intelligence?" Amen-Nati asks.

Amen-Nati knows Menkh's mind. The *Nomarch of Wast* is also a commoner. Most of Pharaoh Thut-Moses' top army officers are veterans of the northern wars and are commoners. They rose through the ranks under Thut-Moses, who was the commander in chief of Pharaoh Amen-Hotep's army. Now pharaoh, because of his marriage into the royal family, Thut-Moses, himself, is a commoner. After Thut-Moses became pharaoh, he began appointing commoners to high offices. Nobles like Menkh took offense. The nobles disapproved of commoners rising up in society. They disapproved of commoners attending the Royal School at Karnak. They especially disapproved of commoners who were independent thinkers. But Menkh's opinion doesn't matter to Amen-Nati. The *Nomarch of Wast* has already decided to send Senen-Mut to the Royal School as the *Student of Wast*. Amen-Nati sent Menkh to question the boy only to observe tradition.

"That boy holds heretical opinions," Menkh asserts.

"The boy utters heresy?" Amen-Nati asks, raising his eyebrows.

"The boy questions Pharaoh's war in the north," Menkh says.

"Your opinion is based on reports you have heard from the temple school," Amen-Nati observes, "not on an examination of the boy's intelligence and fitness, *as I instructed*."

"Since my master has also heard reports of his heresy," Menkh asks, "why do you consider him at all?

"If he holds any heretical views at all," Amen-Nati replies, ignoring the vizier's insolence, "he must have learned them at the temple school."

"Why does my master say that?"

"Where else would he learn them?" Amen-Nati asks. "Certainly you do not believe his heretical ideas originate from his own mind. Isn't it the belief of the nobles *that only the priests* are capable of teaching a student what is knowable?"

"Yes, it is true that all learning is in the hands of the priests and the temple," Menkh admits reluctantly.

"Well then," Amen-Nati says, smiling, "if this student speaks heresy, then he must have learned it at the temple school. That is where you should search for your heretics."

Amen-Nati enjoys putting Menkh in his place. Amen-Nati also knows that the old priest at the temple school only teaches his students the traditional religious myths and that their duty is to obey. But Amen-Nati knows that Menkh cannot admit that a commoner can learn from someone other than a priest. Otherwise, the vizier, himself, would be accused of holding heretical views.

Loyalty! That is what these priests want, Amen-Nati sneers. *But Pharaoh wants people around him who can think and do more than take orders.*

The Nomarch of Wast is committed to giving Senen-Mut an education, not only because he promised Senen-Mut's father, but also because the lad displays remarkable intelligence and a desire to learn. Given the opportunity, Amen-Nati believes that Senen-Mut could become a scribe or even a priest. Menkh represents the old noble class who believes the only role for a commoner is to labor, obey and die. Pharaoh has directed his nomarchs to find talented students no matter their origins. He wants to recruit a new class of administrators and priests. Pharaoh intends to change the old traditions.

"Unless you have made any additional observations of Ra-Moses' son that you wish to share," Amen-Nati smiles, "I have decided to send Senen-Mut to the Royal School at Karnak. This is my decision." And without pausing to allow Menkh to reply, Amen-Nati says, "You may go."

For a moment, Menkh considers launching a protest. Anger and arrogance struggle inside his mind. In the end, however, Menkh knows it's useless to say anything. He bows silently and departs. But even as the *Nomarch of Wast* savors his victory over the noble who is his servant, Amen-Nati knows that he is doing Senen-Mut no favor. In the Two-Lands, what matters most is name and titles. Senen-Mut has neither. At the Royal School, Senen-Mut will meet the sons and daughters of nobles and of the royal family. The offspring of nobles are unsuited for anything but maintaining their own false pretensions and fawning over each other.

The *Student of Wast* receives the royal summons to present himself to the Royal School at the *Palace of Ladies* in Karnak. Hat-Nofer is so excited that, every day for a week, she visits Armant's market, showing Senen-Mut's *Royal Summons* to anyone wishing to see it. The townspeople are as excited. Never before has a commoner of Armant received such an honor. Ra-Moses is so proud that his face is frozen into a permanent smile. Senen-Mut's brothers are also jealous, but only Amen-Nen-Het expresses outright hostility.

"I should have been offered the opportunity to attend the Royal School," he tells anyone who will listen. Most laugh. They remember that Amen-Nen-Het was such a poor student that he barely completed four years at the temple school.

"Amen-Nen-Het reads little and can think even less," the townspeople laugh. "He's fortunate to have his father's flax business."

The day comes that Senen-Mut must depart for Thebes. Both of Senen-Mut's sisters weep, but only Nof-Ret-Hor's tears are genuine. Armed with a scroll declaring him to be the *Student of Wast*, stamped with the Nomarch's seal and addressed to the Royal Teacher, Senen-Mut boards the nomarch's barge moored in the *Wast*'s private harbor to sail the short fifteen-*iteru* journey down river to Thebes.

CHAPTER TWO

"Make way for Wast! Make Way!" The captain of the Barge of Wast shouts out his warnings as he and the pilot maneuver their sleek transport vessel into the great harbor of Thebes. Relying on his rowers, the pilot steers the Barge of Wast into the canal leading to the dock reserved for river barges belonging to Pharaoh's forty-two nomarchs and his other nobles. The nobles' canal continues up to Karnak for the exclusive use of Pharaoh and Pharaoh's co-Regent. Exercising a noble's 'right of way' and relying upon the oarsmen's speed, the Barge of Wast flashes past the fishing, freight and transportation barges maneuvering for access into the docking areas.

Senen-Mut has never seen so many boats in his life. Everywhere he looks there are vessels of all shapes and sizes, from magnificent river ships with three banks of oars to little skiffs and fishing boats. With all the congestion, Senen-Mut wonders how all this water traffic sorts itself out. A great barge loaded with grain barely avoids colliding with a great flatbed ship transporting gigantic blocks of granite. Yet, before Senen-Mut's eyes, traffic sorts itself out, ships reaching their intended docking areas and disgorging the people, goods and materials pouring into Thebes from throughout the Two-Lands and from all over the known world.

"Why does that boat have so many soldiers?" Senen-Mut asks the captain, pointing to a two-masted vessel with two banks of rowers.

"That transport ship brings gold from Nubia or semi-precious stones from the Sinai," the captain replies. "Pharaoh's treasure boats dock up here near the royal storehouses." The captain points out great stone buildings overlooking the harbor.

"And those boats over there," the captain continues, "transport linen, wool, furniture and every other kind of product to the docks that serve the marketplace." All this activity amazes the *Student of Wast*.

The pilot slides the *Barge of Wast* into the royal canal and docks it neatly in a comfortable slip. Then the captain escorts Senen-Mut up to a platform sheltered from Amen's rays by a huge multi-colored canopy. Here the dock master lounges upon a high-backed dais. From his vantage point the dock master enjoys a panoramic view of the great harbor of Thebes.

"Good day, Excellency!" The captain of *Wast* bows low to the dock master whose leather-backed chair is carved to represent the image of a fish. Before becoming the Overseer of the Royal Dock, the dock master spent many years both as a sailor and captain in Pharaoh's naval service.

"Good day, Captain of *Wast*," the dock master replies. "How can Thebes serve *Wast*?"

"This is the *Student of Wast*," the captain says, indicating Senen-Mut. "He carries the *Seal of Wast* to the Teacher of the Royal School at Karnak."

"I will see that the *Seal* and the *Student of Wast* are delivered to the Royal Teacher," the dock master replies.

"I will convey to my master that his captain received much kindnesses from the dock master of Thebes." The *Wast*'s barge captain leaves the customary offering with the dock master's scribe, bows once more and returns to his barge for the return trip.

The dock master signals his scribe to send up a dockworker.

"How may I serve my master?" the dockworker asks from his kneeling position.

"Take this royal student who carries the *Seal of Wast* to Karnak," the dock master orders. "Direct him to the Royal Teacher at the *Palace of Ladies*."

"Yes, master," the young dockworker replies. "Your will be done."

The dockworker is about the same age as Senen-Mut. He wears a soiled loincloth, tattered leather sandals and a filthy skullcap. Though his face is dirty, his eyes are quick and intelligent. The dockworker wears a lop-sided grin that is strangely disconcerting to Senen-Mut. It's as if the dockworker is laughing at him. But Senen-Mut doesn't know why. He finds it disturbing that someone as low as a dockworker, someone at the bottom rung of society, should be grinning as if he were content with his station in life.

You can be certain, Senen-Mut reminds himself, that if Amen-Nen-Het caught any of his flax workers or slaves smiling, he would be certain to give them more than enough work to wipe the smile from the offending worker's face.

"Follow me, *Student of Wast*," the ragged-looking dockworker says. He turns on his heels and heads up to a great dusty road teeming with a river of jostling, pushing humanity. The road passes through a pair of pylons. Here Senen-Mut gazes down upon the unbelievable sight of Thebes, the capital of the Two-Lands and the greatest city in the world.

Thebes is a giant labyrinth, sectioned off by winding streets and crooked alleyways. The capital of the Two-Lands is noisy, over-crowded and smells. Night and day, people from all over jostle each other in the capital's congested streets. The unimaginable smells result from the vermin-ridden family dwellings lacking any sanitation facilities squeezed together in two or three-story mud brick buildings. In the lower section of Thebes, immediately adjacent to the harbor, animals and livestock are domiciled in the same building as family members. Even those administrators and scribes fortunate enough to live high up or near a waterway cannot entirely avoid the smells of the Theban slums. With the exception of those actually living in Karnak, only those with villas or mansions situated in the rolling expanse between upper Thebes and Karnak are completely free of Thebes' foul smells.

Senen-Mut's guide leads him past Thebes' lower slum areas and heads directly into the heart of the market district. Litters and carts carrying petty administrators, minor priests and rich merchants clog the streets. Guards with cudgels force the crowds of yelling and cursing men, women and children to make way for the nobles. Thebes' streets twist and turn so abruptly that Senen-Mut can hardly follow his guide. More than once the *Student of Wast* becomes completely lost, altogether, and is forced to wait until his guide returns to retrieve him.

"Can't you keep up!" the dockworker snaps at Senen-Mut, showing his impatience. "If I don't get back to the dock master quickly, I will lose my position." And without waiting for Senen-Mut to reply, he disappears again, this time scampering in front of a litter and a donkey cart, loaded with goods, all the while yelling, "Keep up!"

They reach a gate that serves as the entrance into the main marketplace. The soldiers stationed at the gate are more interested in their game of chance than watching the surging throng. Different smells now fill the air. The smell of salted fish, beer and bread reminds Senen-Mut that he hasn't eaten since leaving Armant. The dockworker stops to wait for the *Student of Wast* to catch up.

"Master," the young worker says, "my name is Iby." He decides to walk by the royal student's side.

"I am Senen-Mut."

"My entire family works on the docks," Iby boasts, "either for the overseer of the docks, the overseer of freight or the overseer of measures."

"You must be very proud of your family," Senen-Mut replies.

"Every day we handle all the boats coming in," Iby boasts. "Once they've deposited their cargos, we moor them out there in the harbor." Iby points out to the great expansive area where boats bob up and down at their anchorage.

"In what way does your family serve the Pharaoh?" Iby asks, assuming Senen-Mut to be of noble birth.

"My father lives on an army pension and serves the *Nomarch of Wast*," Senen-Mut explains.

The dockworker's face registers disbelief. "You're a commoner?" he asks.

"Yes," Senen-Mut replies.

"There are only two classes serving the *Living God*," Iby says, "those of noble birth who give orders and the commoners who must carry them out. How is it that a commoner is admitted into the sacred sanctuary of Karnak?"

"There are only two types of people who serve Pharaoh," Senen-Mut answers, mocking his guide. "There are the ones who serve the *Living God* with their backs and the ones who serve him with their brains."

Iby considers the *Student of Wast*'s response.

This one is having his jest with me, Iby decides. *He's just like those other noble brats, only this one is a bit cleverer.*

Iby continues hustling Senen-Mut through the Theban marketplace. They pass the stalls where merchants display all sorts of produce, meats and fish. Elsewhere, merchants display goods from all over the world. Instinctively, Iby maneuvers through the twistings and turnings of Thebes' labyrinth until the dirt roads become paved and the streets become wider and straighter. Here the merchants sell their wares in courtyards or inside bazaars.

"This is the upper marketplace," Iby comments. "Here the powerful and their servants do their shopping."

In Thebes' upper marketplace, Senen-Mut notices that the servants all wear smiles plastered across their faces just like Iby. Here people bow to each other. They all seem especially happy to serve their masters. In this upper section of Thebes, workers continually clean the streets and dispose of the filth. Iby leads Senen-Mut past a series of large multi-story buildings.

"Over there are Pharaoh's public houses," Iby points out.

"Public houses?" Senen-Mut repeats.

"Pharaoh's *Houses of Silver*, his *Granaries* and the other buildings where he keeps his possessions," Iby explains.

Senen-Mut nods.

They approach a crowd of people, clustered outside a cook shop. Inside the shop's courtyard, bread is being cooked in the sand. In the next courtyard, a vendor solicits the crowd waiting for the fresh bread.

"Buy my onion seeds!" he shouts out with a musical lilt. "They block snake holes most effectively!"

A litter, trailing two donkeys loaded with goods, heads towards them. Senen-Mut and his guide move aside and the merchant passes. But though the street is relatively wide, there is not enough room for the litter and donkeys to pass the crowd lined up at the bread shop.

From inside his litter the merchant screams at his guards, "Get that scum out of the way!" The guards quickly begin swinging their clubs and pushing at the crowd. "Make way! Make way!" they shout.

Senen-Mut stops to watch.

"*Student of Wast,*" Iby cautions. "Here in Thebes, it is not wise to become distracted by what does not concern you."

Where the path separates, a group of sailors asks directions to the *Street of Pleasure* where they will spend a month's pay in one night. Iby directs them off to the left. Further up they pass the *Street of Barbers*. Here a patron can be rid of unwanted hair while learning the latest court gossip.

"May it be written in the Book of Thoth that I do not intend a bad omen, but I'm just saying that the Pharaoh should be spending more time in Memphis," one of the barbers states. "In Memphis, Pharaoh can protect us from a Mitanni invasion."

"Do you think that the priests would deliver all this loot to the Pharaoh's *House of Gold*, or the Royal warehouses without Pharaoh presence?" another barber responds. "Pharaoh must remain with his gold."

"That's what the Thirteenth Dynasty did and you see where it got them!" a patron, displaying the insignia of an administrator, remarks.

Iby and Senen-Mut pass out of earshot by leaving the shops and bazaars of Upper Thebes altogether. Now they travel down a broad, straight boulevard paved with stone. Here the crowds have dissipated and the few people about appear to be officials or administrators of some sort. Along this boulevard, stele and monuments record the names of great pharaohs and recount their deeds. Here also are parks tended by an army of gardeners. Scattered about are single and two-story mansions and palaces. Uniformed soldiers in groups of twos and threes patrol this boulevard. A pair of uniformed soldiers stops them and demands their insignias. Iby shows his insignia of a dockworker.

"This is the *Student of Wast*," Iby explains to the soldiers. "I am escorting him to the Royal School at Karnak to meet with the Royal Teacher."

A sentry examines the Wast's insignia on Senen-Mut's credential. Then, without comment, he allows them to pass. After walking a great distance down the paved boulevard, they arrive at a great wall with an imposing gate and sentry posts. Behind the wall sprawls the complex of Karnak, home of the gods, Living and immortal.

"State your business!" the officer of the guard barks.

"This is the *Student of Wast*," Iby replies boldly. "He is here to present himself to the Royal Teacher at the *Palace of Ladies*. His credential bears the *Seal of Wast*."

After the officer of the guard inspects the Wast's insignia on Senen-Mut's credentials, he passes him through the gates, and assigns four soldiers to escort Senen-Mut to the *Palace of Ladies*.

"May the gods and fortune favor you," Iby shouts to Senen-Mut. *I will not be seeing that one again*, the dockworker assures himself as he heads back to the great harbor of Thebes.

CHAPTER THREE

The Palace of Ladies is actually a complex of residences and apartments connected by gardens, walkways and secret accesses. The palace is even surrounded by its own walls. Inside the complex, there is the Nursery for the Royal Infants and the Household of Royal Children. The Royal Teacher and his assistants live in the Palace of Ladies and educate the royal children along with the children of nomarchs and other nobility. The students attending the Royal School hold the title Companions of the Royal Children. When Senen-Mut arrives at the Palace of Ladies, his guard presents the Student of Wast's credentials to the Royal Teacher.

"Just what we need," Hapu-Seneb sneers to his assistant, "another commoner."

Hapu-Seneb, the Royal Teacher, is the high priest of Amen's most loyal follower. The Royal Teacher is ambitious and without any sympathy for commoners, especially one identified as a 'heretic.'

"Do not expect any special consideration here, boy," the Royal Teacher glowers at Senen-Mut.

"No your lordship," Senen-Mut responds.

He remains in a prostrate position with his head touching the floor. Hapu-Seneb keeps the new student on his knees far longer than is customary. The Royal Teacher enjoys watching commoners grovel at his feet.

"What do you make of this *Student of Wast*, Mes-Djer?" Hapu-Seneb asks his assistant who wears an owlish look of a person unable to commit the heresy of independent thinking since he has never held an independent thought of any kind.

"Master will undoubtedly be sorely tried by this one," Mes-Djer replies.

"All right, get up," Hapu-Seneb says and then, aside to his assistant, "What's the boy's name?"

"Senen-Mut, Master," the assistant replies.

"Get up, Senen-Mut," Hapu-Seneb says. "Mes-Djer will take you to the *Corps of Pages*. They will see that you are properly settled. You are to learn your duties and *stay in your place*."

The Royal Teacher appraises Senen-Mut with a sly look. "So you aspire to become an initiate, do you?"

"I aspire only to assist Pharaoh in whatever manner my abilities allow me, Master," Senen-Mut replies in a quiet voice.

Hapu-Seneb did not expect such a reasoned and subtle answer from a commoner, recognizing in Senen-Mut's response the workings of a keen mind.

This Student of Wast is well prepared, the Royal Teacher tells himself. *He neither acknowledges nor denies any ambition.*

"You believe that Pharaoh needs the assistance of a commoner like you?" Hapu-Seneb's voice is intentionally sarcastic. "I'd say that your first lesson must be to serve according to your rank."

Senen-Mut withholds any comment, remembering his father's advice. "When in the presence of a noble, if there is nothing to say, say nothing."

The Royal Teacher mistakes Senen-Mut's silence for submission and is satisfied that the *Student of Wast* is sufficiently chastened.

"Now you may take our new student to the Overseer of the Pages and see that he is settled in, " Hapu-Seneb instructs Mes-Djer.

In the dormitory housing the Corps of Pages, the Overseer of Pages assigns Senen-Mut a personal space and a sleeping mat.

"This will be your home for as long as… " The overseer pauses. "I guess we shall see how long you actually remain in the Royal School, shan't we?"

"Judging from this student's behavior," Hapu-Seneb later reports to Seth-Mesy, "Menkh is correct in calling Wast a hotbed of heresy."

"Possibly the Nomarch of Wast himself taught the boy what to say," Seth-Mesy concludes.

"If so," Hapu-Seneb replies, "it was done more subtly than I would have believed Amen-Nati capable."

"This Student of Wast bears watching," Amen's high priest concludes.

One other member of the Corps of Pages is a commoner, nevertheless the Royal Teacher and his assistants educate the entire Corps of Pages along with the Children of the Palace without distinction. All students receive tutoring in mathematics, astronomy and astrology. They each learn the science of number and proportion as the fundamental principle upon which the ancient laws and traditions governing the Two-Lands have been formulated since the beginning of time.

"The eye follows what the form reveals. Sound compels bodies to make certain gestures and to move into certain positions. Form and sound arouse internal reflexes in everyone," lectures Abit, Hapu-Seneb's oldest and most learned assistant. He is also a member of the elite, an initiate of Amen's Inner Temple, the highest order in the Two-Lands.

Abit's lesson on universal principle bores most of his students, but it stimulates Senen-Mut. Abit likes the way Senen-Mut's approaches his lessons. The Student of Wast seizes every opportunity to probe into the ancient mysteries and understand their meanings. Already Abit finds that Senen-Mut has mastered the understanding required for initiation into the outer temple. Abit cannot resist taking the Student of Wast further. And today's lecture on universal principles gives Abit his opportunity.

"Is the universal principle that impacts sound the same principle that works on form?" Senen-Mut asks.

"More than one universal principle works on them both, my son," Abit responds.

"But does the *same* universal principle work the same on sound as it does on form?" Senen-Mut takes advantage of Abit's invitation to probe even though his fellow students grow restless. Abit's interest in the Student of Wast displeases the nobles who are normally indolent and easily bored with Abit's esoteric discussions. They take Abit's interest in Senen-Mut as an insult if not to their intelligence at least to their rank.

"Proportion and sound are fashioned by all of the universal principles," Abit explains, "just as the universal principles fashion everything that exists. What distinguishes a principle's impact on form from its impact on sound is its universal effect."

With his last statement, Abit's draws blank stares from everyone, including Senen-Mut. The teaching assistant explains further.

"Take the principle of vibration," Abit continues. "Vibration impacts form differently than it impacts sound. Vibration alters form but enhances sounds. However, the *effect* of vibration is the same on both form and sound, don't you see?"

"I still do not understand," Senen-Mut says.

"*He still doesn't understand,*" one of his fellow students sneers.

"Principles are universal when they exhibit laws that are inflexible and unchanging," Abit explains. "There is no exception to or recourse from a universal principle."

"Is that why the ancients taught that, to understand a *universal principle*, we must understand proportion and number?" Senen-Mut asks.

"Yes!" Abit replies. "That's it! You've got it."

"So a statue's proportions correspond to a number that is invoked by a particular universal principle?" Senen-Mut says, thinking out loud.

"Yes, again," Abit says. "Anyone who contemplates the physical form of a statue will be affected by that particular universal principle, *even if only at the subconscious level.*"

Asfet, one of Senen-Mut's fellow students, breaks into the conversation. He is the youngest son of the *Nomarch of Hare*. He is very bright when he doesn't let his arrogance get the better of him, which is not very often.

"Aren't you just saying that the bigger the statue, monument or stele," he sneers, "the greater its impact on the observer?"

"Yes," Abit replies, "but there is more to it than that."

"Furthermore, form and sound are ways that the noble class impresses illiterate commoners with the meaning of rank and privilege," Asfet continues, directing his animosity at Senen-Mut.

His fellow students join in the laughter. They are grateful for the interruption. Asfet is always happy to ingratiate himself with students whose families have wealth and titles.

"Asfet points out an important fact of nature that impacts human beings," Abit responds. "Nature obeys such gestures and forms that accord with universal laws. When the wind blows, branches bend; if words of sorrow are spoken, tears flow and if the obelisk touches the sky, the looker wonders in amazement."

"I understand this principle with sound," Senen-Mut remarks. "When the workers sing, their work becomes easier."

Asfet frowns in disgust.

"Is this not the reason," Senen-Mut blurts out, "that none can defy the will of gods, since nothing in nature can defy universal principle?"

Asfet bristles at Senen-Mut's question. "Who is delivering this lecture, the teacher or this *commoner*?"

Abit realizes that he has allowed Senen-Mut to go too far. Questions concerning the gods are not permitted. Even if they were, no student is permitted to speak of the gods in such a sacrilegious, disrespectful manner. Abit dismisses his class, but the damage is done. Hapu-Seneb quickly learns of Senen-Mut's heretical statement. For months afterwards, the Royal Teacher targets the Student of Wast for every petty joke and cruel prank that the Corps of Pages can concoct. After the constant harassment and hazing, Senen-Mut wants nothing more than to escape the Corps of Pages and the Royal School, itself. Yet he knows that he must remain. If he quits, it would break his mother's heart. Even while exposing Senen-Mut to the mysteries of the Outer Temple, the Royal Teacher prods Asfet to lead a vicious campaign against the Student of Wast. Hapu-Seneb wants there to be no doubt that Senen-Mut is nothing more than a commoner and he directs the corp of pages treat him as they would a shadoof worker. And these scions of the 18th Dynasty's most noble families ___ the Two-Lands' future scribes, priests and administrators ____ eagerly impress the contempt and hostility with which they hold all commoners upon the Student of Wast. At this time in the Two Lands of Upper and Lower Egypt, birth matters far more than merit. However, it will not be too long in the distant future when these same nobles will come fawning to Senen-Mut seeking all manner of political favors.

Senen-Mut's life alternates between the exhilaration of being the Royal School's brightest student and the pain of being an outcast. Even the other commoner, the Student of Jackal, distances himself as far as possible from the Student of Wast. Yet, things begin to change. The Royal Teacher assigns Senen-Mut to more interesting and challenging lectures, many of which are conducted by Hapu-Seneb, himself. Even more importantly, the royal couple, the Princess Maat-Ka-Re and her brother, the Crown Prince, Aa-Kheper-Ren-Re Thut-Moses II attend many of these same lectures. Over time, Senen-Mut finds himself in the presence of the royal couple almost on a daily basis. What is more exciting, Senen-Mut feels the Princess Maat-Ka-Re watching him. Sometimes, when she doesn't think he notices. Senen-Mut tries to dismiss his feelings as fantasies. Pharaoh's daughter is the most beautiful woman in all of the Two-Lands. How could she have any interest in the Student of Wast. But one evening, Aron, the Student of Jackal, confirms Senen-Mut's observation.

"The Princess Maat-Ka-Re always seems interested in what you have to say," Aron remarks to Senen-Mut.

He and Aron share a writing table and are engaged in copying decrees for Hapu-Seneb. The Royal Teacher assigns the Corps of Pages secretarial tasks when his regular scribes are fully occupied. But since none of the nobles in the Corps of Pages can be assigned anything other than normal schoolwork, Hapu-Seneb's extra work always falls to Aron and Senen-Mut to complete.

"I have no idea what you are talking about," Senen-Mut replies.

"You know very well what I am saying," Aron laughs. "Your prattling during the lectures has caught the interest of the princess."

Aron's laugh rings with jealousy. Aron's father also served in the Pharaoh Amen-Hotep's Wars against the Northern Nomes, but Aron's father is not a member of the Order of the Golden Fly. This distinction becomes the source of Aron's hostility towards Senen-Mut. Aron is the tallest and most muscular student in the corps. He has a quick wit and a competitive disposition, especially when it comes to Senen-Mut. But Aron is no scholar and does not enjoy his studies. Even so, Hapu-Seneb has been instructed to see that Aron always attends the same lectures as Senen-Mut. Thus the Student of Jackal has ample opportunity to observe Maat-Ka-Re's behavior. And the Jackal is more than a little jealous of the Wast.

"I'm telling you this," Aron confides to Senen-Mut, "so that you don't make things harder on yourself, or me, than they already are."

Senen-Mut doesn't comment, but, inwardly, he is thrilled.

Maat-Ka-Re is interested in me.

Senen-Mut can't believe it. His own feelings stir. The very name, *Maat-Ka-Re*, sends a stream of fire cursing through his body. Whenever he is near her, Senen-Mut feels something akin to a burning inside. He wants to explode. But he knows that he must be careful. He dares not reveal his own feelings to anyone, especially not Aron. It could cost him his position as a Royal Page and Student of Wast, if not his head.

But what will be, will be, especially when Hathor herself enkindles a great and abiding love between a man and a woman. And it does not matter that the woman is the daughter of Pharaoh and the man is the son of a commoner.

Then it happens. One day when the Princess Maat-Ka-Re overhears Hapu-Seneb giving Senen-Mut and Aron a copying assignment, she requests one for herself, as well. Furthermore, Maat-Ka-Re tells the Royal Teacher that she wants the task assigned to Aron. That a Child of the Palace be given an assignment is unheard of. However, the royals are laws unto themselves; they have supreme authority over not only their servants, but also everyone else in the Palace of Ladies.

"I do not want the commoners to learn more than I know," Maat-Ka-Re explains when questioned by her personal tutor, It-Ruri.

Soon Senen-Mut and Maat-Ka-Re find themselves sharing several evenings a week together. They are alone with the exception of her brother, the Royal Heir, Aa-Kheper-Ren-Re, 'Aak,' for short and the princess' ever-present bodyguard, Awab. Over the next several weeks, Maat-Ka-Re and Senen-Mut meet ever more frequently over papyrus scrolls in the Copy Room. The Student of Wast intrigues the Royal Princess.

"He's so unlike the others," Maat-Ka-Re confides to Aak.

"Is that so?" the Crown Prince yawns.

"Yes," the princess smiles dreamily. "He doesn't treat me like a ____."

"Like a what?" the Crown Prince asks.

"Like a woman," Maat-Ka-Re blurts out.

"How does he treat you?" Aak asks.

"He treats me like I'm as important as any of the other students," Maat-Ka-Re replies.

"Even as important as me?" Aak asks. The Crown Prince cannot resist shooting a jibe at Maat-Ka-Re. Even though he loves her dearly, Aak sometimes vents his jealousy over the favors their father showers upon his sister.

"Possibly," Maat-Ka-Re says, doing nothing to assuage her brothers hurt feelings.

One day, when Aak is Pharaoh, he and Maat-Ka-Re will wed. Their marriage will be strictly ceremonial, rather than connubial. Though he and Maat-Ka-Re love each other as brother and sister, the Crown Prince looks forward to the day when his sister must become subordinate to his will. Until then, Aak really doesn't care who Maat-Ka-Re takes as her consort, though a commoner might well fit into his plans. But he will not object to his sister becoming intimate with the Student of Wast.

"You're considering taking this commoner as your consort?" the Crown Prince asks.

"Possibly," Maat-Ka-Re repeats.

So, eventually, the awkward meetings between Pharaoh's daughter and the *Student of Wast* in the Copy Room become trysts in secret places, away from prying eyes, all over the Palace of Ladies.

"Tell me about your family," Maat-Ka-Re asks coyly one evening as the young lovers hold hands in one of the many private gardens inside the Palace of Ladies.

Though Senen-Mut tells her of his father's service to the Nomarch of Wast and his family's flax plantation, he discloses his own deep conviction about his father's success. "But without my mother's devotion, my father would be nothing," he confides.

Maat-Ka-Re stares at her suitor. "Tell me about your sisters," she urges him.

"When Nof-Ret-Hor and I were children, we could enter each other's dreams," Senen-Mut relates.

"I would like to enter my brother's dreams," Maat-Ka-Re exclaims. "Do you think you can teach me?"

"I can try," Senen-Mut replies. But he quickly learns that this js a mistake.

"I don't want you to try," Maat-Ka-Re says sternly, "I want you to do it!"

Senen-Mut is confounded. He doesn't know what to say. But on this occasion, sensing his distress, Maat-Ka-Re relents. She draws upon her experiences in manipulating both her father and Aak. She knows that if he is to further her plans this is not the time to force Senen-Mut into submission. Now she needs her future consort's devotion, not his fear. So, in their secret meeting places all over the *Palace of Ladies*, the lovers are engaged in more than idle discussions about family and dreams. More frequently, the lovers find themselves engaged in each other's arms.

Soon Karnak begins buzzing. Stories about the princess' scandalous behavior circulates all over Pharaoh. Their secret meetings, never very secret, are now under constant observation. Maat-Ka-Re even recruits Aak to cover for them, but to no avail. All of Karnak talks of nothing more than the affair the Royal Princess is having with the Student of Wast. Finally Maat-Ka-Re decides that all her attempts fail at keeping her affair a secret.

"No fish swim in my pond," Maat-Ka-Re complains to Senen-Mut. They meet in the garden adjoining her private apartments. "Even though my servants fill the pond with fish everyday, they all quickly disappear."

Maat-Ka-Re looks up to Senen-Mut. A comically serious look is frozen on her face, as if the absence of fish in her pond is of major importance.

"I have heard that you know how to get fish, even the rare species of fish, to swim in any pond you choose," she says, measuring the impact her words have on the man she has chosen as her consort.

Maat-Ka-Re loves to tease Senen-Mut. She begins by treating him tenderly as if to say, *"I love you!"* Then she behaves as if to tell him that 'only fools fall in love.' Senen-Mut is no fool, but he has certainly fallen in love with the most beautiful woman in the Two-Lands. Maat-Ka-Re is playful, impulsive and amazingly self-willed. None of this matters to Senen-Mut. If Maat-Ka-Re wants fish in her pond, Senen-Mut will put fish in her pond.

"I can get fish to swim into any pond that I choose," he boasts.

"So you can fill my pond with fish?" she asks smiling coyly.

"I'll bet he can't," Aak sneers. The Crown Prince tires of listening to the lovers teasing each other.

However, Aak actually likes Senen-Mut. Maat-Ka-Re's brother admires the Student of Wast for his intellect and his health.

"I'll get fish to swim in your pond," Senen-Mut promises.

From then on, the Student of Wast along with many fish of the Nile become frequent visitors to Maat-Ka-Re's pond in her private garden in Pharaoh's Mansion of Millions of Years.

"Senen-Mut," Maat-Ka-Re shouts, "come see the fish gathering in my pond."

Today she, Senen-Mut and Aak enjoy the cooling, gentle breezes wafting off the Nile. Maat-Ka-Re and Senen-Mut have forsaken their meeting places in the Palace of Ladies and for months meet almost daily in her private garden. Counting the fish, Maat-Ka-Re squeals with joy. Aak is also impressed, although he is not nearly as exuberant. The Crown Prince has a weak heart. It has been weak from an early age. And from Aak's early age, Maat-Ka-Re has cared for her little brother. One day, Aak will become Pharaoh, Ruler over the Two-Lands. But, for the time being, he spends all his time with his sister. It is important to Maat-Ka-Re that Senen-Mut win Aak's respect and approval.

"Look Aak!" Maat-Ka-Re claps her hands together as she races around her pool. "Look at that one. He's a whopper!"

Pharaoh's daughter beckons Aak's litter bearers to bring her brother closer. She wears a filmy linen slip that stretches from just below her shoulders to her ankles. A side slit, from the ankle to the knee, allows her to walk comfortably. Her firm, young breasts are barely covered by the shoulder straps supporting her dress. The straps are beaded and cut in a V-shape. Maat-Ka-Re's skin glows with the luminescence of youth, her eyes are lovely and clear. Her full lips are moistened and colored with red ochre. She perfumes her body with exotic oils from throughout the Two-Lands. Senen-Mut likens her fragrance to Hathor's breath; it overpowers him. She speaks softly with a musical lilt. To Senen-Mut, the sweetness of sounds flowing from her mouth makes her whole body a musical instrument. Her hair is curious. Sometimes it is dark brown with golden highlights. Then at other times it seems her hair is as black as lapis lazuli. Maat-Ka-Re walks with graceful, unhurried steps; her rounded hips, trim thighs and well-formed legs exude a sensual eroticism.

"One day, my brother," Maat-Ka-Re says looking over at Aak, "Senen-Mut will unite all in the Two-Lands under your rule as he brings me these fish."

"Dear sister," Aak replies, "I believe your prophecy, but I can take no comfort in it."

"You are a terrible grouch," Maat-Ka-Re says gaily, "what ails you today?"

Aak says nothing. He does not wish to spoil his sister's happiness with his depression. Maat-Ka-Re turns back to Senen-Mut.

"Your father," she asks, "Pharaoh Amen-Hotep gave him land?"

"My father saved the life of General Amen-Nati, now Nomarch of Wast," Senen-Mut replies.

"Did you know that distinguished women actually saved Egypt from the asiatics and the Nubians?" the princess asks. Her face becomes serious.

Senen-Mut stares at Maat-Ka-Re. He's never certain what she will say next.

"How did they do that?" he asks, trying to keep the skepticism from his voice.

"When Pharaoh Seqenen-Re Tua-aa II died fighting the asiatics, his wife, Queen Ah-Hotep, my great-grandmother, led our military campaigns. She fought on the battlefield until she expelled all the asiatics out of Egypt. Then she ordered the executions of all the Egyptian nomarchs, administrators, scribes and priests who collaborated with our asiatic enemies."

"When my father fought for Pharaoh Amen-Hotep," Senen-Mut says quietly, "long after the death of your great-grandmother, Egyptians were still killing Egyptians. My father always believed there was some other reason for the war in the north."

"My grandmother, Queen Ah-Moses Nefer-Tiri, Queen Ah-Hotep's daughter, directed the bloody purge of all nomarchs and their families because for two hundred years they served the Hyksos kings," Maat-Ka-Re replies. Her voice is calm, but she resents Senen-Mut's impertinence. "The 'Eyes of Horus' provided the list of those to be exterminated."

Senen-Mut senses Maat-Ka-Re's irritation and says nothing.

"My great-grandmother was invested into the Order of the Golden Fly, the highest military order in Egypt," Maat-Ka-Re continues. "All of the members of this order fought and displayed valor in battle." The princess scrutinizes the Student of Wast. "Your father is a member of the order, isn't he?"

"Yes," Senen-Mut replies, "he's a member. But he still questions why the war killed so many Egyptians."

"Four Pharaohs gave their lives in bloody battle, along with thousands of soldiers. They died to liberate the Two-Lands from the asiatics," Maat-Ka-Re says. "We fought to repel the invasion of our land from the north. The heads of those who allowed the asiatics to freely wander about our land were put on poles along with their families and soldiers. Queen Ah-Moses Nefer-Tiri personally led the army against these traitors. This is her enduring legacy."

Senen-Mut decides it is unwise to displease his lover with his father's doubts. He takes her hand and pulls her to his side.

"As I said," Maat-Ka-Re continues, "the queens of Egypt have played an important role in saving Egypt. And so will I."

"I know you will, my princess," Senen-Mut tells her. "And I will serve you."

"Yes," Maat-Ka-Re says, "for you were sent to me by Hathor."

"Why did Hathor send me to you?" Senen-Mut asks, affecting a look of innocence.

"Because I prayed to Hathor every day," Maat-Ka-Re smiles, "and she sent me you."

"Is that royal brat still consorting with that commoner from Wast?" Seth-Mesy asks.

"I am afraid so, your Excellency," his assistant replies. "Hapu-Seneb reports that, not only does Maat-Ka-Re keep company with the Student of Wast, but also shares his independent way of thinking. Together they challenge everything."

"See how heresy grows, day by day," Seth-Mesy exclaims. "What began in Thebes will be sweeping across the Two-Lands." The high priest's eyes blaze with zeal. "Daily those who should obey, question the will of god!"

"The Royal Teacher informed me that the Student of Wast even questioned the source of the god's authority," the assistant adds.

"The heresy has returned to Karnak, and is taking root in the royal family," Seth-Mesy says. "Amen wills that it shall go no further!"

"It's intolerable," Seth-Mesy's assistant echoes.

"Centuries of unwavering obedience make possible the traditions of the Two-Lands," the high priest says. "We cannot allow this heresy to destroy our traditions."

"Hapu-Seneb reports that the weak-willed Royal Heir has fallen under the spell of this commoner as well," the assistant continues.

"I will not have it," Seth-Mesy declares. "I do not care what you do! Slit that commoner's throat and feed him to the crocodiles, if you must. But separate that commoner from the royal couple, immediately!"

"Yes, lord," the assistant responds.

"Hi, Senen-Mut!"

The unfamiliar figure just appears in the Copy Room. Hapu-Seneb has given Senen-Mut and Aron the task of reproducing twenty scrolls before the morning. Maat-Ka-Re isn't with them this evening. As a matter of fact, it's been almost a week since Senen-Mut last saw her. She hasn't attended any of his lessons, nor has she responded to any of his messages, left discreetly in their secret spots. Senen-Mut tries to distract himself with work, but he's worried. It's because he is distracted that the Student of Wast hadn't noticed this stranger slinking up to the table. But now he notices the stranger staring directly at him, a strangely comical grin plastered on his face. There is something vaguely familiar about him.

"Don't you remember your guide, Student of Wast?" the stranger asks.

Senen-Mut takes a better look. It's the dockworker that escorted him here to Karnak.

"Iby!" Senen-Mut shouts, genuinely surprised. "Is that you?"

"This is the guide who brought me here," Senen-Mut explains to Aron.

Aron nods but continues with his work.

"Why are you here?" Senen-Mut asks.

Iby wears a dark woolen cloak over a dark linen tunic.

"I came to get you, Senen-Mut," he says quietly. "But not so loud."

"You've come to get me?"

"Yes." Iby gives the Student of Wast a crooked smile "How long have you been attending the royal school now?"

"Almost two years."

"Two years!" Iby exclaims. "I bet 20 copper debens that you would be gone before the end of your first month." Iby shakes his head in disbelief. "Well, time to get going."

"Get going?" Senen-Mut asks. "I'm not going anywhere."

"Oh yes you are, Student of Wast!" Iby says. "I've been instructed to get you and the Student of Jackal here out of Karnak as quickly as possible. Your lives are in danger!"

"But why?" Senen-Mut asks with a look of innocence.

In an instant Aron understands the situation. Aron looks first at Iby then at Senen-Mut

What a fool! he tells himself, but to Iby he says, "Our friend, here, believes that Pharaoh takes kindly to a commoner being intimate with his daughter."

With that, the Student of the Jackal drops his stylus and says, "I'm ready!"

So that's why I haven' heard from Maat-Ka-Re, Senen-Mut thinks, remaining seated.

"Just because Pharaoh knows that Maat-Ka-Re and I love each other doesn't mean that I should go slinking off into the night," he tells Iby.

Aron is putting on the dark tunic and robe proffered by the dockworker.

"No?" Iby snorts. "Well what if I were to tell you that, if you return to your sleeping mat at the Corps of Pages tonight, you will certainly meet with a fatal accident."

Senen-Mut feels a cold and clammy chill running through down his spine.

"How do you plan for us to escape?" Senen-Mut asks, somewhat chastened.

Iby thrusts the dark tunic and cloak into Senen-Mut's hands.

"Just leave that up to me and do what I say," Iby says. "These cloaks will help conceal you from the sentries. Don't worry. No one is looking for you. At least not yet."

Outside the Palace of Ladies, Iby picks his way over dark paths that would have been difficult to find even during the day. Not even the sentries standing watch on the wall surrounding the Palace of Ladies are aware of the dark figures slinking through the palace's secret passageways. They exit through a hidden gate in the wall surrounding the Palace of Ladies. Passing through the reeded canal area near the royal dock, Iby leads the Royal Students' escape through the main wall surrounding Karnak and over an indirect route back to Thebes. It is almost dawn before the three travelers, weary from their trek, arrive at a small cluster of mud huts a short distance from the harbor.

"Stay here!" Iby tells the runaways. "I'll be back."

The Theban night is chilly. The wharf is silent. The darkened hulls of river boats are barely visible in the predawn gloom. Here and there lights, glowing inside alabaster vases, twinkle on the decks of boats that gently rock to and fro upon gentle waves. Down near the reeds, knots of people huddle around open fires set up high on brick mounds. Somewhere an owl lets out a mournful series of hoots welcoming a new day. After awhile Iby returns.

"At first light, the Eyes of Horus will see you safely aboard the *Barge of Wast* ," Iby says. "They will provide us transportation down to Memphis."

"The *Barge of Wast?*" Senen-Mut exclaims. "You mean the Lord Amen-Nati knows about this?"

"Of course," Iby replies. "Who did you think was responsible for saving your life?"

"That must mean my father knows, as well," Senen-Mut murmurs, almost in tears. He buries his face in his hands. Then he rises up again. "The Eyes of Horus?" Senen-Mut questions. "Who are they?"

"The Eyes of Horus are the 'eyes and ears' of Pharaoh," Iby explains. "You must have made an impression on someone. My uncle says that without the help of the Eyes of Horus, you would have been left in the red sand as a snack for the jackals. Okay, lover boy, try to get some rest. And consider yourself expelled from the Royal School."

"But where am I going?" Senen-Mut asks.

"We," Iby corrects Senen-Mut.

"What do you mean, *we?*" Senen-Mut asks.

"You, Aron and me ..., *we!*" Iby explains. "It was my fee for getting the two of you safely out of Karnak. The Lord of Wast and the Eyes of Horus have decided where to use your unique talents."

In the gloom, Aron sits in the chilly mud hovel and wonders what trick of fate has caused him to end up here. And pulling his cloak around him for warmth, Aron realizes that, as much as he disliked Senen-Mut before, he really hates him now.

In the Mansion of Millions of Years, a coded knock sounds on the door of Mut-Sherif, Pharaoh's Grand Vizier. A servant allows a watcher for the Eyes of Horus to enter.

"Master, the Student of Wast and the Student of Jackal are headed north," the watcher says.

Mut-Sherif nods and dismisses the messenger. *So much for Seth-Mesy's plot to slit the Student of Wast's throat.* Pharaoh's Grand Vizier congratulates himself.

The next morning a number of Pharaoh's closest advisors, including his Grand Vizier and the high priest of Amen, meet in Pharaoh's Seal Room.

"The Eyes of Horus inform me that the Wast's independent thinker has escaped having his throat slit," Mut-Sherif announces to Pharaoh. "Even now, he is heading towards Memphis."

"Let us hope that our students will take better advantage of their opportunities at Horus Nest," Pharaoh observes. He looks at Mut-Sherif as the two share their private joke.

Seth-Mesy, on the other hand, is quite annoyed.

"If the Student of Wast knew where he was going," Pharaoh's Royal Scribe observes in a high-pitched squeaky voice, "the lad might have chosen to have his throat slit."

Other council members politely ignore the scribe's tasteless remark. If he were sent away, the Royal Scribe would most likely faint at the very mention of Horus Nest.

Senen-Mut, Aron and Iby speed down the Nile on the seven-day trip that will end in the harbor of Memphis. Shu, the wind god, is the oarsmen's friend. He blows into the *Wast's* brightly colored sails, easily propelling the barge over Hapi's white-capped waves towards its destination. When the *Barge of Wast* arrives in Memphis, the oarsmen praise Shu for making their toil so easy.

Horus Nest is Pharaoh's great military fortress located apart from the island city of Memphis. Horus Nest is the headquarters for Pharaoh's War Council. After arriving at Memphis, the three companions are taken directly to the section at Horus Nest reserved for training new recruits.

"The three of you have completed your studies at the Royal School at Karnak, I understand?" the officer in charge asks. "We've been told to expect you."

Senen-Mut and Aron nod their heads; Iby says nothing.

"That must mean that the three of you have completed your education and can read and write."

Again there is no response. The training officer's face frowns into a look of anger.

Eugene Stovall

"When I speak, I expect an answer," he barks. "Have you completed your education, or not?"

"Yes, Master," all reply in unison.

"I have been told that you read and write like scribes. Is this true?"

"Yes Master!" Senen-Mut answers. "All of us can read and write."

"Not I, sir," Iby replies with an impish grin on his face. "I can neither read nor write."

The officer stares at Iby.

"Ah yes," the officer replies, "I've heard about you. You're the one who can slip in and out of Karnak without the Seeing Waters or anyone else knowing you're there."

"Well, sir," Iby replies, "I certainly could not have done it without assistance from the Eyes of Horus."

"Is that so," the officer says. "What is your name, recruit!"

"Iby, sir."

"Well, Iby," the officer laughs, "I'm putting you in charge. I don't care that your friends can read and write and have the makings of scribes, what I need are soldiers. You seem to have the makings of a good one. I'm holding you responsible for these other two."

"Yessir," Iby replies. His lopsided grin spreads even wider on his face.

I think I am going to like the army, Iby tells himself.

BOOK TWO

CHAPTER FOUR

For centuries, Pharaoh's army was an amalgamation of militias raised, trained and supplied by his nomarchs. Though good enough to subdue Nubian tribes in the south and nomads wandering into the Nile Delta from Palestine, Pharaoh's soldiers were hopelessly ill-equipped and ill-prepared to face a modern army. To defend their lands, eighteenth dynasty pharaohs required a modern army charging across battlefields in fast-moving chariots, hacking and slicing with bronze weapons as they flew by, preparing demoralized enemy soldiers for slaughter by hard charging infantry. Like his predecessor, Pharaoh Thut-Moses also wants a well-armed and well-trained army. He needs to continue the centralization of his army under the unified command of his War Council. The War Against The Northern Nomarchs gave Pharaoh Amen-Hotep the opportunity to build a truly national army. Now Thut-Moses wants to continue the process by assuring himself of the personal loyalty of his officer corps. This is why Thut-Moses and his War Council actively recruit officer candidates like Iby, Aron and Senen-Mut.

"Swing the body smoothly, soldier!" the Master of Javelins shouts. "The spear must be one with the arm!" The training officer positions Senen-Mut's arm and body into the correct throwing position. "One day your life will depend on your javelin. And you'll thank me for making soldiers out of you scribes." He derides them because they can read and write. The Master of Javelins considers the officer candidates weaklings, unfit to lead soldiers into battle. To him, they are nothing but bald-headed scribes.

My hand comes back, level with my ear, weight on the right foot. Senen-Mut's mind knows what to do, but his body refuses to obey. *Forward, smoothly! The hand must be one with the spear. Now release!* His spear flies towards its target in a perfect arch. Sailing, sailing... but again it falls short. Three months of training and Senen-Mut has made so little progress in weapons training that his fellow officer candidates mock him.

"Instead of being called the Student of Wast, he should have been the Student of Tortoise," they laugh.

Neither does Senen-Mut manage mace or the *kapesh*. His only competence is with the dagger.

"The dagger is the assassin's weapon," his training officer sneers. "You should be in the Seeing Waters with those sneaky Nubians."

Senen-Mut works even harder at the javelin, but after six months, he still can't hit the target. His efforts produce little more than aching shoulders, sore legs and a completely exhausted body. The running, the physical exercises, the weapons training and the hand-to-hand fighting done under the scrutiny of his training master grinds him down. Senen-Mut is drained mentally and emotionally. Furthermore, training in armor, greaves and helmet saps the little energy he has remaining. Since they are not actually on a battlefield, Senen-Mut reasons it's unnecessary for him to wear armor while doing weapons training.

Unlike Senen-Mut, neither Iby nor Aron have any difficulty with the training. Aron's physical strength and athletic ability makes his training at Horus Nest more play than work. Aron flings the javelin as if it were a throwing stick. Whatever Aron aims at, at whatever distance, he hits. Iby has an inexhaustible store of energy. Though he's of average height and not particularly strong, Iby seems unaffected by the rigors of military training. He runs all day, completes each exercise, meets the minimum requirements for all weapons and is never tired.

Every day Senen-Mut reaches the limit of his endurance. The javelins' shafts blister his hands. Splinters puncture his blistered hands. Pain sears his hand with every throw. At last, out of sheer exhaustion, he voices a complaint.

"I could throw my javelin a lot further," Senen-Mut confides in Iby, "if I could practice without a helmet and this bronze leather jacket. And these greaves on my shins are so heavy that I can't step into my throw."

Unfortunately for Senen-Mut, the Master of Javelins overhears his complaint. The training master concludes that the Student of Wast wants the Javelin Master to overhear him. The battle-toughened training master is physically imposing and towers over Senen-Mut. He has been ordered to pay particular attention to the Student of Wast and curb any tendency that the recruit exhibits towards insolence or disrespect.

"They told me that you recruits were intelligent," the Master of Javelins says, looking at Senen-Mut but speaking loud enough to be heard by everyone on the practice field. "Troops of the Middle Kingdom marched into battle wearing only loincloths. The Hyksos wore body armor. Who do you think had the advantage, recruit?"

The Javelin Master glares down onto Senen-Mut's face. Withering under the Javelin Master's gaze, Senen-Mut stammers, "The soldier wearing body armor, Master."

"The soldier wearing body armor," the Master sneers. "But this scribe, here, questions Pharaoh's compassion for his soldiers. Pharaoh wishes to protect his soldiers from harm while our wise scribe, here, wishes Pharaoh's soldiers to march into battle wearing only a kilt." Then the Master of Javelins addresses Iby. "I thought your men were educated."

Iby just shrugs.

"Captain!" the Javelin Master shouts.

"Yessir!" Iby responds

"I want everyone of your men throwing javelins continuously until I tell them to stop. Do you understand?"

"Yes, Master!"

"*Continuously!*"

"Yes, Master!" Iby shouts once again.

Senen-Mut hurls one javelin after another. *How long have they been throwing?* Each time he releases one javelin, another is thrust into his hands. He hefts the wooden shaft, pain sears down his back and radiates into his arms. His shoulders quiver as he tenses up in preparation for his next throw. After a while, Senen-Mut's legs buckle. When the final javelin is placed into his hands, his throw barely clears his front foot. Actually it isn't a throw at all. Rather Senen-Mut falls forward and the javelin sticks in the ground in front, propping him up without leaving his hand.

Watching Senen-Mut's body quivering in pain, the Master of Javelins smirks. "That is enough for today!" he announces.

Senen-Mut's hand is a bloody mess. But he gets no sympathy from his fellow recruits, only hostile glares. Senen-Mut drags himself to the barracks. He collapses on his sleeping mat and falls into a dreamless sleep.

Four more months of training pass, but now after ten months, the twelve-hour days are not as long. Senen-Mut misses fewer evening meals because of fatigue. His body is now rock hard and, what is more remarkable, he almost tosses his javelin the minimum distance set for officers. Aron, on the other hand, buries his javelin in a target at twice the minimum distance. Now Senen-Mut can batter his opponent, relentlessly, with the mace and can use his kapesh to hack, rip and slash with the best of the recruits.

Swing your body around. Pause. Your hand is set up high, level with your ear. Weight on your right foot. Now swing back. Shift your weight forward in a single movement. Body, shoulder, arm, all at one with your javelin. And throw!

It's Senen-Mut's best throw, ever. He impales his target. Proudly, he shows his target to Iby and Aron.

"How many javelins has he thrown since he's been in training?" Iby asks Aron. "Fifty? a hundred? A thousand? And that's his best throw." They look at each other and burst out laughing.

Over the next several months, in addition to their normal training, the three officer recruits receive lectures on tactics, strategy, intelligence and logistics. Of the thirty officer candidates in training, six, including Iby, Aron and Senen-Mut are selected for additional training at the Temple at Iunu, a short distance from Horus Nest on the western side of the Nile. At Iunu, Pharaoh's handpicked candidates learn to lead soldiers across unfamiliar ground guided only by the stars or reorient an army unit in the desert after a storm. The council needs officers who understand military maneuvers and can complete them on a cloudy day. When their training is almost complete, Senen-Mut and his companions are selected to attend the temple of Iunu where they study astrology, astronomy and mathematics under the tutelage of masters assembled from all over the Two-Lands

Pen-Nek-Heb, high priest of the Aten, holds the hereditary titles, Chief of Observers and Greatest of Seers. Pen-Nek-Heb is the lord of Iunu and serves on Pharaoh's inner council. Pen-Nek-Heb hears much concerning the Student of Wast. It is not everyday that Pen-Nek-Heb has the Consort of the Princess as his student. Pen-Nek-Heb looks forward to meeting the student whose notoriety includes being branded a heretic by Seth-Mesy. Though a high priest, Pen-Nek-Heb's world view, which includes the need for independent thinkers in the army and elsewhere in the Two-Lands, has made him one of Pharaoh's more trusted councilors.

"I am interested in whether you see any promise in this Student of Wast," Mut-Sherif confides in Pen-Nek-Heb. "Pharaoh ordered me to save him from your friend, Seth-Mesy."

"Save him?"

"Seth-Mesy ordered his throat cut."

"Oh!"

"I just hope that we haven't gone to all this trouble for nothing."

"Don't worry," Pen-Nek-Heb promises, "I will give you a report on the student's progress."

For months, astronomers, astrologers and mathematicians teach Senen-Mut and his fellow officer candidates how to observe the movements of the heavenly bodies and record their observations. The recruits learn to measure distances and predict the weather. They learn to predict future events by applying the rules of scientific observations, measuring distances and observing their interactions. Senen-Mut and Aron must assist Iby to record his observations. Iby is not illiterate. The former dockworker can read hieroglyphics quite well. However, Iby has difficulty inscribing his 'glyphs' properly.

Pen-Nek-Heb sends Mut-Sherif regular reports on Senen-Mut's progress. When their studies are completed, the officer candidates must undertake a final examination. They must record astronomical and astrological observations for a thirty-day period, noting the locations of all celestial bodies with their correct names for each day. Using their own observations, the students are required to predict agricultural, climatic and social events. These predictions should be accompanied by the student's judgments of the significance of their observations to Pharaoh, the army and the temple of Iunu. Iunu's scholars require the recruits to submit appropriate mathematical calculations as well as the appropriate astronomical and astrological rules governing each of their forecasts.

Senen-Mut records his daily observations on papyrus scrolls. Weekly he rolls and ties each scroll, individually, and stores them in a leather pouch and deposits his observations at the library. Iunu's wisest scholars evaluate each student's work. All meet the minimum requirements set by the War Council, but Pen-Nek-Heb directs Iunu's Keepers of Records and Possessors of Secrets to store Senen-Mut's observations and predictions in the temple's Vault of Initiates.

Upon returning to *Horus Nest*, Senen-Mut and his friends are advanced to the rank of officers of Pharaoh's War Council and given their army assignments. Aron is assigned to Pharaoh's chariots, Iby to the Eyes of Horus, and Senen-Mut is assigned to the War Council's supply section.

CHAPTER FIVE

Commissioned as watch officer for the Eyes of Horus, Iby oversees the Unit of Ten that patrols Memphis' Street of Pleasures. Soldiers assigned to the Eyes of Horus are responsible for policing the back alley brothels and wine shops operated by the Governor of Memphis. Of special importance are the foreign spies and religious zealots who intrigue against Pharaoh's interests. Mut-Sherif has expanded the Eyes of Horus' functions from merely providing military intelligence to policing the large cities and assisting in the collection of Pharaoh's taxes in villages, towns and homes throughout the Two-Lands. Pharaoh's police, the Eyes of Horus, watch and report on the activities of foreign agents. But they are especially interested in the agents sent by the Persian kingdom known as Mitanni, who are gaining supporters among the nomarchs. Iby already has more experience 'watching' than any other officer in the Eyes of Horus. Iby's soldiers give him daily reports on what they see and hear. The War Council is also interested in their competitors in the Seeing Waters.

Officially the Seeing Waters hold a royal commission to guard temples throughout the Two-Lands. Headquartered at Amen's temple at Karnak, the Seeing Waters are Seth-Mesy's personal intelligence source. Amen's high priest sends Seeing Waters throughout the Two-Lands to observe and report on whatever serves the interests of Seth-Mesy. And what concerns the high priest is heresy. In Iby, Mut-Sherif has a perfect watcher.

"This one has sources up and down the Nile," the Grand Vizier confides to Pharaoh. "He will keep us informed on the activities of the Seeing Waters as well as the Mitanni."

"Soon, because of this young man," the Grand Vizier promises, "we will know everything of any importance happening in the Two-Lands."

One evening, Aron and Senen-Mut visit Memphis' Street of Pleasure. Iby joins his two companions outside one of their favorite beer shops. Anywhere on the Street of Pleasure, the young officers enjoy the privileges of their rank. But as Senen-Mut stares up at the stars, he is unconcerned with rank and privileges. He is thinking about Maat-Ka-Re. Aron, on the other hand, is trying to decide which pleasure house to visit.

"Have you ever loved a woman?" Senen-Mut asks.

"That depends upon what you mean by 'love'," the newly commissioned chariot officer replies.

A great full moon hangs low over the Nile like a great portal into the realm of Nut. "On this perfect evening, our friend here is just 'mooning' over the Princess Maat-Ka-Re," Iby explains to Aron. Both Iby and Aron enjoy a chuckle at Senen-Mut's expense.

"I thought that I'd forgotten her," Senen-Mut sighs, "but I haven't." Out of habit he begins to observe planetary positions to the constellations. "Lately, I've been thinking more about her."

"No I don't moon over any woman," Aron says, laughing in answer to Senen-Mut's question.

The muscular, well-endowed officer of Pharaoh's chariots lowers his voice.

"If I were you, I'd forget all about Pharaoh's daughter." Aron winks at Iby. They both laugh before draining their bread beer. "The next time Iby might not be around to save you and me from the assassin's dagger!"

"Well, if you're worried about that," Iby interjects, "you'd better find a way of curing lover boy, here and quick."

"Why?" Aron asks.

"Pharaoh is leaving Thebes," Iby replies. "In less than a moon, the Lord of the Two-Lands will arrive in Memphis to review his northern defenses." The novice spymaster shoots Senen-Mut a curious look. "The Living God will be accompanied by his Inner Council, as well as his daughter, the Princess Maat-Ka-Re."

Maat-Ka-Re is coming to Memphis! Senen-Mut can't believe his ears. He bombards Iby with questions. "How do you know that she's coming? When will she arrive?"

"Whoa there, lover boy!" Aron interjects. "I, for one, don't want to find myself guarding some patch of desert in Nubia because of you. You've already cost me an opportunity for a royal appointment. I don't want to lose my appointment to Pharaoh's Chariots, as well." Aron's look tells Senen-Mut that this is serious.

"You can't just go around disrespecting the Living God and his household," Aron cautions. "So if you're planning to do anything, don't get me involved or else I'll report you."

Aron's heated words surprise Senen-Mut.

"What do you mean?" he asks. "I thought we were friends."

"*We're not friends!*" Aron snaps. "You're concerned only with yourself. *You have no friends.*"

"Come on, Aron!" Iby says, trying to head off a confrontation. "Admit it! Horus Nest is the best thing that ever happened to you. You love the chariots and the horses. You weren't cut out to be either a scribe or an administrator. If it hadn't been for Senen-Mut, you'd never have made it to the chariots. Neither would I have made it to the Eyes of Horus."

"That may be true," Aron says, "but all the *bad* things that ever happened to me were caused by him, as well. So I'm just warning him, that's all."

Senen-Mut turns his back to Aron. "I want you to tell me when the Princess Maat-Ka-Re arrives in Memphis," he whispers to Iby, "but I will wait until our friend leaves for a pleasure house. I don't want him to inform on you, or me."

A gloomy silence falls upon the three chosen by fate to be companions. After awhile, Aron mumbles something to Iby and stumbles off in the gloom of the evening towards the sounds of high-pitched screams and the laughter of women.

One day, I am going to enjoy crushing that arrogant son of Seth beneath the wheels of my chariot, Aron promises himself.

Pharaoh sits serenely in the Seal Room. Mut-Sherif, Seth-Mesy, some administrators and scribes join him. The Princess Maat-Ka-Re is present, as well. Thut-Moses likes hearing his daughter's advice. Father and daughter usually agree on most matters. Hapu-Seneb is also present. Pharaoh questions the Royal Teacher.

"While he attended the Royal School, did you find the Student of Wast competent at his studies?"

"Yes, Great God," Hapu-Seneb replies.

"What about the other commoner, the Student of Jackal?" Pharaoh asks. "Was he also a suitable student?"

"Yes, Lord."

"What about their intelligence, was any fault found with their reasoning?" Pharaoh asks.

"No, Great Lord," Hapu-Seneb replies. "They could reason, read and write quite well. Neither did Pharaoh's most skilled scribes find any fault with their work."

"These commoners," Thut-Moses continues, "left Karnak under strange circumstances. Isn't that correct?"

Seth-Mesy shifts about uncomfortably wondering where Pharaoh's questions are heading.

"Amen's priests say that 'commoners' are incapable of accomplishing such feats, is that not true, father?" Maat-Ka-Re smiles.

Thut-Moses gives Maat-Ka-Re a subtle wink. The princess remains serene, but she enjoys the sight of Seth-Mesy squirming as much as her father.

It's a shame that my daughter was born a woman, Thut-Moses smiles to himself. *She would have made a great Pharaoh.*

"Would the Living God disrupt traditions that have existed for centuries simply because he has found two exceptional commoners?" Seth-Mesy responds. "They may have been nobles in their previous lives."

Murmurs ripple among the scribes and administrators.

"The days of absolute obedience are gone for good," Mut-Sherif reminds the priest. "We cannot build an army or defend Egyptian territory by telling our soldiers that their only responsibility is to obey." Bowing to Pharaoh, Mut-Sherif says, "I believe that the Student of Wast and the Student of Jackal have shown that commoners possess as much of Thoth's good sense as nobles."

"Heresy! Heresy!" Seth-Mesy screams out. "It's not possible to train commoners to make wise, independent decisions. The masses must obey, willingly, if possible, by compulsion, if necessary."

"Pharaoh has already decided to give commoners choice," Mut-Sherif observes. "He intends to strengthen his army using intelligent planning, not blind obedience."

"Commoners cannot rise above their own selfish interests," Seth-Mesy declares. "Give them choices and they will ignore our ancient wisdom, our universal laws and the will of the gods. If we allow commoners to behave as they will, the Two-Lands will descend into chaos."

Forced to endure Seth-Mesy's insolence, Pharaoh listens quietly. Thut-Moses himself is a commoner. As Pharaoh Amen-Hotep's general, Thut-Moses successfully prosecuted Pharaoh's War Against the Northern Nomarchs. When Amen-Hotep died without an heir, the inner council proclaimed Thut-Moses pharaoh. Thut-Moses holds no prejudices against commoners. On the contrary, Thut-Moses appointed many of his former comrades in arms, including Amen-Nati, to prominent positions inside Karnak and over the forty-two nomes. Seth-Mesy's tirade against commoners amuses Thut-Moses.

"After seeing the greatness of Pharaoh's new army," Mut-Sherif asks the priest, "how can you object to Pharaoh's will?"

"Because to forgo the ancient laws is heresy!" Seth-Mesy's voice cracks with indignation.

"Do you insist that only those who are capable of 'kissing the ground' lead Pharaoh's army?" Maat-Ka-Re asks. She, too, is amused by the pompous little priest.

"I speak not of Pharaoh's administrators or overseers," Seth-Mesy retorts. "They, after all, are nobles." The priest raises his eyebrows, barely giving the princess any eye contact. Seth-Mesy can hardly conceal his contempt at having to respond to a woman, even if she is Pharaoh's daughter.

"You would return us to the days when our soldiers wore loin cloths on the battlefield," Mut-Sherif says, "and claim that their obedience would ward off Nubian arrows or Mitanni battle-axes."

"Well, frankly," Seth-Mesy says, "Amen does not care whether they ward off Nubian arrows or Mitanni battle-axes or not."

"We have nothing to fear from the Mitanni!" Hapu-Seneb asserts, coming to Seth-Mesy's defense. "We have excellent information that neither the Mitanni nor any other asiatic horde plan to invade Lower Egypt."

"Does your information come from the same source that claimed no one could get in or out of Karnak without the knowledge of the Seeing Waters?" Mut-Sherif sneers.

Thut-Moses decides to end the debate. "When I return from inspecting my fortifications in the northern nomes, I intend to deliver to the council my plans for the army. Now, all may leave, except Mut-Sherif."

Maat-Ka-Re is the reason Pharaoh decides to inspect his garrisons in the north. It was months earlier, on a warm, breezy day, when he and Maat-Ka-Re were departing Pharaoh's Hall of Justice, that the decision was made.

"Today, your judgments were well spoken, my daughter," Thut-Moses smiles.

"Thank you, father," Maat-Ka-Re replies. "I speak only as you, or Aak, would approve."

Pharaoh stiffens; he doesn't like being reminded of his son. No one other than Maat-Ka-Re even dares mention the Royal Heir's name in Pharaoh's presence. Even though father and son resemble each other, Thut-Moses hates the sight of his son. Notwithstanding their physical resemblance Thut-Moses, the battle-scarred veteran, finds his son's infirm and frail body offensive.

As a child, Aak suffered a terrible disease. Sores broke out on his arms, legs and body. For weeks, the Crown Prince lingered between life and death. Gradually, the healing priests and Aak's mother nurse the sick child back to health. Even though he recovered, the disease left Aak thin, shrunken and covered with scabs. He reminds his father of one of those orphaned children who slink about the marketplaces begging and stealing food. Thut-Moses hates the sight of his son's weak body. Anyone other than Maat-Ka-Re so witless as to mention Aak's name in Pharaoh's presence risks permanent expulsion from Karnak.

"You know that it distresses me when you mention his name," Thut-Moses chides Maat-Ka-Re.

"I don't care, father," she replies. "He's your son and my brother. And I love him."

Thut-Moses' face turns stony and he sets his chin at a stubborn angle.

"You had a number of petitions from Memphis and the northern nomes," Maat-Ka-Re observes. Her nonchalant manner immediately alerts Thut-Moses to be on his guard.

"And?" he asks.

"Father, I believe that its time for you to inspect your northern fortifications."

Her proposal does not take Pharaoh entirely by surprise.

"My daughter well knows that we visited the Northern Nomes last year."

"So!" Maat-Ka-Re says. "It is well known that a lack of vigilance caused the Hyksos to invade the Two-Lands and overthrow the Thirteenth Dynasty."

"That may be so, daughter," Thut-Moses responds, "but Pharaoh cannot just get into a barge and sail down the Nile to Memphis."

"Why not?" Maat-Ka-Re says.

"I know what you want, Maat-Ka-Re," Thut-Moses says. "It's been two years since you've seen your Student of Wast. So now you're saying that a bargain is a bargain."

Thut-Moses is surprised his daughter's patience has lasted this long. Normally, whenever she wants something, she pesters him until she gets it.

"If the Mitanni launched an invasion of the northern nomes," Maat-Ka-Re says coyly, "would Pharaoh delay leading his army because the Royal Presence was in the delta area, just last moon?"

Thut-Moses seldom denies his daughter anything and he will not deny her this. Thut-Moses directs the Royal Scribe to announce Pharaoh's tour of the northern nomes.

Once the others leave, Thut-Moses steps down from his dais and joins Mut-Sherif on one of the sofas.

"It seems that Seth-Mesy doesn't like our plans for the army," Thut-Moses confides in his Grand Vizier.

"Not only doesn't he like it, Great Lord," the Vizier replies, "Seth-Mesy is actively sabotaging it."

"But why?" asks Thut-Moses.

"The new epoch, predicted by Pen-Nek-Heb, worries Amen greatly," Mut-Sherif replies.

"Why should the new epoch worry Amen any more than the other priests?"

"Because when Seth-Mesy's own seers confirmed Pen-Nek-Heb's prophecy," Mut-Sherif explains, "they concluded... " Pharaoh's Grand Vizier pauses.

"Yes," Pharaoh says.

"They concluded that Amen would be toppled by the Aten!"

"Scribe," the Pharaoh calls out, "read me the prediction of the high priest of the Aten concerning the new epoch."

The Royal Scribe scurries out of Pharaoh's Seal Room. When he returns he carries several scrolls. After inspecting each, the scribe enrolls one and reads:

A long period passes, followed by a new darkness. We are tied to our predecessors by the thread of tradition and their teachings. The teachings that are appropriate for our present epoch can be found in the temples and monuments built by the great pharaohs towards the end of the last black period. Amen-Hotep destroyed what needed to be destroyed in order to conform to the law of the new epoch. Stone blocks from the old temples serve as foundations for the new ones. Thus does the Aten see into the future and foretell events.

"This doesn't sound like Amen will lose his power to me," Thut-Moses remarks.

"Seth-Mesy believes that the unbroken continuity of Egypt's ancient traditions flows through the priests," the vizier replies, "specifically through Amen's high priest."

Thut-Moses considers his Grand Vizier's words. "You must take precautions to guard the Student of Wast and the Student of Jackal," he says.

"It shall be done, Great Lord."

"As I recall," the Pharaoh chuckles, "it was you who encouraged my daughter to observe the Student of Wast for you."

Thut-Moses watches Mut-Sherif for a reaction. With all this court intrigue, it's difficult for Thut-Moses to know whom to trust. He knows that Mut-Sherif serves him well, but woe to anyone who jeopardizes the well-being of Pharaoh's daughter.

"As I understand the situation, the Royal Princess began examining the Student of Wast a little too closely," Mut-Sherif replies, keeping his voice and words well within the bounds of discretion.

"Maat-Ka-Re's young man shows how the army can benefit from officers with commoner backgrounds," Pharaoh says.

"The record of the Student of Wast, as well as those other two commoners convinced your War Council that commoners can make good officers," Mut-Sherif reports. "We are recruiting several more for officer's training at Horus Nest."

Pharaoh smiles. He is pleased.

"The War Council," Mut-Sherif continues, "rates the Student of Wast in its highest officer rank. He could be a general of the army, one day."

"Good! Good!" Thut-Moses is happy that he did not allow Seth-Mesy to slit Senen-Mut's throat.

"If the Student of Wast is the man for you, two years in military school will do him no harm," Pharaoh had told his daughter. "I will save him from Seth-Mesy, but he must attend the Military School at Horus Nest. After all, when you marry your brother, your consort should be more than just a lover."

Maat-Ka-Re loves and respects her father. *He is so practical.* Of course, he is right to require her consort to complete military training. When Aak is Pharaoh, he will need an advisor who understands the War Council. But the enforced separation has driven Maat-Ka-Re mad with desire.

As Seth Mesy and Hapu-Seneb make their way out of the Pharaoh's Seal Room together, their whispers are punctuated with oaths and scowls. The priests are not happy.

"Pharaoh continues to support the heresy," Seth-Mesy whispers.

"It will not end until liberals like Pen-Nek-Heb begin advocating mass education and the commoners are engaged in mass disobedience," Hapu-Seneb agrees.

"When I first put Thut-Moses on the throne," Seth-Mesy snarls, "not a day went by that he wasn't thanking me."

Hapu-Seneb nods his head in agreement.

"Now, he threatens to put my head on a pike!" The high priest's voice rises in anger.

"Pharaoh believes he can ignore god's power," Hapu-Seneb agrees.

"The gods will not permit it!" Seth-Mesy rages.

Once Amen's high priest is certain he and Hapu-Seneb are completely out of hearing, Seth-Mesy whispers, "Bring the agents of the Mitanni to me. Amen will stamp out the poison oozing out of Iunu."

CHAPTER SIX

Maat-Ka-Re gazes once more into her 'see-face'. She takes her bronze mirror from a bag of spun gold slung over her shoulder. Fashion has come only lately to Karnak. But now everywhere in Karnak, young, freethinking daughters of nobles and royals keep the metalworkers on the Street of Goldsmiths busy crafting brooches, collars and rings. The Palace of Ladies is now dictating fashion at pharaoh's court. But court fashion is not only being set by the young women, but the wives of the scribes and administrators, as well. All over Karnak the women of Pharaoh's court try to outdo each other in their array of pendants, brooches and bracelets.

"See how the heresy spreads?" Seth-Mesy harangues Pharaoh's Inner Council.

But few councilors are as concerned with Seth-Mesy's charges of heresy as they are with keeping peace in their household. Court fashion becomes as important a symbol of rank and prestige among the women as the offices and titles held by the members of Pharaoh's Inner Council. The men can deny neither their daughters nor their wives.

"Pharaoh allows the Princess Maat-Ka-Re to carry a bronze see-face in a purse of spun gold." The words echo throughout Karnak and all over Thebes. Noblewomen stretch their household budgets and incur the ire of their husbands to secure for their daughters and themselves their own bronze 'see-faces' and golden shoulder bags. Everyday artisans, jewelers and metal workers all over the Two-Lands and as far away as Megiddo pray to the gods for the continued health of Maat-Ka-Re Hat-Shep-Sut for introducing fashion to Thebes, Karnak and the Palace of Ladies.

So now thousands of women from all over Memphis mob the harbor, hoping for a glimpse of the princess with her bag of spun gold slung over her shoulder. They give the Living God a respectful welcome, but the crowd erupts with wild cheers and expressions of love for Maat-Ka-Re. The people's affection for his daughter pleases Thut-Moses and the princess. For a brief period of time, she encourages the mass excitement by showing off her purse of spun gold. But she quickly remembers that she has come to Memphis not to promote fashion but to satisfy her heart. She begins to seek out in the crowd the one face that she has come to see.

Did he miss me? Will he look the same? Does he still love me? Will I love him? Oh I hope so, the princess questions and answers herself. *I want to love him. Has Hathor really sent me the mate for my KA? Is he the one that I prayed for?* Maat-Ka-Re frowns. *It's been so long, I can't even remember what he looks like. Is he handsome? Is he tall?*

Maat-Ka-Re remembers that the other one, the Student of Jackal, was tall and muscular. But she didn't want a brute for a consort. The princess didn't want someone interested only in fulfilling his needs.

Yes, she smiles to herself. *I remember now. The Student of Wast was so intelligent that I couldn't help loving him.* Maat-Ka-Re knew Senen-Mut was the one to help her fulfill her ambition to be adored throughout the Two-Lands as 'the foremost of distinguished women'.

Amid the tumult of the beating drums, blaring horns and cheering crowds, Pharaoh's golden barge pulls into Memphis' royal dock. Maat-Ka-Re checks her 'see-face' one final time and scans the cheering crowds looking for *one* face, *his* face.

Oh, there he is! She sees him. He stands among Pharaoh's military escort. Her face breaks into a demure smile. When their eyes meet, she is not disappointed. Instantly, there is a hush as everything becomes quiet. Despite the roar of the crowd all the lovers hear is the beating of their own hearts. And for the future female pharaoh and her consort, time stops.

"I don't want Seth-Mesy knowing any more about our affairs than necessary, do you understand?" Thut-Moses instructs his Grand Vizier as soon as he disembarks.

"Yes, Majesty," Mut-Sherif replies.

"No words are to pass between those two," Thut-Moses insists, indicating his daughter and her lover. "I want no Seeing Waters observing Maat-Ka-Re and Senen-Mut together and no reporting any of our affairs back to Seth-Mesy. That priest is like a jackal always nipping at my heals."

"You will be obeyed, Master," Mut-Sherif replies.

Nomarchs and dignitaries from everywhere escort Pharaoh and his daughter to his Mansion of Millions of Years made ready for his majesty by an army of scribes, administrators and servants. Once inside the palace, Thut-Moses occupies himself with his War Council, his administrators and his nomarchs. Maat-Ka-Re is allowed to retire to her own chambers and entertain whomever she pleases. Later in the day, Senen-Mut is summoned to Pharaoh's Mansion of Millions of Years where the lovers are reunited. Finding themselves in each other's arms, drowning in each other's eyes, their long separation fades into a distant memory and the flame of their past love quickly rekindles itself..

For the next several weeks, Maat-Ka-Re's handmaidens, Awab, her bodyguard, the Palace Guard and the Eyes of Horus are the only intruders into the young lovers' privacy. Sometimes they jabber at each other all day long and far into the night. Other times they hardly say a word.

After a week, Senen-Mut is ordered to report back to Horus Nest. Maat-Ka-Re is required to attend her father's receptions, dinners and private audiences. Pharaoh especially requires her presence in the Hall of Justice to hear petitions and arbitrate disputes. When Pharaoh leaves Memphis on a three-week tour of his fortifications in the Sinai with his viziers, Maat-Ka-Re accompanies her father. The lovers are desolate. This second enforced separation is worse than the first. Once Pharaoh completes his inspection, he and Maat-Ka-Re return to Thebes. A month later, Senen-Mut and Iby receive orders to report to Mut-Sherif at the Eyes of Horus headquarters at Karnak.

"Our mission," explains the young officer escorting Senen-Mut and Iby into the Eyes of Horus building, "is to give Pharaoh sight over the whole of the Two-Lands."

They pass through a secret entrance and down a dark corridor.

"You'll get accustomed to the darkness, after awhile," the officer assures them. "We don't have the power of the obelisk down here." The young man was trained at Horus Nest and knows the signs and countersigns of both the War Council as well as the Eyes of Horus.

But he has never been in battle, Iby observes to himself. *Probably the son of a noble.*

Out of the dark, secret corridor, they emerge into a great hall filled with bustling officials. The walls of the hall are made of sandstone. They join at the ceiling to form a pyramid. Windows are clustered together on each side of the hall, in an ingenious pattern, symbolizing Horus. The pyramid building has four levels. At the top level is a door, a garden, a wall and a gate.

"How many pharaohs have the Eyes of Horus served," Senen-Mut asks their escort.

"We are taught that as long as the Golden Horus has ruled over the Two-Lands, we have been his eyes," the young officer replies.

The sun's light enters the pyramid's windows and reflects off the bronze panes mounted upon limestone walls. The sun bathes the entire hall in light. In one area, knots of army officers confer with each other while scribes sit at long tables consulting papyrus scrolls and maps. A continuous stream of messengers and pages scurry in and out of the hall carrying pouches filled with scrolls. On either sides of the hall, passages lead to the banquet room, the kitchen and sleeping areas. Senen-Mut and Iby are escorted to a rock-cut staircase leading up to a mezzanine where the doors open into a courtyard. At the rear of the courtyard, two Palace Guard stand at double doors eight cubits high secured by an intricate set of locks imprinted with the Grand Vizier's seal. The doors open directly onto the grounds of Pharaoh's Mansion of Millions of Years. Passing through well-tended gardens, they enter into the palace itself. A short distance down a well-lit passageway they come to a door with a guard posted outside. A knock and Senen-Mut and Iby are admitted into the private audience room of the Grand Vizier Mut-Sherif himself. Both officers bow to their knees, but Mut-Sherif greets them warmly.

"I am happy to meet the two of you, at last," Pharaoh's Grand Vizier smiles. "You may rise. I assume that my captain has shown you the Eyes of Horus headquarters?"

"Yes, Master," Senen-Mut responds.

"That is where you will reside and work." Mut-Sherif gives Senen-Mut a pat on the arm and a strange smile. "After you are settled, report to the Hall of Scribes in Pharaoh's House of Records. There you will receive reports from the Eyes of Horus agents. The captain here will give you whatever you need. You are to bring me whatever you learn that might be of importance to me or to Pharaoh." Mut-Sherif smiles at Senen-Mut once again. "Do you think you can handle this assignment?" the Grand Vizier asks.

"Yes, Lord," Senen-Mut replies.

"Good," Mut-Sherif replies. "Very good. Captain, you may show them back to their quarters."

Meeting Senen-Mut in person convinces Mut-Sherif that the Student of Wast will make an ideal consort for Princess Maat-Ka-Re Hat-Shep-Sut and Pharaoh's Grand Vizier is pleased. Senen-Mut is a commoner of uncommon intelligence. Unlike most of the young nobles that he must deal with, Mut-Sherif finds this young commoner utterly devoid of any political ambition and concludes that Senen-Mut's devotion to the princess will serve Pharaoh's goals for the 18th dynasty very well. *He is the very person to further Pharaoh's plans*, the Grand Vizier smiles to himself.

Months pass. When Senen-Mut is not with Maat-Ka-Re, he is reading and analyzing scrolls as well as writing and dispatching reports. Iby, on the other hand, spends weeks, even months at a time away from Karnak. He travels all over the Two-Lands, across the cataracts into Nubia, through the Sinai desert to Gaza and even into Palestine. At Horus Nest, Iby reports directly to the War Council. Senen-Mut doesn't miss his friend. He is too much in love with his princess.

"I've got a plan to get away all by ourselves," Senen-Mut whispers to Maat-Ka-Re one evening as they lie together in her garden. A pale moon casts shadows upon the grassy bank where they rest after swimming in her pond, still teeming with an amazing variety of fish. Three shadoof workers toil swiveling their poles back and forth from sunrise to sunset, pouring the Nile's waters into this canal every day, so that Maat-Ka-Re's pool remains filled. From where the lovers lay, stately sycamores shelter them from gentle winds. Flowers and shrubs fill the air with the aromatic fragrance of romance. Lying on their backs and staring into the star-filled night, the magic of the evening overwhelms the lovers.

If only Maat-Ka-Re's coterie of onlookers weren't always around, Senen-Mut pouts to himself. He is tired of the prying eyes of her retinue of guards and maids.

"And what might your plan be?" Maat-Ka-Re asks. Her moonlit expression, though playful, is intent, intrigued by the idea of slipping away from her palace.

"Let's sail up the Nile," Senen-Mut laughs, "just you and me."

"...and Aak?" Maat-Ka-Re adds mischievously.

Senen-Mut likes Aak, but he wants to be alone with Maat-Ka-Re. The princess gives Senen-Mut a haughty look reminding him of his place.

"Yes… and Aak," Senen-Mut agrees, not trying to hide his disappointment.

"Good," Maat-Ka-Re says, squeezing Senen-Mut's arm with both her hands, "when do we leave?"

"On the next full moon."

"You know that if my father catches us," Maat-Ka-Re laughs, "he'll be furious."

"Then we'd better not let him catch us," Senen-Mut says quietly. "OK?"

"OK," she laughs. Maat-Ka-Re eagerly anticipates the adventure, but with a far different purpose in mind. She intends to use Senen-Mut's escape as an opportunity to free Aak from his virtual imprisonment inside the Palace of Ladies.

So a month later, on another evening when the moon is once more a great round orb, Iby brings a boat to Karnak's royal dock. The conspirators, Senen-Mut, Maat-Ka-Re and Aak, accompanied by the Crown Prince's personal attendants, the princess' handmaidens and her bodyguard, board a nifty yacht with two sails and four rowers. Slipping out of Karnak, down the canal, they row up the Nile. The next morning, they arrive at Senen-Mut's family home in Armant in the Nome of Wast.

Senen-Mut's parents are overjoyed to see their youngest son.

"You left home a boy," his mother greets him, "now you return a man." Tears of pride pour down Hat-Nofer's cheeks.

But in the presence of the most beautiful woman in all of the Two-Lands, everyone else ignores Senen-Mut. In the presence of Princess Maat-Ka-Re, Senen-Mut's father, brothers and sisters are awestruck. All fall to their knees where they remain until Maat-Ka-Re begs them to rise. Even so, they all avert their eyes from the princess while doing everything they can to make her and Aak as comfortable as possible in their humble surroundings.

Once he has secured his guests in their own apartments with an army of servants to see to their comforts, Ra-Moses dispatches one of his sons to inform the Lord Amen-Nati of the royal couple's arrival. Amen-Nati speeds his Eyes of Horus messenger to Karnak.

Menkh, Amen-Nati's vizier and Seth-Mesy's spy, dispatches a Seeing Waters messenger to Karnak as well. Watchers of the Eyes of Horus intercept Menkh's man and return him to Wast. Amen-Nati's soldiers extract as much useful information from the Seeing Waters as possible before Menkh's messenger dies under the ordeal.

Mut-Sherif dispatches a Hundred Palace Guard to escort the royal couple back to Karnak. He also orders the guard to seize Senen-Mut and Iby, bind them and, after transporting them back to Thebes, throw the pair into a pit. They are to remain in the pit until Pharaoh decides whether to send them to a rock quarry, force them to slave in an underground tunnel or tie them to an oar on a transport barge. Maat-Ka-Re's prediction was correct. *When learning of Maat-Ka-Re's disappearance, Pharaoh became furious!*

"What if the Seeing Waters had found you before my Eyes of Horus?" Pharaoh thunders. "You could be lying in the desert, right now!"

"Father, you know perfectly well that we were in no danger," Maat-Ka-Re replies.

"That is not the point!" Pharaoh shouts even louder.

"And what is the point, Father?" Maat-Ka-Re asks.

"The point is that you exposed the Royal Heir to great dangers," Thut-Moses sputters.

"Ha! That's a laugh!" Maat-Ka-Re taunts her father. "What right have you to say anything about my brother, especially after the way you have treated him all these years." Maat-Ka-Re stares at her father; her look is one of contempt. "Nowhere in the Book of Thoth has any kindness been recorded that you have given my brother."

Pharaoh looks as if someone has struck him. But Maat-Ka-Re takes no pity and deals him another blow.

"Even while suffering from his childhood afflictions, my brother shows more courage and nobility than any other in your court," Maat-Ka-Re says. "Yet you continually deny him a father's love and fail to give him the preparation he needs to become Pharaoh."

Thut-Moses wilts under his daughter's rebuke like a flower that has been denied water. He buries his face in his hands and tears flow down his cheeks. But Maat-Ka-Re is relentless.

"I expect you to free my military escorts, immediately," she says. "Officers Senen-Mut and Iby assuredly protected me from any assassin that spindly-legged toad, Seth-Mesy, might have sent. Besides, if you condemn them, you must hold your own Eyes of Horus responsible for allowing us to escape."

With that Maat-Ka-Re gathers herself in the self-righteous indignation of a loving sister and exits Pharaoh's Seal Room, leaving her thoroughly confused and agitated father alone with his thoughts.

"Mut-Sherif, my old friend, what would you do?" Thut-Moses asks, looking woefully over to his Grand Vizier.

"About what great lord?" Mut-Sherif makes it a practice never to make himself a target of Pharaoh's anger, if he can help it, which, in this instance, he certainly can.

"Don't give me that 'great lord' stuff," Pharaoh groans. "You know about what. About my daughter. How did she grow up fast and so independent! *And how did it happen right under my own eyes?*"

"With such a daughter, the Living God has much to be proud of," Mut-Sherif offers.

"I suppose that when Amen gave me a son like Aa-Kheper-Ren-Re he gave me Maat-Ka-Re in compensation."

"Such a gift is the foremost of distinguished women," Mut-Sherif responds, knowing that praise for Pharaoh's daughter is never a mistake.

"Do you believe that Maat-Ka-Re planned this escapade just to chastise me for my treatment of her brother?" Pharaoh asks. "Or was it done on some whim?"

"Pharaoh has the words of the Princess Maat-Ka-Re," Mut-Sherif replies. "She accuses you of failing to prepare the Royal Heir for his role of Pharaoh?"

"I suppose she must have planned it all along," Pharaoh concludes. "She wants me to see how badly I've treated her brother, who she loves."

"With such a daughter you have been blessed," Mut-Sherif congratulates his master.

As a child, Senen-Mut's mother oft taught him, "A good woman of noble character is food that comes in a time of hunger." So he is not surprised when he and Iby are released from their pit on the orders of the Princess Maat-Ka-Re. And once he is reinstated into the Eyes of Horus, Senen-Mut is elevated to the rank of captain in Pharaoh's own elite Personal Guard.

CHAPTER SEVEN

"I will not allow Seth-Mesy's Seeing Waters to bully the dynasty back to the old ways!"

The fierce look upon Maat-Ka-Re's face is the one that she assumes when she practices being the foremost of distinguished women. But to Senen-Mut, this look only enhances her beauty.

Maat-Ka-Re and Senen-Mut hold hands under an arbor intertwined with convolvulus and ivy. The convolvulus' trumpet-like white and bluish flowers intertwine themselves within thick leaves of green ivy. Iby brings news from his most recent journey into Palestine. Iby has been given the responsibility for operating a special spy unit composed of orphans, street urchins and petty thieves who have slept among the reeds of Thebes' harbor, lived by their wits and taught Iby how to survive. These commoners are Iby's family—his only family. Many of them are now sailors, pilots and dockworkers. Iby promises any of his 'brothers' who join his organization of spies an elevation in status.

"Once my group is in place," Iby boasts to his friends, a crooked smile plastered onto the side of his face, "nothing will happen between the shores of the Great Green Sea and the Sixth Cataract that my 'family' won't know about."

Though Senen-Mut no longer receives Iby's reports, he continues to review every report filed at Eyes of Horus headquarters for Mut-Sherif. Upon occasion, Mut-Sherif requests that Senen-Mut report directly to Pharaoh. Thut-Moses is pleased to receive reports from Maat-Ka-Re's consort.

"My daughter was right to save those two from a rock quarry," Thut-Moses remarks to his Grand Vizier.

"Was she also correct about the treatment of your son, Master?" Mut-Sherif asks.

"Yes," Thut-Moses replies. "She was right about that as well."

But Pharaoh remains conflicted. Ever since Maat-Ka-Re rebuked him for his treatment of her brother, Thut-Moses has allowed Aak to render judgments in disputes brought to Pharaoh's Hall of Justice. But when Aak sits in judgment, Thut-Moses, embarrassed by his son's frailty and feebleness, finds it convenient to absent himself from the proceedings altogether. Believing Aak's infirmities reflect upon him, Thut-Moses closes his eyes and imagines the nobles saying, *"What do you expect from a commoner?"* Thut-Moses is certain the women at the Palace of Ladies ridicule him. It is difficult for Thut-Moses, the soldier, to handle the silent smirks and noisy whispers referencing his sickly, litter-ridden son. So Thut-Moses avoids being in the same room with Aak whenever possible.

Aak depends upon Maat-Ka-Re to assist him with his official duties and public appearances. The princess handles every situation with ease and grace. Maat-Ka-Re and Mut-Sherif bring Aak into Pharaoh's Hall of Justice and seat him upon a specially constructed dais that props him upright throughout the proceedings. Maat-Ka-Re sits by his side and Mut-Sherif stands close by. Aak always renders fair and just decisions. Though Pharaoh has the natural pride of a father, he experiences a sense of relief each time one of Aak's public appearances is concluded. Nevertheless, the more Aak appears in public, the more confident the Crown Prince becomes dispensing justice in his father's court. This experience gives Aak the confidence that he will perform well when the time comes for him to assume the throne. Aak's only concern is that when he and his sister are together, Maat-Ka-Re always dominates him, forever playing her 'I'm the foremost of distinguished women' role. And when she hears Iby's latest report concerning Seth-Mesy's latest conspiracy against her father, today is no different.

"Seth-Mesy intends to rule the Two-Lands with fear," Maat-Ka-Re asserts. "He is using the Seeing Waters to bully us back to the old ways, and it's up to us to stop them."

"Them," Aak says mildly. "Seth-Mesy you mean, don't you, sister?"

"Of course, Seth-Mesy, brother, but there are others as well." Maat-Ka-Re says.

"Like who, sister?"

"Like all the priests who challenge Pharaoh with their threats of heresy," Maat-Ka-Re replies. She lets Senen-Mut's hand slip and gets up. "Do you know what will happen if we allow the priests to force the people back into absolute obedience?"

"I really don't know," Aak replies, stifling a yawn, "but I'm certain that you will tell me."

Maat-Ka-Re ignores Aak's sarcasm and continues. "Allowing the priests to accuse and punish our people for heresy will make them fearful. Sons will distrust their fathers, mothers will distrust their daughters, husbands and wives will distrust each other. When fear rules the land, do you know who the people will trust?"

"No."

"*Foreigners!*"

Long ago, Maat-Ka-Re's mother taught her daughter about the three Egyptian queens, the distinguished women who saved the Two-Lands from foreign domination by leading battles against the Hyksos and their Egyptians collaborators.

"And you, my daughter, will be the 'foremost of distinguished women'," Maat-Ka-Re's mother promised.

"If Egypt is to be saved," Maat-Ka-Re reiterates, "we must force these priests to obey the will of Pharaoh."

Aak does not agree.

Where will this heretical thinking leave me once I'm Pharaoh and Maat-Ka-Re is queen? Aak wonders. But he decides not to challenge his sister directly. Rather he asks, "What about the gods?"

Maat-Ka-Re pauses to consider Aak's question.

"The gods love the Two-Lands of Upper and Lower Egypt," she argues. "They'll not support a priest who challenges a Living Member of their own celestial body."

She looks to Senen-Mut and Iby for confirmation. Neither of them is rash enough to take sides. After they were rescued from Pharaoh's pit, Mut-Sherif taught Senen-Mut and Iby a valuable lesson about expressing their opinions to the royals.

"I hope the pit taught you something about court etiquette," Mut-Sherif lectured the foolish officers, "otherwise the next time nothing and no one will save you."

"What was the pit supposed to teach us?" Iby asked.

"The pit was supposed to teach you never to forget that you serve the Living God and the Royal family. You are not their equals. You are not as valuable as the horses that propel Pharaoh's chariot. Their majesties, the royal couple may speak with you and even seek your opinion. However, never forget that you are dispensable and can be replaced. The royal couple is indispensable and irreplaceable."

"I do not understand what is wrong with the old ways," Aak continues the argument with his sister.

Maat-Ka-Re remains silent. She purses her lips, unaccustomed to Aak or anyone else disagreeing with her. Aak seems not to notice and continues.

"We need our traditions, sister," Aak emphasizes. "I believe that if all of us moderated our attitudes towards Seth-Mesy, he might moderate his views on this heresy nonsense." Aak doesn't give his sister an opportunity for her 'I know what I'm talking about' outburst, but continues, even though he is out of breath from his exertions. "I don't want to become Pharaoh and have the entire priesthood against me."

"You won't have the *entire* priesthood against you," Maat-Ka-Re mutters. Being contradicted by her brother puts her into a bad mood.

"Didn't our tutors teach us that '*There is no possibility, what-soever, of systematically infusing the masses with wisdom*'?" Aak asks trying to reason with her.

"Yes!" Maat-Ka-Re snaps.

"So that's why we need the priests to get the people to do what we want them to do," Aak concludes. "The priests convince the people to do what is best for the Two-Lands, otherwise Pharaoh must always use coercion."

"What's that to do with anything," Maat-Ka-Re responds. *What's Aak talking about,* she wonders, *and why is he contradicting me? And this is not the first time. He knows when he contradicts me that it makes me really angry.*

Aak is unconcerned with Maat-Ka-Re's feelings. He continues, "My point is simple."

"What is your point, dear brother?" Maat-Ka-Re's voice oozes sarcasm.

"If we don't demand absolute obedience from the people, how will I be able to rule when I become Pharaoh?" Aak makes his meaning even clearer. "*Sister, when I am Pharaoh, I—not you—will rule the Two-Lands!*"

But Aak's conciliatory nature will not allow him to leave the discussion there. He tries to soften his message, "After all, when I am Pharaoh, I shall be the Golden Horus and the Living God, shall I not?"

Senen-Mut smiles to himself. He wonders if Mut-Sherif taught Aak his lesson on court etiquette—at least as far as Maat-Ka-Re is concerned.

"You shall be the Golden Horus and the Living God as long as the Two-Lands of Upper and Lower Egypt are defended by an army of well-trained and well-equipped soldiers," Aak's sister responds. "We cannot train such an army if the priests are given the author-ity to substitute fear for wisdom."

"Then, dear sister, I must ask my original question, once again," Aak says, in a soft, patient voice. "How do I rule when the people do not absolutely obey all my commands?"

Maat-Ka-Re looks over at the next ruler of the Two-Lands.

"Dear brother," she smiles sweetly, "you will rule over the Two-Lands of Upper and Lower Egypt with *my* help, of course!"

CHAPTER EIGHT

Nobles, in litters emblazoned with insignias identifying their rank and relationship to Pharaoh, gather in front of Karnak's newest building. Thut-Moses had wanted to commemorate his daughter's ascent to the co-Regent's throne and her consecration as God's Wife with a monument that would endure throughout the ages, but Mut-Sherif informed Pharaoh that there was little time to construct such a massive building. Furthermore, Seth-Mesy had gathered enough council support to delay the construction of such a memorial. Amen's high priest used the scandal over Pharaoh's choice of a female co-Regent to justify his obstruction to the memorial. Seth-Mesy was assured of council support. But years of military campaigning taught Thut-Moses that there are many avenues to one's objective.

"You know my will for Maat-Ka-Re's memorial?" Thut-Moses asked Mut-Sherif.

"Yes, Great God," Mut-Sherif bowed.

"Then I expect these instructions to be accomplished without delay and without any mistakes? Am I clear?"

"Yes, Master," Mut-Sherif bowed lower.

"Connect Karnak's fourth and fifth pair of pylons with a roof and decorate this hall as a memorial to my daughter, Maat-Ka-Re Hat-Shep-Sut. None of my Inner Council need know my will except those who supply workers and materials."

"It will be done as you command, Great Ruler of the Two-Lands."

"I do not want any opposition from Seth-Mesy," Thut-Moses ordered. "If he gets in the way, *kill him!*"

In this way, Thut-Moses created a massive memorial commemorating his daughter's consecration. Only three persons with knowledge of Pharaoh's will, two workers and a scribe, broke the secrecy surrounding the roofing between the fourth and fifth pairs of pylons. They paid with having their tongues slit; those they told were not as fortunate. But before the royal court of Karnak was aware of what was happening, Pharaoh created a magnificent hall where today the nobles of Karnak gather.

The gates surrounding Pharaoh's Mansion of Millions of Years open. A magnificent twenty-wheel carriage towed by a team of sixteen white oxen exits. Upon the carriage is mounted a golden platform, overhung by a crimson canopy. At each corner of the platform is affixed golden standards emblazoned with the insignia of Aa-Kheper-Ka-Re Thut-Moses, Pharaoh over the Two-Lands of Upper and Lower Egypt. The crimson canopy shades two carved thrones from the blazing Egyptian sun. Thut-Moses sits erect in the higher, more elaborate throne. He holds across his chest the crook and flail, symbols of his authority to lead and power to punish. Radiantly beautiful, Maat-Ka-Re sits upon the lower throne as serene as a goddess. The litters of the assembled nobles fall in behind the carriage of the Living God and his daughter. The great procession proceeds towards the royal docks. In his litter, Mut-Sherif tries to still his own misgivings over Pharaoh's blatant departure from tradition. The appointment of Maat-Ka-Re, co-Regent over the Two-Lands, instead of the Crown Prince, Aa-Kheper-Ren-Re Thut-Moses II may still have serious repercussions. *But, considering the excitement and enthusiasm his fellow nobles are demonstrating,* Pharaoh's Grand Vizier thinks looking over the procession of the most important people in Karnak. Pharaoh is correct in assuming that none will oppose his break with tradition from any of his councilors.

Mut-Sherif remembers how insistently he and the council had urged Pharaoh to appoint his co-Regent. They thought that once the co-Regent was named, their problems would be over. No one believed that Pharaoh would appoint his son, co-Regent, so everyone believed that he would choose Seth-Mesy. But, Thut-Moses outmaneuvered his council.

Mut-Sherif continually pestered Thut-Moses about appointing a co-Regent. But Pharaoh ignoreed his Grand Vizier. Finally, Mut-Sherif resorted to sarcasm.

"Since the Living God has resolved that he doesn't need a co-Regent, he must certainly have discovered a method of becoming the Golden Horus, *in fact as well as in myth.*"

"And what does my Grand Vizier mean by that?" Thut-Moses asks.

"I am merely inquiring whether or not the Living God can fly about the Two-Lands whenever his presence is needed?" Mut-Sherif's dared to chide Pharaoh.

"If I didn't know better," Pharaoh replied, allowing his Grand Vizier's insolence to pass, "I would think that you also believe that I am a heretic."

Thut-Moses enjoys matching wits with Mut-Sherif. It forces him to consider opinions that differ from his own. Thut-Moses is enough of a general to know that sometimes someone else has a clearer picture of the battlefield than he. The council approved of Thut-Moses because they thought to control him. Thut-Moses knows that the nobility are blind to the fact that their world has changed. Few are capable of perceiving a world where nobles do not rule. Neither do his councilors understand that Thut-Moses has two passions: an undying love for his daughter and far-reaching plans for an invincible army, both of which caused Thut-Moses to push Amen's pompous high priest aside as soon as he became Pharaoh. Seth-Mesy is a hindrance to Thut-Moses' plans for a well-trained, well-equipped national army and to raise Maat-Ka-Re to a level no woman has yet achieved. Pharaoh's ingratitude has caused Seth-Mesy to campaign against Thut-Moses' heresies. In this contest of wills, Pharaoh's Grand Vizier battled Amen's high priest over Pharaoh's appointment of a co-Regent. Mut-Sherif watches as his bearers bring his litter into the most prominent place in the procession following Pharaoh and his daughter. The procession proceeds to the royal docks where the royals board the royal barge for Luxor.

"You expect your Grand Vizier to obey just like Seth-Mesy expects his priests to obey," Mut-Sherif complained to Thut-Moses.

"How is that?"

"You expect *blind obedience!*"

Pharaoh did not respond. He had made up his mind; he would not appoint Aak co-Regent. Thut-Moses preferred leaving the office vacant and ruling alone, but neither his Grand Vizier nor his Inner Council would permit it. This played into Pharaoh's hands.

"For the good of his people," Mut-Sherif pleaded, "Pharaoh must appoint a co-Regent. Someone needs the authority to act as Pharaoh when you are not present."

"My son is the Royal Heir," Thut-Moses responded. "If I should fall, he will take my place."

"It is not enough that your son is the Royal Heir," Mut-Sherif replied.

"You know my son is unfit for the office," Pharaoh demurred. "Why do you pester me?"

"None of your council shares Pharaoh's aversion to the Crown Prince's disabilities. None believe that infirmities interfere with his judgment. Many have praised your son for his wise decisions rendered in Pharaoh's Hall of Justice. The council does not know what prevents Pharaoh from following tradition and appointing his son, co-Regent."

"Don't play dumb with me," Thut-Moses snapped in his sternest military tone. "You know as well as I that the Royal Heir is unfit to serve as co-Regent."

"But if you do not appoint a co-Regent," Mut-Sherif said quietly, "you will soon find that Seth-Mesy has assumed the position for himself."

This was a warning Thut-Moses could not ignore. Amen's high priest already makes his life difficult, enough.

"All right, then," Thut-Moses said, raising his hands in resignation, "you may tell the council that I will appoint a co-Regent."

Thank Thoth for his wisdom, Mut-Sherif prayed silently. Even Pharaoh noticed the shoulders of his Grand Vizier imperceptibly rise, as if some great weight had been lifted. "Should I wait until after you have informed the Royal Heir before I make the announcement to the council?" the Grand Vizier asks, "or do you want me to reward some of His Majesty's friends by letting them know of the Living God's decision beforehand?"

Thut-Moses knows that the successful outcome of any military campaign depends upon deception. And the wily, battle-tested veteran saw that he has quite deceived the council. Pharaoh's weather-beaten face cracked into a faint smile.

"You, my friend, may decide when and to whom you'll make the announcement," Thut-Moses said, "especially since you may experience some difficulty in getting the council to accept my choice of co-Regent."

"Why is that, Great Lord?" Mut-Sherif asked in a weak voice. His shoulders slumped back into their former position. And then, with almost instant precognition, Mut-Sherif anticipated Pharaoh's terrible pronouncement.

"I am not appointing the Royal Heir co-Regent," Thut-Moses said, his face breaking out into a broad grin. "I have decided to appoint my daughter, the Princess Maat-Ka-Re!"

Even as he heard Pharaoh's words, the color drained from the Grand Vizier's face. Mut-Sherif turned an ashen grey as if he were being prepared for the underworld. Mut-Sherif is confounded by his own gullibility. He should have realized that Thu-Moses intended to appoint Maat-Ka-Re co-Regent all along.

Though he mades a masterful presentation to the Inner Council, as expected, the Grand Vizier encountered intense council resistance against Maat-Ka-Re's elevation organized by Seth-Mesy.

"I have been warning the council of the consequences of heresy," Amen's high priest thundered. "First we depart from ancient practices and traditions that even the Hyksos observed." Murmurs of agreement circulated in the council. "Now we are asked to defy our most cherished traditions, pass over the Royal Heir, and appoint *his sister* co-Regent." Seth-Mesy surveyed the council. "This is what results from putting a commoner on the throne."

"Here! Here!" council members cried out in agreement.

"Pharaoh may even try to make his daughter *the Royal Heir*," one councilor said out loud.

The Audience Chamber rang with shouts of '*Heresy! Heresy!*'

Seth-Mesy nodded his head. "Yes, heresy!" he said matter-of-factly. "None can deny that Pharaoh has ignored the Crown Prince's training. Now we are told that the Crown Prince is unfit for the co-Regency. Why are we not surprised?"

Again nods and murmurs. Seth-Mesy continued.

"Pharaoh's vizier asks us to accept the consecration of Pharaoh's daughter as co-Regent. Would anyone be surprised if Amen completely forsakes his chosen people for consenting to such a blasphemous act?"

"No! No!" the councilors cried out.

Seth-Mesy's attacks forced Thut-Moses to reconsider his daughter's appointment.

"Majesty," Mut-Sherif offered, "you can win over your council if you appoint Seth-Mesy as your co-Regent."

But Maat-Ka-Re gave him the decisive argument. "You are Pharaoh," she reminded her father. "You are the Living God, the Divine Horus. What care you for these yapping jackals. They *must* obey your will! Even Aak believes that I should become the co-Regent."

"He does?" Thut-Moses responded. Thut-Moses was genuinely surprised. Despite being humiliated by his father since his debilitating illness, Aak has always worshipped Thut-Moses and would do anything to please him. Aak would support whomever his father chooses as his co-Regent.

"Do you believe your brother?" Thut-Moses asked.

"Yes," Maat-Ka-Re said. "Aak knows that I am far better suited to be Pharaoh's co-Regent, than he. I can leave Karnak at anytime and go anywhere. Aak moves slowly and must rest often. It might take Aak almost the entire day to travel from Karnak to Luxor."

Maat-Ka-Re touched her father's hand to emphasize the truth of what she said.

"Aak knows that the Two-Lands needs a co-Regent. The people want their grievances heard and a fair judgment rendered. In this manner our dynasty will earn stability and longevity."

Thut-Moses agreed with his daughter's reasoning.

"Believe me father, there is nothing Aak wants more than to become Pharaoh over a Two-Lands that is happy, peaceful and prosperous."

"Your brother speaks wisely," Thut-Moses concluded, "that is if these are, indeed, his words."

"They are his words," Maat-Ka-Re said quietly. "After all, he is your son."

"This is true," Thut-Moses sighed.

"Actually, Aak has another reason for supporting me as your co-Regent," Maat-Ka-Re said in a conspiratorial whisper.

"What is it?" Thut-Moses asked.

"He wants me to have the experience so that I can serve as *his* co-Regent when he becomes Pharaoh." Maat-Ka-Re smiled. "Your son knows that it would be impossible for him to appoint me his co-Regent unless I already held the title."

"Did you hear that?" Thut-Moses almost shouted at his Grand Vizier. "The boy already thinks like a Pharaoh."

Mut-Sherif nodded.

"I want the inner council's approval for Maat-Ka-Re's appointment as my co-Regent," Thut-Moses instructed his Grand Vizier, "and I want it immediately." The warrior's face became stern as Pharaoh uttered his instructions. "If any councilor opposes me in this, strip them of their rank and titles, evict them from their lands and fill the vacancy with my supporter. And I expect the first vacancy to be the position of Amen's high priest!"

Once Mut-Sherif explained Pharaoh's will to the Inner Council, it quickly approved Maat-Ka-Re's appointment over Seth-Mesy's muted opposition. However, on this day of Maat-Ka-Re's coronation, Mut-Sherif still remains apprehensive though the litters of the rich and powerful emblazoned with insignias of office, proclaiming titles and ranks of their occupants all seem to support their new co-Regent, completely.

Along the procession route, the aroma of sweet-smelling incense arises from burning braziers. Pharaoh and his co-Regent stop before the shrines of Khonsu and Mut led by dancing priestesses who sing hymns and play reed pipes, harps and lyres as they stream out of each temple and join the procession. At the royal docks father and daughter board the royal barge, every part of which is overlaid with gold. Between its great golden masts stand two obelisks mounted by the Golden Horus. On the prow and stern are the heads of Amen's rams, crowned with atef and uraeus. Gangs of men haul ropes tied to Pharaoh's barge and tow it slowly up the royal canal towards Luxor. Jubilant crowds line both sides of the canal. As the people engage in wild rejoicings, hysterical shouting and fervent praying, Thut-Moses strikes a pose, standing upright in full view of his people, holding the steering rudder as if he were personally sailing his royal barge up to Luxor.

Meanwhile, the procession of nobles in their litters and the gay entourage of priestesses and musicians parade down the Avenue of Sphinxes. They are joined by an even greater company of priests, scribes and administrators. Pharaoh's Palace Guard in full battle array lines the Avenue of the Sphinxes with their military standards blazing in the sun. The noise of the procession, greatly enlarged by thousands, reaches an ear-splitting volume. Periodically trumpets blare out, signaling the progress of Pharaoh's barge.

Seth-Mesy is understandably reluctant to join Princess Maat-Ka-Re's coronation procession. He is forced to swallow more than one bitter draught on this day. His dreams of becoming Pharaoh's co-Regent have been dashed as even are his secret aspirations of, one day, becoming pharaoh. Amen's high priest is not even chosen to conduct the co-Regent's consecration ceremony. Instead Maat-Ka-Re requests Pen-Nek-Heb, high priest of the Aten, to consecrate her. And this insult intensifies the enmity between Seth-Mesy and Maat-Ka-Re.

Upon Pharaoh's arrival at Luxor, princes, princesses, nobility and high officials from all over the Two-Lands line up to greet the Living God and make their offerings. Aak takes precedence over all others, including Pharaoh's other children, wives and relatives. They all arrange themselves behind the Royal Heir. After 'kissing the dust' at Pharaoh's feet and receiving his father's blessings, Aak gives thanks to the gods. Then he greets his sister.

"Beloved," Aak says, "may Amen shower you with blessings on this day."

"And may the Aten bless you as well," Maat-Ka-Re responds, "for it was you who made this day possible, my love." She holds Aak's face with both her hands and kisses him on both cheeks as well as upon his forehead. Afterwards Aak's attendants assist their master back into his litter.

Then the royal family, nobility, nomarchs, overseers and scribes greet Pharaoh and his co-Regent in order of their rank, titles and family. In the background the cheering of the crowd continues unabated. Bouquets of flowers are piled high on platforms along with offerings of bread, beer, alabaster and linen. Fattened and festooned oxen are also led to where a regiment of scribes carefully tally and record every gift and offering.

After the offerings are received, Pen-Nek-Heb leads Pharaoh and his co-Regent into a dark and mysterious chamber deep within Luxor's temple. The secret ceremony is brief and Pharaoh and Pen-Nek-Heb reemerge to present the newly crowned co-Regent to the people. Upon her head Maat-Ka-Re wears the symbol of her office, a golden diadem with a jeweled cobra in a raised position, poised to strike any of the co-Regent's enemies.

Then comes the feasting and dancing that continues throughout the day, into the night and for the next several days and nights. Pharaoh and his party quietly return to Karnak. For her trip back, the newly crowned co-Regent boards her own personal golden barge, another gift from her doting father. Maat-Ka-Re asks Aak to return with her. Neither seems concerned that as co-Regent, she now outranks the Royal Heir.

CHAPTER NINE

ak!" Maat-Ka-Re addresses her brother.

"Yes?"

"Our teachings tie us by a thread of tradition to our ancestors. Isn't that right?"

"I suppose so." he replies.

"These teachings can be found in the temples and monuments. Isn't that also true?"

"I guess," he replies again.

"And what is cut in stone has already taken place, hasn't it?"

Aak tires of Maat-Ka-Re's questions.

"What are you driving at?" the Crown Prince asks. Usually, his sister's devious mannerisms do not bother him, but today they do.

"My point is this," Maat-Ka-Re says. "If we are to protect the Two-Lands from new invasions from the north, none of these traditions can assist us."

"I never thought of it that way," Aak agrees. "I suppose you're right, but what of it?"

"I'm concerned about the priests?"

Not the priests again, Aak mutters under his breath. "What about the priests, dear sister?" He doesn't try to hide the sarcasm in his voice.

"Their intelligence network," Maat-Ka-Re purrs.

Aak knows what's coming. He believes that his sister is too reckless. She's been campaigning to destroy the Seeing Waters ever since becoming co-Regent. But Aak knows she really wants to eliminate Seth-Mesy altogether.

But I'm not letting that happen, Aak tells himself. *If she had her way, she wouldn't stop until the entire Two-Lands was plunged into a full-scale civil war.*

"Why should the army's intelligence network concern the priests?" he asks her.

"Senen-Mut and Iby are building a separate intelligence organization that will rival the Seeing Waters in every respect, numbers, resources, experience and commitment," Maat-Ka-Re says. "Isn't that right, Senen-Mut?"

Pretending that he has not heard the question, Senen-Mut just stares into space. Maat-Ka-Re bristles at being ignored, but she continues.

"The Seeing Waters are little more than paid assassins who serve the highest bidder," Maat-Ka-Re asserts.

"Don't you think that's being harsh?" Aak replies. "The Seeing Waters have been temple guards for centuries. They protect Amen's temples as well as the temples of the other gods. They even guard Pen-Nek-Heb's Temple at Iunu. I don't know how you can say these things."

"The Seeing Waters cannot be trusted," Maat-Ka-Re insists. "Isn't that right, my little brother?" She addresses Senen-Mut by his pet name, though she normally uses it only when they are alone.

"The new army has many uses for the Eyes of Horus," Senen-Mut replies. Senen-Mut decides neither to confirm nor deny Maat-Ka-Re's assertion. He is certain Maat-Ka-Re uses his pet name to cause friction between he and the Royal Heir. Aak doesn't take the bait.

"What of it, sister?" Aak asks.

"The Eyes of Horus are prepared to die for Pharaoh," Maat-Ka-Re says. "They are soldiers. They are neither frightened nor corrupted. The priests have no power over them."

"Whatever their loyalties," Aak says, "I will not permit your antagonism with Seth-Mesy to foster hatred between the Eyes of Horus and the Seeing Waters. The Two-Lands need both and when I am Pharaoh, and *so will I*."

"This is why the priests concern me," Maat-Ka-Re says. "They don't want to lose their ultimate weapon."

"Which is?"

"The power to curse a heretic with an unpleasant afterlife," Maat-Ka-Re says.

"That may be, but what does that have to do with the rebuilding of the army?" Aak asks. "What you are proposing sounds like treason."

"Tell my brother what you know," Maat-Ka-Re tells Iby.

Iby is reluctant; he remembers only too well his time in the pit and Mut-Sherif's lecture about court protocol afterwards. Maat-Ka-Re glares silently at the Eyes of Horus spymaster. Given no choice, Iby begins.

"Great One, I have received a number of reports from interrogations of bandits and nomad tribesmen in the north. It seems that the Mitanni are planning something." Iby looks over to Senen-Mut for support, but gets none, so he continues. "The War Council concludes that soon Pharaoh will face an asiatic invasion."

"What has this to do with the priests and the Seeing Waters?" Aak asks.

"The army will follow Pharaoh as long as they believe that he will defend them," Senen-Mut responds. "But if our people get caught on both sides like before… "

Prudence prevents Senen-Mut from completing his thought.

"I still do not understand the concern," Aak says.

"We believe that the Seeing Waters are communicating with the Mitanni," Iby blurts out.

"The Mitanni?" Aak frowns. "Sister, do you know of these Mitanni?"

"Yes brother dear," Maat-Ka-Re replies, now confident that she has his attention.

"I guess you would," the future Pharaoh replies. "Father includes you in all the important matters."

"It's only because our father does not want you to lose your strength that he doesn't burden you," Maat-Ka-Re lies. "He knows that you drain your energy when you worry over affairs of state. The health sages predict that if you are prudent you will live to an old age, so Father doesn't want you wasting your energy needlessly."

"You must tell me about these Mitanni," Aak demands.

Wearing a pleasant smile, Maat-Ka-Re nods to Senen-Mut. Now she knows she has Aak's attention.

"The kingdom of the Mitanni is ruled by a Persian dynasty," Senen-Mut begins. "Its capital is beyond Palestine in the lands of Syria, near the Tigris River."

"The Mitanni kingdom is continually expanding towards the Two-Lands," Iby says. "Even now, they are infiltrating agents into Lower Egypt. Their people are especially numerous in Avaris, where asiatics have settled since the time of the Hyksos. The Eyes of Horus keep a close watch upon these Mitanni."

Aak considers Iby's revelation in silence.

"You see, dear brother," Maat-Ka-Re explains, "the Eyes of Horus are convinced that the Mitanni are following the same strategy as the Hyksos. First they infiltrate their people into our towns and villages. Then they will claim entire sections of Lower Egypt. Even now the Eyes of Horus reports that Canaanite tribes allied with the Mitanni control whole parts of the Anubieon from the Bahr Yussef canal all the way to Lake Moeris."

"The Mitanni are busy recruiting anyone related to the traitors executed for serving the Hyksos," Iby confirms.

"And dear brother," she says. driving home her final point, "we have reports that the Mitanni have Seeing Waters agents in their employ."

Aak bites his lip, trying not to react just yet.

Is this just another one her ploys to recruit me into war against Seth-Mesy, he wonders, *or do these Mitanni really threaten the Two-Lands?*

Aak reacts far differently than Maat-Ka-Re hopes. Considering the information laid before him, Aak reasons that now there is an even greater urgency to heal the rift between Seth-Mesy and his father, especially if the Mitanni are actually planning to attack the Two-Lands. Aak believes that Maat-Ka-Re's intrigues are making things worse for the dynasty, not better.

"Sister, what you say convinces me that we must rely even more heavily upon our ancient traditions to guide us," Aak says quietly.

Thut-Moses also ponders what to do about the Mitanni. His War Council advises him that his army is still unprepared for an all-out war with the asiatics.

"Amen-Nati has served me well," Thut-Moses tells Mut-Sherif. "The information that Senen-Mut and his friend, Iby, has delivered is invaluable. The problem is what to do with it."

"It is clear, Great One," Mut-Sherif replies. "Since eventually it seems that you must repel the Mitanni, your first task must be to prepare your army."

"By that you mean?" Pharaoh asks.

"We have learned much since the time of the Hyksos, Great One," Mut-Sherif observes. "It is certain that the Mitanni have learned much as well. Their success in battle and their federation of Canaanite tribes in Syria, Lebanon and Palestine prove this fact."

"I will hear my War Council's opinion on this matter," Thut-Moses says.

"Great one," the commander of Pharaoh's Isis regiment observes, "the army would become better prepared and more quickly if we were actually engaged in a war."

"What do you say to my general's suggestion, Mut-Sherif?" the Pharaoh asks. "I think it has merit."

"Of course, the army will become more effective once it becomes battle-tested," Mut-Sherif responds, "but how many soldiers can we spare? In an ill-conceived war against the asiatics, Pharaoh's army could be overwhelmed and lost."

"I suggest the Living God direct his will against those rebellious Nubian Bowmen in the Land of Kush," another general suggests. "The black people were never punished for supporting the Hyksos during our time of troubles. And our watchers report that even now Mitanni agents incite the Nubian tribesmen to rise up against us. Let Pharaoh toughen up the army by quelling the Nubians' rebellious spirit. We should lose very few soldiers to the Nubians and the war will prepare our army for fighting the asiatics."

Pharaoh instructs Mut-Sherif to obtain his council's support for the plan. Surprisingly, Seth-Mesy offers no objection to a war with the king of Nubia and Pharaoh receives his Inner Council's unanimous approval.

Throughout the Two-Lands there is a frenzy of military activity. Most important is the recruitment and training of additional soldiers. The facility at Horus Nest exceeds its capacity to train new recruits. The War Council establishes another training camp south of Thebes in the Nek-Heb valley where Pharaoh's Palace Guard is headquartered. Mut-Sherif orders Senen-Mut to the Nek-Heb valley facility to assist with the training and become Mut-Sherif's eyes and ears. Thus Pharaoh's mobilization against the king of Nubia separates the co-Regent and her consort for weeks at a time. Maat-Ka-Re is pleased that her father is building up his army, but she misses Senen-Mut dreadfully. After a particularly difficult month of separation, Maat-Ka-Re becomes desperate. She sends a message under the seal of the co-Regent to the commander of the Nek-Heb Valley training camp ordering Senen-Mut to report back to Karnak, immediately. What else can Maat-Ka-Re do? She may be the co-Regent, but she's still a woman and still needs her man. And right now, she needs the sight of his face and the feel of his arms around her body.

Maat-Ka-Re hurries through the gardens of Pharaoh's Mansion of Millions of Years to where the co-Regent and Senen-Mut have their own apartment, a private 'love nest' when they need absolute privacy. The pungent scent of rare herbs fills the air, as she scampers over the hidden path. Eager with anticipation, she is startled by the heavy crash of some animal fleeing through the reeds in the evening shadows, probably frightened by the scent of Natee, Maat-Ka-Re's pet lion, who pads in front of his mistress. When Awab is not around, Maat-Ka-Re always takes Natee with her when she leaves the palace.

The evening breeze is cool, but their private hideaway is warm. Maat-Ka-Re slips into Senen-Mut's arms where she spends the rest of the night. The next morning, Maat-Ka-Re teases him.

"Little brother, why do you love me when there must be at least a hundred dancing girls more beautiful?"

"Loving sister," he answers, trying to hide the hurt, "any other would be as the moon to your sun. To me you are the wind and my forehead is always cool. You are the river that keeps my garden fertile. You are the wine and my cup is never empty."

Maat-Ka-Re buries her head in Senen-Mut's lap so that he cannot see the tears in her eyes. She does not like showing him her sentimental side. After awhile they make love once again. Later in the afternoon, Maat-Ka-Re grills Senen-Mut thoroughly about the preparations underway at the Nek-Heb Valley training camp.

Meanwhile, Seth-Mesy prepares for the war against the Nubian king as well. His preparations, however, have an entirely different purpose. Amen's high priest prepares to place someone more malleable. He is determined to replace Pharaoh with the weak Royal Heir.

"What news of your plans to rid me of this heretic?" Seth-Mesy asks Hapu-Seneb.

"Lord High Priest," Hapu-Seneb responds, "we have informed the Nubian king that the heretic plans to invade his land, but, frankly, I don't believe he has much chance of defeating Pharaoh's army."

"Chance! What is chance?" Seth-Mesy chides his follower. "Amen's plans have less to do with chance and more to do with the will of the gods."

The man is too cautious, Seth-Mesy tells himself. I want my servants to act on faith rather than on fact. Why must I endure all this

Eugene Stovall

thinking? he asks himself. But, for the time being, he must rely on Hapu-Seneb.

"Have the Mitanni agents been sent to the Nubian king?" Seth-Mesy asks.

"Yes, Excellency," Hapu-Seneb responds. "Even as we speak Seeing Waters are escorting the Mitanni to Kerma."

"And I trust that the Mitanni have sent their best agents?"

"Yes, Master," the Royal Teacher replies once again.

"And which Seeing Waters are escorting them?" Seth-Mesy asks with a gleam in his eye.

"We have assigned our Medjay," Hapu-Seneb responds.

"And their instructions?" asks Seth-Mesy.

"Kill Pharaoh!"

CHAPTER TEN

The Dangola Reach, nestled within a great curve in the river, is Nubia's only stretch of agricultural land and the center of the Nubian kingdom. Inside the Dangola Reach, various Nubian tribes settle in their own villages and towns and pay allegiance to the king of Nubia at his capital of Kerma.

At the time when the 13th Dynasty is the economic center of the known world, the king of Nubia evicted a small tribe from its village inside the Dangola Reach. The king of Nubia demanded the tribe give him women for his soldiers' brothel, including the daughter of the tribe's headman. When the tribe rebuffed the king, he forcibly dispossessed them from their village and their land. The king condemned this tribe, known the Medjay, to live in the Sudanese desert searching its barren reaches for water and food. In their wanderings, the Medjay approached the remote desert outposts, established to protect Pharaoh's Saharan trade routes. These outposts, garrisoned by Egyptian soldiers, provided the Medjay with food and water in exchange for female diversions.

Over time, the Medjay attached themselves to the Egyptian's desert outposts, performing menial tasks like carrying water, washing clothes and cooking daily meals. When the soldiers were ordered to leave their outpost to escort a caravan past hostile Nubian tribes, the Medjay accompanied them, bearing the Egyptians' weapons and supplies. Gradually the Medjay became valuable sources of information and passed messages concerning the comings and goings of trade caravans bound for Thebes from one garrison to another. So attached to the Egyptian army became the tribe of Medjay that the army commissioned them to garrison several of Pharaoh's more isolated Saharan outposts. Soon with the Medjay providing the army information about when and where the Nubians will attack, Pharaoh's caravan losses were dramatically reduced.

The Medjay even spied on Kerma itself, providing the Two-Lands with the information it needed to defeat the Nubian army time and time again. So important did the Medjay become to Pharaoh's army that his officers refers to them as their 'Seeing Waters'.

When the 17th Dynasty found itself in a life and death struggle with the Hyksos, the Medjay not only informed Pharaoh of the Hyksos-inspired Nubian insurrection, but they supported Pharaoh's War for National Liberation. With the final Egyptian victory, Pharaoh rewarded the Medjay with a royal commission to guard palaces and temples throughout the Two-Lands. The Medjay's commission included all Amen's temples, including his temple at Karnak. Thus id Seth-Mesy inherit the services of the Medjay and the intelligence network known as the Seeing Waters.

A group of black-robed priests pass inside Karnak's main gates and make their way to Amen's Temple. The priests arrive from Amada, Amen's Nubian temple. The priests are scheduled to receive instructions in arcane rituals. The temple servants welcome the visitors and escort them to their sleeping quarters. Unnoticed, two of the priests detach themselves from the group and disappear into a secret passage that leads upstairs to Seth-Mesy's private chambers. They flash the sign of recognition to the Seeing Waters guards and are immediately allowed into the priest's chambers. Seth-Mesy hardly recognizes his own Seeing Waters 'kissing the dust' at his feet. The normally grizzled and fuzzy-haired Medjay are completely clean-shaven with eyes heavily outlined with black antimony in the custom of Amen's priests.

"Is all in readiness?" Seth-Mesy asks.

"Yes master," the Seeing Waters captain replies. "Even as we speak, fifty Medjay and twenty Mitanni are on their way to Kerma. Once Pharaoh invades Nubia, he will not return to Thebes alive."

"Why don't you just admit it?" Senen-Mut says.

"Admit what?" Iby asks.

"Admit that I could be just as good in the field as you!"

"Any time you show me any of your skill as a field operative, my Master," Iby says in a voice tinged with sarcasm, "I will gladly admit it. But it just so happens that this is not one of those times."

The pair trudge down a dusty path to Abu Simbel. The road is filled with travelers, mostly on foot. Every so often, a donkey cart passes them, kicking up even more dust and sand.

"Poor villagers, laborers seeking work, farmers hoping the bartering is better in Nubia," Iby says, "these are the people who must travel hot dusty roads, not officers in Pharaoh's service."

"Yes but no one will report that we are trailing the Mitanni agents into Nubia," Senen-Mut replies.

"Look," Iby says, "you need to understand something."

"Which is?" Senen-Mut asks.

"Everybody knows everybody!"

"What's that supposed to mean?" Senen-Mut asks.

"It means that you have no chance at catching a band of Mitanni with Medjay escorts unawares in Nubia. We should have just taken a boat upriver and saved all this walking." Iby often travels to Nubia but he has never walked around the first cataract. "This is the road that travelers without the means use. One can remain invisible to the Seeing Waters and still sail upriver. My contacts could have sailed us around the first cataract all the way to Kerma." Iby does not wear his normal grin. He is not happy.

"Maybe I'm not able to recognize the important things that you see, or speak several different languages or know every sailor on the Nile by their first name," Senen-Mut says, "but how am I going to learn if I don't get some field experience?"

"Being a watcher for the Eyes of Horus is not an experience," Iby says, trying to keep the emotion out of his voice. "It's a way of life. We were born to it, you were not, *Master*."

Senen-Mut gladly accepts Iby's sarcasm in exchange for a bit of camaraderie.

"But the only way that I can get you and the others to accept me as a member of your group and not just another scribe is to go out on a mission, *like this one*," Senen-Mut explains. "After all, we are trying to save Pharaoh's life."

"What's so important about being accepted by my men?" Iby asks. "You're the co-Regent's consort. She is the most beautiful woman in all of the Two-Lands. Her father, the Living God, has promised you the title of '*Royal Advisor*'. Why are you risking all of that, as well as your life, to get the respect of *my people*?"

"Both my father and the Lord of Wast are members of the Golden Fly," Senen-Mut responds. "Can I do any less than they?"

"Being a member of the Golden Fly won't mean very much if you're dead," Iby sniffs. "Besides, are you certain that membership in the Golden Fly is the only reason you're following Mitanni agents into Nubia?"

"What do you mean?"

"Aren't you trying to impress your *beloved* Maat-Ka-Re?" Iby laughs with his mouth, but his eyes remain intensely serious.

"Well, what of it?" Senen-Mut tries to match Iby's belligerence with his own. "Why shouldn't I get the experiences that Maat-Ka-Re will need from me when she's on the throne?"

Iby puzzles over Senen-Mut's motivations. He has never understood the Student of Wast. Commoners and nobles alike can only dream of the life he has been given as the consort of Pharaoh's daughter. Yet he is still busy going out of his way to cause problems.

Is he just so much in love that he can't see that she's using him? Iby wonders. *They're all using him! Or maybe he's just plain dumb*, Iby decides that it's a combination of both.

"When she's on the throne… " Iby begins.

"Don't you mean when Aak is on the throne?" Senen-Mut asks.

"Yeah, I guess," Iby says, backing away from what he intended to say. *Everyone knows how ambitious the Princess Maat-Ka-Re is. Even Aak can see it. She wants the throne! The only one who doesn't see it is Senen-Mut. Is his master pretending not to know about the co-Regent's ambitions?* Iby asks himself. "And what will happen to me if those Nubian bowman put your head on a pole outside the gates of Kerma?" Iby asks.

"I suppose, in that case," Senen-Mut says, smiling, "you will have to work it out on your own, since Anubis will be leading me before the Scale of Djeheuty and the Forty-Two Judges in Thoth's Hall of Justice."

Senen-Mut and Iby are following the centuries-old path south, chasing Mitanni agents and their Seeing Waters guides down to the Dangola Reach and the Nubian capital of Kerma. Senen-Mut's idea to walk rather than take a barge makes no sense to Iby, since they already know where the Mitanni are headed. But believing that there are no secrets on the river, especially where the Lord Iby and the female co-Regent's consort are concerned, Senen-Mut thinks to keep his quarry unaware of their presence as long as possible.

"Besides," Senen-Mut responds, trying to use humor, "you are my servant. It's your duty to protect me in all circumstances. You cannot allow me to suffer any misfortune like having my head affixed to a pole on Kerma's gates. Otherwise your KA, will out-weigh a feather of Maat and become a tempting a meal for the Forty-Two Judges." Senen-Mut's pitiful attempt at humor in no way distracts Iby from the physical demands of the trek. "You must agree that this is an opportunity for me to show Pharaoh and Mut-Sherif what an officer who uses his initiative can accomplish."

Iby says nothing. The rays of Amen are beating down sapping his energy. *Talking to this fool is not worth the effort,* Iby concludes.

Both are covered with the fine red dust of the western desert. Sand is in their eyes, noses and ears. Sand even lodges between their teeth. Iby wishes he had never told Senen-Mut about the

Mitanni agents. It is by accident that they met each other at the Eyes of Horus headquarters.

"I thought you were in Memphis," Senen-Mut said. He was preparing to report back to the Nek-Heb Valley training camp after his tryst with Maat-Ka-Re.

"I've been following Mitanni agents."

"*Mitanni agents!*" Senen-Mut says. "Where?"

"They're meeting with Seeing Waters here in Thebes."

"How many are there?"

"*Several!*" Iby looked about knowing that he had already said too much. For the past year, Iby reported only to the War Council. Senen-Mut had been unaware of his most recent activities.

"Well, come on!" Senen-Mut said. "Give me the rest of it!"

"Okay!" Iby shrugged. "Watchers report Mitanni agents leaving Avaris, Sais and Bubastis, singly and in groups of twos and threes. They have all arrived in Thebes within days of each other and have been seen meeting with Seeing Waters."

"What do you suppose they're doing here?" Senen-Mut asked.

"I don't know yet," Iby replied.

"Well, I can't tell Mut-Sherif or Pharaoh that the Mitanni have sent agents to Thebes but we don't know why, can I?" Senen-Mut said.

"I intend to follow them," Iby explained. "And when I learn their intentions, I'll report back to you."

"That's a good idea," Senen-Mut said. "When do we leave?"

"We?"

"Of course 'we'," Senen-Mut smiled. "I'm coming with you."

So this is how the Iby finds himself following the trail of the Mitanni and Seeing Waters Death Squad to the Nubian capital of Kerma *on foot*. When, at long last, they arrive at Abu Simbel, they must find a place to rest. The next day Iby secures passage for the two of them aboard a fishing boat heading towards the second cataract. By late afternoon, the wind begins to die down and at dusk they are at a dead calm, ending all travel for the night.

"You still believe the Mitanni are heading to Kerma?" Senen-Mut asks.

"If I didn't we've come a long way for no reason," Iby says, risking his deadpan humor on Senen-Mut. Actually, Iby is quite humorless. He takes everything seriously, especially traveling into Nubia. "Where else would the Mitanni and Seeing Waters be heading except to Nubia's fertile valley? There's nothing else down here but desert. You don't have to come to Nubia for desert, there's plenty of desert in the Two-Lands."

"And why would they be going to Kerma?"

"To meet with the Nubian King," Iby answers. *Boy, he can ask some dumb questions.*

"I remember reading that the Hyksos sent agents into Nubia to stir up trouble for the 17th dynasty."

"Yes, but unless the Mitanni arm and train the Nubians, they'll be no match for Pharaoh's army."

"True enough," Senen-Mut concedes. "But on the other hand, the Mitanni must be planning something to help the Nubians defeat Pharaoh's army. It's our job to find out their intentions."

The following day, a fresh breeze fills the sail carrying the fishing boat further up the Nile. Here and there are scattered the skeletal remains of boats and shadoofs sticking out of muddy embankments. Along the water's edge, gaunt palms make their last-ditch struggles against winds and waves that are determined to uproot them. By mid-morning the fishing boat reaches the second cataract. Here Senen-Mut and Iby must earn their passage by assisting the boat crew in the backbreaking work of sliding the fishing boat over the granite rocks that obstruct their passage. It takes hours of tugging and pulling, but by mid-afternoon, the fishing boat clears the rocks and once again gains the Nile's deep waters. The crew eats a hot meal and rests before reassembling the boat, hoisting the sails and lowering the keel. By mid-afternoon, the fishing boat catches a brisk wind and is once again skimming south up the Nile, towards its final destination, the fertile Nubian valley of Dangola Reach.

Around a great bend in the Nile, where the palms of Wadi Halfa, blue in the distance, heave into sight, the air suddenly turns cold. Iby and Senen-Mut shiver in their thin linen cloaks. Neither is prepared for the cold. But by early evening, the fishing boat pulls into the dilapidated dock in Kerma's neglected harbor. Before the pair take their leave, the boat's pilot tells Iby where he can find a bed, a meal and information.

Kerma is far less than what Senen-Mut expected. Compared to Thebes or Memphis, Kerma is a wretched little village. It's most important public work is the stone boulevard that leads from the main gate to a three-story mud brick building that serves as the king of Nubia's palace. Even though partially enveloped in the palm, coconut and date trees, the king's palace shimmers in the African sun and dominates Kerma's landscape. The palace is surrounded by a wall that stands higher than the wall encircling Kerma, itself. The palace guards wear reinforced leather armor and leather helmets and carry bronze-tipped javelins, double-bladed daggers and Egyptian styled swords, gifts from the king of Mitanni.

"If the rest of his army is armed like these guards," Senen-Mut whispers to Iby, "the Nubian king will be a formidable adversary."

"Only the guard is armed like these," Iby assures Senen-Mut.

The Nubian king locates his granaries, houses of silver and other storehouses containing his wealth of Nubia down the right side of the royal boulevard. On the left side are located open thatched roofed sheds containing prisoners whose arms are pinioned behind their bodies and tied to poles in such tortured positions that many slump over motionless, already dead. The prisoners who are still alive await their trial or their execution. Skulls stacked waist high encircle the entire prisoner compound.

Wrapped from head to toe in the filthy linens common to desert dwellers, Senen-Mut and Iby enter Kerma disguised as nomads. But as they join the throng of people, pushing through Kerma's gates, a soldier armed with a wooden spear approaches them. Iby moves up to the Nubian officer and, uttering a few words, he drops several cowry shells into the officer's palm. Giving the two desert nomads not another look, the Nubian guard returns to his post.

"How did you know the Nubian guard would let us in?" Senen-Mut asks.

"Desert nomads have been bribing their way into marketplaces for centuries," Iby smiles. "Besides we sailors have our secrets."

Inside, Senen-Mut and Iby join the boisterous crowd streaming along the dusty path besides Kerma's earthen wall, past the king's gardens, olive groves and vineyards and onto a broad plain, populated by a great variety of tents, huts, pens, and stalls that serves as Kerma's marketplace. Here people gather from all over Nubia and other parts of Africa, as well, showing off their distinctive dress and decorative jewelry. The men wear tunics tucked under their belts and tied in fronts in butterfly bows. Women wear square pieces of cloth with tassels dangling from the lower edges. Both men and women wear as many decorated headbands, jeweled bracelets and golden armlets as they have in their possession. Each one tries to outdo the others in wearing supple leathers, fine linens and feathers of every color and description. The Nubians all strut about the marketplace flashing their jewelry and showing off their gold and silver as if that were their sole purpose for living. Each eyes the bangles dangling from his neighbor's ears and the rings on the fingers, toes and lips of his neighbor's wives, sisters and daughters. They inspect each other's finery with a jealous spirit and a thieving heart, all the while shouting epithets and insults.

"These Nubians do not seem to be preparing for war," Senen-Mut observes to Iby.

"When have they ever prepared for war?" Iby sneers.

"What I mean is that these people think the war will be fought over on the western plains," Senen-Mut explains. "Obviously the Mitanni spies have not informed the Nubian king that Pharaoh's *War Council* plans a different kind of war."

"All the better that they enjoy themselves now," Iby observes. His wry smile indicates a total lack of sympathy for the devastation that these Nubians are about to experience. "Possibly they will

Eugene Stovall

enjoy putting a few more rings in their ears or through their noses, before they die."

Iby leaves Senen-Mut to discuss Nubia's war preparations with a carpet weaver.

"Old man," he says, "I have heard that the Egyptians are planning a war. What say you?"

"Always has the African trade route passed through Kerma," the weaver replies. "Kerma's marketplace is not like the marketplace at Thebes; it's not wondrous. But Kerma has a great supply of what the world wants, ostrich feathers, cowry shells, ivory, copper and gold." Iby can see, from the wrinkles in his face, that the old weaver has seen many things. "Wars have been waged on the great plain for centuries, but Kerma's market has remained untouched. We do not fear Pharaoh or his army, so long as we have the things Pharaoh wants,"

Iby thanks the carpet weaver and gives him a few cowry shells.

"You're right," Iby tells Senen-Mut, "they're not prepared."

"What else did the weaver say," Senen-Mut asks Iby. "We're not here to learn about Kerma's defenses. What word of the Mitanni and the Medjay? What of them?"

Without a word, Iby turns his back on his master and, once again, mingles with the crowd, discreetly inquiring about the Mitanni and paying generously with cowry shells for any information. When Iby returns, this time his face is twisted into his familiar lopsided grin.

"What did you learn?" Senen-Mut asks.

"I learned that the Medjay have taken the Mitanni to Amen's temple at Amada."

Outside Kerma, a short but forbidding mountain range rises abruptly out of the eastern desert. Within these rocky heights, lies a valley that even the hardiest desert nomads bypass. The Nubians call this valley *Seth's Retreat*. It is rumored that any Nubian caught trespassing inside Seth's Retreat is compelled to labor there for the remainder of his short, miserable life. *Seth's Retreat* is not only the home of the Temple of Amada, but also the location of Nubia's richest gold mine. A high priest administers the temple, the mine and everything else in the valley. It takes a while, but Iby finds the owner of a donkey cart, who will accept his cowry shells in return for taking them out to *Seth's Retreat*.

CHAPTER ELEVEN

"No! No!" the driver gesticulates wildly with both hands. Senen-Mut and Iby have spent most of the afternoon bouncing up and down in his donkey cart. They have come to this desolate mountain-top spot. Their behinds are sore and their legs are stiff. They can see Amada's gates are still some distance away, down a road that winds down to the valley floor, a great distance away. It is a distance that neither Senen-Mut nor Iby care to walk. But the donkey cart driver is adamant. He refuses to take them any further and continues to wave them out of his conveyance.

"Down there!" Iby shouts. "Down there!"

But the driver abruptly turns his cart around and heads back to Kerma. Senen-Mut and Iby leap from the moving cart. For the next hour, Amen hides himself within puffy, pink clouds bouncing his rays off of distant peaks. But the sun's rays fail to penetrate the shadows enveloping the rocky road descending into Seth's Retreat. Two hours after Amen has completely descended into the underworld, the intrepid pair after picking their way down the mountain path that meanders its way directly to the gates of Amada.

A walled stronghold, Amada nestles at the bottom of the rocky, semi-arid valley behind a massive wall several cubits higher than the wall encircling Karnak. Behind the wall lay Amen's temple, clusters of shops, and a barracks for the garrison, storage facilities and stables. Behind the buildings are several sections of unexpected greenery. Gardens, orchards and vineyards spread over the left side of the valley like a quilt. A canal bordering the fields and orchards cuts through the mountain connecting directly to the

Nile. Amada has sufficient wharf area to allow transport barges to dock, load their cargo and return to Thebes. Each month Amen's high priest is responsible for transporting the mine's entire output back to Pharaoh's *House of Silver*. Senen-Mut and Iby could see some of what lay beyond the walls as they approached Amada's gates. Fortunate for Senen-Mut and Iby that the Captain of the Guard, though *Seeing Waters*, acknowledges the *Eyes of Horus* recognition signal and, after inspecting their insignias of rank hidden within the folds of their rags, admits them inside Amada's gates. The guard captain leads the pair past a pylon dedicated to the 13th Dynasty's victories over the Nubians, through Amada's pillared hallways, past sanctuaries and shrines and up a secret staircase to a private audience hall.

"The Lord Dantha, Overseer of the Pharaoh's Nubian Mines, Collector of Pharaoh's Nubian Taxes and high priest of Amen's temple at Amada," the Captain of the Guard recites sonorously, "will join you at his will. Remain here. I will inform the Lord Dantha of your presence."

The *Seeing Waters* captain orders six of his soldiers to watch the two Eyes of Horus. He then disappears through a door at the rear of the Audience Hall and passes into an administrative office teeming with activity. A middle-aged cleric wearing the black robe of Amen's priest catnaps in a great chair near the wall while an army of administrators, scribes and messengers, scurry all about him like a swarm of honey bees. The sleepy priest is Dantha, lord of Amada.

Dantha's offices, though quite large, are rather austere compared to the gilded magnificence of Seth-Mesy's chambers. Dantha's principal furnishings are a great ebony desk and highbacked chair cushioned with soft leather. Dantha's army of scribes keeps meticulous account of Amada's bustling activities. They occupy writing tables and high stools, scattered about Dantha's chambers in no particular order. Shelves filled with scrolls line the walls and shards are packed into several alcoves. Administrators converse anxiously to one side as messengers and pages rush about. Individually, they carry out their assigned tasks as they collectively, relieve Nubia of as much of its mineral and material wealth, as possible. But the napping priest seems oblivious to the frenetic activity surrounding him. Dantha has a couple of hours before conducting Amen's evening rituals so he has time to nod in his chair. His wife often scolds him for not getting enough rest, but he has a ready answer.

"What time do I have to sleep with all that is expected of me?" he asks her.

Yet, even though his eyes are closed and an occasional snore passes his lips, the seasoned administrator is fully aware of everything going on around him. He is satisfied that the daily mining and income reports tallying the gold shipments leaving his dock are accurate. He is also aware that his *Overseer of Mines* threatens a reduction in output unless he receives more slaves. Dantha's overseer never seems to have enough Nubian slaves to dig out the precious yellow metal.

"You really must take better care of your workers," Dantha lectures his supervisor. "I don't have an unlimited number of slaves. You must do with what you have until after Pharaoh's war. We should have plenty of slaves then."

"I hope so," the *Overseer of Mines* grumbles, "else you will not be meeting Pharaoh's quota."

"Don't you mean that *you* won't be meeting Pharaoh's quota?" Dantha spine-chilling look reminds the *Overseer of Mines* of his place.

"Master!" The *Overseer of Mines* falls to his knees.

Dantha knows how to keep order and maintain obedience. He is not only responsible for Pharaoh's mine, he also collects and stores Pharaoh's Nubian taxes, silver, gold, foodstuffs, animal skins everything collected on behalf of Pharaoh as well as Amen. Dantha is meticulously honest. He is a man of rigid honor, absolute loyalty and endless devotion to Amen. Whatever he collects in Nubia arrives in Thebes. Dantha is trusted by Seth-Mesy as well as Mut-Sherif. Few hold such a distinction. With all he must do and the little time he has to do it, the high priest of Amada is annoyed at being disturbed by his Captain of the Guard.

"What is it *this* time?" the priest mutters. "Did I not say that I was not to be disturbed?"

"My master ordered that he was not to be disturbed *unless* by Amen or Pharaoh," the captain replies. "My master's visitors carry the insignias of the *Eyes of Horus* and Pharaoh's Palace Guard." The guard bows low. "I thought my master would want to know of their arrival."

Preparations for Pharaoh's war with Nubia saddle Dantha with even more responsibilities. Pharaoh's *War Council* is staging the assault on Kerma from Amada and has taken over *Seth's Retreat*, completely. Barges filled with soldiers dock at Amada's wharf and disrupt Dantha's transport schedules. Amada's wharves and docks are small and barely accommodate normal water traffic. The sudden increase in military traffic causes Amada's tiny docking area to be continually congested. Daily, the *War Council* sends thousands of soldiers to Amada, without any schedule. Already the congestion has caused three collisions that closed the docking facilities for several days. Dantha is surprised that there haven't been more accidents considering the number of military barges trying to exert their "right of way' over Amada's transports. Not only has Pharaoh's *War Council* disrupted Dantha's shipping schedules, but the *War Council* also calls upon Amada to feed and bivouac the thousands of soldiers arriving daily, which is why Dantha gets so little sleep. But when his captain informs him of his *Eyes of Horus* visitors, the obedient priest puts the golden insignia of his office around his neck and shuffles into his private audience room expecting to hear more demands for housing and food for another contingent of Pharaoh's invasion force. But, instead, Dantha is surprised by the unexpected appearance of the two dirty, ragged nomads.

"You are from Thebes?" Dantha asks.

"Yes, master," Iby responds, giving the priest the respect due him.

Dantha is suspicious. The priest first studies the *Eyes of Horus* before asking to see their insignias. Their insignias are proper and their mannerisms, despite their outward appearance, convince the priest that they are, indeed, young army officers.

"How can Amada serve the young *Eyes of Horus?*" Dantha asks, cautiously.

"As the Lord of Amada must know," Senen-Mut begins, "we represent Pharaoh's *War Council.*"

"Daily I meet officers representing Pharaoh' *War Council,*" Dantha says. His tone is matter of fact. "Though none of the others look nor dress like either of you."

"We have come to Amada on a matter of military urgency," Senen-Mut says.

"Everyone arriving at Amada, these days, arrive on military urgency, of one sort or another," the priest shrugs. "Usually they want me to feed and house their soldiers. You have heard that Pharaoh is about to wage a war, I presume?" Dantha studies the reaction of the nomads before him.

"This emergency involves the personal safety of Pharaoh," Senen-Mut replies. He begins sizing up the Lord of Amada.

"I pray to Amen that no misfortune *befalls* the Pharaoh," Dantha replies.

"It is our duty to see that no misfortune does *befall* the Living God," Senen-Mut replies.

"It's my duty to intercede with Amen for the continued Life, Prosperity and Health of the *Living God.*" This discussion bores Dantha. He takes mental notes. "Since you have come a great distance on your mission to save the *Living God* from misfortune, please state how Amen's humble servant can serve you, young *Eyes of Horus?*"

"Even now, the *Living God* assembles his hosts to chasten Kerma," Senen-Mut says.

"Of this, I am well aware, young overseer," the priest responds. He wonders if Seth-Mesy would approve of his giving these nomads any information.

"Yes master," Senen-Mut says, "I am certain that you are." Then thrusting his face closer to the priest, Senen-Mut continues. "You may also be aware that we have been following Mitanni agents being escorted by Medjay traitors. We believe these Mitanni are here in Amada." Senen-Mut notes that now Dantha's eyes widen and his arrogant manner disappears.

"Yes," Dantha responds. He decides that Seth-Mesy would want him to cooperate with these *Eyes of Horus* officers especially since there is a possible threat to Pharaoh's life. "Those of whom you speak arrived several days ago." The priest pauses. *How much more should I reveal*, he wonders. He has been uncomfortable ever since the Mitanni and *Seeing Waters* arrived. *I'd better tell it all*, Dantha decides. "They did not confide the nature of their mission, but they bear the insignias of Amen," Dantha begins. "Their leader warned me not to reveal their presence to anyone, not even to the *War Council*."

Dantha is unfamiliar with political intrigue. When he tells his wife about the strangers, she becomes uncharacteristically quiet. She starts wearing *cowrie shells* for protection against the evil eye and a *scarab* for good luck. His wife also demands that Dantha wear the *ankh of life*. She warns her husband that he faces grave danger.

"How many are there?" Senen-Mut asks.

"There are a hundred of them," Dantha replies. "They requested private quarters. Their leader, a Medjay Captain, invokes *Pharaoh's secrecy* and threatened anyone breaking it with the loss of a tongue and possibly a head."

"Did you recognize the captain?" Senen-Mut asks.

"Yes," Dantha responds. "He captain's the garrison of Amen's Temple at Karnak."

"Seth-Mesy's personal guard?"

"Yes! "

Dantha looks from one *watcher* to the other. The smaller one, wearing the silly grin, serves the other, high priest decides.

"Amen's Captain of the Guard is leading Medjay and Mitanni in an attempt to assassinate Pharaoh," Senen-Mut says, quietly.

The priest gasps and intones a silent prayer.

All Egyptians join with Pharaoh in their hearts. He lives so they live! All divergent opinion finds unity in the Living God. Pharaoh unites truth as he unites the Two-Lands. No words are of any importance other than those of submission to Pharaoh's will. Correct behavior is found in Pharaoh's wisdom. All other behavior is an offense against the Gods!

"Yes, Officer of the Hundred," the priest concludes, "I believe that you speak Thoth's truth. I await your instructions".

Senen-Mut's mind races. Pure impulse has driven him this far, but not until this moment does Senen-Mut realize that the purpose for his mad dash into Nubia is to remove this threat to Pharaoh's life. He cannot fail.

"Where are they now?" Senen-Mut asks.

"They remain in their quarters."

"Thank you lord of Amada for this information," Senen-Mut says. "My friend and I wish your hospitality until we report back to our master, the Grand Vizier, Mut Sherif."

Dantha's eyes widen with this revelation. These two officers report directly to Pharaoh's Grand. *Truly I have decided well*, he murmurs to himself. "You may have all the hospitality Amada can give, young overseers of the *Palace Guard*." With that Dantha instructs his personal servant to see to their needs.

"Thank you, Lord of Amada," Senen-Mut says. "And please send me your *Captain of the Guard*."

"That is if you think he can be trusted," Iby interjects. He trusts no *Seeing Waters*.

"Also send for a representative of Pharaoh's *War Council*," Senen-Mut continues as if Iby had not spoken. "Tell them to bring enough soldiers to subdue these rogues and assassins."

The *War Council* sends three Palace Guard units taking the Mitanni and Medjay death squad by surprise. The Mitanni intruders and their Medjay guides put up not struggle. Over the next several days, all of the intended assassins are questioned. The Medjay and Mitanni officers are tortured and executed; their heads are delivered to Karnak for Pharaoh's inspection. Dantha hands the remainder of the assassination squad to his *Overseer of Mines*, who is overjoyed to receive eighty more slaves.

Eugene Stovall

CHAPTER TWELVE

Thousands line both banks of the Nile, hoping to catch sight of Pharaoh sailing back to Thebes after his spectacular victory over the Nubian king. The crowds are wild. They dance to the beat of throbbing *menits* and rattling *sistras*. Periodically competing groups of women cry out their high-pitched wails from both sides of the river. The people are ecstatic.

At the prow and the stern, Pharaoh's great ship curls upwards into the sky. At the highest peak of the prow is enthroned the golden Horus, the hawk god. Upon the stern's highest peak is the ram of Amen, crowned with the *atef* and a golden *uraeus*. In between, the barge explodes with gold and silver. At its widest point the royal barge can hold five chariots side by side. In the center of the barge, the sanctuary of Amen faces Pharaoh's golden throne. Holding the crook and flail across his chest and wearing the double red and white crown upon his head, Thut-Moses, the *Golden Horus* and *Ruler of the Two Lands* returns to Thebes as *Smiter of Nubia*. As the crowds catch sight of their *Living God*, sitting high upon his golden throne in absolute majesty, they shower him with their adoration and love.

Thut-Moses is pleased with his people. Their merriment is contagious. Pharaoh suppresses an urge to jump up and join in the dancing and merry making. Ever since he took over the throne, Thut-Moses has been plagued with doubts about his fitness as Pharaoh. Today the doubts have disappeared. He is the *Living God*, Ruler over the Two-Lands, Pharaoh of Upper and Lower Egypt. This is his day. His war was successful at every level. The army performed well. His soldiers killed and enjoyed killing ____ which, after all, was the only purpose for this war. The *War Council* performed well. Planning, mobilization, supply, transportation, battle plan and intelligence each contributed to the overall success of Pharaoh's war.

On the battlefield, Pharaoh's chariots drive great gaps through the Nubian ranks, raining death with javelin and arrow, slicing through them with their sharp-edged swords. The infantry charges through the gaps. Egyptian soldiers surround and isolate pockets of Nubians and hack them to death. Even where the Nubian have numbers, wooden spears and reed shields are no match for bronze swords and two-headed battle-axes. Defenseless from the outset, the Nubian army is annihilated. Pharaoh's army drives the remnants towards the gates of Kerma, slaughtering every Nubian in its path. But Kerma's gates and low walls offer scant obstruction to the rampaging Egyptians. Nor do the famed Nubian Bowmen, at the top of wall, hinder Pharaoh's infantry from smashing through Kerma's gates opening the way for Pharaoh's chariots to stream inside Kerma's walls. A bloodlust descends upon Pharaoh's soldiers. Like a pack of wild animals, they slaughter every man in their path and rape and physically assault every woman before hacking them to pieces as well. Their murderous onslaught continues until they confront the high walls and disciplined troops defending the Nubian king's palace. Pharaoh's rampaging soldiers are taken by surprise. They had thought the war had been won. They learned that the fighting had just begun and the Nubian guard had begun doing the killing.

The Nubians wield weapons of the highest quality, bronze swords and bronze tipped-spears. They wear leather body armor that keeps them in the fight even after receiving vicious blows. The Nubian king's palace guard is more than a match for Pharaoh's soldiers. These Nubians hold their lines and keep themselves from being cut off. Only the superior number of Pharaoh's soldiers forces the Nubians off of the walls and into the palace courtyard. Even then the king's guard does not falter. Instead it redoubles its

Eugene Stovall

efforts, fighting even more furiously. More of Pharaoh's soldiers lose their lives. The Nubians deliver thrust for thrust, slash for slash, and blow for blow. The king's personal guard is taller and stronger than the Pharaoh's soldiers and use the War Council's fighting tactics, a coordinated defense against onrushing adversaries. This tactic allows three or four guards to attack Pharaoh's onrushing soldiers one at a time. Time and time again, groups of Nubians catch one of Pharaoh's soldiers between them and deal him a disabling or death blows from back and front.

The Nubian king, himself, coordinates the defense of his palace deploying and redeploying his fighters to meet the Egyptian attacks coming from different directions. The king's Nubian bowmen, high up in guard towers, direct a steady hail of bronze-tipped arrows upon Pharaoh's chariots forcing them back from the wall. But neither the Nubian Bowmen nor the Nubian Palace Guard are able to hold out. After a gallant stand, the sheer number of Egyptian soldiers overwhelms them. In his triumph, Pharaoh spares no one, neither Nubian soldier, nor palace guard, nor Nubian bowmen, nor any Nubian, male or female, bearing a battle wound ____ nor even the life of the Nubian king, himself, who had done nothing to deserve Pharaoh's wrath, other than being black and weak.

On his triumphant journey downriver, Thut-Moses orders the king's body draped over the prow of his ship. The Nubian's wooly head, cutting through the waves of the Nile, smooths Pharaoh's way home.

Sailors lower mammoth crimson sails emblazoned with Pharaoh's insignia as they enter Thebes harbor and the oarsmen row Pharaoh's barge up to the royal dock. As the great ship glides into the royal berth, amid the cries of his people, Thut-Moses is enveloped in serenity, daydreaming about the etchings he will have placed upon his monuments.

Pharaoh, Smiter of Nubia, *with his mighty arm and in individual combat, slays the Nubian king,*

Thut-Moses smiles. *I like that. It will be carved on my mortuary temple.*

Mut-Sherif and Maat-Ka-Re are the first to welcome Thut-Moses as he descends from the royal barge onto the dock. Behind them waits a crowd of family, nobles, administrators and priests. At the sight of his daughter, Thut-Moses permits himself a slight smile. All 'kiss the dirt' at Pharaoh's feet.

Over the din of the crowd, Thut-Moses shouts, "Rise my daughter and welcome your father back from his labors!"

Maat-Ka-Re slowly rises. Her sensuous body is enveloped in a diaphanous linen gown lined in gold. Around her neck she wears a golden collar, embellished with semi-precious stones and engraved with her titles. Then Maat-Ka-Re cries out, in a lilting voice,

"Pharaoh of Upper and Lower Egypt, Aa-Kheper-Ka-Re, Son of Ra, Thut-Moses, living for ever and ever, you are the victorious Horus, thy hands are strong against all lands. The sun rises at thy pleasure, the water in the rivers is drunk at thy will and the air in heaven is breathed only when permitted by thy word."

Maat-Ka-Re steps up and embraces her father, kissing him on both cheeks. Thut-Moses bursts with pride. Maat-Ka-Re steps back and takes the hand of her brother standing, unassisted, along-side his litter. Manfully, though in great pain, Aak walks up to his father. Bowing low, his head touches the ground. The nobles, close by, hold their collective breath. Then rising when bidden to meet his father's emotionless eyes, the Crown Prince and Royal Heir, in a surprisingly loud voice, says:

"Living God, Great Pharaoh, Aa-Kheper-Ka-Re, Son of Ra, Thut-Moses, King of Upper and Lower Egypt, Speaker of Truth, Beloved of Ra, the Golden Horus, Lord of the Diadem, Lord of the Cobra, Conqueror of Nubia, it is just and fair that you call my sister fore-most among distinguished women and foremost among your children as well." Tears well up in Aak's eyes, as he continues. *"For you are the sun around which all draw life. And though it is not much, this life that I possess, I give it to you, as I have always given it, for you to do with it as you see fit."*

Aak's simple statement of love pierces Thut-Moses' heart. And, on the day of his triumphal return to Thebes, though Thut-Moses will receive many expensive gifts and offerings from his nobles, administrators and relatives, but none will he value more than his son's simple declaration of love. From this day, Thut-Moses attempts to show the Crown Prince a little more consideration.

Seth-Mesy stands among the court officials. His face twists into an evil sneer barely masking his hate. Not only does his failed plot humiliate him, but fear of Pharaoh's retribution clutches at the priest's entrails, as well. Seth-Mesy joins the others bowing low with his face touching the ground.

Why did Dantha disobey my orders? Seth-Mesy fumes. *I should have known that fool was not up to the task.* Seth-Mesy now must wonder when, and how, Pharaoh will take his revenge.

Even as Pharaoh eyes his enemy, no change in his expression betrays his feelings or what he is thinking. *Thoth will decide the time and the place for the Scales of Djeheuty to be brought into balance for the high priest of Amen,* Pharaoh decides.

With tears of joy streaming from her eyes, Maat-Ka-Re claps her hands and a bevy of dancing girls and musicians appear. Maat-Ka-Re leads her father to a great platform born by a hundred Nubian bearers. Upon the platform, Pharaoh is carried back to Karnak escorted by a company of palace guards. In front of him, priestesses dance, sing and play their musical instruments; behind follows a great procession of the nobles, court officials, priests, administrators and scribes. At his *Mansion of Millions of Years,* Maat-Ka-Re addresses her father once again.

"*Thy hands be on the Beauteous one, O enduring Pharaoh, on the ornament of the Lady of Heaven. May Nub give life to thy nose, may the Lady of the Stars join herself to thee. Let the goddess of Upper Egypt journey north and the goddess of Lower Egypt journey south each uniting and joining in the name of Thy Majesty. May the Uraeus be set upon thy brow. Thou hast delivered thy subjects out of evil. May Ra, lord of the lands, show thee grace. Hail to thee! The horn of thy bow is slacked, thine arrow loosened.*"

The moon rises up from the Nile, an immense pale orb casting a great stream of pale light over the waves. The two lovers sail into eternity. Senen-Mut and Maat-Ka-Re float down the canal towards their lover's hideaway in a boat with a prow resembling a swan. Four rowers and a pilot man the boat. They sail for the *Nome of Wast* and a cottage retreat not far from the home of Senen-Mut's parents. Only Natee accompanies Maat-Ka-Re on this journey. Though the lion frequently sails with his mistress, the big cat is uncomfortable on the water and paces back and forth.

Maat-Ka-Re has wanted to escape Karnak ever since Pharaoh's victorious return. However, other events intervene, Pharaoh rewards Senen-Mut for tracking down the would-be assassins with a golden bracelet and membership in the *Order of the Golden Fly*. Pharaoh's War Council wastes no time sending Senen-Mut, Iby and a unit of *Eyes of Horus*, into the lands of the asiatics. They spend two years traveling through Palestine and into Syria, reporting on everything of military importance. The *War Council* uses their information to plan a pre-emptive attack against the Mitanni and their Canaanite allies. When all is made ready, Thut-Moses leads three regiments of infantry and two regiments of chariots northward, sweeping up into Palestine and crushing all opposition. Within a year, a host of Canaanite, Syrian and Mitanni princes declare their allegiance to Thut-Moses. Victorious once again, Pharaoh brings boatloads of plunder back to the Two-Lands and tells stories of a strange river, called the Euphrates, whose waters run *backwards*. Now, after four years and two wars, Senen-Mut and Maat-Ka-Re have Pharaoh's permission to steal away from Thebes for two full moons of uninterrupted bliss.

"How much do you remember of me, beyond the river?" Maat-Ka-Re asks. She loves looking into Senen-Mut's eyes. They seem to know what she's about to say before she says it.

I wonder where his intelligence comes from? Maat-Ka-Re asks herself.

"The moon is aglow and love is in the air," Senen-Mut responds. Maat-Ka-Re feigns annoyance.

"Answer my question," she pouts. "You know it makes me cross when you ignore me." She is angrier with herself than with Senen-Mut for loving him so much. So she moves to the other side of the boat and begins playing with Natee, daring Senen-Mut to come closer. The lion seems to know how his mistress feels and bares his fangs to Senen-Mut. Then Maat-Ka-Re sees the wooden box with the symbol of Isis attached to an ingenuous seal. It wasn't there before.

"What's this, my love?" Maat-Ka-Re squeals. She picks at gilded symbols and carvings.

"I was going to give it to you when we arrived," Senen-Mut says.

"May I open it?"

"Of course," Senen-Mut replies. "Its yours."

With a cry of pleasure, Maat-Ka-Re breaks the seal on the lid, opens the box and takes out an exquisitely fashioned silver and gold necklace with a golden pendant inlaid with semi-precious stones and inscribed with hieroglyphics.

"What is this strange symbol?" Maat-Ka-Re asks. "I have never seen the like before. *Mut-Ka-Re!* Is that what it says?"

Again Senen-Mut does not respond but merely flashes an enigmatic smile, similar to the lopsided grin Iby always uses to hide his feelings.

"It's suppose to be a mystery," Senen-Mut says.

Maat-Ka-Re does not throw a tantrum. Instead she says, "Whatever it's meaning, nothing I possess is quite as beautiful."

Maat-Ka-Re glides over to Senen-Mut and gives him a slow sensual kiss. Then, turning her back and nestling upon him, she says, "Help me put it on."

Their nearness makes putting the necklace around her neck a near impossibility. Senen-Mut trembles with emotion and Maat-Ka-Re glows with sensuality. The necklace just gets in the way of their complete union ___ as lovers.

Long after the moon disappears and their passions are spent, Senen-Mut and Maat-Ka-Re arrive at Wast. They remain on their boat until Amen is high in the morning sky. Then climbing up the quiet dock, hidden away from the regular canal traffic, they follow a secret limestone path through flowering shrubs and a grove of sycamore trees. Upon a grassy knoll sits a wooden pavilion attached to a single story cottage. Here Senen-Mut and Maat-Ka-Re spend two months of delightful bliss. They wander about, explore themselves and, avoiding all other people, do the things that come naturally to lovers. Sometimes they swim in a special pool where Amen warms the waters tumbling over a gentle waterfall. Sometimes they take walks into an arid valley where a unique tree, whose flowers give off a wondrous fragrance, grows. Maat-Ka-Re gathers the tree's fragrant buds to use in her perfumes. In the evenings, they watch Amen blaze his path onto the western horizon before cooling himself in Nut's nurturing darkness. Some days they do nothing at all.

One evening after enjoying a light supper of baked fish, fresh fruit, bread and barley beer, Maat-Ka-Re reaches over and takes Senen-Mut's hand.

"Isis is a moon goddess," she whispers. "Isis gives birth to Horus, the god of the sun. Together, Isis and Horus create and sustain all life. Isis and Horus are the saviors of our people."

Senen-Mut does not reply.

Maat-Ka-Re continues, "Isis teaches women how to grind corn and make bread, spin flax and weave cloth."

"Yes," Senen-Mut agrees, not knowing what else to say, but deciding that he had better say something.

"I am thinking about how my father's army has eliminated the threat of an asiatic invasion only by becoming an invader himself," Maat-Ka-Re continues. She is pensive.

"Yes," Senen-Mut agrees, "your father has done much to restore security to the Two Lands. Truly he is the *Living God*."

"As long as my father is strong, our northern border is secure," Maat-Ka-Re agrees. "But what will happen when its Aak's turn?" Maat-Ka-Re faces Senen-Mut. "How will Aak maintain Egypt's security?"

"You will be at his side, no Pharaoh could have a better co-Regent."

"You really think so?" Maat-Ka-Re asks.

She really is a gentle soul, Senen-Mut thinks. *She is going to need all the help I can give her.*

He responds with "As your father has named you, so it is true. You are 'the foremost of distinguished women'. Besides, you needn't worry about Aak."

"Why not?" Maat-Ka-Re asks, quietly.

Senen-Mut must be careful not to suggest that Aak could rule the Two-Lands without Maat-Ka-Re' help. Such a thought would spark an immediate reaction.

"Don't get angry," Senen-Mut says. "I only mean that your brother seems to be doing quite well, now that he has given Pharaoh, a grandson."

"Yes," Maat-Ka-Re says, "and that's what worries me."

"Why so?"

"We should have killed that snake, Seth-Mesy, when we had the opportunity," Maat-Ka-Re reflects. "Now we must live under the threat of that assassin. He might even have Aak killed and proclaim Aak's son as Pharaoh with Seth-Mesy as regent."

Though Maat-Ka-Re called for Seth-Mesy's head, Mut-Sherif counseled against it. Pharaoh's *War Council* was planning the *War in Palestine* and could not risk a civil war.

"Open opposition to the priesthood, especially while planning to invade the asiatics in the north, is unwise," Mut-Sherif counsels. "Pharaoh gains nothing by risking a civil war instigated by the priests."

Senen-Mut agrees. Maat-Ka-Re fumes over the decision.

"Pharaoh is not so secure within his borders as to risk a civil war while his army is engaged in an all-out war in Palestine," Mut-Sherif reminds the spoiled princess.

Maat-Ka-Re allows the matter to rest. Seth-Mesy uses the temples of Amen throughout the land and the activities of his Seeing Waters to pursue his ambitions. But now that her father is home and the asiatics "kiss the dust" at Pharaoh's feet, Maat-Ka-Re believes the time has come to eliminate Seth-Mesy, *for good.*

"Amen connives directly with the Mitanni," Senen-Mut warns her. "Even though Pharaoh has defeated the asiatics in battle, you must realize they will certainly intervene if a civil war disrupts the Two-Lands."

"Do you remember when our Sages noted that a movement in the sky indicated an important change in the future of the Two-Lands?" Maat-Ka-Re asks.

"Yes," he replies.

"A new epoch is coming, a new, mysterious epoch. Transition to this epoch is fraught with peril, not only for us, but also for all of mankind. Priests now operate in the dark of Amen's rays and instill fear in the people. In the new epoch, priests will all operate in the light of the Aten at his full height and power. We must prepare the way."

"How so?" Senen-Mut had never believed in the predictions of priests. They always seemed so self-fulfilling.

"Isis teaches her people to read and to pass on the secrets of agriculture and medicine," Maat-Ka-Re says. "Isis teaches women how to tame men well enough to live with them."

"So are you planning to tame me?" Senen-Mut chuckles.

"You need no taming, my love," Maat-Ka-Re smiles reaching over and kissing his fingers. "But when one sees the appearance of animals, plants and minerals for which no seed is known to have existed, then one knows that a new age is beginning. The seeds from the old age become exhausted as do the seeds of an old man. The previous age appears exhausted before it disappears altogether. Priests like Seth-Mesy are symbols of an exhausted age. They and their rituals of fear and obedience must be brushed aside to make room for the new."

"So what is your plan?"

"I plan to follow in the footsteps of the great queens," Maat-Ka-Re laughs gazing into the distance. "I want to be remembered as a god, like the Two-Land's other distinguished women."

Eugene Stovall

Furthermore, she thinks to herself, *I want my independence from the domination of men.* She looks over at him, *and especially from you.* But for now he need not know her intentions, she decides.

"Does not the great *Scale of Djeheuty* weigh the *KA* of women as well as men?" Maat-Ka-Re asks staring into Senen-Mut's eyes. "Is not my woman's *BA* and *KA* required at the *Place of Records?*" The Hall of Records is where the *keepers* test those seeking admittance into the afterlife. "Mustn't I, too, pass the test?" Maat-Ka-Re asks.

"What test is that?" Senen-Mut asks, as if he did not know what every child learns at a very early age.

"You know, very well," Maat-Ka-Re chides him. "No *KA* of the recently dead may pass the judges unless it can balance a *feather of Maat* on the great *Scale of Djeheuty.*"

"What has that to do with wanting to eliminate the priesthood?" Senen-Mut asks. "Why should all priests be punished for Seth-Mesy's crimes? *Why should anyone be punished simply for obeying orders?*"

"I don't want to eliminate the entire priesthood, dear," Maat-Ka-Re says. Her voice imitates Natee's purring. "I just want the throne and the dynasty protected from the schemes of Seth-Mesy."

Senen-Mut knows it is senseless to argue. Maat-Ka-Re will do as she will.

"So you must agree that as we move toward the new epoch, we move more towards the worship of Isis." Maat-Ka-Re stares at him; her eyes are seductive. "This is why I say that Isis trains women to train their men." Maat-Ka-Re flashes an impish smile "They must be of some assistance when their son is born."

This last comment catches Senen-Mut completely by surprise. "Son? You, you mean that _____."

"Yes," Maat-Ka-Re laughs, "you're going to have a son." Running over to where he sits in bewilderment, Maat-Ka-Re encircles his neck with her arms. "You my darling will be responsible for raising him to be Pharaoh. And upon you I now bestow the name and title, Senen-Mut, Chief Steward of Pharaoh's Son."

Months later Maat-Ka-Re and Senen-Mut have a child ____ a girl child. Maat-Ka-Re names her, Neferu-Re. But her grandfather, Thut-Moses does not live to see his granddaughter. The Eighteenth Dynasty's second pharaoh, the great general and conqueror of Nubia and Palestine, meets his KA and travels to the underworld before Maat-Ka-Re enters her sixth month of pregnancy. The Royal Heir and his sister bury their father. Then in a private ceremony, conducted by Seth-Mesy at Aak's insistence, brother and sister marry each other and enter into a traditional, uneventful reign of Pharaoh Aa-Kheper-Ren-Re Thut-Moses II, *Living God* forever and ever and his co-Regent, Queen Maat-Ka-Re Hat-Shep-Sut. Aak appoints Senen-Mut his Royal Steward with total control over the Mansion of Millions of Years. Aak bestows upon Senen-Mut the additional titles of Hereditary Prince, Great Favorite of *God's Wife*, Pharaoh's Treasurer of the of the Two-Lands and Chief Steward of the Princess, Neferu-Re. Aak's son, Thut-Moses III and Maat-Ka-Re's daughter, Neferu-Re become inseparable. Undisturbed by temple plots, Nubian insurrections or asiatic invasions, Aak rules serenely secure on his throne. However, even though Maat-Ka-Re relieves Aak of the day-to-day stress of handling the *Seal Room*, she can see the burden of office gradually grinding upon her brother's weak heart. Though she does everything possible to relieve the strain of being Pharaoh, after a short reign, Aak's frail body meets his KA and departs for the underworld. Aak is buried in the Valley of the Kings, very near his revered father. But as the time that Queen Maat-Ka-Re has long prepared for, arrives, her bitter rival, Seth-Mesy, also lurks. Aak's son and heir, Thut-Moses III, is still a child and Seth-Mesy makes his bid for supreme power in a bold move to eliminate Maat-Ka-Re Hat-Shep-Sut, *Foremost of Distinguished Women*, once and for all.

Eugene Stovall

CHAPTER THIRTEEN

As far as life in the Two-Lands is concerned, everything re-mains as it was when Pharaoh Thut-Moses II ruled. Maat-Ka-Re Hat-Shep-Sut was co-Regent under her father, as well as under her brother and remains co-Regent now. Hat-Shep-Sut as she is now known, continues to preside over the daily brief-ings in Pharaoh's *Seal Room*, sign royal proclamations and ren-der judgments in disputes brought before her in Pharaoh's Hall of Justice. When her father fought his wars against the Nubians and the asiatics, Maat-Ka-Re conducted the whole of Pharaoh's affairs, dispensed justice and accepted the advice of Pharaoh's In-ner Council. As Aak's wife and co-Regent, Hat-Shep-Sut assumes responsibility for the daily decisions made in the *Seal Room*, the nerve center of the Two-Lands.

However, from the beginning, Iset, the mother of Aak's ten-year-old son, the Crown Prince and Royal Heir, stirs up trouble. Iset demands that the Inner Council immediately place her son on the throne and that she be named Thut-Moses' Regent and Seth-Mesy his co-Regent. Seth-Mesy pleads her case before Pharaoh's Inner Council.

"Iset insists on moving Thut-Moses and herself into the *Mansions of Millions of Years*," Senen-Mut informs Hat-Shep-Sut.

"That's not surprising," she replies. "Iset has wanted to move into the palace ever since Aak's son was born." Hat-Shep-Sut laughs at the idea. "Imagine that common concubine thinking my brother would move her into his *Mansion of Millions of Years*. She is fortunate to be living in the *Palace of Ladies*."

"But Seth-Mesy makes a strong case for a Royal Steward with total control over the *Mansion of Millions of Years* moving the Royal Heir into the palace," Senen-Mut insists. "And once Seth-Mesy moves the Crown Prince into the palace, Thut-Moses will shortly be wearing the Two Crowns and Seth-Moses will be making all the decisions."

"How often did I tell my father and Aak that Seth-Mesy needed to be eliminated?" Hat-Shep-Sut snaps.

"Yes I'm afraid that you were right all along," Senen-Mut nods, "now your old enemy is seizing control over the Inner Council."

Senen-Mut has sat on Pharaoh's Inner Council from the time he serves Hat-Shep-Sut's father as Pharaoh's Advisor, under Aak, Senen-Mut became Royal Steward over the entire *Mansion of Millions of Years,* a position that gave him a position of authority over the Inner Council. When Aak was Pharaoh the council came to trust Senen-Mut. Even Seth-Mesy and Hapu-Seneb consult him on occasion. Senen-Mut never seems a partisan of one faction or another; he always forwards ideas that resolve issues in a way that all parties are satisfied. Only the high priest of Iunu, Pen-Nek-Heb is more admired by the council and Senen-Mut considers Pen-Nek-Heb mentor.

"What is the mood of the council?" Hat-Shep-Sut asks.

"Seth-Mesy influence has grown since your brother's death," Senen-Mut replies. "His influence is even increasing with the nomarchs of the north."

Seth-Mesy has reason to be pleased with himself. And his devotion to Amen will be vindicated when the young Thut-Moses is crowned Pharaoh and he, Seth-Mesy, becomes the boy's co-Regent and the supreme authority in the Two-Lands.

When he assumes power, the priest intends to return the Two-Lands to its tradition of absolute obedience and class privileges.

Abruptly his door opens and his personal servant barges in and prostrates himself at Seth-Mesy's feet.

"What is it?" Seth-Mesy asks. He tries not to sound too irritated. After all once he becomes the most powerful person in the Two-Lands, he must expect these intrusions.

"Master, the Lady Iset wishes a word."

"Bring her in," Seth-Mesy says, giving his face the severe, haughty look that he plans to wear as Pharaoh, *one day.*

The servant disappears, returning with a chubby middle-aged woman who wears a black wig with braids falling below her shoulders. Her face might have been attractive once, but now it is so encrusted with eye liner, rouge and lip gloss that is difficult to tell what she really looks like. Around her neck, Iset wears an enormous beaded collar with a large golden scarab in the center. The collar barely covers her plump, sagging breasts. Her linen shift is dyed safflower yellow and she wears leather sandals gilded with gold. Entering Seth-Mesy's chambers, Iset has the good sense to bow low and 'kiss the dust' as Seth-Mesy expects of all commoners.

"Rise Lady Iset," Seth-Mesy commands. "What brings you to Amen's chambers?"

"I want to know, priest of Amen, when my son will be declared Pharaoh so that he may move into the *Mansion of Millions of Years* as is his right?" Thut-Moses' mother stares at the high priest, her eyes wide with expectation.

"Your son will be notified when Pharaoh's council decides the time is appropriate," Seth-Mesy replies in his sternest tone.

"And when will that be?" she asks. Iset has known a number of men in her life, including a Pharaoh; Amen's high priest does not intimidate her.

"Is your son prepared to appoint me his co-Regent?" Seth-Mesy's lips twist in anticipation.

"Once he, and his family, have moved into the palace and *that woman* is gone, I will inform my son to appoint you his co-Regent." The Lady Iset knows that she must maintain her advantages especially over the wily Seth-Mesy.

"Well, then Lady Iset," Seth-Mesy smiles, "you may go prepare your son and I will prepare the council for the announcement." The priest who seldom smiles now grins like a crocodile.

Satisfied, Thut-Moses' mother waddles from Seth-Mesy's chambers with a grin plastered upon her face. Everything is fitting nicely into place for the two conspirators. Seth-Mesy removes a quill from his desk and, finding a shard, writes a short message. Then he calls for a messenger.

"See that this message is copied and have it delivered to Hapu-Seneb and the others listed on this scroll." Seth-Mesy gives the servant the shard and a papyrus listing his council supporters.

"As you command, Master," the servant replies.

" Then report back to me."

"It shall be done, Master."

Amen! Seth-Mesy prays. *You have spared me to accomplish this great task. Thy will be done!*

"What are you going to do?"

Iby shows Senen-Mut the message Seth-Mesy sends to his supporters.

At the next Inner Council meeting, I will proclaim Menkh-Kheper-Ru-Re Thut-Moses III, Pharaoh, Ruler of Upper and Lower Egypt, Speaker of Truth, Beloved of Ra, the Golden Horus, Lord of the Diadem, Lord of the Cobra. Prepare to prostrate yourselves before Pharaoh for evil will befall anyone who would disturb the serenity of the Living God.

"Have there been any more reports of our asiatic vassals refusing to pay their tribute?" Senen-Mut asks. Since Aak's death, Thut-Moses' Palestinian vassals refuse to pay Pharaoh's tribute. Though Iby wonders what this has to do with Seth-Mesy's naked bid for power, he replies to Senen-Mut's question.

"Daily our Palestinian tax collectors are turned away empty-handed by the village headmen," Iby reports. Iby is now Captain of Captain over the *Eyes of Horus*. Since Mut-Sherif's death shortly after Aak became Pharaoh, Iby has reported to Senen-Mut as well as to the *War Council*.

"Good," Senen-Mut exclaims.

"*Good!*" Iby repeats surprised by Senen-Mut's reaction. "You do realize that the asiatics' refusal to pay tribute is the first indication of their intention to invade, don't you?"

"Even better," Senen-Mut replies. Ignoring Iby's strange look, Senen-Mut signals a scribe over. "Get your reports to the council before the next meeting," Senen-Mut instructs Iby. Then he nods to the scribe. "Take the Lord Iby's complete report and provide all of Pharaoh's councilors with a copy," Senen-Mut orders.

"As you will, master," the scribe replies.

Senen-Mut returns to Hat-Shep-Sut's chambers to inform her of Seth-Mesy's plans.

"What would happen if our meddlesome priest had an accident," Hat-Shep-Sut asks.

"The council still might proclaim your step-son, Pharaoh," Senen-Mut replies. "I've got a better idea."

"What you have in mind?"

"Neither the nomarchs nor the priests will rest comfortably knowing that a ten-year old Pharaoh and a treacherous Amen are all that stands between them and an asiatic invasion," Senen-Mut asserts.

"But what they don't know is that the asiatics are planning an invasion," Hat-Shep-Sut responds.

"Well," Senen-Mut says, "I think its time we tell them."

Pharaoh's Great Audience Hall in the *Mansion of Millions of Years* overflows with administrators, scribes and minor court officials. Pharaoh's entire Inner Council, all forty-two nomarchs, the *War Council*, the high priests of all the temples, the overseers of Pharaohs harbors, public buildings, houses of silver and granaries are also present. Crown Prince Thut-Moses III sits on his throne trying to remember his mother's instructions.

"Don't fidget!" she whispers from behind.

But the delay is too much for the ten-year old; he can't help fidgeting and squirming all over his throne. Then he stands up. A hush falls over the hall; everyone falls to their knees. Iset comes from behind the Crown Prince's throne, and forces him back down on his seat. She whispers her instructions, but the child doesn't listen. The ten-year old Thut-Moses has a short attention span and resumes his fidgeting. The ten-year old looks less like a *Living God* than like a willful child. He is unconcerned with the proceedings that occupy the adults.

Thut-Moses wears a double white and red crown that is too large for his head. With Royal Heir's fidgeting about, the crown falls to one side of his head. The Royal Heir appears quite ridiculous.

Iset fumes. She knows that her royal highness, *Queen* Hat-Shep-Sut, is delaying the ceremonial announcements.

She is deliberately trying to make him look foolish, Iset tells herself. *Well when my son is Pharaoh, Queen Hat-Shep-Sut will not only be out the Mansion of Millions of Years, she'll find herself unwelcome anywhere in Karnak.* Even though my son is only ten years old, he is Crown Prince Menkh-Kheperu-Re Thut-Moses III, King of Upper and Lower Egypt, Speaker of Truth, Beloved of Ra, the Golden Horus, Lord of the Diadem and Lord of the Cobra. Not even the foremost of distinguished women can oppose me taking my rightful place along with her son inside the Mansion of Millions of Years.

Then comes a wail of trumpets and a beating of drums. Inside the Great Audience Hall, Pharaoh's court begins to stir with anticipation. The trumpets herald the approach of her royal majesty, Queen Maat-Ka-Re Hat-Shep-Sut. Pharaoh's court ripples with excitement. The blare of the trumpets grow louder, the beats of the drum grow stronger, the shaking of tambourines, the banging of *menits* and the rattling of *sistras.* Then the court hears the singing of priestesses joined by the deep-throated voices of the Aten's red-robed priests chanting ancient songs, in *praise of Pharaoh.* The music is thrilling, the beat, irresistible and reaches a crescendo just as the doors are thrown open and Maat-Ka-Re Hat-Shep-Sut enters the Great Audience Hall upon a raised throne carried by twelve Nubian slaves and escorted by armed guards. Senen-Mut leads the Palace Guard in full military uniform, his *Order of the*

Golden Fly insignia hanging about his neck. Standing at Hat-Shep-Sut's feet is Natee, her great golden-maned lion and behind her throne stands her faithful personal bodyguard, Awab.

A shout goes up, "The Living God enters!" As Hat-Shep-Sut enters, all in the Great Audience Hall bow low and 'kiss the dust" at her feet. Accompanied by the Palace Guard in their glittering bronze armor and drawn swords, Hat-Shep-Sut ascends to her throne.

Then Pen-Nek-Heb, flanked by the User-Amen, Aak's former Grand Vizier, marches through the center of the hall up to Hat-Shep-Sut's throne. The high priest of the Aten cries out:

Pharaoh Thut-Moses has gone forth in triumph to mingle with the gods. His sister and wife, Hat-Shep-Sut, settles the affairs of the Two Lands by reason of her plans. Egypt must labor with bowed head for her whose will is to preserve Maat. She is of the excellent seed of Amen and came forth from him and is now declared in Regnal Year Seven, Horus Powerful of KA, Female Horus of Fine Gold, Two Ladies Flourishing of Years, Divine of Diadems, Maat-Ka-Re Hat-Shep-Sut, Foremost of Distinguished Women, Pharaoh of the Two-Lands of Upper and Lower Egypt.

BOOK THREE

CHAPTER FOURTEEN

The Princess Maat-Ka-Re has achieved her ambition. Throughout the Two-Lands she is recognized as Pharaoh of Upper and Lower Egypt, Maat-Ka-Re Hat-Shep-Sut Khenmet-Amen, *Foremost of Distinguished Women*.

Pen-Nek-Heb's support of the female Pharaoh increases Amen's bitterness towards the Aten. This bitterness gnaws at the vitals of religious authority and undermines the traditions and authorities that have directed the course of the Two-Lands for three millennia. This bitterness becomes so destructive that, during the reign of a future pharaoh of the eighteenth dynasty, Amen and the Aten will engage in a bitter civil war. Some might say that this war was inevitable. Religious values and core religious beliefs had eroded. But now, even if they desired, the priests cannot oppose Hat-Shep-Sut. Her control over instruments of control is too powerful. She has been God's Wife for her father and her brother. The people love her.

Princess Maat-Ka-Re decides that Seth-Mesy will never achieve his ambitions. Never will Amen's high priest ever become co-Regent or Pharaoh. The transition to the reign of the *female* Pharaoh is remarkably smooth and orderly.

But, Seth-Mesy does not give up. He decides that, if he is to have any influence in Hat-Shep-Sut's court, he must influence Pharaoh's selection of *God's Wife*.

God's Wife is the most important religious position in the Two-Lands. *God's Wife* speaks to the people. She tells them about the *Living* and *Eternal Gods*. The priests do not speak directly to the people; they need *God's Wife* to tell the people to obey the priests. While the priests conduct their ceremonies and rituals within the secrecy of their temples, *God's Wife* performs her rituals in public sight for all the people to see. Ceremonies conducted by *God's Wife* allow the people partake in the religious experience and feel the presence of the gods. The people share a special bond with *God's Wife*.

God's Wife decides which priests are permitted inside the god's temples. She declares whether Amen's black-robed priests or the Aten's red-robed priests or any other priest are sufficiently pure. *God's Wife* alone conducts the ceremonies necessary to purify both the priests' bodies and KAs. And only she affirms whether or not a priest is fit for office. And when called upon, *God's Wife* mediates disputes between temples.

By tradition, *God's Wife* is the wife of Pharaoh, the Queen of the Two-Lands and the mother of Pharaoh's heir. All the *distinguished women* held the title, *God's Wife*. The Princess Maat-Ka-Re had been and extremely popular as *God's Wife*. Senen-Mut uses Hat-Shep-Sut's popularity with the people to convince the Inner Council that her ascension to the throne would cause the least disruption throughout the Two-Lands. But after being on the throne over two years, despite all Seth-Mesy's intrigues, Hat-Shep-Sut refuses to appoint anyone to the position of God's Wife and Pharaoh's most loyal supporters grow dissatisfied over her failure to follow tradition.

"I want to do away with the title of *God's Wife*, altogether and assume the functions myself," Hat-Shep-Sut tells Senen-Mut. Her consort is now Grand Vizier. "The people will love me more than they have loved any other Pharaoh!"

"You've done more to end the rivalry between Seth-Mesy and Pen-Nek-Heb already," Senen-Mut advises. "This is not good, now that the priests are cooperating they could easily find a pretext to declare you unfit for office. If you eliminate the title of *God's Wife*, you will weaken your authority within your own council."

The council beseeches Senen-Mut to get Pharaoh to appoint *God's Wife*. The council wants her to choose either Pen-Nek-Heb or Seth-Mesy. "It will restore order and symmetry to the Two-Lands," they urge. Her council wants a man appointed God's Wife, but Senen-Mut dares not mention this to Hat-Shep-Sut. She reacts badly to any reference to her sex, even the most innocent. But her Grand Vizier emphasizes the council's concern.

"Majesty, you must appoint *God's Wife* soon," he councils.

Hat-Shep-Sut is silent; she does not agree with Senen-Mut.

I am Pharaoh now, she tells herself. *No one can force me to do anything that I do not wish to do.*

"Too much time has passed already," Senen-Mut continues. "Seth-Mesy enjoys the backing of the Crown Prince's mother and he is beginning to gain support among the nomarchs in the north. He even speaks openly in the council against your delay. Everyday he grows bolder."

"Bolder?" Hat-Shep-Sut snaps.

"Seth-Mesy argues that, by putting you on the throne, the Two-Lands lost both a Pharaoh and *God's Wife*.

"You spend too much time worrying about the council and not enough time worrying about me," Hat-Shep-Sut retorts.

"I spend all my time worrying about you," Senen-Mut replies. "That is why I believe that you must appoint *God's Wife*."

"My council needs to understand that it is my will that there be no *God's Wife*," Hat-Shep-Sut replies. "Why must I repeat myself? Am I not Pharaoh and *is this not my will?*"

Senen-Mut is caught. Pharaoh and her council are locked into a contest of wills. Hat-Shep-Sut is oblivious to the growing cooperation between Amen and the Aten. Senen-Mut worries that even worse things could happen if she doesn't act soon.

Pen-Nek-Heb enters Senen-Mut's private office with a direct access to the *Eyes of Horus* headquarters, the office formerly belonging to Mut-Sherif. At the Aten's temple at Iunu, Pen-Nek-Heb is accustomed to solving problems and unraveling mysteries.

The Aten's high priest is the master of measures. When the end of an epoch arrives, the master of measures understands how to abandon the old boundaries to give free access to the new ones. He hands over for destruction that which is corrupt, so that only the indestructible remains. Pen-Nek-Heb made it possible for Hat-Shep-Sut to become Pharaoh. Now he believes that he has the influence necessary to advise her on the best course for her rule. The priest is wrong. Hat-Shep-Sut treats Pen-Nek-Heb as just another council member to be used as she sees fit. And for the time being, Hat-Shep-Sut does not see fit to listen to Pen-Nek-Heb or even see the priest. Even his momentous predictions fail to interest Hat-Shep-Sut.

"But why will the *Living God* not meet with me?" Pen-Nek-Heb asks Senen-Mut. "I wish to discuss the great changes that the Two-Lands are about to undergo."

The high priest's pleas to Senen-Mut fall on deaf ears. The priest cannot believe that his own initiate refuses to obey him.

Another sign of the coming epoch, Pen-Nek-Heb sighs to himself. "Pharaoh must understand that her decisions will bring either prosperity or ruin upon the Two-Lands," the high priest pleads to Senen-Mut.

"When Pharaoh is interested in her council's opinion," Senen-Mut explains, "she will attend a council meeting or invite the council to her *Seal Room*." Senen-Mut stares blankly at Pen-Nek-Heb. He shows no sentiment. "For the time being, the *Living God* has not seen fit to listen to you."

"She cannot defy our ancient traditions without incurring a cost that her people may be unable to pay," Pen-Nek-He says.

"Pharaoh believes in the most ancient of traditions governing the Two-Lands," Senen-Mut responds.

"Which traditions are those?"

"The traditions that tell the people that the will of Pharaoh is law because her words are infallible."

This is as plain as Senen-Mut can say it. Hat-Shep-Sut will tolerate no one's opinions over her own, not even those of the enlightened priest who made it possible for her to seize the throne. "Pen-Nek-Heb," Hat-Shep-Sut instructs Senen-Mut, "is not to even attempt to exercise any control over Pharaoh's will."

My own initiate refuses me an audience with Pharaoh? Pen-Nek-Heb rages within. *This is not the way things are done.*

Pen-Nek-Heb normally wears a solemn look. Now his face twists into a stern scowl. Never before has the man, known in the council as the wisest in the Two-Lands, second-guessed himself. Never before has the sage of Iunu ever entertained the idea that he has made a mistake, But today, the high priest of the Aten regrets his decision to defy three millennia of tradition and support a female Pharaoh.

The Aten's high priest pulls himself up to his full height, almost a head taller than Senen-Mut.

"Please inform the *Living God* that I await her pleasure," Pen-Nek-Heb's words seethe with anger.

"Lord Pen-Nek-Heb, it troubles me to say this, but I do not believe her Majesty wishes to discuss this subject at this time."

"You must find a way to convince the Great God that she has very little time before it is too late," Aten's high priest warns. But in the end, Pen-Nek-Heb departs Pharaoh's *Mansion of Millions of Years* without receiving an audience. And Hat-Shep-Sut avoids listening to another lecture on the importance of her appointing *God's Wife*.

Later, Senen-Mut brings up the subject in their private chambers.

"I received a visit from Pen-Nek-Heb, today." Senen-Mut affects a nonchalant manner knowing how to pique her curiosity.

"What did the Aten want?"

"He wanted an audience to discuss the importance of appointing *God's Wife*."

"I suppose he believes that he is the best person for the position." Hat-Shep-Sut eyes Senen-Mut, expecting him to support Pen-Nek-Heb's request.

"If even my most loyal supporters do not obey my will," Hat-Shep-Sut continues, "how can I expect those who plot against me to obey?" Her voice is deceptively soft. "Did you promise the Aten an audience?"

"I did not believe that your Majesty wished to listen to the Aten's lecture," Senen-Mut says.

"You were correct in your assumptions," Hat-Shep-Sut says.

"But the priests of your council are telling members that the absence of *God's Wife* is evidence of the god's disfavor." In bringing the issue up once again Senen-Mut decides to reduce it to its simplest terms. "Seth-Mesy argues that your obstinacy shows why Pharaoh should be a male."

"And why is my *female will* any different than a *male will?*" Hat-Shep-Sut snaps.

"Because *God's Wife* is a goddess to the people," Senen-Mut says. "The land is restless without her. She is important for the people's well being. *She guarantees the continued existence of the social order.*"

"Are you saying that I'm unfit to be Pharaoh because I am a *woman?*" Hat-Shep-Sut fumes. "I will tolerate no slander upon my sex, *is that clear?*" She's really angry. "And I'll permit no one to tarnish my image as the *foremost of distinguished women,* not even you."

There is a point in human affairs that future events begin to take place. Senen-Mut and Hat-Shep-Sut have reached this point in their relationship. This is the time when Hat-Shep-Sut stops loving Senen-Mut and begins treating him like a rival.

"Great Majesty and Lord of the Two-Lands," Senen-Mut replies, "You cannot eliminate the people's only connection to Amen and expect them to love you. *Majesty, you already know this!*"

Hat-Shep-Sut fights to control her emotions.

He thinks he knows what's good for me! she murmurs to herself. *BUT I AM PHARAOH!* Her scream is silent, but emphatic. She fights to calm herself down. Once she has retrieved her serenity,

Hat-Shep-Sut asks, in a quiet voice. "Do you and the council presume to oppose my will?"

"Majesty! Senen-Mut prostrates himself. "I mean no disrespect. My only concern is how to answer your council members' inquiries about Pharaoh's intentions to appoint *God's Wife*."

He pauses before continuing.

"I have encouraged your council to engage in extended debates over the suitability of any candidate that Hat-Shep-Sut might choose."

"*You* have encouraged?" Now Hat-Shep-Sut is really angry.

"How dare you!" she shouts. "*You* have presumed to encourage them to debate what, you know, *opposes my will?* Instead of helping me resolve the problem, *you're* making it worse. *You're still discussing the issue?* If you'd make my will clear to them, the issue would go away!"

Senen-Mut does not respond.

"I've encouraged them to discuss the matter so that Pharaoh's enemies won't debate another issue," Senen-Mut replies.

"What issue is that?" Hat-Shep-Sut huffs.

"Depriving Pharaoh of her throne."

He knows that this forceful tone offends her. He braces himself for another outburst. But after several minutes the only sound escaping her mouth is one of exasperation.

"No matter what I do, my enemies will continue their attempts to deprive me of my throne," Hat-Shep-Sut says. She uses the resigned tone that Senen-Mut knows is meant to put him off, but Senen-Mut senses she is weakening.

"You don't want Seth-Mesy to control your friends on the council, do you?" Senen-Mut asks.

"If the council wants *God's Wife*," Hat-Shep-Sut says, "then I shall give them *you*."

"Of course I am greatly flattered by the esteem that your majesty shows me," Senen-Mut responds, certain that her proposal is not meant to be serious, "but I cannot accept the title."

"Why not?" Hat-Shep-Sut asks.

"God's Wife is a priestly title with revenues, servants and significant authority," he explains. "God's Wife burns the names of Egypt's enemies. God's Wife presents offerings to the seventeen gods. God's Wife purifies all priests residing in all temples located within Karnak's walls. No priest may perform his duties without the permission of God's Wife."

"That is why you must be God's Wife," Hat-Shep-Sut argues. "I would not have a moment of peace if anyone else held that title. I have too many enemies as it is."

"But I cannot hold a priestly title," Senen-Mut reminds her. "The ancients did not permit dual service or divided loyalties. I am your Grand Vizier, Overseer of the Inner Council as well Royal Treasurer. Someone else must be God's Wife."

"But who can I appoint?" Maat-Ka-Re asks. "Certainly you must see that if I appoint either Pen-Nek-Heb or Seth-Mesy, I have but increased my troubles."

Senen-Mut nods in agreement.

"As I see it, you have only two equally bad choices."

"Which are?"

"Thut-Moses or Neferu-Re."

"I thought you intended a military career for my step-son."

"I do," Senen-Mut responds. "But the last time I spoke to the royal heir, he was defiant." "What's he saying?"

"He says that unless you allow Neferu-Re to accompany him to Horus Nest, he's not leaving."

Hat-Shep-Sut enjoys a rare fit of laughter. "Can't you just see Thut-Moses as a priest?" she says. "He's more bloodthirsty than Neferu-Re." Her laughter breaks the tension between them. "My stepson is never happier as when he is hurling a wooden javelin or swinging a mace."

"If you exclude Thut-Moses, then your only other choice for God's Wife is Neferu-Re," Senen-Mut continues.

Senen-Mut notices a peculiar look in Hat-Shep-Sut's eyes.

Is that a look of triumph? he asks himself. She must know that the council's opposition to Neferu-Re will be fierce. But now Senen-Mut

Eugene Stovall

realizes what Hat-Shep-Sut has been planning all along. *Very clever! Either they accept Neferu-Re as God's Wife or leave the office vacant. Either way, Pharaoh wins. Very clever, indeed!*

"So it seems that my only choice is my daughter," Hat-Shep-Sut replies, a sly smile playing at the corners of her mouth.

Now, it's her turn to appear nonchalant as if to camouflage her intentions. He doesn't know whether to be happy that Hat-Shep-Sut will finally appoint *God's Wife* or to fret over giving Neferu-Re such awesome power. Senen-Mut fears that they both may regret this decision.

"What is it, my Lord Consort," Hat-Shep-Sut asks. She waits several minutes for his reaction. "Do you not favor my appointing your daughter *God's Wife?*"

Hat-Shep-Sut enjoys watching Senen-Mut squirm. She knows how difficult it will be to get council to approve Pharaoh's selection.

"On the contrary, Majesty. Neferu-Re will make an ideal *God's Wife* and her appointment will help resolve the other issue."

"The *other* issue?"

"Getting the Crown Prince to begin his military training at *Horus Nest*," Senen-Mut smirks. Hat-Shep-Sut wants Thut-Moses and Neferu-Re together as much as possible. She intends that her daughter marry her stepson, just as she had married Aak. Senen-Mut knows that the thought of Thut-Moses and Neferu-Re being separated while he takes military training at *Horus Nest* will make Hat-Shep-Sut very unhappy. She had even contemplated sending Thut-Moses to train at the Nek-Heb Valley Training Camp with the Palace Guard. Nek-Heb Valley is much closer to Thebes. But even the palace guard receives its basic training at *Horus Nest*. Even though Hat-Shep-Sut is unhappy that Thut-Moses and Neferu-Re must be separated, she is even unhappier contemplating Neferu-Re leaving Karnak.

"Practically speaking, Great Lord," Senen-Mut says, lowering his voice to a conspiratorial tone, "you and I, and half of Thebes, believe that Neferu-Re keeps Thut-Moses here in Karnak to promote her own ambitions."

"You speak the truth," Neferu-Re's mother replies. Hat-Shep-Sut cannot allow her consort to know too much of her plans. *But it doesn't matter whether he knows or not*, she decides, *just as long as he does what he is told and obeys the will of Pharaoh*. However, she decides that prudence dictates that their conversation take a different direction.

"I blame it on that nurse, Tuua," Hat-Shep-Sut says. "I should have had her poisoned long ago." Senen-Mut spots the insincere look on Hat-Shep-Sut's face, the look she always wears when she's trying to deceive someone. She is actually trying to copy Iby's foolish grin, Senen-Mut laughs to himself. He knows all of Hat-Shep-Sut's looks. They tell him exactly what she is feeling as well as what she is thinking. For example, there is the look of motherly pride that flickers across Hat-Shep-Sut's face whenever Neferu-Re's name is even mentioned. Then the haughty expression she wears when she wants to appear to be the *Living God* completely disappears. Hat-Shep-Sut even has a look that makes her appear less beautiful, though to Senen-Mut, her beauty is timeless and never changes. She uses this look to discourage his amorous advances, which she has done quite often, lately. But the look that Senen-Mut never tires of seeing is Hat-Shep-Sut's expression of happiness. When she is happy, her face glows with the beauty of Isis. Hat-Shep-Sut knows that her consort can see into her Ka. She hates him for it. It is unwise for Hat-Shep-Sut to allow her enemies to see what makes her happy. So, even though she changes her expression, she knows that she has not put her consort off the scent.

"Once you appoint your daughter to the position of *God's Wife*," Senen-Mut observes, "there will be no reason for Neferu-Re to keep Thut-Moses here in Thebes."

"Why do you say that?" Hat-Shep-Sut asks.

"*God's Wife* will outrank the Crown Prince."

On the day her Grand Vizier announces the Princess Neferu-Re's appointment as God's Wife, the Great Audience Hall of

Pharaoh's *Mansion of Millions of Years* is filled to capacity. Rumors had been circulating throughout the Two-Lands for months.

"She will appoint Pen-Nek-Heb," some say.

"It will be Seth-Mesy," others insist.

Nomarchs and top administrators who seldom attend Inner Council meetings make rare appearances. Senen-Mut dreads the outcome. Hat-Shep-Sut smiles with anticipation, marveling at how well her plans are succeeding.

The announcement shocks Pharaoh's court. Neither Seth-Mesy nor Pen-Nek-Heb expected that Hat-Shep-Sut would name Neferu-Re God's Wife. Yet, both were practical men. Furthermore, each was content that the other had not secured the coveted honor. In the end, Pharaoh's choice was a wise one.

CHAPTER FIFTEEN

Hat-Shep-Sut paces back and forth. Her servants conceal themselves behind the colorful linen drapes that divide her royal chambers into separate sections. The servants keep their distance, out of eyesight, but within earshot. Even Natee is more attentive than usual, watching his mistress moving back and forth from his usual spot in front of her high-backed chair. Occasionally, the massive lion expresses his sympathy with a low, rumbling growl.

The object of Pharaoh's anger is a golden scroll lying on the table where Senen-Mut dropped it. The offensive scroll emblazoned with Amen's insignia upon its seal arrived less than an hour ago. It reads:

Pharaoh Aa-Kheper-Ren-Re Thut-Moses II went forth into the afterlife in triumph. Having mingled with the gods, his son, Thut-Moses III stands in his place, Pharaoh over the Two-Lands. Ruler upon the throne of the one who sired him, Thut-Moses' stepmother, the Divine Hat-Shep-Sut, now settles the affairs of the Two Lands by reason of her assumption of office and Egypt labors with bowed head.

For this reason, Amen-Ra calls for a renewal of the Living God, Horus Powerful of KA, Female Horus of Fine Gold, Two Ladies Flourishing of Years, Divine of Diadems, Pharaoh of Upper and Lower Egypt, Pharaoh Maat-Ka-Re Hat-Shep-Sut Khenmet-Amen, at the forthcoming Opet-festival.

May the Foremost of Distinguished Women remain enduringly and may her blessings prosper the Two-Lands.

"I will avenge this is an insult!" Hat-Shep-Sut shrieks. "I will not tolerate it! Bring me that priest's head!"

The high priest's proclamation is a challenge to Hat-Shep-Sut's authority.

"How dare he?" Hat-Shep-Sut fumes. She paces about her chambers, but it does nothing to calm her anger.

"I appointed that ingrate to his position," Hat-Shep-Sut continues to rant. *"Now I want his head!"*

Pharaoh stops pacing and glares at the Captain of her Palace Guard. The officer shifts uncomfortably at his station, hesitating to carry out Pharaoh's instructions. He glances over at Senen-Mut as if to ask for help.

"Great One!" Senen-Mut cries out falling down to his knees.

It is the charade that Senen-Mut and Hat-Shep-Sut must play whenever others are present. At all times the *Royal Consort* acknowledges Pharaoh's divinity with exaggerated gestures of obeisance and humility. Not only does his submissiveness please Hat-Shep-Sut, but the Grand Vizier's behavior reminds everyone to use prudence in Pharaoh's presence. So, Pharaoh's Captain of the Palace Guard imitates Senen-Mut and fall to his knees, as well. The Grand Vizier pleads for restraint.

"Certainly, Amen's high priest intends to justify his announcement before your council."

Senen-Mut wants to buy some time to find out who is behind Dantha's bold challenge to Pharaoh's authority. But already Hat-Shep-Sut's explosive temper and vindictive disposition threatens to limit the time he needs. *Someone has concocted a very clever scheme for toppling Hat-Shep-Sut,* Senen-Mut concludes, *and there's more to it than an announcement of a pharaonic jubilee at this year's Opet-festival.*

"Majesty," Senen-Mut suggests, "this thing is not what it seems."

He wants to warn her that whoever is behind this attack wants Pharaoh to be the architect of her own downfall.

But Hat-Shep-Sut will have none of it. "This is but another indication of Amen's contempt towards me," Hat-Shep-Sut retorts. Senen-Mut signals the captain of the Palace Guard. *"Leave now and I will give you instructions, later."*

Visibly relieved, the captain hurriedly rises and departs. Storming the Temple of Amen and seizing the high priest by force is not something the captain relishes. The *Seeing Waters*, guarding Amen's temple, are battle-tested Medjay. They would never yield to his palace guard. The Medjay would defend the temple to the last man. But 'the last man' might very well be one of his palace guardsmen. Storming Amen's temple and taking Amen's high priest against his will would require an entire regiment of Palace Guard commanded by someone of a much higher rank than a captain. Even if the palace guard were successful in capturing and executing Dantha, the resulting civil war between the army and the Medjay would tear the Two-Lands apart. Many soldiers, particularly those who remain loyal to the nomarchs of the north, would side with the Medjay. Senen-Mut realizes that this is not a situation where Pharaoh can behave rashly. So from his bowed position, Senen-Mut urges caution and reason.

"Great Lord, please remember how fickle your council might be in such a situation. There are still many, especially among the northern nomarchs, who prefer your step-son on the throne."

"You may rise," Hat-Shep-Sut says fixing him with a cold stare.

Of late, Senen-Mut has become more aware of Hat-Shep-Sut's animosity. Senen-Mut doesn't understand what he has done to cause this animosity and is hurt by it. But he never allows Hat-Shep-Sut's anger to cause him to act precipitously.

And ordering the palace guard to put Dantha's head on a pole, Senen-Mut tells himself, *is a very precipitous act.* Senen-Mut rises cautiously. He is concerned as he watches Hat-Shep-Sut clenching her small fists until her sharp, painted fingernails dig deeply into the palms of her hands.

"Certainly, there are more persons involved in this plot than that doddering old fool," he asserts. "You do not intend to execute

Dantha before discovering who else is responsible for disturbing your serenity. Possibly, the other conspirators are among your own advisors. You need to know all the facts, before you act, don't you think?"

"I have all the facts I need!" Hat-Shep-Sut responds. "Once I have dealt with that ingrate in Amen's temple, then I will deal with the others." Hat-Shep-Sut's eyes narrow and she frowns at her Grand Vizier. "Besides, I do not intend to have him beheaded immediately, I want him tortured, as well. That way you can find out who else plots to take away my throne." Her eyes blaze with anger. "But, in any event, I will have Dantha's head for this insult _____ *and I want him brought before me now!*"

Senen-Mut's mind races. Hat-Shep-Sut's anger is like a volcano and it's getting ready to blow.

What can I do to calm her before the eruption? he asks himself. *Think! Think quickly!*

Senen-Mut understands that Hat-Shep-Sut has suffered an emotional shock. Whoever is behind this thing planned it well. Even if Hat-Shep-Sut were not the sensitive, high-strung person that she is, Dantha's attack would have still been a terrible blow. For Amen's high priest to propose a *pharaonic jubilee* is a direct accusation that the *female* pharaoh is unfit to rule.

According to ancient tradition, a jubilee celebrates Pharaoh's accomplishments and renews *pharaonic* rule. Jubilees are never proclaimed by Amen's high priest before the end of the seventh regnal year and, normally, not until the fifteenth. Dating from the death of her husband, Hat-Shep-Sut has been Pharaoh barely six years. Senen-Mut actually agrees that Hat-Shep-Sut should respond to Dantha's announcement by decorating a pole with the rascal's head. *But, not yet!'*

Normally, Hat-Shep-Sut would allow Senen-Mut to calm her down. But her love for her consort has now turned into bitter resentment over his influence. She chafes when he forces her to listen to his counsel. Today, in particular, she doesn't want to hear any of his advice; she only wants him to obey her commands.

He's always thwarting my will. I'm the Living God. My will is what matters! Hat-Shep-Sut seethes with emotion.

He not only wants to tell me what to do, now, he's telling me that I must endure the insolence of Amen's priest. A commoner tells me that I must endure the unendurable!

When she was *God's Wife*, Hat-Shep-Sut observed priests at close hand and found them greedy and full of pride. Now that she is Pharaoh, she believes the priests have exceeded even their own normally cynical and corrupt behavior. Daily they demand even greater shares of what the people produce. They press for a greater share of the land, a greater share of the taxes and a greater share of the people's loyalty. Ever since Hat-Shep-Sut became Pharaoh, the priests behave as if they ruled over the Two-Lands.

I must have an end to these priests and their schemes. And my Grand Vizier must learn that it is I who wields the crook and flail and not he.

"Whatever decision you make, you must have the full backing of your council," Senen-Mut lectures. "You especially need the backing of the priests."

Hat-Shep-Sut just glares at him.

"*You* never seem to have any trouble getting your friends in *my* Inner Council to do *your* bidding," she spits. She aims her barb where it will hurt him most, like a scorpion's sting. "My inner council does nothing I tell them to do unless my Grand Vizier approves." Hat-Shep-Sut often complains to Neferu-Re that *her father believes that he's Pharaoh!*

But all Senen-Mut wants to do is to serve the woman he loves and keep her safely on the throne. And, in reality, Senen-Mut is all that stands between Hat-Shep-Sut and the nomarchs, nobles and priests who daily plot to dethrone her. Like jackals after carrion, many of her council are making fortunes by siding with the priests against the female Pharaoh. They hope to amass even more wealth by awarding Hat-Shep-Sut's double crown to her stepson,

Thut-Moses III. Senen-Mut must be constantly on the alert for their endless plots. He works to retain council support for Hat-Shep-Sut's rule by making concessions, awarding projects and bestowing titles. Senen-Mut always supports the endless petitions of nobles and commoners alike so long as the petitioner pledges loyalty and devotion to the Living God, Hat-Shep-Sut. Each day, before Amen spreads his first flickering rays across the eastern horizon and far after Amen departs for the underworld. Senen-Mut is fully occupied instructing his overseers, issuing proclamations and meeting with members of Pharaoh's Inner Council, separately and in groups. It is only long after the creatures of Mut, begin their evening celebrations deep inside the Nile's moon-swept marshes, that Senen-Mut ceases his labors, grabs something to eat and then snatches a fitful sleep before beginning again the next day. And though he has not shared Hat-Shep-Sut's sleeping mat for several months, Senen-Mut continually serves her interests.

Senen-Mut even planned the *accident* that killed Seth-Mesy, eliminating Hat-Shep-Sut's most hated enemy. Seth-Mesy met his *KA* under one of the two great obelisks Senen-Mut erected for Hat-Shep-Sut at Karnak. He also won council approval for Dantha as Seth-Mesy's replacement. Hat-Shep-Sut believed that she could control Dantha far easier than she could control Seth-Mesy. Hat-Shep-Sut believed the doddering high priest of Amada would be happy to do her bidding. The council wanted to replace Seth-Mesy with Hapu-Seneb. The Royal Teacher was already one of them. He was familiar with the way things were done in Karnak. To secure Dantha's appointment, Senen-Mut had to wrangle, threaten and deal. When Pharaoh's Grand Vizier, after considerable difficulty, rallied the Inner Council behind Pharaoh, many throughout the Two-Lands thanked Thoth for Senen-Mut's wisdom in directing Pharaoh's affairs. Unfortunately, Hat-Shep-Sut was not one of them. She believed that her Nubian priest would end the feud between the *Living God* and Amen and that her troubles were at an end. Pharaoh could rule as Pharaoh wills. But Hat-Shep-Sut could not be more wrong.

The priests control fully one third of all the land in Egypt ____ temple complexes, farms, ships, mines, quarries, towns and villages. Massive numbers of slaves labor in the temples and upon temple land. Everyday priests receive loaves of bread, jugs of beer, sacks of grain, wines and meats from thousands even while temple lands produce surpluses of grain matched only by the production from Pharaoh's own royal nomes. The priests hoard their vast wealth behind the high walls and temple complexes. As the guardian of Amen's wealth, Dantha is not the weakling Hat-Shep-Sut expected. As soon as Dantha takes control of Amen's Temple at Karnak and assumes authority over all of Amen's other temples throughout the Two-Lands, he leads the council opposition to every one of Hat-Shep-Sut's projects. After all Dantha was Seth-Mesy's favorite protégé most of the councilors remember. Worse yet, Dantha possesses an amiable manner that wins him a hearing from councilors who would never have listened to Seth-Mesy. As it turns out, Hat-Shep-Sut could not have appointed a more effective opponent to her projects and proposals than the Amen's Nubian high priest.

"Pharaoh's obelisk caused my predecessor's death and almost bankrupted the royal treasury," Dantha argues to Pharaoh's Inner Council. "Limits must be placed on Pharaoh's buildings and the safety of the workers should be considered before work is begun."

This last comes as a surprise to Dantha's fellow council members. No priest ever expressed any concern about the welfare of the workers before. Priests concern themselves with cutting costs and saving time. They are far more concerned with protecting slabs of precious limestone than protecting the lives of the workers or their families. With her normal impatience, Hat-Shep-Sut rushes one building project after another to completion without any concern for the safety of the workers. Dantha uses the issue of worker safety to attack the female Pharaoh urging that she slow her building projects and direct her Director of Buildings to observe traditional safety measures. He argues that Pharaoh's construction projects are killing too many laborers. The priest's comments resonate at

Pharaoh's court. Dantha becomes as popular with Pharaoh's Inner Council as Seth-Mesy was disliked. Seth-Mesy never successfully disrupted any of Hat-Shep-Sut's projects. Dantha stops some projects, permanently, and delays several others. One project, Dantha fails to stop, however, causes so much animosity between Pharaoh and Amen's high priest that, Senen-Mut believes, it caused Dantha to call for Hat-Shep-Sut's premature jubilee.

The all-out struggle between Dantha and Pharaoh begins when Hat-Shep-Sut directs her *Director of Buildings*, the high priest of Anubis, to construct a sparkling, beautiful chapel made of red granite dedicated to the Aten. Pharaoh's red chapel sits upon a raised platform directly facing and towering over the temple of Amen. Dantha is scandalized. Amen is the chief deity of Karnak and ruler over the Two-Lands. Hat-Shep-Sut's red chapel overthrows Amen's rule. To make matters worse, Hat-Shep-Sut surrounds her red chapel, as well as Amen's temple, with a series of interconnected shrines depicting her own divine conception, birth and early childhood as the daughter of Amen, himself. Pen-Nek-Heb, the Aten's high priest, had proposed the project to Hat-Shep-Sut before Seth-Mesy's unfortunate accident. And Hat-Shep-Sut seized upon the idea as the most effective method of diminishing Amen's power.

"A chapel honoring the *Aten* in Karnak," Pen-Nek-Heb counseled, "will create balance between the *Aten* and Amen. Your chapel to the *Aten* will declare that Pharaoh rules in the light of true intelligence."

The high priest of Iunu furnishes the *Director of Buildings* with the plans, the labor and the material necessary for Pharaoh's red chapel. Though her Grand Vizier advises caution, Pharaoh removes Seth-Mesy and installs the 'witless' Dantha to head off any opposition. Then she orders her Director of Buildings to begin the project while Pen-Nek-Heb argues in her Inner Council that, since the project will employ workers from the north, Pharaoh's red chapel will heal the ill feelings still lingering in the northern nomes. Nevertheless, Hat-Shep-Sut's red chapel outrages Amen's priests and when Dantha assumes the duties of Amen's high priest, his opposition is as vigorous and effective as Seth-Mesy's would have been shrill and self-defeating. But since the *Aten's* high priest completely funds the building of Hat-Shep-Sut's red chapel complex, Dantha is unable to obstruct the project and Pen-Nek-Heb gains an immense advantage with Pharaoh over his rival.

"This is a blasphemy against Amen!" Dantha thunders. "It's another departure from tradition. It's is heresy!"

Amen sends priests to preach against Pharaoh's heresy, up and down the Two-Lands. His dire warnings are read in the temples of Ptah, Isis, Thoth as well as Amen. Everywhere Amen's priests call for the cessation of work on Pharaoh's red chapel and her ouster from the throne.

"There can be no peace in the Two-Lands when Pharaoh attacks Amen," Dantha vows. "The Aten chapel is an affront to Amen."

"The gods be saved from Pharaoh's heresies," priests tell each other. "The *Aten* never intrudes upon the affairs of men. The Aten is too powerful, too mighty, even for the *Living God!* The Aten is Life, itself. Calling upon the Aten will bring disaster upon Pharaoh's house and destruction upon the Two-Lands."

Despite Dantha's opposition, Hat-Shep-Sut completes her red chapel and surrounds it with shrines. Daily, Dantha must watch the Aten's red-robed priests, serenely indifferent to Amen's prerogatives, conduct their ceremonies at the *Aten's* chapel and before Hat-Shep-Sut's shrines. Now with his proclamation of pharaonic jubilee, it seems that Dantha is retaliating against Pharaoh's red chapel and Pharaoh, herself.

Nice and neat, Senen-Mut thinks. *Too neat!*

Hat-Shep-Sut stops her pacing and faces her Grand Vizier.

"Dantha's treachery," she hisses through her tight jaws, "gives me ample justification with your friends on the council for what I'm about to do." Her remark is calculated to hurt Senen-Mut, once again. And seeing the hurt in his eyes gives Hat-Shep-Sut some satisfaction.

Please Thoth, Senen-Mut says, *let her be persuaded by your wisdom.*

Senen-Mut decides to gamble on getting her out of this dangerous mood and making her see reason.

"Pharaoh's councilors might see Amen's execution in an entirely different manner," he argues.

"How so?" Hat-Shep-Sut snaps.

"They might believe that you are overreacting because the plot was not aimed at you as Pharaoh, but because it was aimed at you as a *woman.*"

Senen-Mut prepares for the eruption that follows whenever her *sex* his mentioned. But, strangely enough, Hat-Shep-Sut does not react, instead she responds reasonably.

"I need scarcely remind you that this council would not have treated my father so contemptuously."

This is good, Senen-Mut thinks. He decides to press the point further.

"Great Majesty!" he continues. "Even though you are the *Living God,* the ancients provided that when Pharaoh becomes exhausted, she must be renewed *even if it is necessary for Amen to remove her from office and choose her successor.* Whatever else you do, Mighty One, you must answer the high priest's call for a jubilee or face an insurrection. Even Thoth in his wisdom cannot know the outcome of such a catastrophe. A civil war could cause the fall of your family's dynasty. A civil war could cause the Mitanni to invade the Two-Lands. Is the head of Dantha on a pike worth the destruction of everything your dynasty has accomplished thus far?"

There! He has said it. Senen-Mut scarcely breathes as he waits to see whether or not his words have their desired effect. She stops pacing and struggles against an emotional outburst. Finally she deliberately walks over to an ivory-topped table laden with food. Roasted beef, mutton, antelope and goat overfill great platters, fowl, geese, duck, pintail and pigeon roasted with rosemary, parsley and coriander, simmering on serving spits and vegetables, onion, lettuce and cucumber-filled bowls. With subtle, almost imperceptible, nods, Hat-Shep-Sut makes her selections before sitting down in a high backed chair at her ivory dining table. Her servants race about, filling golden plates and pour mugs with wines and beer. Hat-Shep-Sut focuses upon her food. She sits silently nibbling away at the food until only well-picked bones remain on her plates. When she finishes, Pharaoh turns to Senen-Mut, as if there had been no interruption in their conversation.

"Go on," she says.

"Whenever Amen summons a pharaoh to a jubilee and renewal ceremony," Senen-Mut continues, "the gods stand ready to judge a pharaoh's fitness to rule. The fact that this call has come earlier for you than for any past pharaoh does not alter the fact that you have been summoned. *By ignoring a call for renewal you risk a civil war. They could deprive you not only of your throne but of your life as well!*"

"So be it," Pharaoh responds, stifling a yawn.

"The council might take it as bad omen if you have Dantha executed for doing Amen's will," he points out. "Your ministers might even ask: *'Who's next?'*"

"Okay! I get it." Hat-Shep-Sut feels angry once again. She refuses to look Senen-Mut in the eye. She hates his arrogance and his disapproving looks. He acts as if he were disciplining a child.

One day, Hat-Shep-Sut says silently, *I'm going to wipe that smug look off of his face. But,* she decides, *not today.* "What do you propose?" she asks, rising from the table and going over to where Natee rests. She strokes his golden mane and the big cat begins purring.

"We need to know a lot more about this scheme before Pharaoh acts, don't you agree, Great Lord?" Senen-Mut asks.

"What more need I know?" Hat-Shep-Sut replies, her voice drips with sarcasm, "Pharaoh sees past, present and future."

"Indeed, Majesty?" Senen-Mut answers. Now the discussion degenerates into a contest of wills.

"I don't care what was planned and who is behind it!" Hat-Shep-Sut screams. "That priest has insulted my royal dignity and *HE MUST PAY!*"

As Senen-Mut watches Hat-Shep-Sut, it seems that this last outburst was a bit too sudden and her words are too shrill.

She's putting on an act, Senen-Mut surmises. *What is she up to?*

He starts to voice his suspicions, but thinks better of it. Senen-Mut is usually frank and honest with Hat-Shep-Sut. But now he has a dilemma. He is torn between telling her of his suspicions and maintaining the silence that will kill their love.

Neferu-Re, and her mother are just alike, Senen-Mut reminds himself. *The two of them can be very unreasonable.* Senen-Mut decides *to treat Hat-Shep-Sut the way he treats Neferu-Re when his daughter is out of control.*

He goes over to a pile of cushions and, seating himself, silently watches Hat-Shep-Sut. She resumes pacing back and forth. Seconds pass, then minutes. A servant coughs. Silence again. Hat-Shep-Sut's slippers make a squeaky sound sliding across the woolen carpets. Natee opens his gigantic maw. A growl turns into a yawn. The silence between Hat-Shep-Sut continues to build. Again the curtains rustle. But, in the end, Senen-Mut's patience is rewarded. Hat-Shep-Sut breaks the silence with something reasonable.

"I will listen to my vizier's concerns before I cut off that traitor's head," she offers. "What are they?"

"Great One," Senen-Mut responds, "allow me to question the *Eyes of Horus* and some of your individual ministers. They may have information about how this plot was hatched. Dantha didn't suddenly decide to deliver this affront to the *Living God* on his own."

"Alright," Hat-Shep-Sut sighs. She gives her consort an icy stare. *How could I have ever loved this weakling,* she wonders. "I will do nothing until bring that ingrate to my Great Audience Hall."

She rises up and, for the benefit of her household staff, dismisses Senen-Mut with a wave of her hand. Hat-Shep-Sut eyes the retreating figure of her consort. But as her Grand Vizier backs towards the apartment's massive ebony doors, Dantha's golden scroll in hand, Hat-Shep-Sut is unable to resist one final barb. "That priest should thank Amen for staying Pharaoh's hand and *his friend* for saving his life ____ at *least for now!*"

When he departs and the doors are closed. The fury on Hat-Shep-Sut's face is replaced by a faint smile. *Men are such fools,* she thinks. *I will follow his guidance for the time being, but I will enjoy exacting a full measure of revenge for the indignities he has given me. And afterwards when I have cast off this hateful yoke of male domination, all will know that I am truly the foremost of distinguished women.*

Her mood lightens. And feeling quite satisfied, she calls for her handmaidens to attend her.

CHAPTER SIXTEEN

Outside Pharaoh's palace, Senen-Mut spots Iby accompanied by two officers of Pharaoh's Palace Guard approaching him from across the courtyard. The spymaster and his aides all bow to Senen-Mut and salute him by crossing their arms across chests.

"What's the alarm?" Iby asks, the ever-present grin plastered across his face.

"Dantha announced a *pharaonic* jubilee for the upcoming *Opet-festival*," Senen-Mut says, passing Iby the high priest's scroll.

After reading Dantha's announcement, Iby asks, "Do you want me to bring the high priest to the palace?"

Iby has no doubt what Hat-Shep-Sut wants done.

"We don't need him just yet," the Grand Vizier replies. "But I find it strange that your *watchers* didn't inform you of Dantha's intentions."

Iby stares narrowly at Senen-Mut. *This is not good*, he tells himself. *They're going at each other again.* The grin disappears from Iby's face. He says nothing and awaits Senen-Mut's instructions.

"I want the palace guard placed on alert." Senen-Mut says. "Full battle dress, double guard on the temples and palaces, understand?"

"Yes, Master." Iby clenches his fists and crosses his arms over his chest in another salute.

Senen-Mut turns away and heads towards the *Palace of Ladies*. Iby notices how tense Senen-Mut seems. *A sure sign that he's about to do something really unpleasant*, Iby tells himself.

"Notify the Captain of Pharaoh's Guard that the entire watch is to stand on alert!" Iby tells one of his aides.

"Yes, master," the officer replies. He salutes before rushing off.

Then addressing the other Eyes of Horus officer, Iby says, "Direct the *Captain of the Watchers* to meet me here in Pharaoh's palace."

"As you command, master," comes the officer's prompt reply before he, too, scurries away.

Within the hour, a thousand guardsmen in full battledress, more than double Amen's garrison, take positions throughout Karnak. Inside the temples of Mut and Khonsu, Iby doubles the guard. Within Hat-Shep-Sut's Red Chapel the guard is quadrupled. Iby then hurries over to *Eyes of Horus* headquarters to make his own inquiries.

How did Dantha prepare an announcement for a pharaonic jubilee without his watchers knowing about it? the spymaster wonders.

"Show me the latest reports from our agents in the *Seeing Waters*," Iby instructs the head scribe in the *Hall of Records*. The scribe consults his records on Nubian Medjays and their families. He gives Iby two scrolls. Each merely lists the names of the *Seeing Waters* garrison at Amen's Temple. "Is this all that you have?" Iby asks.

"Yes, Master," the scribe replies.

"Well," Iby decides after glancing over the lists, "Karnak seems secure."

"Master, the entire Palace Guard regiment has taken up their positions." One of his lieutenants reports back.

"Every officer with the *Eyes of Horus* has been given an assignment. *Watchers* have been dispatched to Pharaoh's palace, the *Palace of Ladies* as well as Amen's Temple."

Though Iby is better at collecting information than analyzing it, the spymaster is certain that he knows exactly who is behind Dantha's so-called *plot*. He does not believe Karnak was ever in any danger. Not only does Iby know who is behind Dantha's 'plot', he believes both Senen-Mut and Hat-Shep-Sut know who is behind the plot, as well.

A very clever charade, indeed! He smiles to himself. *But why are these two pretending?*

Once he is satisfied that Senen-Mut's instructions have been carried out, Iby returns to Pharaoh's palace to take up his vigil outside Pharaoh's Great Audience Hall.

Of course Senen-Mut knows who's responsible for Dantha's attack on Hat-Shep-Sut and he suspects that Hat-Shep-Sut knows, as well.

How could she not know? Senen-Mut asks himself. Unlike Iby, however, he finds no humor in the situation. Dantha's attack could topple the dynasty.

Only one person could have forced Dantha to call for a *pharaonic* jubilee. Only one person would benefit from the resulting turmoil. Only one person would be happy to see her mother toppled from the throne. As difficult as it may be for Senen-Mut to accept, only the Princess Neferu-Re could have instigated Dantha's call for a *pharaonic* jubilee at the upcoming *Opet*-festival, which is why Senen-Mut next calls upon his daughter's apartments at the *Palace of Ladies*. All along the way, Senen-Mut asks himself the same question over and over. *Why would Neferu-Re plot to embarrass, if not actually to dethrone, her own mother?*

The closer he gets to the *Palace of Ladies*, the worse Senen-Mut's mood becomes. He just can't fathom the workings of Neferu-Re's mind. He loves his daughter, but she doesn't return his love. She despises him because he's a commoner. Furthermore Senen-Mut has always known that it is Hat-Shep-Sut who encourages Neferu-Re to disrespect him. When it comes to mother and daughter, Senen-Mut just an outsider. He understands neither of them. Both take immense pleasure in making his life, as well as the lives of every other man around them, as miserable as possible. Whenever Neferu-Re pulls one of her stunts, like this one, Hat-Shep-Sut goes into denial.

All that pacing up and down and all her histrionics over Dantha's treachery, Senen-Mut tells to himself. *She was just covering-up for Neferu-Re.*

At the *Palace of Ladies,* the guards salute Senen-Mut as he passes through the open gates. But he strides, resolutely, down the marble path to Neferu-Re's apartments ignoring their presence, his thoughts on the task at hand. Neferu-Re was only three years old when she pulled her first stunt. Senen-Mut remembers it like it was yesterday.

Aak was still Pharaoh when Senen-Mut, Hat-Shep-Sut and Neferu-Re accompany Aak, little Thut-Moses, and Iset on a royal progress to the Temple of Dendera. The golden barge transporting the royal couple down the Nile actually belonged to Aak's father. Aak believed constructing a new barge for him to be a needless extravagance. Aak is happy to use his father's barge where he can sit upon the throne where his father, the *Smiter of Nubia* and *Conqueror of Palestine and Syria* once sat. Iset sees the matter differently and continually nags Aak about his thrift.

Poor Aak! Senen-Mut remembers. *Even pharaohs find it difficult to escape the tongue of a woman.*

At Dendera, Pharaoh and his co-Regent will attend the annual festival of the *Reunion of Hathor and Horus.* Neferu-Re is three years old and under the care of her nurse, Tuua.

Neferu-Re is a precocious child. She gets into everything. In her parent's cabin, Neferu-Re rummages through her mother's belongings. She happens upon the wooden boxes containing her mother's cosmetics. As small as she is, Neferu-Re opens up pots filled with green malachite, black antimony and red ochre, spills the contents on the floor and spreads the messy mixture all about. Then she goes to Thut-Moses' crib and smears the baby with a thick layer of the red, black and green *goo.* Thut-Moses screams at the top of his lungs. But the more the baby screams, the more Neferu-Re smears him. When Senen-Mut and the others reach the children, Neferu-Re looks up at him and flashes her now well-known look of defiance as if to say, *"And this is only the beginning!"*

Neferu-Re occupies her own two-story mansion inside the walled compound of the *Palace of Ladies*. Her personal guard is instructed not to allow anyone, including her parents, entrance without prior permission. But today, Senen-Mut is in no mood for his daughter's foolishness. He brushes past her guards and marches directly into Neferu-Re's public room. Tuua, who lurks just out of sight, notes that her guards fail to prevent Senen-Mut's entrance. The nurse begins experiencing physical pleasure merely contemplating the punishment she will inflict upon them. Tuua enjoys beheadings, but she also likes sending victims to the rock quarries, where she can visit and enjoy their misery. Knowing that she is responsible for a man toiling endlessly in a rock quarry, brings Neferu-Re's nurse immense pleasure.

"Neferu-Re!"

Senen-Mut's shout brings servants flocking into his daughter's public room like startled pintails bursting from a thicket of papyrus. They all 'kiss the dust' before the Grand Vizier. Only Tuua remains upright. She gives Pharaoh's Grand Vizier an insolent look.

"Where is she?" he bellows.

Senen-Mut immediately regrets frightening the servants. Between their mistress and her evil nurse, they already live in constant fear. The servants whisper that, when Neferu-Re was a child, Tuua nursed her on serpent's venom. The servants constantly glance over to where Tuua lurks. The crone watches everything and everyone.

"You needn't shout like that, Father!" A rather high-pitched female voice pierces the room, all noise stops and all eyes turn to a platform where Neferu-Re seems to have materialized. "I'm right here."

Neferu-Re is almost an exact replica of her mother. Slender, almost willowy, like a lotus blossom in full bloom. However Neferu-Re's breasts are voluptuous and she is taller than most Egyptian women, taller even than Hat-Shep-Sut. Neferu-Re is dressed in a demure sheath covered by an ankle-length gown of the finest quality linen, embroidered with semi-precious stones and trimmed in gold. Neferu-Re's honey-colored skin glows with the vitality of youth, but her eyes flash with the arrogance of royalty. Like her mother, she distains wearing wigs. Neferu-Re prefers her own thick brown hair. Senen-Mut's knows how to hurt her father and put him in his place.

Showing her father not the slightest hint of affection, Neferu-Re glides from the staircase to a raised golden dais inlaid with ivory and semi-precious stones.

"Besides which, shouting is rude and common," Neferu-Re sneers.

"It was you, wasn't it?" Senen-Mut says.

Neferu-Re gives a slight nod and all her servants, except Tuua, depart. The room is silent while Neferu-Re decides whether to be truthful or not. Father and daughter play a 'cat and mouse' game with each other. After awhile, the haughty teenager draws her lips drawn back in a contemptuous sneer not bothering to mask her hate. Senen-Mut speaks again.

"You tricked Dantha into sending out that proclamation, didn't you?" His accusation is rather quiet. "You orchestrated that call for your mother's pharaonic jubilee."

"Let me see," Neferu-Re responds. "You received the proclamation, deduced it was me and got over here in less than an hour. Not bad for a *commoner*," she smirks. "It certainly disproves the priest's teaching that commoners have no intelligence." Neferu-Re casts a wicked smile in Tuua's direction. "Or was it mother who told you?" With that Senen-Mut's wicked daughter gives an evil laugh. "Tell me father, did you alert the palace guard as well?" Her mocking eyes match her impudent tone.

"Yes, as a matter of fact, I did," Senen-Mut replies.

"You should have known that alerting the guard was totally unnecessary," Neferu-Re scoffs. "Had I wanted an insurrection,

I wouldn't have used the priest." Neferu-Re laughs once again. "And everyone says that you're such a *brilliant* thinker!"

Neferu-Re looks down her narrow nose that is similar to her father's. Hat-Shep-Sut has a prominent Thut-Mosid nose. Neferu-Re's narrow nose positively identifies her as Senen-Mut's child, which several servants and at least one noble are unwise enough to comment upon. Neferu-Re has them sent to rock quarries where they slave alongside Nubians for the remainder of their lives. On the other hand, when she looks into her bronze 'see-face', Neferu-Re is pleased that her nose makes her more beautiful than her mother.

Once I push her out of my way, Neferu-Re decides, *I shall be a more beautiful and grander pharaoh than my mother ever was.*

Two Nubian slaves enter the room and take up a position behind their mistress. They carry a pole, around which is wrapped a twenty-foot snow white Rock Python. Neferu-Re makes a clicking sound and the python uncoils from the pole and glides over to his mistress, wrapping itself upon the chair's legs and resting its head upon her lap.

"How did you trick Dantha into risking his head?" Senen-Mut asks.

"Am I not Pharaoh's Daughter, Pharaoh's Sister and *God's Wife*?" Neferu-Re asks, thinking to taunt her father with her titles. Then she pauses, as if to relish her next insult. "Oh! I'm sorry!" the princess smiles. "I forgot. Commoners are unacquainted with the privileges of the noble classes." Once again she lets out a mocking laugh. "I didn't trick Dantha into doing anything." Neferu-Re strokes the snake's head. "I command and he obeys."

And there is the simple truth of the entire matter. It's as Senen-Mut had surmised. He knew even when he persuaded Hat-Shep-Sut to appoint Neferu-Re *God's Wife*, years earlier, something like this might happen.

No matter, he tells himself. *What's my next move?*

But just then, a masculine figure with a military bearing descends the staircase and takes a seat on a sofa near Neferu-Re.

"I see we have a guest," the handsome young man says.

Senen-Mut bows to the waist and salutes the co-Regent and future Ruler of the Two-Lands, Menkh-Kheperu-Re Thut-Moses III. Aak's son is muscular and athletic, remarkably free of the infirmities that ravaged his father.

"Hail Majesty," Senen-Mut says. "I did not realize the co-Regent was here in Thebes."

"Neferu-Re asked me to come home for the announcement," Thut-Moses replies.

Thut-Moses reads the surprise in the Grand Vizier's face.

"Your majesty has come to Thebes for what announcement?" Senen-Mut asks.

"The announcement of Pharaoh's jubilee, of course," Thut-Moses replies. Though his face is masked in innocence, his eyes glow in anticipation.

Thut-Moses' muscles ripple from the continuous exercise they receive in *Horus Nest's* officer training program reminding Senen-Mut of his own training and those grueling days hurling the javelin. Thut-Moses wears a short linen tunic and golden sandals. A single-edged, bronze dagger is stuck into the scarlet band wrapped around his waist. He is bare-chested with a shaved head. His eyes are as unblinking as the hawk that symbolizes his destiny. Yet, for all his youthful vigor and muscular appearance, Thut-Moses retains a childlike innocence and a noble charm that endears him to priests and soldiers, alike. When he was a child, Thut-Moses always tagged after Neferu-Re. And even now, Thut-Moses remains as infatuated with Pharaoh's daughter.

But on the other hand, the Royal Heir has become as shrewd and intelligent a claimant to Pharaoh's crook and flail as any of the eighteenth dynasty. Thut-Moses has an intense desire to win whenever he competes. And his love of war now rivals his love for Neferu-Re. Potentially ruthless and given to cruelty, Thut-Moses fondest desire is to lead men into battle and witness the carnage of war. Senen-Mut receives an insight. He now knows how he can resolve this situation.

"Pharaoh expects your presence in her Great Audience Hall within the next hour," he says gravely. Then neither uttering another word nor giving *God's Wife* the customary bow, Senen-Mut strides out.

Once she is certain her father is out of earshot, Neferu-Re turns to Thut-Moses and says, "Only Seth knows how I *detest* that man!"

Thut-Moses goes over to comfort her. She lays her head upon the Crown Prince's chest.

"I hate him and I hate her," she repeats. "I can hardly wait to take her place so that I can see him working in a rock quarry, somewhere." With that she begins to sob uncontrollably.

"*You* want to take her place?" Thut-Moses asks. He fixes Neferu-Re with a quizzical look.

"I mean I can hardly wait until *you* take *your* rightful place on the throne and I am by your side," Neferu-Re corrects herself.

Indeed, my dear sister, he corrects her silently, *when I, not you, become Pharaoh!*

Though tall for an Egyptian, Pen-Nek-Heb's age bends him over. The high priest looks as if the weight of the world is on his shoulders. But this is the way he looks normally. Whether enjoying the friendship of his colleagues at Iunu, or when in the presence of Pharaoh, Pen-Nek-Heb always appears stern. From all over the Two-Lands, the influential and powerful seek Pen-Nek-Heb's advice ___ and his friendship. No one is more influential at court or in the secrecy of Pharaoh's *Seal Room*, than the high priest of Iunu. On the morning of Dantha's announcement, Pen-Nek-Heb is not altogether surprised when, from his second story apartment, he sees Pharaoh's Palace Guard taking up positions all over Karnak. Nor is he surprised when one of the Grand Vizier's servants knocks on his chamber door.

"Lord Senen-Mut requests that you meet him in the Great Audience Hall within the next hour," the officer announces.

"Tell the Lord Senen-Mut that I hear and obey," Pen-Nek-Heb replies.

"Also," the messenger continues, "the Lord Senen-Mut directs that you inform the high priest of Amen that he may also attend to the Grand Vizier, as well. However, the Lord Senen-Mut warns the high priest of Amen that Pharaoh, herself, will be in attendance. And, at present, the *Living God* does not hold the high priest, Dantha, in high regard."

"You may tell the Lord Senen-Mut that I will inform the high priest of Amen of this request," Pen-Nek-Heb replies. "Please inform the Lord Senen-Mut that Amen's high priest must decide for himself whether or not to attend Pharaoh's pleasure."

"I will inform the Lord Senen-Mut of your reply," the officer answers. Bowing low and giving a military salute, the officer takes his leave.

Pen-Nek-Heb hobbles over to Amen's Temple to deliver Senen-Mut's message.

Dantha rises and comes over to greet the high priest of Iunu. Even bent over, Pen-Nek-Heb towers over Amen. Pen-Nek-Heb notices that Dantha appears worn and disheveled. His face looks tired. His robe, normally freshly cleaned is dirty. He has not changed it in several days. Dantha's eyes are sallow and puffy, not blazing with the power of an *initiate of the inner temple* and master over the most powerful priesthood in the Two-Lands.

"Amen bless my good friend," Dantha greets Pen-Nek-Heb, "and welcome."

Without any preliminaries, Pen-Nek-Heb states the reason for his visit. "The Lord Senen-Mut's summons me to Pharaoh's presence within the hour." Amen winces, noticeably. "I am directed to inform you of the meeting, as well."

"Are they asking for you to deliver my head, or do they expect me to deliver it, *personally?*" Dantha's feeble attempt at humor is wasted on Pen-Nek-Heb. The Aten's high priest, in the best of times, is humorless. Nor does Pen-Nek-Heb find humor in the present situation.

He may have courage, Pen-Nek-Heb observes, *but not much sense.*

Taking a seat in a wooden chair, backed and cushioned with leather, Pen-Nek-Heb studies the man who dares insult Pharaoh.

"Tell me, priest of Amen for truly I must know," Pen-Nek-Heb begins, "was it your intention to strip Pharaoh of her throne when you issued your call for a jubilee? This is no idle question. If Pharaoh calls upon me to speak, I want to know your thinking, if indeed you were thinking."

"Of course, I didn't intend ___. " Dantha pauses in mid-sentence. His shoulders slump and he rests his head face in his hands. After awhile, he rises up and looks directly into Pen-Nek-Heb's eyes. "As Thoth is my witness, I don't know what I intended."

Dantha searches Pen-Nek-Heb's face for pity, but he finds none. Neither does he find any antagonism. The face staring back at him is solemn and stern, like a statue carved from stone.

"You know how much pressure I've been under," Dantha continues. "You've been under pressure, as well." Dantha struggles to make himself coherent.

"I have not challenged the *Living God*," Pen-Nek-Heb reminds Dantha.

"Pharaoh's heresy ___, " Dantha begins, but then decides upon a different train of thought. "Delegations of priests from Karnak, Luxor and all over the Two-Lands ___."

Once again, his thoughts fail him and his words become jumbled.

"What could I do?" Dantha asks, finally. "Pharaoh would not listen to me."

Pen-Nek-Heb rises from the chair and extends up to his full height with back, unbowed.

"It is no mean feat to challenge Pharaoh, even for Amen," Pen-Nek-Heb says quietly. "I hope your intentions were pure and that when you stand before the *Scale of Djeheuty*, you remain unafraid."

"Please do not leave yet." Dantha says. The priest claps his hands and a servant brings a pitcher of beer and two mugs. The beer is thick and rather sweet. The *Aten's* high priest sips his beer and listens politely to Dantha's continued ramblings.

"Daily I pray for wisdom, my friend." Dantha shakes his head trying to win over his fellow priest. "But what wisdom is there for me who daily must witness Pharaoh's un-initiated priests stopping at each of those blasphemous shrines that encircle my temple. One day a week, her priests even bring a mob from Thebes into our sacred precincts as participants in her heresies. She calls this day, *Sun Day*."

"Why did you proclaim a *pharaonic* jubilee for the upcoming *Opet*-festival?" Pen-Nek-Heb ignores Dantha's insult to the *Aten*. "You must have known that Pharaoh would react. Were you so eager to join your wife in the afterlife?"

Dantha considers Pen-Nek-Heb's question. "*God's Wife* threatened to withhold purification from Amen's priests unless I announced a jubilee," Dantha acknowledges. "She even threatened to send your red robed priests into Amen's temple to perform *my* rituals."

This man is an idiot, Pen-Nek-Heb concludes.

"*God's Wife* threatened to withhold purification from the priests unless you declared a jubilee?" Pen-Nek-Heb asks raising his eyebrows in mock sympathy. "Didn't you know that *God's Wife* couldn't carry out such a threat?" Pen-Nek-Heb decides to tell Dantha exactly what he thinks. "I don't believe you were ever afraid of *God's Wife*." The *Aten* glowers at Dantha. "I believe that you decided to use her threats as your opportunity to attack Pharaoh in retaliation for building her Red Chapel to the *Aten*?"

Everyone at Pharaoh's court is familiar with Neferu-Re's childish games and her silly court intrigues, none take her seriously. *God's Wife* has been known to cause a man to loose his head, if he is not careful. But Pharaoh's teenage daughter could not have made an experienced priest and administrator like Dantha behave this foolishly, unless, of course, he was already a fool. Dantha looks furtively from side to side. Obviously, the situation has gotten beyond him.

"Amen wants no innovations practiced, none of the old ways changed, nor a woman as Pharaoh," Dantha asserts, defiantly. He

Eugene Stovall

seeks solidarity with his fellow priest. "Pharaoh has plunged the Two-Lands into heresy. The ritual of a jubilee and renewal is the only answer."

"Pharaoh moves with the stars," Pen-Nek-Heb reminds his fellow cleric. "You must pay homage to the *Master of the World*. Amen gilds all the earth and spread life in profusion. Who refuses the will of the *Living God?*"

"The initiates of the Inner Temple have paid homage to Amen since the beginning of time," Dantha responds. "That is our function, that is our purpose for being."

"Let me tell you what I see," Pen-Nek-Heb says. "Amen determined our past in his lunar aspect. But the movements of the sky portend the coming of a great event, a new epoch. This new epoch is Amen manifesting his solar principle and it is through Pharaoh Maat-Ka-Re Hat-Shep-Sut that the new solar age will be known. Neither you nor that child of Set, Neferu-Re, can prevent the lunar Amen from passing into the solar Amen under the aspect of his daughter, Hat-Shep-Sut. This most mysterious epoch and the transition from the lunar to the solar cult, is fraught with the greatest peril, not only for us, but also for all of mankind. *And you, my friend, must find the courage to obey the will of the Living God!*"

Pen-Nek-Heb's words sting Amen's priest. "So you also support Pharaoh's heresy?" Dantha sneers.

"If that child sitting on the throne, fulfills her destiny, Egypt's spiritual lineage will continue as mankind's depository of the *Sublime Knowledge*. If she fails, mankind will be plunged into chaos, barbarism and fear. You, my friend, should know this better than anyone."

Pen-Nek-Heb believed that he had seen all of Dantha's faces, the scholarly cleric, the grieving widower, the jovial priest, the thundering prophet. Now Dantha shows Pen-Nek-Heb his true face, the face of a scheming priest and wicked administrator, the face of one who used any deception to force black Nubians to slave in Pharaoh's mines. Dantha became the most powerful priest in the Two-Lands, but he sought to be more powerful than Pharaoh.

Pen-Nek-Heb concludes that Dantha is the author of the affront to Pharaoh and does not deserve any sympathy. Dantha deserves the same contempt that Pen-Nek-Heb held for his predecessor, Seth-Mesy.

"We must attend to Pharaoh," the priest of Iunu says as he rises from his chair. "I know not about you, but for me Pharaoh remains the *Living God.*"

Watching Pen-Nek-Heb depart his chambers, Dantha wonders how things turned out so badly. Never before had any of his plans failed so miserably. At Amada, his affairs always went well. No one ever suspected his involvement in the attempted assassination of Hat-Shep-Sut's father. Even at Karnak, things have gone well. He sits on Pharaoh's Inner Council, the royal brats, Neferu-Re and Thut-Moses, are his allies, the Royal Teacher, Hapu-Seneb, supplies him with information and does his bidding and the Nubian brotherhood follows his leadership eagerly awaiting an opportunity to take revenge upon the Two-Lands. *How did things get so out of hand?*

Senen-Mut smiles. Despite his daughter's dangerous antics, everything seems to be settling into place. But before he returns to Pharaoh's *Great Audience Hall* where he intends to resolve this matter, Senen-Mut decides to check Thebes, itself.

God's Wife has power over the masses, Senen-Mut reminds, himself; he would not put it past Neferu-Re to hatch a plot among the very commoners she claims to despise. Escorted by palace guards, Senen-Mut tours the shops on the *Street of Barbers* and the houses on the *Street of Pleasure.* He even visits the beer and cook shops. All seems well. *Watchers* assigned by the *Eyes of Horus* to patrol Thebes' marketplace give the Grand Vizier the *'all's clear'* signal. Pharaoh's Grand Vizier strolls through the bazaars and shops in Thebes' upper marketplace. He listens to servants haggling over the prices of bread, meat and vegetables concerned with saving their masters copper *debens* rather than stocking up in case of a civil disturbance. Senen-Mut listens to the latest court gossip repeated by servants of administrators and scribes. From the *Street of Barbers* to the upper marketplace, activities are no different today than on any other day. The people gossip about infidelities, the prices of food and the possibility of a drought. No one speaks of a plot against Pharaoh. Street hawkers passing by the Grand Vizier, bow respectfully. None seem aware that anything is amiss. Pharaoh's soldiers scan the crowds, accost thieves and round up illegal Nubians. The soldiers salute the Grand Vizier. None report anything unusual. Satisfied that, in Thebes, all is well, Senen-Mut returns to Karnak.

"There's too many blacks around the marketplace," Senen-Mut remarks to Iby when they meet outside Pharaoh's chambers.

"There's always a lot of *Nubians* around," Iby replies.

Iby doesn't share Senen-Mut's aversion to the blacks. Nubian sailors are among the Nile's best pilots. Iby learned everything he knows about sailing from them. Anyone sailing above the first cataract would be a fool to attempt it without a Nubian pilot.

"I want your *watchers* to round up the Nubians and the asiatics, here and in Memphis," Senen-Mut orders. "Most of them are spies. Find out what they're up to, then send them to the quarries."

"It will be done, Lord," Iby answers.

CHAPTER SEVENTEEN

Hat-Shep-Sut prepares for her ordeal.

I'm as strong as any woman in my family, she tells herself. *Today I must prove it. After today no one will doubt that Pharaoh Maat-Ka-Re Hat-Shep-Sut is sole ruler over the Two-Lands. And no defiance of Pharaoh will go unpunished!*

Hat-Shep-Sut plans great changes for the Two-Lands. Pen-Nek-Heb's predictions of a new epoch inspire her to initiate new traditions and new ideas. The new epoch predicted by Iunu's stargazers will be Hat-Shep-Sut's epoch____ the time when women rise up and end male domination. And *the foremost of distinguished women,* intends to usher in the new epoch by exercising more control over her well intentioned but common-thinking Senen-Mut.

I tried to find a way not to do what must be done, Hat-Shep-Sut sighs, *but I failed. Now my Senen-Mut must pay the price.*

Hat-Shep-Sut's handmaidens bathe Pharaoh from head to foot in the gentle pool close by her sleeping chambers. Afterwards, they perfume her body with oils and unguents, rubbing her skin until it glows golden. They lightened her face with a special crème and rouge her cheeks. She stares into her 'see-face' and sees the image of a wondrous *neter,* whom her people cannot help but adore. Her handmaidens apply green shadow above her eyes and then line them with black antimony.

For the occasion, Hat-Shep-Sut chooses a golden sheath over which she wears the plaited golden kilt worn only by Pharaohs. Jeweled pectorals cover her breasts and upon her feet, she wears golden sandals. Golden armbands, bracelets and rings are put upon

Eugene Stovall

her fingers, around her arms and over her wrists while she clutches the *crook and flail*. Next her servants strap a ceremonial beard to Hat-Shep-Sut's chin. Hat-Shep-Sut soon intends to banish the beard from her *pharaonic* regalia.

But that must wait for another occasion, she tells herself. *This is not the time. Not today.*

After they affix the beard, her servants place a great black wig upon her head. The wig is plaited with thick braids and interweaved with gold leaf that tumbles over Pharaoh's shoulders and down her back. The wig is heavy and uncomfortable which is why Hat-Shep-Sut seldom wears one. But today the wig must be worn. Upon the wig, her handmaidens put in place the specially fitted double Red and White crown. The terrible red-eyed uraeus, poised to strike any of Pharaoh's enemies is mounted in front.

Hat-Shep-Sut takes a final look in her 'see-face'. She sees a woman with the strength strong enough to do what must be done. She holds out her hand and Natee's handler gives Hat-Shep-Sut the lion's leash. Then Pharaoh orders her *Palace Overseer* to open the doors and prepare the guards to accompany her to the *Great Audience Hall*. Hat-Shep-Sut's handmaidens hurry the pygmy slaves carrying their great ostrich feather fans into their places behind Pharaoh's litter. But just as the procession prepares to depart, a handmaiden delivers Pharaoh a message.

"Great Lord," the handmaiden announces, "the *Overseer of Pharaoh's Chariots, General of the Army of Lower Nile* and *Pharaoh's Friend*, the Lord Aron has arrived and awaits upon Your Majesty's favor so that he may know how he may serve the *Living God*."

Hat-Shep-Sut smiles.

"Escort the overseer into my private meeting room," she tells the servant, "and instruct him to await my pleasure."

Hat-Shep-Sut never learned why Senen-Mut and Aron stopped being friends. She suspects that they *never* were friends.

Possibly there is a little more than destiny involved, she smiles.

"Go to my *Great Audience Hall*," she instructs a messenger. "Tell those present to await Pharaoh's pleasure. I will arrive shortly."

Bowing and kissing the dust in front of her, the messenger races off. Hat-Shep-Sut returns to her dressing rooms and orders all of her *pharaonic* regalia removed. Then she dresses in a simple linen sheath with a jeweled uraeus and joins Aron in one of her private meeting rooms.

"Aron!" Hat-Shep-Sut exclaims, giving her visitor a warm welcome. "It has been too long since I have last seen my good friend. Thank you for answering my summons."

Hat-Shep-Sut's private chambers are grand and spacious with a completely circular ceiling supported by fifty pillars. The palace guard, stationed outside the circle of pillars, is screened off by great linen drapes, embroidered with Pharaoh's cartouche. Hat-Shep-Sut's private chambers are separated into sleeping, bathing, dining and lounging areas. Two separate rooms adjoining her private chambers serve as Hat-Shep-Sut's private audience rooms where she entertains visitors that she doesn't like or doesn't trust. Aron is neither. She invites him into her lounging area.

"Majesty," Aron bows to the floor 'kissing the dust' at her feet.

Hat-Shep-Sut notices that her chariot captain has lost none of his muscular build or his rugged good looks. She wonders what would have happened had she fallen in love with the *Student of Jackal* instead of the *Student of Wast*. She remembers her father did not approve of the *Student of Jackal*.

"That one's a killer!" her father declared. "I'll not have someone who loves killing as my daughter's consort."

I guess some things are meant to be, Hat-Shep-Sut smiles.

On a gold chain, she wears the pendant awarded to Senen-Mut when he was invested into the *Order of the Golden Fly*. Senen-Mut gave her his most precious possession as a symbol of his love and loyalty. Aron spies the pendant; his eyes betray his emotions.

Good, Hat-Shep-Sut thinks seeing how Aron reacts to the pendant. *I believe that I can rely upon my Chariot Captain to carry out my will.*

Eugene Stovall

"Why has my good friend been absent for so long from my presence," Hat-Shep-Sut asks in a voice that purrs like Natee when she rubs the lion's mane.

"Majesty, to be in your august presence has ever been my sole desire," Aron replies.

"Has the Captain of Pharaoh's Chariots heard how greatly Amen's priest, Dantha, has offended me?" she asks staring deeply into Aron's eyes.

"Yes, Great God!" Aron replies. Though unsure why Pharaoh has summoned him, Aron senses an opportunity for advancement. "Scarcely anyone who breathes in the Two-Lands doesn't know of Amen's call." Hat-Shep-Sut notes how greatly the chariot officer exaggerates the truth. It pleases her.

"What do you think of Amen's treachery?"

"The *Living God* has but to command and Amen will pay for his vile deed *with his head*." Aron's declaration makes Hat-Shep-Sut's heart leap.

He will do!

She beckons Aron to share her sofa. Moving nearer to him, Hat-Shep-Sut says, "My great grandmother cut off the heads of thirteen nomarchs, their military officers, their families and their servants for betraying Pharaoh." She gazes steadily into Aron's eyes. "And now my own Grand Vizier, who I believe was once your friend, stands in the way of my cutting off the head of this vile and treacherous priest who calls for my renewal ahead of time."

Aron tells Hat-Shep-Sut all that she needs to know. "Say but the word, Majesty, and by the grace of Ra, I will deliver Amen's head wherever Pharaoh directs and leave the rest of him rotting in the western desert."

"Yes that is what I want!" Hat-Shep-Sut whispers. Her words are seductive. "Amen flaunts Pharaoh's wishes and ignores Pharaoh's orders." She then lowers her voice even more. "But not right now." She leans against Aron, her body nestling against his, as if for protection. Aron stirs uncomfortably. He is unsure how he should react to Hat-Shep-Sut's physical presence. It overwhelms him.

"Our quarrel is not with Amen but his greedy priests, "Hat-Shep-Sut confides. "I need you to take care of Dantha." Hat-Shep-Sut looks earnestly into Aron's eyes, "but I will tell you when." Then, on the spur of the moment, Hat-Shep-Sut adds. "Furthermore I want you to learn who else plots with Amen and *dares challenge Pharaoh.*"

"And if your step-son, the Crown Prince, Thut-Moses is involved?" Aron asks.

"Thut-Moses?" Hat-Shep-Sut's eyes twinkle. "I do not believe that the Royal Heir is involved. But if your friend Senen-Mut were somehow involved with Amen, it would not surprise me."

"I obey thy will, Great One."

"Have you any trusted men in the *Eyes of Horus?*" Hat-Shep-Sut asks in wide-eyed innocence.

"Yes, majesty," Aron responds, "I know many trustworthy watchers. It was they who informed me of the proclamation by Amen's high priest."

"Good!" Pharaoh says. "Make certain that they are prepared to act when the time comes." With that Hat-Shep-Sut rises, peremptorily dismissing her chariot captain. "You may join the others in the *Great Audience Hall* and await my pleasure. Please tell my chamberlain and the gathering that Pharaoh has been delayed."

"I hear and obey, Majesty," Aron pledges.

Watching the tall, muscular charioteer depart, Hat-Shep-Sut is satisfied with the progress she is making unshackling herself from *male supremacy*. She has now the weapon she needs to control Senen-Mut and possibly Neferu-Re as well. Yes, Pharaoh is very satisfied.

CHAPTER EIGHTEEN

From her perch high upon her golden throne, Pharaoh surveys the assembly gathered in her Great Audience Hall. Her stepson and co-Regent, Thut-Moses sits to her right. Moody and introspective, Thut-Moses doesn't really enjoy this court intrigue. He is here only because Neferu-Re insisted, otherwise he would have remained at *Horus Nest* and allowed his stepmother her drama. Despite the rumors on the Street of Barbers and the urgings of different court officials, especially the priests, Thut-Moses has no interest in deposing Hat-Shep-Sut, nor sitting on her throne, at least not for the time being. The Crown Prince prefers to enjoy the company of females rather than battle with them. In Memphis as well as in Thebes, Hat-Shep-Sut's stepson is well known on the Street of *Pleasure*. He visits the houses there, quite often.

Senen-Mut was right, Hat-Shep-Sut thinks, looking over at her stepson, *Thut-Moses is well suited for a military career. Senen-Mut is right about so many things,* Hat-Shep-Sut sighs. She already feels remorse over what she must do. *If only he was less brilliant and more humble.*

But at the royal school, Hat-Shep-Sut learned never to second-guess herself.

"Doubting yourself is like doubting the gods," Hapu-Seneb warned her and Aak. "The royal will and the god's will are the same." So Hat-Shep-Sut sits there wrapped in serenity, suppressing her emotions so that she can see her plans through.

Neferu-Re sits to Hat-Shep-Sut's left and a step lower. As powerful as the co-Regent and far more ambitious, Neferu-Re appears uncomfortable before this gathering in Pharaoh's hall. She feels naked in front of Hat-Shep-Sut's court, as if they can see her see ambitions hanging down from her shoulders like a linen cloak. Periodically she glances at her mother, envious of Hat-Shep-Sut's goddess-like serenity. However, Neferu-Re's ambitions for herself are not nearly as great as Hat-Shep-Sut's ambitions for her. Hat-Shep-Sut intends Neferu-Re to become the eighteenth dynasty's next female Pharaoh. But before that can happen, Hat-Shep-Sut must eliminate her Grand Vizier's influence over her Inner Council. Her council will never obey her as long as they can circumvent her will by going to Senen-Mut. And she cannot allow sentiment to get in her way. Gazing over her court, Hat-Shep-Sut contemplates how one day all these looking up at her will be women. The men now looking up at her will have loss their privileges and their powers.

Pharaoh's *Great Audience Hall* twitters like nests of birds welcoming the rising of Ra in the early morning. Far in the rear, the tweets are especially noisy among her junior administrators and scribes. The entire court anticipates a dramatic and bloody conclusion to this confrontation between the Divine Horus and Amen's high priest.

Dantha, escorted by Pharaoh's palace guard, enters. A hush falls upon the assembly. All eyes fix themselves upon the pathetic priest shuffling into Pharaoh's presence. Now his ceremonial leopard skin robe and golden insignia are not so much symbols of power as badges of shame.

Dantha seems confused. He hesitates to take his accustomed place with the other council members. Pen-Nek-Heb comes to the high priest's aid and escorts Dantha to his customary place. Fifty black-robed priests accompany Dantha to the *Great Audience Hall*. Senen-Mut orders the palace guard to detain the priests in the palace courtyard.

Once Amen's high priest assumes his place, an air of expectation seizes the hall, a tense silence hovers about. The passing time seems an eternity. Just as it seems that the strain upon the court is about to burst, Pharaoh rises and calmly gazing about the hall, calls out in a clear, musical voice.

"Thoth guides the affairs of gods and mortals with wisdom."

Pharaoh's words impress themselves upon the restless crowd.

"Thoth's severe nature symbolizes kindness, but I love Sekhmet whose husband is Ptah. Sekhmet is wise. She is wise as a woman is wise. May Sobek, the crocodile god, grant me long life so that Sekhmet will guide me to fulfill my destiny."

Her court is intrigued. Her words are mesmerizing. None dares makes a sound.

"I am Horus, the Golden Falcon. Upon my head I wear the two crowns. One for Nek-Heb-Bet, the vulture god of Upper Egypt, land of gold, incense and black Nubians whom I detest; the other for Wad-Jet, the cobra god of lower Egypt who strikes Pharaoh's enemies whoever they are and wherever they hide."

Her words are magical. Even the more cynical councilors feel the *Living God's* presence. And the eyes of many administrators and scribes eyes shine with devotion to their Pharaoh and Lord.

"Ra journeys through the sky in his many aspects. It does no harm to cloth the unknowable in the forms of what is known. When we honor he who is greater than ourselves, we reduce our KA to a *'feather of maat'*. Then Thoth is pleased and he stays the hands of his forty-two judges." Hat-Shep-Sut knows that she has her court completely under her spell; the impact is dramatic. "Pharaoh's serenity has been disturbed. The happiness of her people is diminished." The assembly stirs uncomfortably. "The serenity of the Two-Lands has been disturbed by a *heretic!*"

Heretic? Only priests brand their enemies, heretics. The word coming from Pharaoh's lips startles her court. Her council holds its collective breath. Senen-Mut's face freezes into a mask of inscrutability. No one can tell that he is as uncertain as everyone else about what Pharaoh intends to say next. But these are not *his* words. These are not the words the Grand Vizier gave Pharaoh to say.

Now Pharaoh's voice rises with emotion, but it is not shrill, rather it is sibilant and ethereal.

"I intend to eliminate these *heretics* from my court, now and for all times." Imperceptibly, her councilors move away from Dantha.

"Without the selfless devotion and the unstinting service of all who serve the gods, *living* and eternal," she lectures, "the Two-Lands would drift like a rudderless barge. Priests are, in no way, exempt from faithful service to both *living* and eternal gods."

Pharaoh's eyes bore through to Dantha's *KA* as an awl bores through the heart of a wooden plank. The movement away from the priest, who Pharaoh brands a *heretic*, becomes more noticeable. Dantha twitches, his eyes are glazed and his tongue darts in and out of his mouth, trying to moisten his parched lips.

"Priests!" Hat-Shep-Sut lifts her gaze and directs her comments to the red, black and white robed clergy in the rear. "Do not be misled by the *heretics* among you. Devote yourselves to duty and purpose. Serve the people. Do not stray as some of you who roam outside your temples and participate in treasons and conspiracies."

Murmurs ripple about the hall. The palace guard stiffens. Two hundred officers and soldiers surround the audience chamber. Another hundred *watchers* patrol the remainder of Pharaoh's palace. Neferu-Re has brought her own personal escort; they remain in the courtyard watching Dantha's black-robed monks.

Satisfied that her words have had the desired impact, Pharaoh turns to Senen-Mut and in a deceptively soft and lyrical voice, announces:

"Now, my Grand Vizier will report his findings." With that Hat-Shep-Sut returns to her throne, as regal a Pharaoh Karnak has ever seen. Relieved that Hat-Shep-Sut returns to their script, Senen-Mut offers Thoth his thanks before turning to face Pharaoh's court.

"A proclamation of a *pharaonic* jubilee and renewal for the Great God and Living Horus was delivered to Her Majesty this morning," Senen-Mut begins. "It is known that the proclamation was commanded by the Princess Neferu-Re, *God's Wife*."

Once again murmurs ripple throughout the hall. A number of Pharaoh's councilors had surmised who was behind the announcement, but few are prepared for the Grand Vizier's candor. Hat-Shep-Sut glances over at Neferu-Re.

"Is this true, my daughter?"

"Yes," Neferu-Re answers defiantly. "I, *God's Wife, Priestess of Amen, Overseer of the Purification of Priests*, decree that either Pharaoh be adjudged fit to rule over the Two-Lands by Amen or that *one more fitting* be found to take her place."

"And will you explain your reason for announcing the renewal ceremony?" Pharaoh asks.

"Thut-Moses needs to know when he shall be given his rightful place on the throne," Neferu-Re responds.

The lioness is eager to follow in the footsteps of her mother, Senen-Mut shudders to himself.

All eyes turn towards Pharaoh; again silence grips the hall in a deathly stillness.

How will Pharaoh react to such an open challenge from her daughter? the court wonders.

"The blood of the *distinguished women*, that flows in my own veins, flows in veins of my daughter," Pharaoh intones. "All the women in our line have distinguished themselves. It is no wonder that my daughter wishes to follow in their footsteps. It is her destiny."

The court is hushed and hangs upon Hat-Shep-Sut's every word.

"*God's Wife* has announced my jubilee," Hat-Shep-Sut declares. "So for the greatness of my reign, it shall be done. Furthermore, in order that my jubilee be properly prepared, I declare that the appropriate date for the celebration shall be set at an *Opet*-festival no less than seven years hence."

An audible gasp escapes one of the councilors. Senen-Mut flashes a quick look at Dantha. This is his cue. Pen-Nek-Heb leans over and whispers to the priest.

"Pharaoh has given you a chance to save your head. Take it!"

Dantha leaps to his feet.

"In seven years hence, Amen will be pleased to celebrate a jubilee in honor of Pharaoh Hat-Shep-Sut's glorious reign," Dantha announces.

Pen-Nek-Heb steps forward. "Your Majesty is the *Living God*. Thoth sees wisdom in this approach. Pharaoh's Inner Council thanks the *Aten*, Thoth and all the gods, for the wisdom of our *Living God*, Pharaoh Maat-Ka-Re Hat-Shep-Sut."

One by one Pharaoh's viziers rise to echo their praise of Pharaoh's wisdom and state their desire for a triumphant jubilee and renewal ceremony seven years hence. The crisis ends and Pharaoh's dignity and serenity are restored as the Two-Lands is allowed to continue its domestic tranquility. Dantha is especially pleased that his head remains resting on his shoulders. But many nomarchs, especially those who have been around awhile, know that, seven years from now, Dantha will not be around to announce another *pharaonic* jubilee.

"When the celebration of my jubilee takes place " Hat-Shep-Sut announces, "the *Aten* will be content to insure my people's happiness."

Pharaoh rises and the entire hall bows, "kissing the dust" at her feet. Natee leads the way from her *Great Audience Hall*. Passing through, Hat-Shep-Sut catches the eye of her handsome *Captain of Chariots* and gives him an imperceptible nod, sealing the fate of Amen's bothersome high priest.

Much later that evening, as a great pale moon bathes the Nile's gentle waves in a brilliant white glow and Isis feels Nut's gentle caress, a slim figure slips from a secret passage in Pharaoh's palace and hurries along a path that lead to the *Palace of the Ladies*. Slipping past the guard, the figure enters Neferu-Re's palace through a private entrance and delivers a shard containing a message to Neferu-Re from her mother. The servant does not wait for a reply, but hurries back to the *Mansion of Millions of Years*. Tuua takes the shard containing Pharaoh's message to her mistress.

"Your royal mother is quite pleased with your performance today," Tuua cackles.

Neferu-Re snatches the message from the nurse's hand, and then plops back down on the masses of woolen pillows and great linen blankets covering her sleeping mat and Thut-Moses.

"Mother says that all went well today," Neferu-Re tells the pleasantly intoxicated Crown Prince. "She sends us her congratulations."

Thut-Moses is more interested in Neferu-Re's Palestinian wine than her mother's palace plots. "What was all that nonsense about the *distinguished women?*" he asks, slightly slurring his words.

"It was nothing, dear," Neferu-Re replies. "Here, let me pour you some more wine."

"It didn't sound like nothing," Thut-Moses observes.

Thut-Moses is sprawls naked across their sleeping mat. Neferu-Re glares down at the man she intends to marry, half amused, half disgusted.

He is such a man, she complains. God's Wife actually prefers her handmaidens to Thut-Moses.

"It's just a part of my plan to remove mother from the throne, my love," Neferu-Re says. She flops down on the sleeping sofa and snuggles up close to him. "And my plans are going quite well."

Thut-Moses stares back at her, but remains silent.

"Once I remove her," Neferu-Re whispers, "you will be Pharaoh."

Pulling away, the Crown Prince sips more wine. Then looking over at the ambitious teenager, Thut-Moses retorts, "I shall be Pharaoh whether you remove your mother or not."

Neferu-Re tries not to show her annoyance. Recently, Thut-Moses had become increasingly independent. Each time he returns from Memphis, he is more difficult to control. There was a time when he would jump at her every word. Now he is distant and preoccupied. But Neferu-Re decides not to worry.

After all, she tells herself, *mother is arranging everything, quite nicely.*

Many moons have bathed the Nile in shimmering light since Amen proclaimed Pharaoh's jubilee and renewal ceremony. The gods continue to prosper the Two-Lands, bestowing their bounty upon those who farm the land, fish the river and tend their cattle and sheep. The great ones, royals, nobles and priests, continue their scheming, because they know nothing else. Gradually the antagonisms between Pharaoh and the priests diminish. After the untimely death of Amen's high priest, the Lord Dantha Maat, spreads her wings over the Two-Lands. Dantha is stricken by a terrible illness. Sekhmet's priests, wise in the arts of healing, rush to Dantha's chambers to find him wracked with fever. One priest takes up a vigil to banish the evil spirits invading Dantha's body by periodically reciting special prayers and burning the proper incense. Another priest places a figurine of Sekhmet upon Dantha's chest and recites the words that will encourage Sekhmet to draw the sickness out of Dantha and into her figurine. A third priest concocts an herbal tea from saffron, pomegranate bark and calamus sweetened with honey. The priest administers the tea to his patient every hour. However, none of the priests' ministrations prevent the disease from ravishing Dantha's body. Two days after he is stricken, Amen's high priest convulses in a fit of coughing and then, with a final gasp, dies.

Hat-Shep-Sut gives Dantha high funerary honors and declares a full seventy-day mourning period. She even summons her royal embalmer, Amen-Hotep, the high priest of Anubis, from his temple at Hardai and orders him to personally prepare Dantha's body for his journey into the afterlife. Amen-Hotep conducts the rituals proscribed in the *Book of the Dead*. Pharaoh's court marvels at Hat-Shep-Sut's piety and wisdom.

Eugene Stovall

CHAPTER NINETEEN

H at-Shep-Sut watches Neferu-Re and Aron out of the corner of her eye.

Are they passing secret looks between them, she wonders? But she knows the idea is preposterous. *There's nothing between her daughter and her consort,* she sighs. *I'm just getting old.* Pharaoh is barely in her mid-twenties.

Actually she's just looking for any excuse to get rid of Aron.

After the first several months of their 'consorting' together, Hat-Shep-Sut begins to reconsider her decision to replace Senen-Mut. Hat-Shep-Sut can barely tolerate her *Captain of Chariots*. Lately she is never happier then when Aron joins Thut-Moses at *Horus Nest*. Everyday, Pharaoh thanks the gods that her co-Regent and her consort are such close friends.

But the women at Karnak ____ the servants and handmaidens as well as the wives and daughters of nobles and priests ___ speak of Pharaoh's consort as a bronzed god. They talk about his great chest, rippling muscles and good looks. Once in awhile, Aron accompanies Thut-Moses on one of his rather infrequent trips to the Palace of Ladies to visit his mother. Iset does everything but throw herself at Aron. Since the deaths of both Seth-Mesy and Dantha, Iset has no influence in Hat-Shep-Sut's court. She is now an old woman who dreams that, one-day, she will steal away Pharaoh's consort. But Iset's looks, which were never that great before, have long since vanished. She now must depend on her pots of cosmetics just to appear presentable. Aron encourages neither Thut-Moses' mother nor any of the other willing women in Pharaoh's court. Even though, Iset cannot seduce Aron, his visits with her son give her ample authority to gossip.

"Aron has not visited *her* sleeping mat for several weeks," Iset tells the court ladies.

The gossip spreads around Thebes like butter on bread. Court women flock to Iset's quarters to hear the latest news about Hat-Shep-Sut and her consort. And Iset rarely disappoints them. Tittering like nesting swallows, the court women hang on Iset's every word.

"But you can't blame him," Thut-Moses' mother says. "They are *both* so masculine."

The women laugh among themselves, enjoying not only Iset's gossip but her wine and food, as well.

Outside Karnak's *Palace of Ladies*, the gossip flying through Pharaoh's storehouses and circulating among her administrators tell a different story about Pharaoh's consort.

"He's lazy! He's stupid!" Pharaoh's administrators complain.

"What do you expect? *He's a commoner!*

Hat-Shep-Sut appoints Aron her *Collector of Grain* but her administrators complain they lose a day's work whenever he's at the granary. Aron *is* an incompetent administrator and he knows it. As far as Aron is concerned, if it doesn't involve horses or fighting, *or both*, Aron is not interested. "They keep Pharaoh's consort with the chariots," they laugh on the *Street of Barbers*, "because only the horses understand him."

The jokes about Aron in the *Houses of Pleasure* are not so polite. It doesn't take long for Pharaoh's consort to resign from the granary altogether, to the relief of both administrators and scribes.

"Thank, Thoth that Pharaoh needs her consort to replace the Grand Vizier in her bedchamber only," the court laughs, "or else we'd soon be sending tribute to Nubia."

"The Two-Lands are blessed that the Lord Senen-Mut continues to guide Pharaoh's affairs by what *sits upon his shoulders* instead of what *rests beneath his kilt*." Even Hat-Shep-Sut must concede that Aron is hopeless as an administrator.

Would that he had a little less muscle and a lot more brains, Hat-Shep-Sut tells Neferu-Re.

Yet, Pharaoh's brawny consort has at least one skill. Thankfully, at council meetings, Aron is wise enough to keep his mouth shut. And whenever he expresses any opinion, he expresses it only to Thut-Moses. Aron becomes indispensable as Thut-Moses companion.

Hat-Shep-Sut directs Amen-Hotep, her Director of Buildings, to construct a palace at the far western edge of Karnak. She plans to move Senen-Mut out of her *Mansion of Millions of Years* before she removes him from her Inner Council and out of her life altogether. Even before Pharaoh makes the official announcement, rumors fly around Karnak and throughout Thebes. The new palace even becomes known as the *Grand Vizier's Palace*.

"Its Thoth's truth," one wag on the *Street of Barbers* declares.

"No, you son of Seth!" another barber laughs.

"It's true! The Lord Senen-Mut agreed to assist Amen-Hotep with the construction of the *Grand Vizier's Palace, just in case*."

"Just in case!" remarks an insignificant scribe in a small section in Pharaoh's *House of Silver*. "In case of what?"

"In case Pharaoh asks him to move there," the barber cracks.

Barbers and patrons alike, howl with laughter. But the gossip is true. The palace has personal quarters for the vizier, an audience hall, a banquet room, servant's quarters and stables. It can also house an army of scribes and administrators. Within ten months, Amen-Hotep completes the *Grand Vizier's Palace*. Though weighed down by melancholy, Hat-Shep-Sut notifies the council of her decision.

"My Lords," Pharaoh announces. "Please hear the proclamation that I have ordered to be read in every nome and temple throughout the Two-Lands.

Pharaoh Maat-Ka-Re Hat-Shep-Sut declares that:

Amen, Lord of the Thrones, gives sovereignty to his daughter over the black land and the red land. None rebel against the Living God in any land. All lands are subject to her will.

So does she, Pharaoh Maat-Ka-Re Hat-Shep-Sut, intend to reward her Grand Vizier, Lord Senen-Mut, for his loyal service to the person of the Living God and his devotion to Princess Neferu-Re, God' Wife, daughter of the Living God.

So let it be known that, Pharaoh Maat-Ka-Re Hat-Shep-Sut bestows on the Lord Senen-Mut his own palace, an annual income from Pharaoh's Treasury and the servants necessary for the good order and efficient operation of his household.

Furthermore, in addition to his various titles, Pharaoh inscribes the name, Senen-Mut, among the Companions of Pharaoh *on all doors not only at the Grand Vizier's Palace but at Djeser Djeseru and all other temples of Upper and Lower Egypt where the* Living God, Pharaoh Maat-Ka-Re Hat-Shep-Sut is honored.

And so it is done. Hat-Shep-Sut kicks Senen-Mut out of her *Mansion of Millions of Years.* He was her first and only love. But by this act, none will doubt that she is Pharaoh, the sole ruler over the Two-Lands of Upper and Lower Egypt.

Weeks later Hat-Shep-Sut stands at her *Window of Appearances* to witness Senen-Mut's departure. A sea of administrators, scribes and household servants pour out of her palace. They are bearing baggage, furniture, personal belongings and public documents.

"What is this crowd in the courtyard," Hat-Shep-Sut asks.

Chaos rules. Ox drawn wagons, donkey carts and litters are sprawled everywhere. Every resident of Pharaoh's entire *Mansion of Millions of Years* seems to be accompanying Senen-Mut to his new home.

Hat-Shep-Sut has invited her *Circle of Advisors,* Thut-Moses, Neferu-Re, Pen-Nek-Heb, Aron, Amen-Hotep and the newly appointed high priest of Amen, Hapu-Seneb, to join her at the *Window of Appearances.* She wants them to witness the Grand

Vizier's humiliating dismissal from Pharaoh's *Mansion of Millions of Years*. But a mass exodus is not what she intended.

"Who are all these people and where are they going?" she shouts.

"They report directly to your Grand Vizier," Amen-Hotep replies. "They join the Grand Vizier in his palace."

"Why are all my people leaving me?" Hat-Shep-Sut screeches.

"They administer Pharaoh's operations for the Grand Vizier and must remain together," Pen-Nek-Heb confirms.

Pen-Nek-Heb and Amen-Hotep work closely with Senen-Mut during the construction of the *Grand Vizier's Palace*. The Aten's high priest acts as a go between for Senen-Mut and Amen-Hotep and he accommodates all of Senen-Mut's staff at the new palace. Pen-Nek-Heb knows that the number of people leaving Pharaoh's palace exceeds all of her expectations, but neglects to inform her. Iunu's high priest remembers that Pharaoh once denied him an audience.

"There are hundreds out there!" Hat-Shep-Sut wails.

"They must leave, if your majesty is to maintain serenity throughout the Two-Lands," Thut-Moses replies. He, too, finds the situation amusing.

"Who's responsible for this?" Hat-Shep-Sut shouts over the noise of the crowd milling in her courtyard.

"You are, mother dear," Neferu-Re replies.

"How am I responsible for *this*?" Hat-Shep-Sut asks Neferu-Re.

"Don't you remember telling us that no details of father's move should be discussed at council meetings?" Neferu-Re smiles.

"You wanted everything kept secret," Thut-Moses chimes in. He is also enjoying his stepmother's discomfiture.

Neither Aron nor Hapu-Seneb says anything. Hat-Shep-Sut watches, helpless as administrators, scribes and messengers stream out of her palace. She feels that, once again, Senen-Mut has thwarted her will. Further, she sees that Neferu-Re and Thut-Moses enjoy her embarrassment. Though he maintains his silence, Aron's deadpan look infuriates Hat-Shep-Sut even more.

Can't I depend on this muscle-bound fool for anything! Hat-Shep-Sut screams silently. But she knows that, no matter what, she must re-gain her serenity. Hat-Shep-Sut fixes Aron with a long, penetrating stare.

"I thought you have *watchers* in the *Eyes of Horus* who report to you," she says.

"I do, Great Lord," Aron replies. *Why is she so upset with me?* he wonders. *She was the one who ordered him to move.*

Hat-Shep-Sut expresses her the exasperation. "If *Eyes of Horus watchers* report to you," she asks, "why didn't you tell me that half of my people were leaving with the Grand Vizier?"

"I didn't know that I was supposed to tell you who was leaving," Aron says. His voice quivers with irritation. "Besides how are my *watchers* to know how many were planning to leave with Senen-Mut? You ordered that no one was to know how many even reported to him?"

Now it's Pen-Nek-Heb turn. Hat-Shep-Sut glares at the statesman whose steady unblinking eyes return Pharaoh's look. She decides to say nothing.

He knew what Senen-Mut was planning, she tells herself. *I will not forget Iunu's deception.*

"What good are the *Eyes of Horus*, if I am still blind?" she asks Aron. "You told me that your *watchers* keep you informed!"

"I have always told you what I have learned," Aron replies defensively.

"Then you must keep your brains in a canopic jar!" Hat-Shep-Sut snaps.

The others avert their eyes. Aron suffers Pharaoh's abuse, in silence.

All the while the merry chaos in the courtyard continues. Servants and handlers load the baggage belonging to hundreds of people. Carts and wagons rumble their way through the pylons. And a long line of people stream towards the western side of Karnak, towards the *Grand Vizier's Palace*.

Watching, helplessly, Hat-Shep-Sut can only cry out her frustration. "MUST I DO EVERYTHING?"

Pharaoh marches back to her chambers. This morning, sadness over their separation overwhelmed her. She even considered asking him to remain with her. Now she is enraged. Once again, she feels less than the absolute ruler over the Two-Lands. And once again, she vows to have her *revenge*.

Alone with Aron inside her chambers, Hat-Shep-Sut studies her consort.

"Your *watchers* are of no value to me," she decides. "I intend to eliminate the *Eyes of Horus*."

"But, Majesty, how will the military receive its information?" Aron asks.

"From now on, I want Hapu-Seneb and his *Seeing Waters* to report everything they know directly to me!"

"The *Seeing Waters* are of no value to the military," Aron counters.

"Nor to Thut-Moses either, I trust," Pharaoh sneers. "I'm tired. You may leave!"

With that she dismisses her consort.

"I don't see how you do it," Iby shakes his head. The two outcasts share quarters at Senen-Mut's new palace and on this particular evening they share several jugs of wine, as well. Under the influence of wine, the new palace feels like home.

"How I do what?" Senen-Mut asks.

"How can you continue serving a woman who has scorned you for another man?" Iby slurs his words. "And not just some other man, someone you considered a friend and a comrade in arms."

Outside, in the hall, the voices of chamberlains, porters and servants echo about, dragging baggage and furniture into the unfamiliar surroundings. It's been several months since the move. Senen-Mut's staff is still unsettled in their new quarters. Despite months of planning, the move causes massive disruptions. Pharaoh's *House* of Silver, Granaries and the other departments under Senen-Mut's control are mired in chaos and confusion.

Senen-Mut and Iby lounge in an open circular room. Sofas, cushions and small eating tables are available for their comfort. Two halls connect the lounge to sleeping and bathing areas. Working and sleeping areas for his administrators and scribes are located in separate areas of the palace. Compared to Pharaoh's *Mansion of Millions of Years*, the *Grand Vizier's Palace* is cramped and rather austere. However, Senen-Mut is quite pleased with his new home.

Senen-Mut scratches his head in response to Iby. He tries to mimic his friend's comical expression plastering a lop-sided grin on his face more because of the wine than any skill he might possess in mimicry. Actually, both are slightly intoxicated.

"I but serve Pharaoh," Senen-Mut replies, "as I would serve the *Will of Ra.*

"Don't treat me as a false friend," Iby says. "I remember when you were the *Student of Wast* who I rescued from the Royal School some years ago."

Pharaoh's top spymaster raises his wine cup. Senen-Mut, acknowledges the silent toast, before draining his wine cup of its contents. Iby reflects on how his master has matured since his days as the *Student of Wast*. Senen-Mut wears the look of a statesman, reflective, wise, distant, neither harsh nor solemn. Iby likes that Senen-Mut is neither obsequious like Hapu-Seneb, nor dour like Pen-Nek-Heb. Nor has his fall from Pharaoh's favor depressed or angered him. Iby admires Senen-Mut as he admires no other man or *woman*. Senen-Mut's imitation of Iby's silly grin tells his friend to change the subject.

"What do you think of Pharaoh's latest adventure?" Iby asks changing the subject.

"Which one?"

"The war against *Pharaoh's Enemies in the Northern Nomes*," Iby replies. "I brought you the information. It should be around here

Eugene Stovall

somewhere. I hope you didn't lose it." Iby looks hesitantly about the Grand Vizier's chambers

"I read your report," Senen-Mut replies.

"Well?"

"How can I disagree with what she's doing?" Senen-Mut asks. "We did the same thing to solidify her father's rule, remember?"

"Her father invaded Nubia," Iby observes. "There's a big difference between attacking tribesmen, without armor, using wooden spears, and taking on an army of asiatics. The people of the north have the finest armies in the world!"

"If Pharaoh wants to attack her enemies," Senen-Mut says slurring his words, "we have no choice but to support her. Besides she plans to attack the squatters not the Mitanni."

"The *Eyes of Horus* wonder _____," Iby begins.

"The *Eyes of Horus*?" Senen-Mut rises up. "What are the *Eyes of Horus* wondering?"

My friend had better watch himself, Senen-Mut thinks to himself. *He'll soon be considered a heretic.*

"They wonder when you're going to step in?"

"You may tell them that I will *step in*, as you say, when Pharaoh asks me." Senen-Mut gives his friend a wry look. "But you and I know she's not going to ask me. So I'm just going to let her be Pharaoh."

Tribes of nomads have been wandering down from the Sinai desert into the northern nomes and squatting on land east of Saqqarah known as the *Anubieon*, land that runs westward alongside the *Bahr Yussef*, the canal of Joseph. *Anubieon* Canaanites are peaceful, yet Hat-Shep-Sut wants these squatters driven out of Egypt. And she wants to punish the nomarchs who permit Canaanites to squat along the *Anubieon*.

"She's giving Thut-Moses free reign in Lower Egypt," Iby continues. "She's even preparing her memorials?'

"So, my clever spy, you *do* know that Pharaoh's war will not be against the asiatics," Senen-Mut smiles. "Are you trying to trick me into something?"

"Even if she's only planning to attack those squatters from Canaan, its still a bad idea," Iby protests. "And I'm not trying to trick you into anything."

"Then, out with it, oh *Master of Spies*. What do you want?"

"Listen to the words she directed inscribed:

'I have done these things by the device of my heart. I have never slumbered as one forgetful, but have made strong what was decayed. I have raised up what was dismembered by the asiatics when they first invaded Avaris with roving hordes. In the midst of their overthrowing, they ruled without Ra. I banish these abominations to the gods and remove their footprints from the earth.'"

"I see nothing wrong with Pharaoh's words," Senen-Mut shrugs. "She follows the footsteps of the *distinguished women*. Who is to say that the words on her *stele* are untrue?"

"How can Pharaoh memorialize the extermination of peaceful settlers?" Iby asks. "And you seem fully aware of what Pharaoh intends to do." Iby voice trails off, worried that he has overstepped himself.

For his part, however, Senen-Mut is pleasantly inebriated and unconcerned with Canaanites squatting alongside the *Bahr Yussef*, whether peaceful are not.

"Don't you recall what your father and the *Nomarch of Wast* told you about the war they fought against the Egyptians and foreigners in the time of Amen-Hotep I?" Iby continues. "Those people embraced the gods of the Two-Lands and paid their taxes to Pharaoh."

"Yes," Senen-Mut replies. "And your point is?"

"It's the same thing, all over again," Iby says.

"It's not the same at all," Senen-Mut argues. "Your own *Eyes of Horus* confirms that the Pharaoh's campaign is being carried out against asiatic settlers in northern nomes. There is no fighting taking place between Egyptians."

Iby looks at Senen-Mut and shakes his head. "If we were taking out agents working for the Mitanni, I could understand. The Mitanni continue to infiltrate their spies into Avaris, Saqqarah and even Memphis. But the Canaanites of the Anubieon could become valuable allies for Pharaoh."

"It doesn't appear that Pharaoh wants allies," Senen-Mut replies. "Besides what would you have me do? It should be apparent, even to you, that I have lost my influence with Pharaoh."

"I know that Pharaoh has excluded you from the planning," Iby says, "but you could do *something.*"

Actually, Senen-Mut plays a more active role in planning the *War Against Pharaoh's Enemies in The North* than Iby realizes. At the very outset of the war, the decision was made to exclude Iby and the Eyes of Horus from planning information. The War Council knows ties of intermarriage exist between the Anubieon Canaanites and watchers with the Eyes of Horus especially those watchers recruited by Iby. Even some of Iby's own relatives live among these Canaanite tribes. All the information used to plan Thut-Moses war comes from *Seeing Waters* sources without Iby's knowledge. Senen-Mut provided Pharaoh's *War Council* with the information in the secrecy of Pharaoh's *Seal Room* on several occasions. Both Pharaoh and her co-Regent agree that the security of the Two-Lands require a continual purge of asiatic settlers from all Lower Egypt. Senen-Mut smiles at the irony.

While he and Aron exclude Iby from Pharaoh's war plans in the Anubieon, Hat-Shep-Sut and Aron conspire to kick me out of her palace. What a clever woman!

Though Senen-Mut assisted the female Pharaoh's rise to power, now in order to retain any influence at court, he must tread lightly. Nor does he wish to destroy all of his friend's illusions. Iby, Captain of Captain over the *Eyes of Horus* is too valuable to be sacrificed so early in the game.

"Of course I feel some remorse," Senen-Mut confesses. "No one wants to see innocent people butchered." He pauses to see whether his words have any impact on his friend. Iby remains noncommittal. "If either my father or Amen-Nati were alive today both would be disappointed that I didn't do more to prevent the *War on Pharaoh's Enemies in the Northern Nomes.*"

"Your banishment could be seen as a punishment for your failure to act," Iby observes.

Senen-Mut decides to play along.

"You and Pen-Nek-Heb warned me that Pharaoh's stepson wanted war, but I didn't listen," Senen-Mut confesses.

Senen-Mut decides that Iby's silly grin won't work for him in this situation, so he tries to affect a look of innocence. "But I must continue to serve Pharaoh as best I can, don't you see?"

"None of this is your fault," Iby says, sympathizing with his master.

Seeing that he has Iby's sympathy, Senen-Mut continues. "When Pharaoh submitted her plans to conduct military exercises in the northern nomes, I thought it was a good way to keep Thut-Moses occupied. I know how Pharaoh worries about a palace coup. *If Thut-Moses is involved in the north*, I thought, *Pharaoh would rest easier on her throne*," Senen-Mut pauses to see if his words have any impact. "Believe me," he continues, "I thought this would be a rather harmless pursuit to keep the Crown Prince busy."

"Harmless," Iby gives a mirthless laugh. "She's launching a large-scale military operation. Thut-Moses' army is raging through asiatic settlements not just in the *Anubieon* but all over the delta."

"Thut-Moses' attacks are to deny the Anubieon squatters supplies and support," Senen-Mut replies off-handedly. "Remember how firmly the Hyksos held their control over Lower Egypt before any pharaoh challenged them."

"What I don't understand," Iby says, "is why you persist in defending her even when you know she's wrong? You know that Thut-Moses is not only killing asiatics; he's killing Egyptians, as well!"

"What are you suggesting that I do?" Senen-Mut asks his friend.

"If asiatics like the Mitanni or some other Persian tribe invade Lower Egypt with their regular armies," Iby declares, "the squatters, as Thoth is my witness, will support the invaders. Even Pen-Nek-Heb argues that this war could provoke a Mitanni invasion."

"So you've heard about his pleas to Pharaoh in her *Seal Room?*" Senen-Mut remarks.

"Of course," Iby replies.

"Then you must know that Pen-Nek-Heb failed to persuade Pharaoh to reconsider her war," Senen-Mut says. "As a matter of fact, it was at that meeting that Pharaoh decided that eliminating all Canaanite settlements in Lower Egypt would *prevent* a Mitanni invasion."

Iby says nothing; The conversation is interrupted as servants bring meat and vegetable dishes along with fresh fruit and dates. Senen-Mut orders more jugs of wine. After they have eaten Senen-Mut tries to cheer his friend.

"I have just realized how much I have taken your loyalty and faithful service for granted," Senen-Mut says.

"Not so, master," Iby replies. "You have been most generous in your blessings to me."

Senen-Mut is not put off.

"The ancients valued and encouraged intelligence wherever it was found. So when a highly intelligent individual, like yourself, gives faithful service, he should receive the rewards he deserves."

Iby shrugs, showing off his lop-sided smile and wondering what Senen-Mut getting at.

"When you took command of the *Eyes of Horus*," Senen-Mut says, "it was just another incompetent group of soldiers carrying out whatever orders it was given. You and your wharf rats transformed the *Eyes of Horus* into a force that gives Pharaoh and her *War Council* the capability of striking the enemies of the Two-Lands whenever and wherever they please."

"Such lavish praise is unnecessary," Iby remonstrates.

"Many who have not contributed half as much as you, my friend, have received farms and villas for their service. Even I have been given this beautiful palace." Both look around, lift their cups, and toast Senen-Mut's new home. "Everyone has received something, except you, my friend."

"I have received much from you, master," Iby reminds Senen-Mut. "When I met you, I was a dock worker. Now I am a Captain of Captains in Pharaoh's army, Overseer of Pharaoh's *Eyes of Horus*, a *Friend of Pharaoh's Grand Vizier* and a member of Pharaoh's Inner Council. Believe me, master. I have no complaints. I have been well compensated for my service to you and Pharaoh."

Iby raises his mug once more to his lips, caring more for his friend's wine than his words.

Is he trying to retire me, just as things are getting interesting? Iby wonders. *I live for the game.*

Iby laughs to himself, though he is not quite as certain of Senen-Mut's motives as he was before.

Eugene Stovall

CHAPTER TWENTY

"Do you think we can win a war against the Mitanni?" Hat-Shep-Sut asks.

The question is directed to her Grand Vizier who, along with other key advisors, meets with Pharaoh in her *Seal Room*.

"It will be as it has always been," Senen-Mut replies. "The army fights when Pharaoh leads them."

"And will the army follow Pharaoh Hat-Shep-Sut?"

"If the Two-Lands go to war against the Mitanni, Majesty," Senen-Mut responds, "Thut-Moses must lead the army." He gives Hat-Shep-Sut a grave look that says, *"Don't take this distinguished woman thing too far."*

"Thank you, my ever faithful vizier," Hat-Shep-Sut sneers, "but that was not the question I asked." Hat-Shep-Sut draws herself up into an aura of full royal dignity. "I repeat. *Will the army follow Pharaoh Maat-Ka-Re Hat-Shep-Sut against the Mitanni?*"

"Yes, Great Lord," Senen-Mut responds, "the army will follow Pharaoh Hat-Shep-Sut against the Mitanni. Does the female Pharaoh, foremost of Distinguished Women intend to lead the army of the Two-Lands against the asiatic invader?"

The contest of wills continues, silently. The two stare directly at each other; neither blinks. Abruptly, Hat-Shep-Sut rises and strides out.

Watching Hat-Shep-Sut storm out of the Seal Room, Pen-Nek-Heb remarks to Senen-Mut, "You seem, once again, to have offended the *Living God.*"

"The Living God is unable to face any truth that offends her," Senen-Mut replies. "Especially when it concerns the fact that she is a woman."

"She should understand that few men are capable of leading the army," Iby chimes in.

"She is unable to live in truth," Senen-Mut says. "It doesn't matter whether the Mitanni invade or not, her concern is remaining upon the throne."

The three of them depart the Seal Room and head down the marble steps to their litters.

"Bound for the *Grand Vizier's Palace?*" Pen-Nek-Heb asks. His eyes flash a hint of amusement.

"Yes." Senen-Mut replies.

"May I join you?" Pen-Nek-Heb asks.

"We are honored by Iunu's company," Senen-Mut says, "however we normally walk."

"My healer priest has recommended that I walk more ____ unless you think I might slow you down."

"The company of the *Aten* and my master is always welcomed," Senen-Mut bows.

And without any preliminaries, Pen-Nek-Heb launches into the subject of the day.

"Do you believe she will actually try to lead the army against the Mitanni attack?" he asks.

"Of course not," Senen-Mut replies.

"She doesn't believe there will be a war," Iby adds.

"Neither does the council," Pen-Nek-Heb says. "Most of them believe that Thut-Moses' atrocities are deterring a Mitanni invasion."

"She has the council's overwhelming support," Senen-Mut replies. "As far as they are concerned, she can do no wrong."

"But Thut-Moses' assaults are becoming more indiscriminate," Pen-Nek-Heb grumbles.

"His soldiers have acquired a love of slaughter and plunder," Iby observes: "Many on the council are acquiring wealth from the soldiers' plunder."

"Pharaoh believes the war will establish her reputation as the '*foremost of distinguished women*'. So your concerns about the war mean nothing compared to her ambition to use the war to become a god, not only in name, but in *deed*."

"Where do you stand with Pharaoh's ambitions?" Pen-Nek-Heb asks Senen-Mut.

"As always, I serve the will of Pharaoh."

"So you agree with her," Pen-Nek-Heb says.

"Not necessarily," Senen-Mut responds. "But on the other hand, what she's doing makes sense if she wants to remain Pharaoh. And since she doesn't believe the Mitanni will invade because of Thut-Moses' war, she is now concerned about her stepson's reputation and his popularity with the council."

"What do *you* say, Lord of the *Eyes of Horus*?" Pen-Nek-Heb asks. "Certainly you agree that Pharaoh's war on her own people is disastrous and will work against her keeping her throne in the *long run*, don't you?"

Iby glances over at Senen-Mut as if asking permission to speak. The Grand Vizier gives an imperceptible nod.

"I agree with the concerns of the Lord of Iunu," Iby replies. "They are the same as mine. However. I agree with my master that Pharaoh has no other strategy if she is to retain her throne. She knows that, if the Mitanni invade, her council will have no choice other than to make Thut-Moses, Pharaoh. Hat-Shep-Sut cannot lead the army. No one expects her to. She must continue the war in the north to prevent a Mitanni invasion. She hasn't come this far just to turn everything over to Thut-Moses."

"Nor should she," Senen-Mut adds.

"So what can we do to stop this war?" Pen-Nek-Heb asks.

Pen-Nek-Heb wants to stop the war for an important reason. Pharaoh's war could delay and even corrupt the *new epoch* predicted by his *star-gazers*. Pen-Nek-Heb fears that if fratricide and war ushers in the *new epoch*, all the amazing discoveries and inventions made at Iunu will only serve to deceive and debase mankind rather than lead to enlightenment and truth. Pen-Nek-Heb had supported Hat-Shep-Sut's claim to the throne, because he believed that under a female pharaoh, the Two-Lands would benefit from a most productive transition into the new epoch.

"Pharaoh decides what should be done," Senen-Mut shrugs. "We but follow her will."

"If she were to ask your advice ___."

"If she were to ask my advice," Senen-Mut cuts the priest off in mid-sentence, "I would advise her to find a way to make peace with the Mitanni before they send their hordes into Lower Egypt."

"Why not mobilize the army?" Iby asks. "We could strengthen our forts all along the border."

"Mobilizing the army will take her where she doesn't want to go," Senen-Mut replies. "If the Two-Lands and the Mitanni wage war, win or lose, Thut-Moses becomes the next Pharaoh."

"We can't just sit back and let things happen," Pen-Nek-Heb argues. "*Pharaoh must stop this war.*"

"What do you recommend?" Senen-Mut asks.

"One thing I don't recommend," Iby offers, "is that the *Living God* lead the army against a Mitanni invasion."

"Well, let's hope that it doesn't come to that," Senen-Mut interjects.

"I take it that you believe that the Egyptian army is unprepared for a war against the Mitanni, whoever leads it," Pen-Nek-Heb says.

"The army is prepared," Iby says, "it's Pharaoh who isn't."

"Whether or not the army is prepared," Senen-Mut says, "we all agree that an asiatic war must be avoided." Senen-Mut face brightens and a sly smile plays at the corner of his mouth. "And I think I know how to do it."

"Well, tell us," Pen-Nek-Heb snaps. He's irritable. The walk has proven more difficult than he imagined. "What's your plan?"

"We need an economic program of buying and selling!"

"A *program of buying and selling*," Pen-Nek-Heb replies. "What are you talking about?"

"You've said it yourself," Senen-Mut recalls. "Our northern borders would be doubly protected if the Two-Lands built market-places, instead of forts."

"And?"

"And if we began pouring gold into the land of the asiatics through our marketplaces in Canaan, Lebanon and in Syria, the asiatics would be more interested in trading with the Two-Lands than warring with us."

"The only way your plan will be successful is if they become more interested in accumulating gold than accumulating plunder," Iby observes.

"You're right! Senen-Mut agrees. *You're absolutely right!*" Then he looks over at Pen-Nek-Heb. "Remember those builders who petitioned the council to allow them to negotiate with the Mitanni for Lebanese wood?

"Yes," Pen-Nek-Heb replies, "what about it?"

Then Senen-Mut asks Iby, "And what was the name of that Mitanni agent who wanted to discuss establishing a market somewhere in Palestine?"

"That *bandit*?" Iby responds.

"Yes, " Senen-Mut says, "that *bandit*. And I want the names of those merchants who operate caravans between the cataracts and Minoa. I want to contact everyone else who loves gold and trades with the Mitanni. I want them to represent us."

"Represent *us*?" Iby asks.

"Yes," Senen-Mut says. "I'm going to establish markets to trade goods for gold."

"What about Persia?"

"Yes!" Senen-Mut shouts. "Even in the lands where the rivers flow *backwards!* Wherever we can find asiatics more interested in trading goods than in waging war," Senen-Mut says.

"You think that this might stop a war with the Mitanni?" Pen-Nek-Heb asks.

"It might."

"How?" Iby asks.

"I'm giving away a lot of gold."

One by one Senen-Mut's administrators establish Egyptian trade missions in foreign lands north of the Sinai and east of the Great Green Sea. Merchants with goods from everywhere flock to Senen-Mut's marketplaces. They are eager for gold. Supporting his protégé, Pen-Nek-Heb even encourages northern nomarchs to send their asiatic settlers back into Palestine as traders, interpreters and bankers. Senen-Mut instructs the nomarchs to accept everything. Soon products, wine, wood, livestock and manufactured goods, pour into the Two-Lands.

"Now you no longer have settlers in the *Anubieon*, Pen-Nek-Heb tells the nomarchs, "you now have merchants bringing their goods to the Two-Lands."

For a relatively small amount of gold, Senen-Mut's plan is an immediate success. In less time than anyone could imagine, Pharaoh's war begins to dwindle and Thut-Moses runs out of enemies. Lower Egypt is overrun with traders and merchants granted immunity from harm by tradition. Everywhere Thut-Moses' soldiers find Canaanite merchants instead of Canaanite squatters. The asiatic nomads vanish across the Sinai desert to return as merchants, translators and bankers, facilitating asiatic access to Egyptian abundance.

Army morale erodes. Thut-Moses' soldiers, especially the officers, find Senen-Mut's marketplaces a means of disposing of their plunder. Over one three month period, the *War Council* finds that a quarter of its army has disappeared into Palestine. The desertions force the *War Council* to suspend military action and withdraw its soldiers back into *Horus Nest*. Within a year, the popularity of Senen-Mut's marketplaces brings a smile even to Pen-Nek-Heb's normally dour face. But upon Hat-Shep-Sut's face, whose will is thwarted, once again, her Grand Vizier's marketplaces bring a grimace.

CHAPTER TWENTY-ONE

Amen, the Lord of the Thrones of the Two Lands says:

Come, come in peace, my daughter, the graceful, who art my heart,

Pharaoh Maat-Ka-Re Hat-Shep-Sut.

I will give thee Punt. I will lead your soldiers by land and by water, onto the mysterious shores that join the harbors of incense, the sacred territory of the divine land and my abode of pleasure.

From Punt take as much as you like.

"Thut-Moses has resumed his attack's on settlers in the north," Pen-Nek-Heb complains at a council meeting. "He must be stopped!"

"We were told that the Grand Vizier's marketplaces have all but eliminated the threat of a Mitanni invasion."

"The marketplaces have diminished the asiatic threat," the priest agrees, "But after Thut-Moses' soldiers ran out of plunder, they returned to butchery."

"And well they should," another councilor says. "Look how well the policy has worked."

Pen-Nek-Heb is well aware that many members of Pharaoh's Inner Council are becoming quite wealthy trading for goods from abroad. Those who can supply horses especially mares, become extremely successful. War Council officers, *overseers, captains, captains of captains and generals*, also become wealthy. Pharaoh's army needs tin and copper to manufacture weapons. They help themselves to Pharaoh's supplies, food, and transportation. The nomarchs, especially those in the south, willingly supply the War Council's needs. Few nomarchs support Pen-Nek-Heb's call for an end to the slaughter. The majority benefit from the wealth pouring into their nomes. Indeed, all of Karnak talks of nothing else than how wealthy the nobles are becoming. Fashion among the noble's wives and daughters now includes the costliest silks, the most elaborate cloaks, the daintiest sandals and the most exquisite jewelry, imported from around the world.

Hapu-Seneb, now Amen's high priest, supports Pen-Nek-Heb's opposition to the renewed bloodshed in the north. Because Hapu-Seneb believes the flow of wealth pouring into the Two-Lands brings corruption in its wake.

"I agree with the *Aten's* high priest," Hapu-Seneb tells the council. "The Two-Lands must return to its ancient traditions and sacred beliefs before it is too late."

Hapu-Seneb issues dire warnings against adopting the heresies of new ways.

"Egypt's black earth is overly fertile," Hapu-Seneb warns. "Amen's blessings spring much too quickly and life in the Two-Lands is far too easy."

From the beginning of time, priests accept as their solemn duty the task of saving the people from the *evils of paradise*. The priesthood represses any desire by the common people to rise above their station in life. The priests warn the people of the dangers in acquiring luxuries and superfluous comforts predicting that once commoners experience material comforts, they will demand material comforts as a matter of rights. The priests maintain that luxuries and comforts distract people from carrying out their duties towards their rulers and their gods.

"If the people were allowed to pamper their bodies," Hapu-Seneb declares, "they will become lazy and ignorant and descend into a brutish, self-centered existence. Social life would be a beastly struggle of all against all."

Pharaoh's councilors remain unconcerned. One replies.

"Priests sanctify Pharaoh's authority," he says. "You tell the people that Pharaoh's authority comes from the gods so that the people will toil with enthusiasm and without question. Why do you lecture us about your role? We seek only to carry out the will of Pharaoh."

"You teach that those who labor for Pharaoh's benefit are never sad," another nomarch responds.

"Yes, this is true," Pen-Nek-Heb agrees, "but those who seek after their own pleasure are never happy."

The successful nomarchs smile and poke each other in the ribs as they become extremely wealthy.

"Continue to urge the people to work, sing and worship the gods," the nomarchs laugh. "We do not object."

The priests teach that song turns toil into joy; joy points out the humor in life, humor binds the people into a brotherhood and belonging to a brotherhood or a fellowship makes their lives fulfilling and meaningful." Everyone has learned these sayings from when they attended temple school as children.

"Well said," council members applaud, yet dismiss Pen-Nek-Heb's entreaty to end the violence in the north. And the Grand Vizier directs the council's attention onto other matters.

Thut-Moses' war in the north forces Pen-Nek-Heb to join the Hapu-Seneb's crusade to return the Two-Lands to the ancient traditions.

"Our time has finally come, my brother!" Hapu-Seneb exclaims.

They meet in Amen's temple at Karnak in the personal quarters of Amen's high priest. Hapu-Seneb's eyes shine with enthusiasm as if already beholding a beatific vision of people throughout the Two-Lands obeying the will of Amen in accordance with the ancient traditions, a vision where the heresy of disobedience has been stamped out. Hapu-Seneb almost dances with glee.

Possibly, he's a little too gleeful, Pen-Nek-Heb thinks. He asks Hapu-Seneb, "How will Amen accomplish this happy result?"

The elderly priest's dour countenance masks the skepticism on his face if not in his voice. Pen-Nek-Heb is still uncertain how well an alliance between Amen and the Aten will work.

"Throughout the northern nomes," Hapu-Seneb smiles, "white and black-robed priests have pledged themselves to our holy crusade. Soon Amen will reassert his authority as the true ruler over the whole of the Two-Lands, the usurping, female heretic will be deposed and the Two-Lands will enjoy peace and serenity under the rightful rule of the Crown Prince and Royal Heir, Thut-Moses III."

Hapu-Seneb looks furtively over his shoulder, fearing that, even within the secure walls of Amen's Temple, the *Eyes of Horus*, though greatly diminished might learn of his plot.

"Now you, Pen-Nek-Heb, high priest of the Aten, must choose whether to join our crusade or suffer along with that female usurper." Hapu-Seneb rubs his hands with anticipation. "What is it you want me to do?" Pen-Nek-Heb asks.

"Convince Pharaoh to send a trade mission to the Land of Punt," Hapu-Seneb smiles. "She trusts you."

"What is your plan?"

"As soon as, Pharaoh's caravans begin their return trip from the land of Punt, Nubian tribes from as far south as the great falls and as far west as the burning sands, will attack."

"They must be fools!" Pen-Nek-Heb replies.

"How so?" Hapu-Seneb asks.

"Nubian Bowmen cannot defeat the army of the Two-Lands," Pen-Nek-Heb sniffs. "Pharaoh's soldiers are as numerous as the desert sands. Their chariots will easily crush any Nubian formation. I think you need a *better* plan."

"You may be correct," Hapu-Seneb smiles. But you want to end Thut-Moses' war in the north, don't you?" Hapu-Seneb barely disguises his contempt for his rival. "My plan will accomplish what you want. Thut-Moses' army will be sent to protect Pharaoh's trade mission to Punt. The north and your precious Anubieon will be left in peace. That's what you want, isn't it?"

"Yes," Pen-Nek-Heb agrees.

"A real war in Nubia, might diminish Thut-Moses craving for battle."

Pen-Nek-Heb knows that as long as Thut-Moses remains in the north, he has no chance of stopping the war. *The mission to Punt will get Thut-Moses out of Lower Egypt for a while. A Nubian attack upon Pharaoh's trade mission might force Pharaoh to reconsider her entire war policy.* Pen-Nek-Heb closes his eyes and prays silently for the KAs of those who will depart for the underworld when Amen chastises Pharaoh.

Hapu-Seneb observes his fellow priest.

Pray well, my friend. When Amen controls the Two-Lands once again and everyone is compelled to obey their masters, I will take care of you and your heretical priests at Iunu. And I will especially enjoy eliminating that trouble making whose throat commoner. I should have slit when he was still the Student of Wast.

"I did not banish Senen-Mut from my *Mansion of Millions of Years*," Hat-Shep-Sut screams at Aron and Neferu-Re months earlier, "only to hear all of Karnak singing his praises."

The past evening, during a court dinner honoring the *Lord of Harbors*, Pharaoh is mortified sitting through a performance of dancers, musicians and singers, celebrating Senen-Mut's marketplaces in Gaza, Syria and Minoas. The next day amidst her buzzing court. Hat-Shep-Sut's enmity towards Senen-Mut intensifies.

"I should have dismissed him from my court, long ago," Hat-Shep-Sut fumes.

Neferu-Re and Aron join Hapu-Seneb and Pen-Nek-Heb in Pharaoh's *Seal Room*.

"Majesty, you can't dismiss Senen-Mut without risking a revolt in your council," Hapu-Seneb counsels. "The council will attempt to put Thut-Moses on the throne. There will be chaos and a civil war."

"*I want him out!*" Hat-Shep-Sut screams.

"But mother," Neferu-Re remarks, "who will come to your defense, if your *Eyes of Horus* and possibly your own Palace Guard support Thut-Moses?"

Pharaoh hates being told not to do something, even by her daughter. She does not respond.

"Please Majesty," Hapu-Seneb advises, "be patient for a little while longer. We will find a way of ridding you of this pest."

"Why won't he just go away," Hat-Shep-Sut complains, looking up as if to find the answer in the heavens. "Doesn't he know we neither need nor want his services?"

Hapu-Seneb nods imperceptibly to Pen-Nek-Heb.

"Majesty," the high priest of Iunu begins, "why not send your own mission to the Land of Punt. All over the Two-Lands, Punt is famous for its wealth. When your trade mission returns from Punt laden with riches, for which the *Living God* has paid virtually nothing, none will speak kindly of your Grand Vizier, who empties your coffers of gold for the benefit of your enemies. When your mission returns from Punt, Karnak will speak only of the wisdom of the *Living God*."

Hat-Shep-Sut listens to Pen-Nek-Heb. His idea intrigues her. When she was young, her father had told her of Punt and its fabled wealth.

"Who was the last Pharaoh to send a trade mission to Punt?" Pharaoh asks the Royal Scribe.

The scribe immediately scurries out of the *Seal Room*. When he returns, his arms are filled with papyrus scrolls.

"Great Lord," the royal scribe announces, "Hene-Nu writes of a journey to Punt during the eleventh dynasty. The mission was ordered by Men-Tu-Hotep. Pharaoh's ships transported three thousand men through Wadi Hammamat and down the Red Sea to Punt."

Pharaoh notices the furtive looks between the priests of the Aten and Amen.

What goes between them? she wonders. But then as quickly as the question occurs to her, she dismisses it. Hat-Shep-Sut knows the rivalry between Amen and the *Aten* is as intense as ever. *Pen-Neb-Heb is probably wondering whether or not Hapu-Seneb will support his idea*, Hat-Shep-Sut tells herself.

"Great Lord," Pen-Nek-Heb offers, "if Pharaoh's mission to the Land of Punt is successful, the *Living God* will have a story worth telling on a monument or even in her funerary temple at Deir el-Bahri. It will amaze all who read it."

These words convince Hat-Shep-Sut to send a trade mission to the Land of Punt.

"Great Majesty, *Living God*," exclaims the little wizened-face man who "kisses the dust" in front of Pharaoh's throne.

His name is Neshi. He's an administrator from her Nubian *House of Silver*. Aron recommends him as Pharaoh's viceroy to the Land of Punt. The court whispers that Aron has made a wise selection, for once. Neshi serves as Pharaoh's Nubian tax collector and has visited Punt on many occasions. Though physically repelled by Neshi's black skin and Negroid features, Hat-Shep-Sut approves of her consort's selection.

"What dangers will my trade mission experience in Punt?" Pharaoh asks Neshi.

"Great *Living God*, I have traveled to Punt with a *Unit of Ten*," Neshi says from his bowed position. "None have troubled me. The king of Punt has no army. He and his people live to eat. They waddle about and allow anyone to take what they please from their land."

"What is there in Punt that others have not picked over?" Hat-Shep-Sut sniffs.

"Majesty," Neshi assures Pharaoh, "I will bring such treasures from Punt that all will wonder in amazement."

"How do you propose to accomplish your boast?" she asks imperiously.

"We will caravan the wealth of Punt across Nubia's eastern desert, load it onto barges at Dakka, above the Fourth Cataract,"

Neshi declares, "and, before the moon is half hidden, place Punt's treasures at Pharaoh's feet."

Hat-Shep-Sut has second thoughts about forcibly entering a peaceful land for the purpose of raiding and pillaging. The reason Neshi seems so repellent is because she fears that the people of Punt will *see Pharaoh* in the image of *Neshi*.

You see what you make me do? Hat-Shep-Sut glares over at her Grand Vizier.

But by claiming the Land of Punt's wealth, Hat-Shep-Sut will show Karnak and the entire Two-Lands that Pharaoh can inhale the wealth of a far land in one breath. But Hat-Shep-Sut knows that, regardless what her trade mission to Punt brings back, her court will not forget the wines, the horses nor the slaves, recently acquired from across the Sinai. She will need something even more dramatic to make her council forget about Senen-Mut's market-places and return to the old traditions of unconditional obedience to Pharaoh's will.

"When do you leave?" Hat-Shep-Sut asks her newly appointed her viceroy to Punt.

"Within three moons, Majesty," Neshi replies.

"Pen-Nek-Heb," Hat-Shep-Sut declares, "you have rendered faithful service to Pharaoh in recommending a trade mission to the Land of Punt." Pharaoh flashes Senen-Mut a contemptuous look. "For this you have earned Pharaoh's gratitude and thanks. Let all in my council know that when this Neshi delivers to Pharaoh the wealth of Punt, the *Aten* will be granted his full share."

The co-Regent is pleased with this new adventure.

"Is there a prospect for battle?" Thut-Moses, asks, smiling at Aron

"If there is, I'll be pleased."

Thut-Moses loves carnage and enjoys killing. And during battle he likes having Aron, his muscular, battle-tested comrade, at his side.

"Hat-Shep-Sut can remain Pharaoh as long as she pleases," Thut-Moses shouts out, "just as long as I have war!"

Aron decides not remind the co-Regent that the trade mission to Punt is to be peaceful and killing, even killing unarmed nomads in isolated settlements, is not easy. During his *War Against Pharaoh's Enemies*, Thut-Moses learns that superior numbers, advanced weapons, ample supplies and accurate information about the enemy, wins battles.

"Take no prisoners and seize all their belongings!" Thut-Moses orders his soldiers.

But sometimes the headmen and even the nomarchs themselves, warn the squatters about his pending attack. Often the squatters put up a fight. His soldiers can't just charge headlong into their settlements without a plan. Thut-Moses and Aron favor the *"pincer movement"* launching their attacks by surprise and from two separate locations. The chariots charge from one direction and drive the squatters into a line of oncoming infantry. Thut-Moses intends to use the same tactics against the king of Punt. Thut-Moses invites Neshi to *Horus Nest*.

"We will transport the army in great sailing ships from Memphis over the canal connecting the Nile to the Red Sea at Al-Quseir," Thut-Moses announces. "We will follow Pharaoh Men-Tu-Hotep's route."

"Lord," Neshi warns Thut-Moses, "you may take your army by sea, but so many animals on such a long voyage _____." The black man pauses; he does not want to seem insolent.

"What do you suggest viceroy?" Aron asks understanding how seasick the animals can become.

"Barges, Great Lord," Neshi replies. "Barges up the Nile to Dakka and a caravan across the eastern desert to Punt."

"Barges up the Nile?" Thut-Moses replies. "I cannot transport an army of five thousand men in barges, march them across the desert and then ask them to fight a war."

"But Great Lord, how will we bring back the wealth of Punt, if your great ships sailing the Red Sea carries your army and your supplies?"

Thut-Moses frowns.

"He's right, you know," Aron says. "My horses will be unfit for over a week after being such long time at sea."

"I want my army in Punt," Thut-Moses declares. "I don't want to be at the mercy of those savages."

"Then why not take your army by ship," Neshi suggests, "and allow me to take transport barges up the Nile. We can caravan the wealth of Punt back to Dakka and your army can return home the way it came, by ship."

"That way," Aron interjects, "I can transport my horses and chariots by barge and they will be prepared for war when we meet you."

"Another pincer movement, eh, my friend?" Thut-Moses smiles.

"Yes Lord," Aron replies, but the chariot captain is apprehensive.

"What is it?" Thut-Moses asks.

"Lord, we will have overwhelming numbers, superior weapons and more than enough supplies, but ___," Aron says.

"But, what?"

"We have no intelligence," Aron observes. "We know nothing about the land or the people of Punt. Neshi is our only source of information."

"And ___?"

"This is a weakness in our plan of attack."

Neshi intercedes to put Aron at ease.

"The people of Punt are peaceful," Neshi assures him. "They have no army. Even the weakest Nubian tribe, wandering onto their land, takes whatever it will."

"You see?" Thut-Moses tells Aron. "Don't worry! Neshi has all the information we need."

So in the second week of Athyr, Akhet's third month, the season of flooding, a flotilla of great sailing vessels, each powered by three banks of oars, transport Thut-Moses' five-thousand man army from Memphis over the Al-Quseir canal to the Red Sea. Bedouin line the banks at Al-Quseir to watch the great fleet pass. None can remember such a sight and afterwards the Bedouin construct their calendar from the day Pharaoh's wondrous fleet passes down the Red Sea.

For their part, Aron and Neshi board a nearly as impressive fleet of river barges transporting the thousand animals, wagons and carts, up to the Fourth Cataract, where they land at Dakka, on the Nile's eastern shore and disgorge themselves an to cross over Nubia's eastern desert to the Land of Punt.

When he was a tax collector, the Nubians allowed Neshi and his bodyguard to travel about their tribal lands unmolested. Neshi always *"misplaces"* a third of Pharaoh's taxes when he lodged as the 'guest' of a Nubian headman. This accounts for Neshi never being molested. Seeing Waters also accompany Neshi's caravan through the Nubian tribal lands. The *Seeing Waters* report on groups of tribesmen who watch the caravan, coveting the horses, oxen and donkeys. But the tribesmen, who have no horses of their own, fear the Egyptian chariots.

Yet even as Neshi, crosses his land, as Nubian chieftain observes their transit.

"The caravan is not yet loaded with the wealth of Punt," he tells his followers. "Prepare for when the Egyptians return."

It is the last month of Akhet. The massive Egyptian fleet pulls into the harbor of Punt and disgorges its thousands of soldiers. The rather surprised king expresses his joy and welcomes his visitors. Days later, the king is again 'surprised' by numberless chariots leading an invasion of ox-drawn wagons and donkey carts out of the eastern desert. The king of Punt and his wife gather their people together and hold a festival in the Egyptian's honor.

For a week, the King of Punt entertains Pharaoh's trade mission. The food is overflowing and the entertainment, lavish. Aron directs an artist scribe to capture the image of the Queen of Punt upon a papyrus scroll for Pharaoh's amusement. The scribe sketches the queen's fat, double-chinned figure with a distinctly curved spine, tree stump legs and arms from which the flesh sags down at the elbows. Hat-Shep-Sut finds the Queen of Punt's image so extraordinary that she orders its likeness to be transferred to a wall of her funerary temple at Deir el Bahri.

Once the feasting and entertainment is completed, Thut-Moses' soldiers and Aron chariots stand guard for a quarter moon while Neshi meticulously loots the wealth of Punt. He plunders orchards of Punt's rare and valuable ebony, frankincense and myrrh trees. He raids storehouses filled with animal skins and ivory tusks as well as cages filled with exotic birds and rare species of monkey. Pharaoh's viceroy fills chests with silver, lapis lazuli and malachite, as well as diamonds, rubies and emeralds taken in trade over centuries. Pens containing short horned cattle, ostriches, peacocks, spotted leopards and lions are raided and the animals seized. Neshi's men even snatch black pygmies living among the people of Punt and cram them into cages, like animals.

"These will make special additions to Pharaoh's household," Neshi gloats to Thut-Moses.

Neshi does not give the king of Punt gold in exchange for his goods, rather he offers the king a selection obsolete copper knives and baskets of colored beads. The Africans' well-known addiction for adorning themselves is shared by the king of Punt. He is delighted with the colored beads and willingly parts with his wealth. Neshi believes the king is wise to accept the Egyptian gifts. The king trades the Egyptians for more than just beads. He is trading for *his life*. Nevertheless, the king willingly accepts baskets of cowry shells, valued so highly by Africans.

It takes Neshi two weeks to pack the wealth of Punt onto the donkey carts, oxen-drawn carriages and the backs of Nubian bearers.

Eugene Stovall

"Great Lord," Neshi finally informs Thut-Moses, "the wealth of Punt has been loaded and is now being transported back across the eastern desert."

"Begin boarding the ships," Thut-Moses orders his ship captains.

So begins the trek home. Neshi's caravan stretches several *iteru* in the distance before the last carriages, carts and bearers depart the Land of Punt.

On the final day, Thut-Moses' prepares to take leave of Aron and board his great transport ship. The army is already aboard. "Are you certain that you can get this caravan to Dakka?" Thut-Moses asks Aron, watching carts and wagons disappear over the western horizon. "This doesn't look as easy as I thought."

Aron's chariot officers try to keep the chaos to a minimum. Assembling the oxen drivers, the donkey carts and bearers in a line of march. Thut-Moses notices that little care given to proper groupings and signs of chaos are everywhere.

"My men are capable," Aron says. "We will deliver the wealth of Punt to Dakka."

"I know you will," Thut-Moses laughs, "because I'm coming with you."

CHAPTER TWENTY-TWO

"We've got a problem!"

Iby stands in front of Senen-Mut's desk; a frown has replaced his normal grin. His master scrutinizes Pharaoh's plans to dismantle her grandparent's sanctuary.

She wants her processional path to extend directly from her Red Chapel at Karnak to her funerary temple at Deir el-Bahri. Though her grandparents' temple is Karnak's only monument to the first pharaoh of the eighteenth dynasty, it stands in the way of her processional path and Hat-Shep-Sut wants it removed. It's not the first monument that Hat-Shep-Sut sacrifices to her own vanity. She caused a scandal at her court that lasted months when she ordered demolished Aak's simple gateway memorial to make room for her own twin obelisks. Few commoners complain, however. Her building projects feed and house thousands of laborers and their families. Hapu-Seneb finds Pharaoh's continual improvement of the commoner's lives as well as the general prosperity throughout the Two-Lands appalling.

"What's the problem, my friend?" Senen-Mut asks raising his eyes from Hat-Shep-Sut's plans.

"Watchers report Nubian warriors gathering in the eastern desert," Iby reports.

"So?" Senen-Mut frowns irritated at the interruption.

"The watchers say the Nubians plan to attack Pharaoh's trade mission when it leaves Punt."

Senen-Mut puts the plans down and gives Iby his full attention. "How reliable is the report?"

Eugene Stovall

"Very," Iby replies.

"You must be joking," Senen-Mut says.

But one look at his friend's face tells the Grand Vizier that this is no joke.

"Why would the Nubians attack Thut-Moses?" Senen-Mut asks. "They can't be that foolish."

"Possibly the wealth of Pharaoh's caravan is too tempting."

"A Nubian has no need for Pharaoh's wealth in the afterlife," Senen-Mut observes.

"Neither does an Egyptian," Iby replies, "but their wealth is packed in their tombs, nonetheless."

Iby smirks. Senen-Mut ignores the heresy.

"Thut-Moses took five thousand infantry and how many chariots? Senen-Mut asks.

"One thousand."

"There you see," Senen-Mut smiles, "the Nubians couldn't possibly be dumb enough to attack five thousand infantry supported by a thousand chariots."

"Thut-Moses sent the infantry back up the Red Sea, the way they came," Iby counters. "Only chariots escort Pharaoh's caravan back across the eastern desert."

Senen-Mut rises from his table. His brow wrinkles as he ponders the situation.

"How did that happen?"

"He had no choice other than sending his infantry back by ship," Iby explains. "They carry barely enough food and water to get the caravan across the desert; they haven't enough supplies for five thousand soldiers. Thut-Moses had no choice other than to send his infantry back to *Horus Nest* by way of the Red Sea."

"Didn't they plan their trip before they left?"

"The infantry was sent as a precaution against the king of Punt's army, not the Nubians," Iby replies. "Neither Thut-Moses nor Aron planned for a Nubian attack."

"The king of Punt has no army," Senen-Mut snaps. "Everybody knows that!"

"Apparently neither Thut-Moses, Aron nor Neshi knew it."

"But Neshi must have known it," Iby repeats. "Aron chose him because he made several trips to Punt and knew the King of Punt, personally.

Senen-Mut analyzes the situation for a while before coming to a conclusion.

"It was unwise of Thut-Moses to split off his infantry from his caravan, but his thousand chariots should still easily beat off any Nubian attack. The distance is short enough that Thut-Moses should reach the safety of the royal barges before the Nubians can assemble enough fighters to overcome a thousand chariots."

"Their poor planning is equaled by their poor intelligence," Iby remarks. "The watchers estimate that two hundred Nubian tribes, nearly five thousand Nubians, will attack."

"You're telling me that every tribe in Nubia are marshalling to attack Pharaoh's mission to the Land of Punt?"

"Yes!" Iby says. "That's what I'm telling you."

Senen-Mut can't believe it.

"Who issued the call? They don't have a king. Why didn't the *Eyes of Horus* warn us?"

"If you recall, the *Eyes of Horus* were not included in the planning," Iby sniffs. "My reports are from watchers already in Nubia."

"Then Pharaoh must have been betrayed!"

Iby nods, "I agree, Master or else _____."

"Or else what?" Senen-Mut replies.

"Or else it's Pharaoh's co-Regent who has been betrayed!"

Medjay scouts inform Thut-Moses of the Nubian tribesmen gathering in his rear. It's the second day and the trade mission's trek out of the Land of Punt has been very slow.

"Do you think they're hostile?" Thut-Moses asks Pharaoh's viceroy.

Neshi hesitates.

"Speak!" Aron commands. "Do these tribesmen intend to attack us?"

Though the Nubians are on foot, they are traveling fast. However, chariot thrusts frighten away the relatively few numbers of Nubian warriors for now.

"One never knows what a Nubian might do," Neshi offers.

"I read on a map that there is a low-lying fortress close by, within easy reach of Dakka," Aron says. "Is it still there?"

"Yes, master," Neshi answers. "Pharaoh Sen-Wos-Ret built several fortresses after conquering Nubia. Most of them, including Baki have been abandoned since the 13th Dynasty."

"Why didn't you mention hostile Nubian tribes during our planning sessions," Thut-Moses asks the little black man.

Neshi looks over at Thut-Moses from his litter.

"Nubians are always hostile," he shrugs. "I recall that my predecessor and his entire Unit of Ten disappeared while visiting a Nubian village. The disappearance of Egyptian tax collectors and their escorts is not a rare occurrence. This is why I did not think it worth mentioning. Besides, you were bringing five thousand soldiers and a thousand chariots how could a few Nubian tribes be of any concern to the Egyptian army?"

Aron had a premonition of danger even before they had departed Punt. His premonition prompted him to suggest they load as much of the wealth of Punt as possible, including the pygmy slaves, onto the transport ships. At the time, Thut-Moses laughed at his friend's caution, but now they are both happy not to have the pigmies along.

"Those little people could never keep up, if we were attacked," Aron had told Thut-Moses.

"Who do you expect to attack us?" Thut-Moses asks.

"I don't know, but I've got a feeling about this return trip," Aron replies.

"What you are feeling is the excitement of another adventure, my friend," Thut-Moses laughs. "Pray that Horus guides our way and that Amen blesses our journey."

But it is Aron's premonition that convinces Thut-Moses to lead Pharaoh's trade mission loaded with the wealth of Punt back across the eastern desert, personally.

As Ra nears his midday height, the great caravan stretches out and disappears over both horizons. The oxen, and donkey carts raise great clouds of dust that can be seen *iteru* away.

"Aron!" Thut-Moses calls out.

"Master."

"Instruct your captains to pull the caravan up tighter. Shorten the column by broadening the front!"

"Yes Master."

"Within the hour, I want to see the last of the caravan in the front of the eastern horizon," Thut-Moses orders. "Am I clear?"

"Yes, Lord."

If after only two days journey, they're strung all over the desert, like this, Thut-Moses muses, *before its over they'll be stretched from the Nile all the way back to Punt. Then even Amen will be unable to save us from a Nubian attack!*

He watches Aron's charioteers ordering the plodding oxen, cajoling donkey carriages and forcing the African porters to move closer and faster. It's a nearly hopeless task. Aron rejoins Thut-Moses.

"We should just stop and let the stragglers catch up," he says.

"No," Thut-Moses replies.

Only one day away from the Red Sea's cooling breezes and here in the eastern desert Amen's rays burn the skin of man and beast. Even barren rock crumbles into dust under the searing heat of Amen's blazing rays. The sun burns gaunt, moisture-starved shrubs and twists plant life into a prickly landscape. Sometimes sand devils, living, thinking masses of dirt and grit, coil up from nowhere, enveloping and consuming everything in their domain. Wind driven sand finds its way into every orifice of the men's bodies. Sand gets into their mouths and chokes off their breath. Sand blows into an animal's mouth so quickly that the beast suffocates. And the sun and sand are not the only miseries. The caravan must contend with pests and creatures, as well.

Flying insects seek moisture everywhere, eyes, nose and mouth. They even get between the legs. Though scorpions and snakes seek after small prey, people and beasts pay the price for being in the way. Scorpions strike before anyone notices that they are about. Snakes slither and hide, waiting to catch its victim unawares. Yet these are minor inconveniences considering the increasing numbers of Nubian warriors steadily marching towards Thut-Moses caravan. His Medjay scouts confirm that the Nubians are hostile and intend to seize the wealth of Punt and take Egyptian lives.

After offering up an evening prayer at the day's end, Thut-Moses gathers his chariot captains together with Neshi and Aron. The officers are exhausted, but they have pulled the caravan together. Thut-Moses served with these officers in the *War Against Pharaoh's Enemies the North*. He trusts them and he is proud of the work they have done today. Already cook fires burn and meals are being prepared, but Thut-Moses must ask even more.

"Men, you did well today," Thut-Moses announces, "but we must put much more distance between the Nubians and ourselves."

There is a shuffling of feet, and some inaudible sounds.

"Listen to my instructions," Thut-Moses continues. "After everyone has eaten, I want to resume our march throughout the night." A groan escapes one of his officers. Neither Aron nor Neshi speaks. "Also I want everyone riding; no one is to walk. Is that understood?"

"But, Lord," Aron interrupts, "where are we to put them? The carts and wagons are full. And we cannot disturb the animals with riders sitting on their cages."

"Put them in chariots, if you must," Thut-Moses replies, "but I want everyone riding tonight."

Thut-Moses knows this night march will make the difference between defeat and victory. This march will be a test of will between the Egyptian charioteers and Nubian rabble.

"Allow all cook fires to remain burning even after we break camp. I want the Nubians to believe we've camped for the night."

After his men eat and, with only the stars as guides, Thut-Moses goads his caravan back into motion heading towards the ancient fortress of Baki. Thut-Moses continues to shorten the length of his caravan by broadening his front as wide as he dares. Men and animals groan from lack of rest. But the tactic works. Believing their quarry is within easy reach, the Nubians camp for the night, resting from their day's march on foot and preparing for the next day's battle. The distance Thut-Moses puts between himself and his Nubian pursuers is the difference between slaughter and survival. Sometime after sunrise, Thut-Moses' scouts find a great depression in the desert terrain. Here Thut-Moses allows his exhausted men and animals to rest.

The depression, in an otherwise level plain of rock and sand, appears once to have been an oasis. But now a few drooping palms and some low-lying shrubs are the only indications that water ever existed here. The depression affords shade and concealment. So when the Nubians stir from their camp, they are surprised to find that the Egyptians have vanished. And Neshi brings Thut-Moses even more good news.

"Baki is less than a day's journey away," he announces. "Thank, Amen," Thut-Moses replies, silently. The co-Regent is thankful to have survived what could have been a nasty crisis hatched by Nubians who would have loved to revenge themselves on those who have oppressed them for centuries.

"We shall rest until Amen is two hours past his midday heights," Thut-Moses instructs his officers. "Then we shall march to Baki."

Thut-Moses watches the exhausted men and animals pour into the depression.

"Allow neither man nor beast to sleep before being fed and watered," Aron instructs his officers. "There will be no time to eat after they wake."

It takes the better part of two hours for the entire caravan to settle safely inside the dry oasis. Despite Aron's instructions, many of the exhausted charioteers, after seeing to their weary horses, forego food, themselves and sleep where they fall.

"How far away are the Nubians?" Thut-Moses asks his Medjay.

"They are five *iteru* away," the leader replies. "Your night march surprised them. They remained in camp from early evening until late morning."

"Do they march now?"

"Yes, Lord."

"How soon will they be at this place?"

"Their advance groups should be here by the time Amen is at his noonday rest," the scout estimates, "the entire mass will arrive when Amen begins his late afternoon descent."

"How well can they fight after marching through Ra's cauldron?" Thut-Moses asks.

The scouts are silent.

"Answer your master," Aron orders.

"Who knows how or when a Nubian will fight?" the Medjay leader shrugs. "We would not have believed so many would have followed this far."

"Okay!" Thut-Moses says, abruptly. "I want you to keep a close watch on the advanced party. I want to know when they are close. I want to know if the advance party camps or intends to attack. I want to know everything about what they are doing. Is that clear?"

"Yes, Lord."

"And I need numbers. How many are in the advanced party? Understand?"

"Yes, Lord."

"See to it!"

The Medjay 'kiss the dust' at Thut-Moses feet and back out of the tent and return to their horses. The arduous march seems not to have bothered them in the least. They glory in their role as Thut-Moses' *eyes and ears.*

Thut-Moses turns to Aron. "We must attack the Nubians before they attack us," he tells his lieutenant. "I want you to arrange it."

Aron can't believe what he is hearing. "My men and horses are exhausted from last night's journey, Lord, " Aron hesitates. "All my chariots were overloaded. They cannot attack!"

Thut-Moses gives Aron a calm look and a pat on the shoulder.

"I need you and your men to attack and disperse their advanced party," he says quietly. "We have no choice. If the Nubians mass, they'll overrun us. We must attack and scatter them before they mass." Thut-Moses stares at Aron. "Do you understand?"

"Yes, Master." Aron says. To his surprise, Aron discovers that his obedience gives him strength.

"Prepare two hundred chariots for an attack on the advanced group of Nubian fighters as they approach our rear," Thut-Moses orders. "They should be tired from their march and easily routed by your surprise attack."

"Yes, Master!"

"Plan it well!" Thut-Moses instructs. "Two hours after Amen reaches his height, I want the captains that you choose to lead this attack, here in my tent."

"Yes Master!" Aron says. "What of the remainder of my chariots?"

"Keep them in the rear," Thut-Moses instructs. "They are to form a barrier between the caravan and the Nubians. As the caravan continues towards Baki, you will rotate your chariots in groups of two hundred. Each will harass and disperse the Nubians, in turn. Do you understand?"

"Yes, Master!"

"Then go and see to my instructions."

Aron clenches his fists and crosses his arms in a salute before departing. Thut-Moses turns to Neshi. "I want this caravan moving two hours after Amen has reaches his height, understand?"

Neshi bows, "Yes Master."

"Appoint assistants and bring them to my tent. I will instruct them. Now go!"

Neshi "kisses the dust" and departs.

Overhead, Amen's rays, finger their way out of the east. Though he believes that Amen is indifferent to the petty affairs of men, Thut-Moses calls for a priest to conduct the morning rituals, just in case. The rites also give the co-Regent confidence.

Baki is not far away, and my chariots should keep them from massing, until we get there. Thut-Moses already visualizes the cheering crowds and a grateful Pharaoh welcoming him back to Thebes bearing the wealth of Punt.

Whoever planned this Nubian attack, miscalculated, Thut-Moses smiles to himself. When he returns to *Horus Nest* he will regale old veterans of the great wars, now commanding his regiments and sitting on his *War Council,* with tales of this adventure in the eastern desert. But even as Thut-Moses enjoys his self-congratulations, a Medjay scout enters his tent to deliver a chilling report.

"Great Lord," the Medjay says, "The Nubians are massing *in front of us.*"

"Where?" Thut-Moses asks.

"Between our front and the Nile."

"How many and how far away are they?" Thut-Moses asks.

"They are not far away and their number is as grain in a field blessed by Hapi," the scout replies.

Too late! Thut-Moses now knows, that the Nubians have set a clever trap ____ and he is caught.

Senen-Mut's reaction to the Nubian threat is immediate. He mobilizes the palace guard bivouacked upriver at the *Nek-Heb Valley* army camp. Within hours, a guard regiment clambers aboard swift transport barges being readied to speed upriver to Dakka. Senen-Mut supplies the regiment with grain, wine and extra weapons. Healer priests and acolytes from Sekhmet's temple take their own barges along with supplies of linens and unguents to dress battle wounds. Horses and chariots are loaded upon their own specially designed transports. Once the rescue mission has been loaded, the flotilla of barges unfurls its sails, embroidered with Pharaohs crimson red insignias, casts off its moorings and glides away from the docks and out into the harbor. Aboard each barge, a single bank of rowers, bend their backs, pulling together according to the steersman's song. Shu is favorable. He billows out the barges' great linen sails, speeding them upstream like flock of falcons, intent upon its prey.

Hapu-Seneb fidgets with the writing quills on his table. First he arranges and then re-arranges his inkpots. Now he plays with his writing shards and sheets of papyrus. The priest awaits news of the fate of Pharaoh's trade mission. Already his *Seeing Waters* reported the mobilization of the Palace Guard Regiment at the Nek-Heb Valley and their deployment upriver.

"It is believed that the regiment is headed to Nubia," they report.

Since then, however, nothing! Hapu-Seneb has no idea *how* his plan is progressing.

Of course, it wasn't my plan, he reminds himself. *It was the will of the Living God.*

Nevertheless, the high priest still frets that, if something goes wrong, he will go the way of his predecessors.

An acolyte escorts a *Seeing Waters* messenger into Hapu-Seneb's chambers. Impatiently, the priest waves the acolyte away. Rise up!" the priest tells the messenger 'kissing the dust' at his feet, "What news have you?"

"My master is the overseer of the *Seeing Waters* assigned to Pharaoh's trade mission," the messenger begins.

"Yes, yes! I know," Hapu-Seneb says impatiently. "Tell me of their progress."

"Pharaoh's soldiers have departed the Land of Punt upon the Red Sea, Master."

"What of the co-Regent?"

"The Great Lord, the Crown Prince, Thut-Moses brings the caravan with Punt's wealth across the eastern desert."

"Everyone in Thebes, knows this," Hapu-Seneb says. "Why do you try my patience? What other news have you brought me?"

Eugene Stovall

The messenger looks from side to side to be certain they are alone. "My master says that all Nubia will celebrate Punt before the next full moon."

"You tell your master that they had better be celebrating sooner than that or else another Nubian will find himself draped over the prow of Pharaoh's barge and floating head-first in the Nile."

The messenger 'kisses the dust' and departs. Pen-Nek-Heb waits outside in the hallway. From the grim look on the messenger's face, Pen-Nek-He surmises that Hapu-Seneb's plot is not going well.

Priests make poor conspirators, Aten reminds himself. They have no understanding of what motivates human behavior. This is what differentiates Pen-Nek-Heb from Hapu-Seneb and all the other priests. Pen-Nek-Heb understands that the people behave according to what they know which is good. People are not animals who must be trained to obey their master's will. *Nor can the new epoch emerge by treachery against the co-Regent.*

Of this, Pen-Nek-Heb is certain. Priests are only clever at planning conspiracies. Never are they clever at carrying them out. Pen-Nek-Heb strides into Hapu-Seneb's chambers, unannounced. Amen seems not to be surprised.

"Have you met with success," Pen-Nek-Heb asks, "or must the Aten prepare for the punishing blow of *Pharaoh's Flail?*"

"No word has come, yet," Amen murmurs, slouching down into his high-back chair, irritated by Pen-Nek-Heb's unwelcome appearance.

"I return to Iunu," Pen-Nek-Heb announces. "There is little more that I can do here. You've received as much of my assistance for your schemes as I am willing to give." He searches Hapu-Seneb's face, but decides that either Hapu-Seneb has learned to hide his thoughts, better, or he doesn't know any more about what's happening in Nubia's eastern desert than Pen-Nek-Heb. He decides it's the latter.

But Hapu-Seneb misinterprets Pen-Nek-Heb's look.

"Are you gloating?" he asks. "Do you believe that Amen is facing Pharaoh's wrath, *alone?*"

Hapu-Seneb wrinkles his nose trying to pull his face back into a snarl. Pen-Nek-Heb thinks that Hapu-Seneb is about to sneeze.

"My *Seeing Waters* have made certain that your name is added to the list of crusaders against Pharaoh's heresy."

"Is that so?" Pen-Nek-Heb smiles.

"Yes!" Hapu-Seneb smirks. "Not only has the *Aten's* opposition to the *War Against Pharaoh's Enemies in the North* been noted, but you are now associated with the Nubian attacks on Pharaoh's trade mission that have jeopardized the life of the co-Regent."

"I am certain it was done even before the ink was dry on the papyrus that I signed in support of your cause," Pen-Nek-Heb says.

"And that Thoth witnessed," Hapu-Seneb sneers, glaring arrogantly at his intruder. "So I would not be so quick to gloat, if I were you!"

Once more the hate between the *Aten* and Amen boils to the surface. It's as if one of them has released stomach gas and is polluting the air with a stench that both must breathe.

"*And that Thoth witnessed,*" Pen-Nek-Heb repeats. "This means that you announced my support for your treason, *even before I agreed to support you.* How well you deserve your reputation for treachery."

"Treachery! I'm treacherous?" Hapu-Seneb sneers. "Pharaoh murders priests as if they were common criminals."

The high priest of Iunu pulls himself up into a stately pose. Giving Hapu-Seneb neither the courtesy of a reply nor the customary bow, Pen-Nek-Heb turns on his heel and strides out of Hapu-Seneb's chambers. Unconcerned with the high priest of Iunu at the moment, Amen returns to worrying over events being played out on in Nubia's eastern desert.

Nubians are massing in Thut-Moses' front and rear. They appear like a great shadow stretching out across the desert, absorbing the land, bit by bit. In this way, black skinned warriors intend to absorb Thut-Moses' caravan and the wealth of Punt.

Thut-Moses calls Aron and Neshi to his tent and orders them to have the chariots form a perimeter and squeeze everyone and everything, wagons, carts, animals, drivers, handlers and porters, inside. The next hour is chaos. Men and beasts jostle each other frantically avoiding the chariots herding them together. Inside the perimeter, great clouds of dust and sand rise into the air. Everyone is choking and gasping for breath. Excess baggage, food, tents even water, is left behind. Only the wealth of Punt is protected from the attack of black-skinned warriors, garbed in colorful feathers and animal skins and brandishing crude knives and wave wooden spears and powerful bows. But even as they mass in their thousands, Egyptian charioteers protected by helmet and body armor, armed with razor sharp bronze weapons weave back and forth among their advancing ranks hacking, gouging and slashing through skin and bone with every stroke. The tribesmen, screaming out in hatred and pain, fill the air with a cacophony of frenzied yells and shrieks.

Some of Neshi's Nubian bearers panic. They drop their burdens and run out to meet the onrushing Nubian warriors. Every one of the Nubians who worked for the hated Egyptians is beaten and gored with wooden spears. A triumphant yell rises into the air as the heads of the bearers are affixed to poles and paraded about.

The Nubians venture nearer, but they seem undecided about how to attack. For the time being the feathered warriors do little more than jump up and down, shrieking their war cries.

"They fear our chariots," Aron comments.

Thut-Moses bellows out to his officers. "Hear my words! Get as many behind Baki's walls as you can?"

As bad as the situations seems, his officers are unwilling to leave the wealth of Punt for the Nubians to save donkey cart drivers, ox herds and bearers.

"Some of this plunder belongs to us," one mutters under his breath.

His fellow officer nods in agreement.

Thut-Moses is not happy. He repeats himself.

"*I said* that we are going to get everyone behind Baki's walls, *is that understood?*"

"Yes, Lord!" This time officers and men shout back in unison.

"That's better," Thut-Moses says.

His confidence is infectious and his fearlessness is inspiring. Thut-Moses gives Aron further instructions. "I want the chariots to wield together to face the Nubian's between us and Baki in a spear-shape formation," he explains. "Then I want you to drive a double wedge through them clear to Baki." Thut-Moses looks to Neshi. "As the spear moves forward, I want your leaders to move their people forward with the oxen and wagons out on the flanks. Keep your porters and donkeys as close to the oxen as possible."

Neshi's sun-darkened face has turned ashen grey. Fear dulls his eyes and causes his body to tremble. Nevertheless, the viceroy, bows to Thut-Moses, and goes out to issue instructions to his overseers.

Thut-Moses turns back to Aron. "Move your chariots slowly like a moving shield. Fill in your gaps between the oxen and chariots as quickly as possible." Thut-Moses gazes into the distance as if to bring the fortress of Baki, closer. "Remember your chariots must not move too quickly, otherwise those sons of Seth will move inside our defenses through the spaces on our flanks. By the time the chariots have completely penetrated, only the oxen should remain at the rear. All the other animals must be up front. Is that understood?"

Aron nods, but he really has no idea how Thut-Moses' plan is supposed to work or what he's supposed to do.

When the time comes, Thut-Moses assembles all his officers. "You know what you must do," he says staring at each man individually. All salute with a short bow and arms crossed. Aron and his officers board their chariots and return to their men. Thut-Moses goes to his knees, prays to Amen, then climbs into his own chariot and orders the driver to move to the point of the attack.

But even with Thut-Moses' well-laid plans, nothing goes right. As soon as Aron's chariots charge and the bowmen discharge their arrows, the Nubians scatter, fleeing in all directions. Charioteers, wielding sword, spear and arrow with deadly efficiency, give chase, cutting a wide swath through the feathered humanity, killing them by the hundreds. The slaughter continues until Thut-Moses recalls his men. But the Nubians reform into another mass and block the caravan's escape route to Baki. Once again, Thut-Moses hurls his chariots directly at the massing Nubians. This time, rather than fleeing, the tribesmen put up a fierce resistance. All along the line of battle, dark-skinned warriors engage in hand-to-hand combat, striking with their wooden spears at horses and charioteers, alike. But their courage is as wasted as their attack; the Nubians are overmatched. Wooden spears and wooden arrows glance harmlessly off of body armor and head protection while the charioteers serve out pain and death with every stroke. Small bands of Nubians maneuver past the chariots and attack the center of the caravan. Black warriors fall upon the defenseless ox herds and cart drivers. Charioteers rush to their defense. The Nubians are hacked to pieces. Once again, the Nubians retreat from the battlefield allowing the caravan to make good its westward escape. And before Amen begins his late-afternoon swift descent below the western horizon, Thut-Moses' leading elements of caravan reach the safety of Baki's protective walls.

Three days later, Senen-Mut's palace guard regiment arrives at Dakka. Once the horses recover, the regiment attacks and disperses the remaining Nubian fighters back to their tribal lands, while Thut-Moses oversees the loading of the wealth of Punt onto royal transport barges and transports it back to Thebes.

CHAPTER TWENTY-THREE

The fool promised me his plan was foolproof.

"You will be rid of the Crown Prince and your Grand Vizier, at the same time," he said. But once more that commoner interferes with my plans, Is there no one upon whom I can depend?

Hat-Shep-Sut awaits the return of Thut-Moses and Aron at Thebes' ceremonial dock in full view of the masses. She poses serenely upon her dais as if she is pleased they survived the attack in the eastern desert. But Hat-Shep-Sut knows they're not all fools. Someone is certain to suspect her.

Well, stiff upper lip, she tells herself, *I must see it through.*

Neferu-Re accompanies her mother to the royal dock.

"Here comes our hero, now " Hat-Shep-Sut sneers to her daughter.

Thut-Moses stands erect at the prow of the lead transport barge enjoying a tumultuous welcome from the thousands lining the harbor, hoping to catch a glimpse of Egypt's newest military hero.

"The way the people sing and rejoice," Neferu-Re observes, "you'd think that he was already Pharaoh."

Indeed, everywhere, thousands of Egyptians continually cheer the Crown Prince Thut-Moses, co-Regent of the Two-Lands, who brings the wealth of Punt back to Pharaoh. And when he lands and the wealth of Punt is unloaded, even Thebes' characteristi-cally sober marketplace goes wild with excitement. Never has such a treasure trove from one mission been seen before. The wild ani-mals, bars of silver and chests of precious stones, rare plants and

Eugene Stovall

trees excite and amaze. But when the black pygmies march into view, excitement turns into hysteria. The crowds surge forward to get a closer look at the black men no taller than small children. The "*oohs*" and "*aahs*" ripple back and forth throughout the crowd.

Hat-Shep-Sut leads Thut-Moses' triumphal procession back to Karnak. Few words pass between her and her co-Regent. Neither has she anything to say to her consort. Her thoughts are upon the damage done to her plans for a female dynasty by Amen's *bumbling priest.*

Who will she get to remove Hapu-Seneb for her? she asks herself. Of course, the priest is not the problem. The problem is Senen-Mut.

"Once again your father has done it again," she tells Neferu-Re.

"Amen's priests are right to concern themselves with heresy," Neferu-Re replies.

"Once I establish my absolute rule," Hat-Shep-Sut vows, "I will never allow a vizier or priest to act on their own discretion, again. Nothing will be done without *my approval.*"

"Father really angered you this time, didn't he?" Neferu-Re laughs.

Hat-Shep-Sut glares at her daughter. "When you become Pharaoh, you will be wise to heed this lesson."

Neferu-Re merely practices affecting the enigmatic smile that Iby had taught her. God's Wife finds it strange that though he is a commoner and friend of the father she despises, she is strangely attracted to the Overseer of the *Eyes of Horus.*

The mood in Pharaoh's Great Audience Hall is quiet and business-like. Administrators and scribes cluster about, speaking in hushed whispers. Seated upon her golden throne, in full view, Pharaoh's face is frozen in a mask of serenity. Beneath her mask, she is as firm, resolute and as cold as a granite statue. The time has come for her to do what must be done ____ *what should have been done some time ago.*

Hat-Shep-Sut watches her court with disdain. All are men. Some wear their heads shaved, others wear wigs and still others the leather skullcap with flaps over the ears. Each proudly wears insignias of office dangling from their necks. Pharaoh notes their expensive robes, golden rings and jeweled amulets. All wear the heavy eyeliner; some even wear women's cosmetics.

Why do these men adorn themselves so, she wonders, *if they do not secretly wish to be women?*

Natee lies at his mistress' feet tethered to her throne by a leather rope. The lion senses Hat-Shep-Sut's anxiety. Ever so often he looks about and growls softly. Gradually a quiet descends upon the court. Anticipation of Pharaoh's words muffles the conversations. Then there is complete silence. Finally, confidant that she has their attention, Pharaoh stands.

"My loyal councilors," Hat-Shep-Sut begins, her voice clear and heard by all. "Had it not been for the leadership of the co-Regent and the courage of my Royal consort, the Nubian insurgents would have brought discord to the Two-Lands and anger to the heart of the *Living God.*" She gazes out at her assembled court with mock concern. "How could such an outrage happen?"

The shuffling silence, with the clearing of throats and muffled coughs, is deafening.

"The reason my co-Regent and my viceroy were set upon by black savages," Pharaoh continues, "was because my trusted Grand Vizier and the *Eyes of Horus* lay about sulking in their palace. Not only did they fail to protect my trade mission and the person of the co-Regent, but they failed in their responsibilities to me, their Pharaoh and *Ruler.*"

Murmurs ripple through the court. Fear clutches at the hearts of the timid. The entire council cowers. Pharaoh's words echo about the Great Audience Hall like a thunderclap. Councilors gasp; priests sigh and even pray, aloud. Worry even lines the brows of scribes who are normally immune from court intrigue.

"Though the Grand Vizier and the *Eyes of Horus* have long enjoyed Pharaoh's favor," Hat-Shep-Sut continues, "the harm done to my serenity makes it impossible for either *man* to continue to enjoy my favor."

All eyes turn toward the Grand Vizier. Senen-Mut's head remains erect, his face displays no emotion and his eyes remained fixed firmly upon Pharaoh's awesome, yet beautiful countenance. Senen-Mut gives no indication that Pharaoh's words have made any impact. Positioned among the court officials, Iby, too, maintains an outwardly calm demeanor. His emotions, as usual, masked by a lopsided grin.

Others ___ councilors, administrators and scribes ____ are not as calm. Pharaoh's words terrify them and Hat-Shep-Sut is pleased. Slowly, with the casual nonchalance of someone in full control, Pharaoh looks directly at Senen-Mut giving him a coy smile. Senen-Mut lowers his eyes, not because he feels any disgrace, but out of embarrassment for the mother of his daughter and for the woman, despite everything, that he still loves. Once more she redirects her gaze over the entire assembly.

"For their outstanding heroism and devotion to the *Living God* while engaged in battle with Pharaoh's Nubian enemies," Hat-Shep-Sut announces, "I direct that the *Order of the Golden Fly* accept both Thut-Moses and Aron into their ranks. Furthermore, I direct *God's Wife* to preside over the ceremony. When all is in readiness for their initiation, let the announcement go forward throughout the Two-Lands."

"Great Lord," Hapu-Seneb rises up to speak, "we are your faithful servants and share your grief over the failure of your Grand Vizier, the Lord Senen-Mut to protect the Crown Prince, Thut-Moses and your trade mission to the Land of Punt."

Despite his timid and humble appearance, made more so by the skimpy leopard skin that flaps about his skinny legs, Hapu-Seneb's voice is strong and rings with authority.

"Is your council, then, to understand that the Ruler of the Two-Lands no longer has one to whom she will speak?"

The council strains to hear Pharaoh's response.

"As of now, Pharaoh has no voice," Hat-Shep-Sut announces solemnly. "No longer is the Lord Senen-Mut permitted to speak for Pharaoh concerning her affairs."

The court is mute, stunned into silence. Hat-Shep-Sut rises and, with Natee leading the way, marches out of her Great Audience Hall. Before the echoes of Pharaoh's footsteps against the marble floor die away, the assembly erupts in a babble of excitement. Few of Pharaoh's court actually know what happened in Nubia's eastern desert, but all know that the Grand Vizier and the *Eyes of Horus* sent a regiment of Palace Guard to rescue the beleaguered trade mission. The one person who actually knows the full facts of the matter is Thut-Moses and his stepmother's denunciation of Senen-Mut disturbs him.

Back at the *Palace of Ladies,* Thut-Moses confronts Neferu-Re. "What is your mother planning?"

"Mother is only concerned with your safety, dearest," Neferu-Re replies. "She believes that it was more than a coincidence that you were attacked."

"Even if there was some sort of conspiracy," Thut-Moses replies, "she cannot believe that Senen-Mut had anything to do with it. Besides he was the one who rescued us."

"Yes," Neferu-Re remarks. "He sent out a regiment of palace guard after it was too late. Had it not been for your bravery and the courage of Aron's chariots, the palace guard would have arrived in time to conduct the sacred rites of Anubis over your dead bodies. Is that not so?"

Neferu-Re pours him a cup of wine. "Mother was very concerned when she learned of your danger. And she wants to make certain there are no more threats on your life."

Thut-Moses is not deceived by Neferu-Re's pretence, but he decides to drop the matter for the time being.

A red-robed priest is shown into Senen-Mut's personal chambers at the *Grand Vizier's Palace.*

"My dear friend," Pen-Nek-Heb greets the disgraced former vizier with an affectionate hug.

"I greet the Lord Pen-Nek-Heb," Senen-Mut says, bowing low before the *Aten's* high priest.

"Now, now, none of that," Pen-Nek-Heb says reaching out and raising Senen-Mut up by the elbow. "We have been friends for too long for that kind of nonsense. I came as soon as I could."

"You have always been a true and trusted friend," Senen-Mut replies. He escorts the high priest of the Aten to a cushioned sofa.

"What do you think she's planning?" The old priest stares at Senen-Mut with a mixture of sadness and concern.

"Pharaoh is probably getting bad advice from Neferu-Re," Senen-Mut offers. "Other than that I don't know what she's up to."

Pen-Nek-Heb considers telling Senen-Mut the whole story including his own role in the plot against Thut-Moses. But he thinks better of it.

What good would it do? He asks himself. *Senen-Mut wouldn't believe that Hat-Shep-Sut was behind the Nubian attack. And even if he believed it, he would still excuse her for doing it.*

Pen-Nek-Heb tells part of the story.

"Amen's high priest was behind the attack," Pen-Nek-Heb says. The priest helps himself to the wine offered by a servant.

"How so?" Senen-Mut asks.

"It's simple," Pen-Nek-Heb answers. "Hapu-Seneb wants to be co-Regent."

"That's ridiculous," Senen-Mut laughs.

"Nevertheless, it is so," Pen-Nek-Heb replies.

Senen-Mut decides to share a revelation of his own.

"Hapu-Seneb knows he won't be appointed co-Regent if something happens to Thut-Moses."

"How does he know this?" Pen-Nek-Heb asks.

"Hapu-Seneb knows that Hat-Shep-Sut will appoint Neferu-Re co-Regent, if anything should happen to Thut-Moses," Senen-Mut explains. Pen-Nek-Heb starts to understand. "So, you see, my good friend, you misunderstood Pharaoh's designs, all along."

"She's going to destroy the Two-Lands!" Pen-Nek-Heb says sharply.

"The fate of the Two-Lands happens not to be her immediate concern," Senen-Mut replies.

"What is her concern?" the high priest of Iunu asks.

"She is determined that Neferu-Re succeed her as Pharaoh, *no matter the consequences*."

Pen-Nek-Heb sees how completely these events have taken their toll on his protégé whose face has matured with worry lines prominently etched upon his brow. "But for now," Iunu's priest advises, "there is little you can do here in Karnak. Come back to Iunu with me. Bring Iby with you."

BOOK FOUR

To Pharaoh Maat-Ka-Re Hat-Shep-Sut, Lord of the Two-Lands, Upper and Lower Egypt, my ally who loves me.

From Barattarna, King of Mitanni, Pharaoh's ally who loves her:

It is well with me and may it be well with thee, thy House, and thy daughter, Neferu-Re, May it be well with thy Nomarchs, thy lands, thy chariots, thy horses, thy soldiers and all that is thine. May it be well with thy Gods.

Grievous news has come to thy ally, Barattarna, that his sister, Hipa-Giluk, wife of Thut-Moses, co-Regent, Crown Prince and Royal Heir, hath died mysteriously at her palace in Karnak. Barattarna weeps for his sister and grieves for thee, my ally, Hat-Shep-Sut.

Grievous also to the ears of Barattarna are the reports he hears of events happening in Pharaoh's land. It is said that thy Nomarch's defy thy commands, thy friends fall away and thine enemies advance upon what is thine. Chaos is said to rule your borders and disrespect rules the behavior of Pharaoh's people. Your rule is weak and no one obeys your commands!

Sad to see that your ambition to be Pharaoh exceeds your woman's ability. What have you to do with chariots, soldiers and war? Egypt needs the firm hand of a man. I understand that it is hard for you to turn to Thut-Moses, especially in this time when he grieves over his dead wife and my dead sister, Hipa-Giluk.

Your ally, Barattarna, who grieves for the loss of his sister and over the troubles plaguing your unhappy land, has spent a cycle of the moon, asking his wise men how he may assist his ally during these troubling times. His wise men suggest to Barattarna to say to Pharaoh Maat-Ka-Re Hat-Shep-Sut the following:

There lives in my palace, my daughter, Mad-U-Kilpa, whose beauty is unsurpassed anywhere in my kingdom. Though she is but ten, she hath learning, knowledge and intelligence. Wed the Crown Prince and Royal Heir to my daughter and replace the wife that he has lost. She will be loving and faithful to Thut-Moses until her death. I, Barattarna, King of Mitanni, promise it.

If you, Pharaoh Maat-Ka-Re Hat-Shep-Sut, wed my daughter, Mad-U-Kilpa, to your stepson, Thut-Moses, all will go well in the Two-Lands of Upper and Lower Egypt. My daughter's beauty and happiness will bless the Two-Lands. All will be well between the Kingdom of Mitanni and the Two-Lands of Upper and Lower Egypt, once again, because this marriage will preserve and renew our alliance.

So I say to my ally, whom I love, may the gods cause our friendship to be renewed and prosper. May Teshop, Lord of Mitanni, and Amen, Lord of the Two-Lands, ordain our friendship, eternally, as it was once and should be again.

I further say to Pharaoh, show me your love by sending your ally gold. I ask gold from my ally for two reasons. First, I must have more war equipment though I know I have more than Pharaoh has already. Second, I must have gold as a dowry for my daughter, Mad-U-Kilpa.

So let my ally send me much gold. Since, in my ally's land, gold is as the dust of the earth, I want gold without measure. And may the gods decree that, from the Two-Lands where gold lies about, Mitanni will receive ten times the gold it expects. Certainly the amount of gold that I request will not trouble my ally's heart. Therefore let my ally send me gold without measure and in great quantity. And I will grant my ally all the peace she requires to continue her rule in the Two-Lands when the Crown Prince and the Princess of Mitanni marry and Pharaoh sends me much gold.

CHAPTER TWENTY-FOUR

"The pig!"

Hat-Shep-Sut fumes with anger. But Pharaoh's anger is not as it once was. In earlier times, her anger reached into Amen's temples, into nomarch's palaces and into foreign lands. Then Pharaoh's anger was feared because the *Eyes of Horus* saw everything. None dared disobey Pharaoh Maat-Ka-Re Hat-Shep-Sut and risk her anger. Now, few fear Pharaoh's anger. Instead the people fear her tax collectors ____ and the co-Regent's soldiers.

Throughout the land, corruption rules at every level. Officials and administrators do not seek *Maat*. They seek wealth and status. They seek titles and property. *They seek gold.*

Spies are everywhere but none spy for Pharaoh. Once soldiers accompanied tax collectors only in Nubia, now soldiers accompany tax collectors all over the Two-Lands. Officers and soldiers collect their *fees* along with Pharaoh's taxes. The officers offer their services to priests who believe the people are withholding temple offerings. In some instances, the wealth of Pharaoh's tax collectors exceeds the wealth of Pharaoh's nomarchs. Soldiers take their orders only from officers appointed by the *War Council*. These officers support themselves and their men by living off farmers and laborers.

Once soldiers pledged themselves to Pharaoh by serving the nomarchs. When Pharaoh needed his army, he ordered the nomarchs to send the soldiers they recruited and trained in their nome. Now soldiers serve only Pharaoh's *War Council*. Nomarchs are no longer permitted to have their own soldiers. The *War*

Council orders any soldier serving a nomarch to either report to *Horus Nest* or be designated as *Pharaoh's Enemy*, and killed on sight. The *War Council* rewards officers who assist in eliminating the personal armies of rebellious nomarchs. The army has five infantry regiments, two chariot regiments and three palace guard regiments ____ nearly ten thousand fighting men. The cost of Pharaoh's national army is expensive. Pharaoh's council raises taxes on the temples to maintain the army. Temple granaries become depleted and the priests turn away the people who come to them for food. Nomarchs who protect their villages and farms from the *War Council*'s tax collectors are denounced as *Pharaoh's Enemies* forfeiting their land, their possessions and even their lives. All of this is reported back to Barattarna.

"If I had the chance," Hat-Shep-Sut snaps, "I'd have my surgeon turn Barattarna into a real woman, instead of the false one that he pretends to be."

"Be that as it may, Great Lord," User-Amen says, "we must send a reply to Barattarna, at once."

Pharaoh's Grand Vizier attempts to impress Pharaoh with the gravity of her situation.

"This is all *Senen-Mut*'s fault!" Hat-Shep-Sut shouts, ignoring her new Grand Vizier's advice just as she once ignored Senen-Mut. "If he hadn't created all those marketplaces and given away all that gold to those dreadful asiatics, I wouldn't be having these problems now."

Hat-Shep-Sut and User-Amen meet in her *Seal Room*. User-Amen was Aak's Grand Vizier. When Hat-Shep-Sut came to power, she appointed User-Amen governor of Thebes to create the vacancy that Senen-Mut fills. Hat-Shep-Sut is comfortable with User-Amen. He supports her policy of ridding the northern nomes of asiatic squatters and raising taxes on the temples to support her army. User-Amen is a patient statesman. He is older than Hat-Shep-Sut, and he exercises a calming effect upon her. User-Amen knows Pharaoh hates men. He knows of her ambitions for Neferu-Re, as well. But he handles Pharaoh's affairs patiently and diplomatically, that is to say, he merely does what she asks. But neither his diplomacy nor User-Amen's willingness to cater to Pharaoh's whims can halt the stagnation and corruption eating at the institutions that govern the Two-Lands.

"My new Grand Vizier is just waiting for the council to depose me and proclaim Thut-Moses, Pharaoh," she confides to Neferu-Re.

User-Amen suggests that Pharaoh bring Thut-Moses back to Karnak, before her rule and the eighteenth dynasty completely collapses.

"Your co-Regent continues to declare his devotion to his Lord, the *Living God*," User-Amen reassures her. "Pharaoh's Inner Council, especially those nomarchs concerned with the welfare of Pharaoh's people, hopes that you and your co-Regent will reconcile your differences before it is too late."

Hat-Shep-Sut bristles at her Grand Vizier's recommendation. *Once again they plot to undermine me,* she tells herself. But out loud she says, "Too bad my co-Regent doesn't look like the king of the Mitanni. Then I wouldn't mind having him at my court. It would amuse me to have a silly man like that at my pleasure."

Indeed, the king of the Mitanni is weak, overly indulgent and effeminate. His blue eyes are dulled by excess and indifference. His black oily hair hangs down over a bloated, painted face. Barattarna reminds Hat-Shep-Sut of a fat cow with sagging udders instead of a manly chest. The Mitanni king paints his fingers, toes and lips and wears such a multitude of bangles, rings and bracelets that he competes with the Nubians in adorning his body.

"Barattarna's letter indicates that he knows that Thut-Moses is planning a war," User-Amen says, the urgency of the situation makes his voice quiver. But Hat-Shep-Sut will have none of it.

"If my step-son defeats the Mitanni," Hat-Shep-Sut responds, "what will prevent him from driving me from my throne?" Hat-Shep-Sut is defiant.

"How then, Great Lord, do we to respond to the king of Mitanni?"

Immediately after their investiture into the *Order of the Golden Fly*, Thut-Moses and Aron enjoy a week of banquets and celebrations at Karnak. Afterwards, they board Thut-Moses' royal barge and, amid thunderous cheering from ecstatic crowds, sail leisurely down river back to *Horus Nest*. A week later, the co-Regent's golden barge glides into its moorings at Memphis' military harbor to an even greater crowd of cheering Egyptians welcoming home the Two-Lands' greatest military hero since Sen-Wos-Ret. Thut-Moses descends from his warship to the sound of guardsmen's swords, clanging, rhythmically, against their bronze shields while shouting altogether surpassing even the din of the crowd. Thut-Moses and Aron leap into waiting chariots and head for *Horus Nest*, accompanied not only by the military escort, but also thousands of wildly cheering people.

Exaggerated tales of the co-Regent's exploits in Nubia's eastern desert circulate throughout the bazaars and marketplaces of every village and town in Lower Egypt. Orphans and urchins, struggling to eke out a wretched existence, gather in the streets, alleyways and footpaths of Avaris, Bubastis and Saqqarah to hear stories of the co-Regent's exploits, told and retold. Now young men from large cities and small villages, as far away as from the coast of the Great Green sea, line Thut-Moses' route hoping to glimpse the *Golden Fly* insignia hanging around the neck of the *Smiter of Pharaoh's Enemies* and *Defender of Pharaoh's Treasure*. Young men, fired by stories of foreign adventures and eager for an opportunity to serve in the army and advance themselves, cry out at the sight of Thut-Moses' golden chariot. By the time he arrives at the granite wall surrounding *Horus Nest*, he is overwhelmed by the crowd's enthusiasm. Thut-Moses estimates that, with such recruits, he could create a *fifty thousand*-man army.

"With these I could conquer Palestine. Syria and the valley where the river runs backward," Thut-Moses boasts to Aron. With these the Two-Lands need never fear the Mitanni."

"And I will be by your side," Aron replies.

Inside the gates of *Horus Nest,* Thut-Moses' regiments are lined up and his soldiers clang their swords upon their shields to welcome their commander in chief. Thut-Moses recognizes their salute as his passes each of the ranks. At his walled palace, Thut-Moses dismounts amid the cheers of his own personal staff of officers and household servants. Weary from his adventures, Thut-Moses looks over at Aron and says, "Its good to be home!"

CHAPTER TWENTY-FIVE

Thut-Moses and Aron both lie on their sleeping mats. Thut-Moses moans. His head is bursting and the pain seems to be pouring out through his eye sockets. The healer priest cannot concoct a potion strong enough to relieve the pain. For the past two weeks, Thut-Moses' commanders have vied with each other to honor the co-Regent with elaborate celebrations. All of Thut-Moses' generals, themselves, are members of Egypt's *Order of the Golden Fly*. Each general in hosting their own separate regimental banquet tries to make it more lavish than the others. Many nomarchs attend the celebrations, bringing valuable gifts. In addition, nomarchs of *White Fortress*, *Northern Shield* and *Prospering Scepter*, themselves honor the co-Regent with celebrations featuring feminine entertainment, sumptuous meals, excellent wine and plenty of bread beer. The bread beer is what causes the two hero their unbearable headaches ___ *or is it the wine?* Thut-Moses clutches his sleeping mat as if he was crossing a cataract aboard a capsized fishing boat. His stomach contracts and tightens with each imagined wave. The two comrades have spent days, laying about in their wretched condition, commiserating with each other.

So great is their distress that neither notices the two royal messengers who have entered the co-Regent's chambers and are 'kissing the dust' at Thut-Moses' feet. Finally he looks over and grants them permission to rise. The *Seeing Waters* deliver a scroll bearing User-Amen's seal.

"Great Prince," one of the messengers says, "the Grand Vizier asks that we, his servants, bring back the co-Regent's reply."

Breaking the scroll's seal, Thut-Moses reads:

Aa-Kheper-Ren-Re Thut-Moses II *went forth to heaven in triumph, having mingled with the gods. Menkh-Kheperu-Re Thut-Moses III, his son, stood in his place as Pharaoh over the Two-Lands, becoming ruler upon the throne of the one who begat him. His sister, the Divine Consort, Hat-Shep-Sut, settled the affairs of the Two Lands. By reason of her plans, Egypt was made to labor with bowed head and back.*

Now be it known that the Living God, Horus Powerful of KA, Female Horus of Fine Gold, Two Ladies Flourishing of Years, Divine of Diadems, Pharaoh of Upper and Lower Egypt, Maat-Ka-Re Hat-Shep-Sut Khenmet-Amen, Foremost of Distinguished Women, announces that Thut-Moses III, co-Regent from the date of Pharaoh's reign in the Regnal Year One and God's Wife, Neferu-Re, are to be united in KA at the upcoming Festival of the Reunion of Horus and Hathor.

Thut-Moses lays down the scroll and smiles to himself.

"I have no reply for the Grand Vizier for now," Thut-Moses tells the messengers. The *Seeing Waters* 'kiss the dust' and depart.

On his sofa, Aron groans. "Have your healers delivered the pain-killing potion they promised, yet?" he asks.

"No," Thut-Moses replies.

"Well, that's not good," Aron whispers. He rolls up into a sitting position, but makes no effort to look at the scroll. "Who were they? What did they want?"

"My step-mother has announced my engagement to Neferu-Re," Thut-Moses says tossing the scroll to Aron almost knocking over an alabaster wine bottle. Aron is prescient enough to allow the scroll to drop while he catches the wine.

"She must be getting desperate," Aron remarks.

"My step-mother is never desperate!" the co-Regent observes. "She only makes you think that she is."

"What do you think she's up to?" Aron asks. The pain inside his head begins to throb. Desperate for any relief, Aron gulps wine from the alabaster bottle. He pauses. The throbbing in his head slackens. Aron drains the alabaster wine bottle. Once his head clears, he rises and goes over to a sofa. The wine dulls the pain. Thut-Moses orders his servants to bring more wine. After awhile both are pleasantly numb.

"When do we go back for the ceremony?" Aron asks.

"In time for the *Festival of the Reunion of Horus and Hathor*," Thut-Moses replies.

"Uhm!" Aron raises his eyebrows and says. "That's several months from now," before he slumps back onto the sofa.

The *Festival of the Reunion of Hathor and Horus* takes place when Hathor leaves her temple at Dendera during Akhet, at the height of the Nile's flood season. Akhet is the beginning of the New Year, a time when stagnation and decay is flushed from the land by the Niles' *new waters*. Hathor, goddess of reproductive energy and source of life, comes to Horus at his temple at Edfu. As she sails up the Nile to meet Horus, Hathor visits many gods including those at Karnak. During her visits, her many worshippers re-enact the reproductive rites that she will perform with Horus at Edfu.

"That woman is ridiculous!" Aron blurts out before realizing what he is saying and to whom he is saying it. "Forgive me, majesty!" he quickly apologizes. "I mean no disrespect to the *Living God* nor did I intend to _____ "

Thut-Moses raises his hand, cutting Aron off in mid-sentence. "Apologies are unnecessary. After what we have shared, you are more than my friend! *More even than brothers!*" Aron much prefers his work on the War Council and serving Thut-Moses at *Horus Nest* than serving Hat-Shep-Sut's mating couch at *Karnak*. Aron actually regards Thut-Moses as his nephew.

"Don't fret!" Thut-Moses smiles. "My supporters on the council know what they're doing. Otherwise they would not have approved of this marriage."

"I wouldn't be so certain," Aron remarks.

The issue has remained unspoken between them since their return from Punt. But now is the time for the words to be spoken.

"Out with it, my friend," Thut-Moses says.

Aron hesitates.

"You believe Pharaoh was behind the Nubian attack, don't you?" Thut-Moses begins. It's half question and half fact.

Aron remains silent.

"Well, even if she were responsible," Thut-Moses continues, "she intended me no harm."

"How do you know that?" Aron asks.

"I decided to lead the caravan across the eastern desert at the last minute, remember? I had planned to return up the Red Sea with the ship. Even you were surprised." Thut-Moses is confident that his step-mother doesn't want him dead.

"Yes that is true," Aron agrees, "I even remember Neshi frowning when he learned that you were coming with us."

"Why didn't you tell me then?" Thut-Moses asks.

"I didn't think it was important."

Thut-Moses reviews his own thoughts about Hat-Shep-Sut, before saying,

"My step-mother has no intention of harming me. She needs me to marry Neferu-Re."

"And after you've married her?" Aron asks. His eyes narrow.

Thut-Moses lapses into short silence before clapping his hands for his wine steward. "First comes the marriage and then we shall see," Thut-Moses says. "But I agree that the *Living God* behaves rather strangely."

"As long as the *Living God* and the co-Regent are with *maat*, I am content," Aron sighs flopping back down in his sleeping mat.

"My step-mother is just self-absorbed," Thut-Moses observes.

"When you become Pharaoh, you'll probably become as self-absorbed, as she," Aron laughs.

"What do you mean when I become Pharaoh," Thut-Moses grins. "I'm already self-absorbed."

The older man rises back up before giving Thut-Moses a hesitant laugh. He is uncertain whether or not his 'nephew' is actually jesting.

"What else can a pharaoh be, other than self-absorbed?" Thut-Moses continues. "Pharaoh is the focus of all who inhabit the

Two-Lands. Whom else can Pharaoh focus on but herself?" Thut-Moses walks over to Aron's sleeping mat and rubs his 'uncle's' bald head. "But possibly when you say that my step-mother is self absorbed, you refer to the *mating couch*." Thut-Moses gives his 'uncle' a probing look. The younger man has always been curious about the relationship between Pharaoh and her consort. But Aron believes there are some things better left unsaid.

The physical relationship between Hat-Shep-Sut and Aron has always been sporadic, at best. He knows that Hat-Shep-Sut never loved him. She used him to get at Senen-Mut. What made matters bad between them was, despite his firm intention to the contrary, he falls hopelessly in love with her and would do anything for her love. What makes matters worse is that he knows Hat-Shep-Sut still loves Senen-Mut. She calls his name in her sleep. Since Aron's return from Punt, their physical relationship has been non-existent. Aron comes to understand that the further away he is from Hat-Shep-Sut the less likely he will suffer Senen-Mut's fate. Once in awhile, he dreams of being with her, again. But he bears the pain of physical separation far easier than having to suffer her aloof indifference and her biting criticisms whenever they are together. Hat-Shep-Sut reciprocates no man's affection; she does not even pretend. As a sculptor uses tools to produce works of art, Hat-Shep-Sut uses men to further her goal of becoming the *foremost of distinguished women.*

"Like mother, like daughter," Thut-Moses blurts out, breaking into Aron's thoughts.

"What?" Aron asks.

"I say that you've never experienced anything, until you been with a woman who spends all her time with a white, twenty foot long snake." Thut-Moses laughs, giving Aron a wink.

"I guess not," Aron replies. He rises up from the sofa; his curiosity is aroused. "What's it like?'

"I can't tell you," Thut-Moses smiles, "but, for a long time, it sure spoiled me for any other woman."

The two men enjoy such a hearty laugh that several of Thut-Moses' servants, wondering at the mirth, peek into his chambers.

"What my step-mother doesn't understand," Thut-Moses says, "is that I prefer a warrior's life to court intrigue. I wouldn't enjoy changing costumes and cosmetics several times each day, as she does. Nor would I enjoy the stream of visitors from distant lands, parading in and out of the Great Audience Hall forcing me to try to behave like the *Living God*."

"I understand your mind," Aron sympathizes. "Even when I was a Royal Student, I was never interested in being an administrator or scribe. Flood and drought reports or harvest forecasts bored me."

"Me, too," Thut-Moses echoes. "I had no interest in trying to remember the minimum reserve levels of grain and livestock. Those lectures would drive me crazy. Pharaoh must keep these things in mind to rule well. My stepmother needn't fear my wanting her position ____ just as I needn't fear her leading my soldiers into battle."

The co-Regent gives Aron an intent stare.

"If we could find a way of working together," Thut-Moses observes, "we could both achieve our ambitions."

"She dislikes you just like her father disliked her brother," Aron observes.

"Why do you say that?" Thut-Moses asks.

"Some god, guides you towards the throne," Aron explains, "just as it guided Hat-Shep-Sut."

"Yes I know," Thut-Moses muses. "But whatever neter it is, it doesn't favor Neferu-Re. And this is what Hat-Shep-Sut really fears." Thut-Moses gathers his thoughts. "No matter what she does, all my step-mother's struggles are useless. My fate and Neferu-Re's fate are sealed." Aron gulps down more wine and says nothing. "Neferu-Re will never rule over the Two-Lands, *even if we do marry*."

Neferu-Re leaves Pharaoh's *Mansion of Millions of Years* and returns to the *Grand Vizier's Palace* that she now claims as her own. Having been left alone, once again, with only Natee for company, Pharaoh's thoughts turn to her consort. Though Hat-Shep-Sut doesn't really miss him, it has been months since Aron shared her mating couch. Even so her body never desires Aron like she still often craves Senen-Mut.

Why is he the only one man capable of satisfying me? she wonders. *Is it because he was the first?*

Thinking about it, Hat-Shep-Sut knows that is not the reason. But now her beauty, radiating eroticism like a lotus in full bloom, is heightened by her enforced abstinence. Her beauty has always served to further her dynastic ambitions rather than her sexual desires. Hat-Shep-Sut manipulated Senen-Mut as well as Aron. Men's desire to possess her has left Hat-Shep-Sut as frigid as any of her stone monuments. Hat-Shep-Sut's beauty strikes men with a malady that addles their brains and makes them yearn for her loving touch. However, she has no love to give. She chills men's hearts with her biting tongue and cruel behavior. But though Hat-Shep-Sut loves her daughter, Neferu-Re rejects the affection for which even Thut-Moses secretly yearns. Neferu-Re finds cannot remain in Hat-Shep-Sut's presence for any length of time. And when her daughter rejects her love and refuses to remain with her in the *Mansion of Millions of Years*, it breaks Pharaoh's heart.

"Oh mother," Neferu-Re exclaims, "I simply must have some time to myself, mustn't I?"

"You have all the privacy you need right here," Hat-Shep-Sut replies. "Besides when I built that palace, I intended it to separate me from your father. Now that you have moved out there, it separates me from you."

"You see," Neferu-Re smiles, coyly, "it still has its uses."

Hat-Shep-Sut ignores her daughter's sarcasm.

"User-Amen has informed Thut-Moses that you and he will be married at the next *Festival of Horus and Hathor*."

"That is wonderful news!" Neferu-Re exclaims. But in the middle of her excitement, Neferu-Re pauses. "How did Thut-Moses respond?" she asks.

"He hasn't responded, yet," Hat-Shep-Sut replies.

"Then please inform me of my official engagement, when he does," Neferu-Re says. Neferu-Re leaves her mother's palace in a huff.

Once mother and daughter were inseparable. It was when both enjoyed conspiring against their mutual 'enemy', *the commoner*, Senen-Mut. Then Hat-Shep-Sut could rely upon Neferu-Re's company. They spent hours discussing ways of getting rid of him. Neferu-Re often proposes bloody methods in their discussions, while Hat-Shep-Sut favors restraint.

"After all, he is your father, " she reminds Neferu-Re.

Both finally agree that banishment, first from Pharaoh's *Mansion of Millions of Years* and finally from Karnak altogether, is the best method of ridding themselves of the *pest*. But once Senen-Mut is finally gone, mother and daughter become estranged. They have nothing else to discuss. Hat-Shep-Sut must send her palace guard before Neferu-Re will spend any time with her. Even when Neferu-Re visits her mother, she seldom stays longer than a week. Only the promise that, one day, Neferu-Re will be Pharaoh gives Hat-Shep-Sut any access to her daughter and even the idea of becoming Pharaoh is beginning to lose its appeal. Once Neferu-Re has her own palace, her own attendants and everything she desires, she stays as far away from her mother for as long as possible. In fact the real purpose behind Hat-Shep-Sut's announcement of Neferu-Re's marriage to Thut-Moses is to recover some measure of control over her daughter.

But Neferu-Re complains to herself all the way back to her palace. Does she really expect me to fawn over her day and night? *She knows Thut-Moses will never marry me. He hates me!*

Hat-Shep-Sut had tried to reassure Neferu-Re that Thut-Moses wants to marry her. "You are so beautiful!"

"Not as beautiful as you," Neferu-Re snaps. "Everyone says so!"

Eugene Stovall

"Thut-Moses has always loved you," Hat-Shep-Sut replies, "If you tried, I know that you could convince him to return to Thebes and share your palace."

"Don't be silly, mother!" Neferu-Re snaps back. "Thut-Moses is as frightened of me as everyone else."

This is not far from the truth. Few other than Tuua and, of course, her mother are unafraid of *God's Wife*, reputed to have condemned hundreds to perpetual toil in the tunnels, in the quarries and behind the oars. In addition, God's Wife orders others executed.

Now that she is alone once again, Hat-Shep-Sut has time to think about Aron.

Oh, well, Hat-Shep-Sut tells herself, *he's probably infatuated with some slave girl.*

Suddenly the idea of her consort with some slave girl makes Hat-Shep-Sut jealous. She claps her hands and calls for her personal scribe, thinking to send Aron a summons ordering him back to Karnak immediately as she had once done with Senen-Mut. But when the scribe answers her summons, Hat-Shep-Sut abruptly dismisses him.

I'll visit Horus Nest, myself, she decides. But just as quickly she knows that such a trip is impossible. Before, when Hat-Shep-Sut wanted someone, she could tell Iby. Her Eyes of Horus Captain of Captains could make anyone appear, *like magic*. Without Iby, the *Eyes of Horus* are no longer effective as Pharaoh's secret police. Even the *Eyes of Horus'* headquarters in Karnak goes largely unoccupied, while hordes of asiatic squatters, pouring into lower Egypt, go largely unreported. Former *watchers* assist administrators acquire gold, land and everything else of value. Corruption and coercion rule the Two-Lands far more effectively than Pharaoh and corruption pays Iby's former *watchers* far better than Pharaoh, who paid them nothing.

CHAPTER TWENTY-SIX

"If the armies of the Two-Lands are to be victorious," Thut-Moses tells Aron, "we need to know as much about their lands, their strengths and their weaknesses as we know about ourselves."

His military activities teach Thut-Moses that war is a science. To be effective, an army must be more than a mass of killers. Making war is more than burning villages, farms and palaces. The successful army needs information before engaging in battle like it needs water before crossing the desert. He was lucky in the eastern desert. If the Mitanni had caught him the way that the Nubians did, defenseless and in the open, his soldiers would have been slaughtered.

"I cannot enter the Land of the Mitanni the way I entered the Land of Punt," Thut-Moses tells Aron. "I must have information. Re-activate the *Eyes of Horus*. Get me Iby."

"You don't mind if I go?" Iby asks the former Grand Vizier for what seems the *thousandth* time.

Senen-Mut closes his eyes and tries to imagine Iby *gone*. Its not that Senen-Mut has lost his regard for his friend, but among the scholars and intellectuals at Iunu, Iby is out of place. Iby is no scholar and being holed up in a temple, reading scrolls and watching stars bores the former spymaster. Iby is unsuited for the cloistered life of a priest. Often, during their enforced ostracism, Senen-Mut has encouraged Iby to leave Iunu for Memphis or even Horus Nest where he could engage in livelier pursuits. Yet,

Eugene Stovall

Iby stubbornly remains at Iunu watching over Senen-Mut like a mother hen convinced that Senen-Mut still needs him.

"I have received a message from Aron," Senen-Mut tells his friend.

"What does Pharaoh's consort say?" Iby asks.

"He wants you to gather a band of former watchers to escort the co-Regent to Gaza and up through the Land of Canaan to the city of Megiddo."

"Is that so?" Iby remarks.

"Yes," Senen-Mut beams. "From Megiddo, he wants to travel up the *Plain of Esdraelon* to Antaradus on the Great Green Sea."

Iby moves closer to his master. "This will be a good opportunity for you to get back into the game," Senen-Mut smiles. "Aron has a lot of confidence in you even though you've been out of action, now, for ___ how long has it been now ___ almost two years."

Iby does not comment, but his sidewise smile seems genuine. "Why has the co-Regent requested me?" Iby asks.

"The co-Regent needs you because he wants neither to alarm Pharaoh nor alert Barattarna about the purpose of his trip."

"Which is?" Iby asks.

"Thut-Moses wants to map the land and learn about the armies of the Canaanite people allied with Barattarna," Senen-Mut replies. "You are to arrange the trip so that it appears to be Thut-Moses' final romp as a bachelor before his marriage to Neferu-Re. They want you and your watchers to spread the rumors that a young noble travels from Memphis to Antaradus so that he and his friends can sample the wine and women of Palestine."

Iby smiles. "As often as the co-Regent and Aron visit the *Houses of Pleasure* in Memphis," he observes, "there shouldn't be any problem getting anyone to believe that story."

But Iby has other reservations. Even though the adventure appeals to him, his concern for Senen-Mut's safety makes him hesitate.

"I don't trust these Seeing Waters here at Iunu," Iby confides to Senen-Mut.

"There is no garrison more loyal to its high priest than the Seeing Waters here at Iunu," Senen-Mut assures him.

But Iby has a secret fear. The former spymaster fears that he has lost his nerve. Iby is not as young, nor as hungry, nor as desperate as he once was ___ and spying is a young, hungry, desperate man's game. "Do you really think I should go?" Iby asks, once more.

Senen-Mut tries to convince Iby that leading Thut-Moses' party into Palestine would be good for both of them. He considers his words carefully.

"Listen, my friend," Senen-Mut says, "if you don't go, who will bring me information about any plot Thut-Moses hatches against Pharaoh?"

Iby has always supported Senen-Mut's unwavering devotion to Hat-Shep-Sut. He supported his master in the past; he will do so in the future.

"If you really need me to bring you information about Thut-Moses' plans, then I'll go," Iby replies.

Silently, Senen-Mut praises Ptah. Now he can continue his researches and observations without having his friend underfoot.

Puffed up with his own importance and wearing a new leopard skin robe, a gift from Pharaoh, Hapu-Seneb ushers two *Seeing Waters* into her *Seal Room*. Hat-Shep-Sut and User-Amen discuss a canal project. Scribes taking notes, attend them. Pharaoh stares serenely forward as the intruders "kiss the dust" at her feet.

"Majesty, I bring words of importance," Hapu-Seneb announces.

"Speak," Hat-Shep-Sut orders.

"These men followed your co-Regent and a party of fifty watchers down the Nile, across the Sinai desert and up to Gaza," Hapu-Seneb relates. Pharaoh reacts with surprise.

"For what purpose has the co-Regent left the Two-Lands?" Hat-Shep-Sut asks turning to User-Amen.

"It is said on the *Street of Pleasures* that the Crown Prince wishes to sample pleasures in the land of Canaan before he marries *God's Wife*," User-Amen replies.

"He plans to visit Megiddo, Antaradus and possibly even the island of Minoas before the *Festival of Hathor and Horus*," Hapu-Seneb interjects.

"My co-Regent travels to Antaradus?" Hat-Shep-Sut storms. "Does the young fool endanger his life prior to his marriage to Neferu-Re, just to spite me?"

Neither User-Amen nor Hapu-Seneb respond.

"Why was I not informed of the co-Regent's departure, sooner?" Hat-Shep-Sut storms at her Grand Vizier.

"Gaza's citizens are loyal to the *Living God*," the vizier replies. *I don't understand this younger generation,* he sighs to himself. *In my day, Thut-Moses would not have dared depart the Two-Lands without Pharaoh's permission.*

"Since the Crown Prince and his party travel incognito, possibly he believes no one knows his identity," Hapu-Seneb snickers.

"The Mitanni knew of the presence of the co-Regent as well as the identities of every one in his party even before they crossed the Sinai," one of the *Seeing Waters* reports.

"The fool!" Pharaoh snaps. "Continue!" she orders Hapu-Seneb.

"After lodging in Gaza for two weeks, the Lord Iby, led the co-Regent and his party up an ancient trade route, through the mountain pass of Wadi Ara to the city of Megiddo."

"The Lord Iby is leading an expedition into the land of the asiatics *without my permission?*" Pharaoh cannot believe her ears.

"Great Lord, many things are done throughout the Two-Lands, these days, *without Pharaoh's permission,*" User-Amen remarks.

His words force Hat-Shep-Sut to acknowledge that her Grand Vizier only speaks the unpleasant truth.

Many things are done throughout the Two-Lands without my permission, Pharaoh acknowledges to herself.

"How many scribes are in the co-Regent's party?" User-Amen asks.

"Many," one *Seeing Waters* replies. "Some scribes make drawings and maps, others compile lists and still others take lunar and stellar readings."

"How long did they remain in Megiddo?"

"The full moon passed into a half moon long before the Crown Prince journeyed up the *Plain of Esdraelon* to the Great Green Sea and the port city of Antaradus."

"How long did he remain in Antaradus?" Pharaoh asks.

"Ships sailed into the port back and forth from Syria and Minoas several times before the co-Regent departs," the *Seeing Waters* say. "Many sailors and pilots knew the Lord Iby. While the co-Regent's party remained in the port of Antaradus, he bought wine and beer for every Minoan pilot and captain and most of their crews."

"The co-Regent's party bought beer and wine for everybody wherever they went," the first *Seeing Waters* adds. "They spent a lot of gold on the *Street of Pleasures* and in the wine and beer shops."

"Enough!" Hapu-Seneb instructs his spies, "tell your *Living God* about the co-Regent's return from Antaradus."

"From Antaradus, they returned to Megiddo."

"If the *Seeing Waters* observed all of their wanderings, then the Mitanni must have observed them, as well," Pharaoh remarks to User-Amen.

Her Grand Vizier nods in agreement.

"Continue," Pharaoh orders.

"Great Lord!" one of the *Seeing Waters* bows. "The co-Regent and the Lord Aron arrived in Megiddo two full cycles of the moon, ago. There they are and there they have remained."

Sitting high up on the Palestinian heights, where the Aruna Pass spills onto the *Plain of Esdraelon*, the city of Megiddo straddles the military and trade routes connecting the Great Green Sea to Palestine, Syria and Lebanon. Any army or caravan transporting soldiers or goods away from or into Palestine must pass close by Megiddo's towering fourteen cubits thick walls, buttressed with guardhouses. Immediately inside Megiddo's walls is the *Place of Artisans and Jewelers*. Here within the safety of their courtyards, unconnected by any streets, the people chat, play music and engage in their primary occupation, the making of jewelry __ necklaces, rings, bracelets and bangles of every size and description. Flat-roofed brick houses completely surround the courtyards. Scaling ladders allow the people to climb from their courtyards to the top of each building and down into individual two and three room apartments with common eating and lounging areas for each of the building's several families.

Across from the *Place of Artisans and Jewelers* is a great, flat plain filled with hundreds of tents, huts and canopied dwellings. These buildings are of every size and description. Here, in Megiddo's marketplace, merchants from all over the known world engage in a frenzy of buying, selling and trading. Though not as large as Thebes, Megiddo attracts merchants eager to obtain the city's locally-produced jewels. Megiddo's marketplace even boasts of one Senen-Mut's original and more successful trading markets. Here the best and finest goods from all over the world are exchanged for Egyptian grain, linen, paper and, of course, gold.

A wide boulevard separates the *Place of Artisans and Jewelers* and Megiddo's marketplace. The great paved road passes several mansions and palaces, as it ascends a gentle hill, before coming to rest on an acropolis overlooking all of Megiddo as well as the surrounding countryside. From the acropolis, the great Plain of Esdraelon can be seen tumbling westward towards the Great Green Sea off in the distance. Directly at the top of Megiddo's acropolis sits the *Temple of Niobe* where worshippers from the far-flung reaches of the Mitanni Empire flock to see the most beautiful woman in the world, Niobe's high priestess and the sister of the King of Mitanni, Hipa-Giluk.

"Doubtless, Barattarna's spies have reported my Lord's presence in Canaan, by now," Iby warns Thut-Moses after they leave Antaradus and begin their journey back to the Two-Lands. "We have yet to survey the coast route between Antaradus and Gaza."

"We have learned much from your guidance, Lord Iby," Thut-Moses laughs. The co-Regent winks at Aron.

"I suggest we return to the Two-Lands by the coast route and avoid Megiddo, altogether," Iby says.

"Your suggestion is wise," Thut-Moses observes. "So now I want you take my scribes and map the coastal route for me."

"But, Majesty ___ ," Iby begins.

"My good friend," Aron intervenes. "You are familiar with the coast and know the information that the co-Regent requires."

"There is much that could be recorded," Iby hesitates. "How can I be certain to include everything the co-Regent and his War Council requires?"

"I trust your judgment," Thut-Moses snaps. "Meanwhile, Aron and I will revisit Megiddo."

Iby stares at Aron. Don't you know how dangerous it is for you to return to Megiddo? his eyes ask. But outwardly, Iby refrains from saying anything and maintains a stone face, absent his characteristically silly smile. Thut-Moses' reckless behavior troubles Iby. *It's as if they believe they can violate universal laws,* he thinks to himself, *and expect their servants to pay the penalties.*

"It will be alright," Aron assures Iby. "The co-Regent just wants to examine the thickness of Megiddo's walls once again, before he returns to the Two-Lands."

Thut-Moses intends to revisit the site of *Armageddon,* but less for any interest that he might have in the thickness of Megiddo's walls than in visiting the person rumored to be the most exotic, erotic courtesan in the world, the high priestess of Niobe.

It was while he was visiting the Houses of Pleasure in Antaradus that Thut-Moses learns of Hipa-Giluk. Thut-Moses learns that the Niobe's high priestess is so adept in the art of lovemaking that after spending but one night with her, men willingly remain at her temple for the remainder of their lives.

"Possibly she can do something a woman who sleeps with a snake cannot," Aron laughs.

"Even if she could," Thut-Moses replies, "I am not so certain I want to find out what it is."

Eugene Stovall

Iby is correct. Thut-Moses should have avoided Megiddo, but you can't put an old head on a young body. Ignoring caution, yielding only to desire, Thut-Moses and Aron arrive at Megiddo. Each actually believes that they are passing through Megiddo's gates unobserved and that they are blending in with the hundreds of other travelers. Nothing could be further from the truth. Even as the two Egyptian princes stride up Megiddo's great central boulevard, past the mansions of powerful Canaanite princes whose tribes occupy all of Palestine and up to the acropolis, many eyes watch and report Thut-Moses' and Aron's every movement.

At the acropolis, they cross through a porticoed courtyard and climb the wide marble stairs up to Niobe's temple. The temple doors open into a great, circular hall. The hall is dark, lit only by torches set upon the wall at regular intervals. In the shadows, Thut-Moses spots the unmistakable though unobtrusive figures of armed soldiers, mingling among the normal pilgrims visiting the temple. Neither Thut-Moses nor Aron are alarmed. Suddenly, they are surrounded by a bevy of bare-breasted priestesses, who playfully tease the pair into following them through a series of hallways. After being half beckoned and half chased through several secret passages where the air is heavy with incense, the visitors begin feeling light-headed and giddy. Finally, Niobe's priestesses lead Thut-Moses and Aron into a spacious hallway in what appears to be a palace adjoining the temple. At the center of the hallway stand great doors guarded by gigantic bare-chested soldiers armed with spears and swords. Slowly the doors open into what appears to be a gigantic private sitting room. The guards and priestesses motion Thut-Moses and Aron inside.

Though the room is large it feels intimate. A fountain, dominates the center of the room while clusters of sofas, low tables and pillows are arranged all around. Over to the side, four marble steps lead up to a golden sofa. Seated upon the sofa is a dark-haired woman, with green almond-shaped eyes. She is clad in a skimpy, diaphanous blue gown that covers very little of her buxom figure. The high priestess of Niobe gazes curiously down at her visitors.

The rumors are all true, Thut-Moses shouts to himself, half stumbling towards Hipa-Giluk's throne. In all of his travels, the co-Regent of the Two-Lands of Upper and Lower Egypt believes that he has never beheld a more stunningly beautiful and perfectly formed woman anywhere in the world.

"Welcome Lord Thut-Moses, co-Regent of the Two-Lands and Crown Prince of Upper and Lower Egypt," she says in a throaty whisper, speaking the Egyptian language, perfectly. "I've been expecting you." Thut-Moses senses a note of sarcasm when she pronounced his titles. Hipa-Giluk rises from her throne and descends the steps in a slow sensuous walk, stopping on the last step directly in front of Thut-Moses, towering over him. Two handmaidens come over to the high priestess. One removes her diaphanous gown; the other slips a linen sheath over her head. The sheath, dyed a golden yellow and edged in purple and blue, drapes down from her shoulders to the floor. The servants secure the sheath about her waist using a wide blue sash. The sheath opens in front to expose the priestess' taut, firm breasts. Hipa-Giluk wears her jet-black hair in gentle curls piled high on her head, held in place by silver pins. On her feet are silver sandals tied in place with colorful blue and yellow ribbons.

The priestess takes Thut-Moses' arm and leads him over to a banquet table where little boys pour pale gold wine from long-necked bottles. The wine tastes like ambrosia, cooling to the tongue and soothing to the palate. The high priestess feeds Thut-Moses different varieties of fish of such delicacy that the flesh almost melts in his mouth. Not even the rare Nile perch is as delicate. Thut-Moses has never tasted the like. The fish is accompanied by varieties of spiced vegetables, baked breads and crisp salads. Following the main courses, the servants offer sweet cakes, toasted almonds, and sugared dates along with several varieties of heavy sweet wines. As they dine, musicians charm the ears and dancers delight the eyes. So tantalizing are the sights and sounds that not only his senses but his desires are inflamed. At the banquet's end, Thut-Moses is overcome with erotic urges. Hipa-Giluk takes him to her bedchamber. Once again the air is heavy with incense. She encourages Thut-Moses to smoke from a calabash containing a mixture of cannabis leaves and poppy resins. During the remainder of the night, Thut-Moses experiences passions that he was unaware ever existed. He remains with Hipa-Giluk for many weeks, engaging in frenetic sessions of lovemaking followed by interludes of drug-induced bliss. When Thut-Moses emerges from his stupor, he learns from Aron that he has married the high priestess of Niobe. Hipa-Giluk then sends her husband back to the Two-Lands to prepare for the arrival of the co-Regent's new wife and the future Queen of Egypt.

"I will not give my palace to that Mitanni whore!" Neferu-Re screams at her mother.

Hat-Shep-Sut refuses to allow Neferu-Re to disturb her serenity.

"First of all, it is not *your* palace; it's *my* palace," Hat-Shep-Sut says.

"But you gave it to me," Neferu-Re whines.

"Secondly," Hat-Shep-Sut says, ignoring her daughter's tantrum, "I don't want that Mitanni woman either in my *Mansion of Millions of Years* or at the *Palace of Ladies*." Hat-Shep-Sut lowers her voice and speaks in an ominous whisper, "In fact, I want her as far away from me as possible."

There is a slight stirring among the palace guard and household servants. Neferu-Re's agitation makes them uneasy. Even Awab, Pharaoh's ever-present bodyguard, gives *God's Wife* a sharp look. Neferu-Re lowers her voice.

At the far end of her chambers, Hat-Shep-Sut rests by the indoor pool. Her handmaidens massage and oil their mistress' body while Neferu-Re lounges on a pillow-covered sofa just outside her mother's bathing area, but well within hearing distance, making it unnecessary for her to shout. On a low table, in front of Neferu-Re, sit platters of food. Dates, figs, grapes and nuts, on one; lettuces, onions, cucumber and garlic on another, braised beef, succulent mutton and a juicy fowl on a third. Neferu-Re picks at the fruit and nuts while alternating between two excellent wines wondering why she even tries using temper tantrums on her mother. They never work. Neferu-Re's tantrums always work on everyone else. At Karnak, Neferu-Re's tantrums are legendary. From the time she is a small child, Neferu-Re behaves as she pleases, insensitive to the consequences of her behavior. Anyone or anything that offends her, people, animals, anything, Neferu-Re orders punished, enslaved or killed. With that sort of power, Neferu-Re quickly learns that her tantrums always get results. Not even her father is exempt from Neferu-Re's vile behavior. Senen-Mut and Neferu-Re often engage in a contest of wills. Neither is ever certain of the outcome. Only her mother is entirely immune to Neferu-Re's temper tantrums. To handle her daughter, Hat-Shep-Sut always does the same thing. At first, her mother exercises patience. When Neferu-Re exhausts her mother's patience, she calls for Tuua.

Just thinking about the nurses' unblinking eyes and snaggle-toothed smile frightens Neferu-Re as much now as when she was a child. From the time Neferu-Re was an infant, Tuua has known Neferu-Re's every thought. Tuua can enter Neferu-Re's dreams and Tuua controls the princess' awareness in the dream state. Whoever, willingly or unwillingly, gives Tuua access to their dreams comes under the witch's control. Tuua needs only look at Neferu-Re and Hat-Shep-Sut's misbehaving child writhes in agony.

As an orphan, Tuua grew up among the rushes and reeds on the bank of the Nile. To feed herself, Tuua learned to beg and steal. When she was still quite young, Tuua met a wise old crone living among the other outcasts. The old woman had once lived in Karnak, but was banished. Tuua never learned the reason for the crone's banishment. Tuua brought the old woman food. In return, the woman taught Tuua the ways of magic and sorcery. By the time, Tuua was a teenager, she was as adept in casting spells as any priest and gained a reputation throughout Thebes. One day, a priest of Sekhmet challenged Tuua to demonstrate her ability casting spells and working spells. Tuua so confounded the priest that he was forced to admit her into Sekhmet's temple where she remained for twenty years, learning the healing arts. In Sekhmet's temple, Tuua became proficient in casting spell that none of the priests of Sekhmet, including the high priest, could remove. With the completion of her studies Tuua was consecrated a priest and an initiate of Sekhmet's outer temple. No woman had ever before achieved a priestly rank. It was during the time when Aak was Pharaoh and she was God's Wife that Hat-Shep-Sut learned of this remarkable woman. Hat-Shep-Sut decided that the first female priest would make an ideal nurse for her infant daughter. Senen-Mut thought it strange that Hat-Shep-Sut would trust the safety of her only child to someone as evil as Tuua. But he was never consulted about the decision.

When she was still quite young, Neferu-Re tried to protect herself against Tuua powers by getting a snake. A palace cook told the princess that a white African python could undo any spell. Too late did Neferu-Re learn that the cult of Sekhmet practiced snake worship. Tuua used Neferu-Re's snake to increase her control over the princess. Tuua spends all of her waking moments developing and encouraging Neferu-Re's evil nature. The nurse even teaches Neferu-Re to hate her father. Tuua never overlooks any opportunity to poison Neferu-Re's feelings for Senen-Mut. And by infecting the daughter with hate, it takes surprisingly little effort for Tuua to turn all of Hat-Shep-Sut's love for her consort into hate, as well. Only in achieving her ultimate aim to have Pharaoh execute Senen-Mut did Tuua fall short. Once Tuua severs all emotional ties between Neferu-Re and her parents, she patiently awaits the opportunity to remove both Hat-Shep-Sut and Thut-Moses so that Neferu-Re can assume Pharaoh's throne. Then Tuua, the Theban orphan, will become the Two-Lands' ultimate authority. But the witch's plans are disrupted by the unexpected arrival of Thut-Moses' Mitanni bride.

"I gave you the palace *after* I took it from your father," Hat-Shep-Sut informs Neferu-Re. "Now I'm giving it to Thut-Moses' new wife *after* I take it from you."

Munching away on her fruit and washing it down with wine, Neferu-Re ponders another approach.

"Why not let her stay in Memphis?" Neferu-Re asks trying to sound innocent of any ulterior motive.

A great stillness settles upon Pharaoh's chambers. The guards, the servants and even the pigmy slaves, who cool Pharaoh's chambers by waving their gigantic ostrich-feathered fans, all hold their collective breaths. Hat-Shep-Sut rises up from her massage and gives Neferu-Re a cold, withering glare.

I didn't realize that the child was such an idiot. She frowns to herself. *How will she rule the Two-Lands after I'm gone?*

"What did I say?" Neferu-Re asks ___ her mother's look becoming unbearable.

"You prefer that the happily wedded couple remain in Memphis?" Hat-Shep-Sut sneers.

Looking off into the distance, and sulking under her mother's jibe, Neferu-Re says nothing. Instead she silently lists those servants present who, she believes, are enjoying her embarrassment. And in the not too distant future, this embarrassment will cause someone to suffer. The idea of watching someone die makes her loins quiver and her body become faint. Neferu-Re looks back at ubiquitous Tuua who knows exactly what Neferu-Re wants and can be trusted to see to the details. For the time being, however, cowed by her mother, Neferu-Re lowers her eyes and concentrates on the food in front of her.

Satisfied that her daughter has accepted her decision, Hat-Shep-Sut lowers back to the table and allows her servants to resume their massaging, oiling and perfuming her still youthful body. Inwardly, Hat-Shep-Sut is pleased. By giving Thut-Moses new bride the *Grand Vizier's Palace*, she accomplishes her goal of forcing Neferu-Re to return to Pharaoh's *Mansion of Millions of Years*.

CHAPTER TWENTY-SEVEN

Hipa-Giluk, accompanied by her three hundred ladies and her guard of five hundred soldiers, travels up the Plain of Esdraelon to the seaport of Antaradus where a flotilla of seagoing ships from the Two-Lands awaits her. The flotilla was sent by Thut-Moses to bring Hipa-Giluk and her entourage to Thebes. These great seagoing ships boast three banks of oars. Thut-Moses' Palace Guard allows Hipa-Giluk's maidens to board, but deny the Mitanni soldiers access. It takes a day to settle the ensuing dispute, but in the end, only the women are permitted to accompany Hipa-Giluk.

Sailing south from Antaradus, the flotilla hugs the Palestinian coast before sailing up into the Nile delta. Hipa-Giluk is in high spirits, pleased that her *little brown man*, as she calls Thut-Moses, is so easily manipulated. The high priestess misses her bodyguard. She is unused to being without male companionship. But these are the sacrifices she must make if she is to assist Barattarna's plans to seize control of Egyptian gold. Hipa-Giluk will do anything to support her brother.

At Antaradus, Hipa-Giluk promises Barattarna that she will deliver the Two-Lands of Upper and Lower Egypt into the Mitanni empire and send him more gold than his storehouses can hold. "A people who have a woman as their ruler are not very intelligent," she scoffs. However, by the time her flotilla enters Hapi's sacred waters, Hipa-Giluk's only concern is *the time it will take her to import some real men into Thebes?*

She tells her handmaidens that she doubts that any of the men of the Two-Lands are capable of satisfying her sexual appetites. They all laugh merrily and promise to help her through this period of enforced *chastity*.

"My little brown man cannot satisfy me," Hipa-Giluk confides to her servants, "but possibly his friend may be of some comfort."

Hipa-Giluk instructs one of her handmaidens to tell Aron that the future queen of Egypt wishes a private audience with him.

"Has the high priestess of Niobe considered a Nubian?" one of the maidens asks. "One of those big strong ones might see you through a lonely night." They all begin titter, imagining the horns their mistress intends to hang up on Thut-Moses' head.

As the flotilla nears Thebes, the crowds line the banks, straining for a glimpse at the co-Regent's bride. But they are disappointed. Thut-Moses orders Hipa-Giluk hidden away from the eyes of profane prior to their wedding. The captain confines Hipa-Giluk to her quarters where she must remain out of sight. However her handmaidens freely roam the decks, cavorting about and teasing the crew. Most of the time they lay about nude, sunning themselves. As he awaits his bride's arrival, Thut-Moses savors the irony that his marriage to Hipa-Giluk will precede his marriage to Neferu-Re.

My unintended marriage will to give my step-mother a important lesson in the universal principle of cause and effect, Thut-Moses smiles to himself.

Hapu-Seneb is also pleased with himself. He enjoys a better relationship with Pharaoh than either of his predecessors. Amen's high priest is now one of Pharaoh's closest advisors called upon to participate in secret *Seal Room* meetings, away from prying eyes and wagging tongues. But with his presence inside Pharaoh's *Seal Room* today, Hapu-Seneb must face Pharaoh's displeasure.

"My inner council must have observed their co-Regent's behavior," Hat-Shep-Sut sneers. "Tell me, how does the council intend

Eugene Stovall

to deal with my step-son's marriage to a woman whose brother wants to rule over the Two-Lands?"

Pharaoh glares at her advisors.

"Majesty," User-Amen responds, "although the co-Regent acted unwisely, your council believes Thut-Moses intent was to serve Pharaoh and the gods of the Two-Lands."

"How does the co-Regent's marriage to the priestess of Niobe *without my knowledge or consent* serve my interests?" Hat-Shep-Sut asks in a slightly amused tone. She wonders whether these men actually take her for an idiot!

Hapu-Seneb throws his support to Pharaoh. "The co-Regent's marriage to that Mitanni woman," he offers, "does not serve the *Living God*'s interest."

User-Amen flashes a contemptuous look at Amen's high priest. But Hapu-Seneb ignores Pharaoh's Grand Vizier's look and seizes the opportunity to further insinuate himself into Pharaoh's favor.

"I do not believe that the co-Regent's visit to the kingdom of Mitanni was meant to serve Pharaoh's interests," Hapu-Seneb continues. "Others on the council agree with me."

"You must have supported the co-Regent's trip to Palestine, as well, or else you would have informed Pharaoh sooner," Neferu-Re accuses Hapu-Seneb.

"I had no knowledge of the co-Regent's plans," Hapu-Seneb replies defensively.

"How can you deny knowledge of Thut-Moses' activities," Neferu-Re asks, "when your *Seeing Waters* followed the co-Regent throughout Palestine and reported his entire journey?"

Hapu-Seneb hesitates. Though the *Seal Room* is warm, he feels a chill. Pharaoh eyes him, suspiciously.

"The *Seeing Waters* have provided reports on the Lord Senen-Mut and the Lord Iby from the time they moved to the Temple of Iunu," Hapu-Seneb sputters.

Pen-Nek-Heb raises his eyebrows and fixes Amen's high priest with a cold, hard stare. "Whom else does your *Seeing Waters* spy upon without my knowledge?" Pharaoh demands to know.

"No one else, Majesty," Hapu-Seneb responds. "The *Seeing Waters* began reporting to me when they observed a member of the co-Regent's personal guard bringing messages back and forth between *Horus Nest* and Iunu."

"Did your *Seeing Waters* read any of the messages?" Hat-Shep-Sut asks.

"No Great Lord," Hapu-Seneb responds, "but when the Lord Aron made the last visit, I was given a full report. I then instructed the *Seeing Waters* to follow either the Lord Senen-Mut or the Lord Iby, if they departed Iunu."

"Why did you not inform me of these activities, *beforehand?*" Hat-Shep-Sut asks.

"Majesty," Hapu-Seneb stammers, "high priests have not forwarded *Seeing Waters* reports to Pharaoh, in the past. The *Seeing Waters* have always believed that the *Eyes of Horus* know what they know."

"But the *Seeing Waters* know that Pharaoh diminished the *Eyes of Horus*," Neferu-Re interjects. She enjoys bringing Hapu-Seneb down. "And when they do not report these matters, Pharaoh is unaware of them."

Hat-Shep-Sut decides to put her Grand Vizier on the spot.

"Why didn't *you* warn me that this was happening?" she shouts at User-Amen.

"Majesty," the old man replies, "you ordered me to replace the *Eyes of Horus* with the *Seeing Waters.*"

"I am surrounded by idiots," Hat-Shep-Sut rages.

In the days when User-Amen served Pharaoh Amen-Hotep, everyone told Pharaoh everything. Now things have changed. No one tells Pharaoh anything. Even Hat-Shep-Sut recognizes how she blinded herself in trying to humble Senen-Mut.

Iby always served me well, she admits. He always kept me informed. But he was too close to Senen-Mut. I had no choice.

Now she realizes the importance of timely and accurate information. She really doesn't know what's happening in the Two-Lands. She doesn't even know what's happening in Thebes.

"Majesty," Pen-Nek-Heb offers, "I also believe the co-Regent was acting to defend the Two-Lands."

"Why so?" Hat-Shep-Sut asks.

"The council knows that Barattarna intends to attack the Two-Lands," Pen-Nek-Heb says. "Without the *Eyes of Horus*, Pharaoh is blind. Everywhere Pharaoh's enemies celebrate the demise of her *Eyes of Horus*." Hat-Shep-Sut's eyes blaze with anger, but she knows Pen-Nek-Heb speaks truly. "The co-Regent was not attempting to establish diplomatic relations rather he was attempting to restore Pharaoh's *eyes*."

"Restore, my eyes?" Hat-Shep-Sut asks. "How so?"

"By undertaking the dangerous mission of acquiring battlefield information about the Mitanni," Pen-Nek-Heb replies. "And by acquiring the services of the *Eyes of Horus*' top spymaster, the Lord Iby."

"Be that as it may," Pharaoh remarks, "if the co-Regent intended to restore Pharaoh's eyes, the council must admit that beginning in the bedroom of the high priestess of Niobe was a strange place to start."

"Few of your Majesty's council would disagree," Pen-Nek-Heb replies.

"Furthermore his actions have cost us more gold than we can afford to give," Pharaoh continues. "Or do you also believe that the amount of gold Barattarna is demanding as a dowry for his sister is of little consequence?"

"Your council has not been informed of Barattarna's demand," User-Amen admits.

"Barattarna's demand for his sister's dowry is far more than what I consider reasonable," Hat-Shep-Sut snaps. "He is demanding what he expects from one of his vassals."

"What if we don't pay what he asks?" Neferu-Re replies.

"It will be war," User-Amen interjects.

"So going back to my original question," Hat-Shep-Sut snaps, "considering the amount of gold Barattarna is demanding as a dowry for his sister, is my council still pleased with the behavior of the co-Regent?" She glares at each of them, before continuing. "*Does the council still want to put him on my throne?*"

Hapu-Seneb and User-Amen look back and forth. Each tries to outwait the other. Finally User-Amen decides to respond.

"Majesty your council continues to serve the *Living* God. We know your desire is always for your people."

"Then go now," Hat-Shep-Sut says. "Inform the council of the terrible consequences of the co-Regent's irrational and foolish behavior. Tell them that I must decide whether or not the co-Regent is even worthy of marrying my daughter, whose father, mother and grandfather all ruled over the Two-Lands of Upper and Lower Egypt as pharaohs. Glumly, Pharaoh's advisors file out of her *Seal Room*. Only Neferu-Re remains.

Hat-Shep-Sut smiles at her daughter. "Now for the first time I have those *men* exactly where I want them."

"And where is that mother?" Neferu-Re asks, sarcastically.

"Groveling in the dust at my feet," Hat-Shep-Sut replies.

"If that is so," Neferu-Re says, "then you must remember to thank your co-Regent for making it happen."

When the Egyptians first began setting up bazaars and market-places in his kingdom, Barattarna thought of nothing other than filling his storehouses with Egyptian gold. So when his spies report that Egypt's co-Regent is lurking inside his kingdom, Barattarna thanks the god Teshop for favoring him with such an opportunity. He calls his chief of assassins and orders an immediate watch placed upon Thut-Moses while he and his advisors develop a plan to kidnap the co-Regent.

"He should be worth a lot of gold," Barattarna cackles to Hipa-Giluk.

But his sister scoffs.

"No matter how much gold they give you in ransom," she says, "it will be a pittance, compared to the amount you can get if you follow *my* advice."

Barattarna likes having fun. He enjoys laughter and frivolity. Hipa-Giluk is far better at intrigue. This is why brother and sister get along so well. Barattarna often tells Hipa-Giluk that the god, Teshop, made an error. His sister should have been the man and Barattarna, the woman.

"If these Egyptians selected some *little brown woman* as their ruler," Hipa-Giluk laughs, "then I see no reason why I shouldn't replace her."

"Please tell me your plan," Barattarna begs his sister.

"Your spies have informed me that this Thut-Moses has an appetite for women, brother," Hipa-Giluk purrs. "And you know how irresistible I am to men."

Barattarna claps his approval.

"I will simply get that little brown man to marry me." Hipa-Giluk smiles. "And I don't think that will be too difficult, do you?"

"No one in my empire is more desirable than you, dear sister," Barattarna attests.

"Any ransom would be a pittance compared to what you could receive for my dowry," she says. "And that's not all."

Barattarna's eyes dance with greed.

"Once I have gone to Thebes and I've become ruler over these *little brown people*, you will have more gold than your storehouses can hold."

"Oh, dear sister," Barattarna winks, "my houses can store quite a large amount of gold."

Thut-Moses weds Hipa-Giluk in a private ceremony. Only the nobility, members of the royal family, nomarchs, senior administrators, the War Council and the favored high priests are invited. Resplendent in their gleaming uniforms and distinctive insignias, members of the *Golden Fly Order* escort Thut-Moses and his bride to Amen's Temple. Hapu-Seneb conducts the ceremony. Neither Hat-Shep-Sut, Neferu-Re nor User-Amen attend the wedding.

Hipa-Giluk strikes an imposing a figure. She wears transparent robes fully accentuating her voluptuous body. But what becomes immediately apparent to all the attendees is that Thut-Moses' bride stands a head taller than every other person in the temple. Hipa-Giluk appears to be a goddess and, standing next to Thut-Moses, dwarfs him as Hat-Shep-Sut dwarfs one of her pigmies. After the wedding, a royal barge delivers Hipa-Giluk's dowry to the King of the Mitanni. The gold shipment, a single shipment from Pharaoh's gold mine at Amada, fills two of Barattarna's storehouses. He is so pleased that each day, for a month, the king visits each of his storehouses and stares at his gold for hours. However, after the marriage, things do not go so well for the Mitanni.

Thut-Moses stands taller than most Egyptian men. He is accustomed to looking down upon others. But his bride stands over three and a half cubits tall. She is a head higher than the co-Regent. To make matters worse, Thut-Moses learns, through a servant, that Hipa-Giluk refers to him as her "little brown man". Thut-Moses is humiliated. Not only has he married an 'amazon', but a woman who ridicules his skin color, as well.

"I'm sure she even ridicules the size of my 'love weapon'," Thut-Moses complains to Aron.

Aron finds the disparity in height between the co-Regent and his bride so funny that for a long time, every time he remembers the 'odd couple' taking their marriage vows, Aron gives a little chuckle. Thut-Moses always knows when Aron is laughing at him. He is not pleased. The co-Regent leaves for *Horus Nest* immediately after the wedding *and* makes no plans to return to his bride at Karnak. Thut-Moses vows never to appear in public with her, ever again. He leaves the high priestess of Niobe isolated in the *Grand Vizier's Palace*, separated from Egyptian society and excluded from Pharaoh's court. Hipa-Giluk is left with only her servants *to make mischief.*

In her isolation, Hipa-Giluk sends her servants all over Karnak making friends, gathering information and laying the foundation for her plans. And her first objective is to disrupt Thut-Moses' impending marriage to Neferu-Re. In order to accomplish this task Hipa-Giluk sets out to gain Neferu-Re's trust. Hipa-Giluk has brought an expert in the art of preparing and dispensing potions. Some of Hipa-Giluk's potions save lives, others make life pleasant. Some of Hipa-Giluk's potions bring an end to life in retching agony or in peaceful sleep.

Though Hat-Shep-Sut steadfastly refuses the Mitanni princess an audience, Neferu-Re is fatally curious about her competitor. After awhile, *God's Wife* journeys to the *Grand Vizier's Palace* to meet the mysterious Mitanni princess. For her first meeting with Neferu-Re, Hipa-Giluk prepares a potion of cannabis leaves. Whenever the high priestess of Niobe adds this potion to a woman's wine, the woman becomes completely subjected to her will. After their first meeting, Neferu-Re and Hipa-Giluk become inseparable.

Once she becomes Hipa-Giluk's friend, Neferu-Re's only goal is to arrange for her new friend to have an audience with Pharaoh.

"What purpose would such a meeting serve?" Hat-Shep-Sut questions her daughter.

"Does her height disturb you?" Neferu-Re replies. "Really mother, she's a very nice person. You'll like her, you'll see."

Yes, Hipa-Giluk's height disturbs Hat-Shep-Sut, but there's something else, something sinister, something she can't identify, but something that she knows is there.

"Oh mother," Neferu-Re insists, "don't be rude. You meet with any man who wags his little finger, but you won't meet with another woman. I'm surprised that someone who calls herself the *foremost of distinguished women* would behave so."

Neferu-Re's insistence begins to wear down Hat-Shep-Sut's resistance. She really has no reason for refusing to see Hipa-Giluk other than the feeling that Barattarna's sister is very dangerous.

Neferu-Re, who usually doesn't like anyone, fawns all over this Mitanni woman. What sorcery has the high priestess of Niobe used upon my daughter? Hat-Shep-Sut wonders.

Whatever it is, Neferu-Re continues to pester her about an audience.

"We have so many things in common," Neferu-Re says. "She's a priestess and so am I. We have fun comparing our rituals." She laughs like a little girl. "But her rituals involve the most unusual practices with men." Neferu-Re starts to giggle. "You should hear what she says about Thut-Moses. Hipa-Giluk is scandalous."

Neferu-Re's laugh is so infectious that Hat-Shep-Sut joins in the merriment and is happy, again.

"I know that all three of us will get along quite well," Neferu-Re declares. "Hipa-Giluk talks of nothing but my upcoming wedding. It's almost like we're sisters."

And since all Neferu-Re does is chatter about the Mitanni princess Hat-Shep-Sut begins to feel a kinship. Until she gets what she wants, Neferu-Re treats her mother like a devoted daughter. And since this is exactly what Hat-Shep-Sut has always wanted, she finally agrees to give Hipa-Giluk an audience.

"Great Queen and kinswoman," Hipa-Giluk says using her most deferential tone, "thank you for receiving me into your august presence."

The high priestess of Niobe gives a short bow but she does not "kiss the dust" at Pharaoh's feet as is the custom. Hat-Shep-Sut is displeased.

"My step-son's wife is welcome to my *Mansion of Millions of Years*, and ____," but before Hat-Shep-Sut completes her words, Hipa-Giluk's eyes stray from Pharaoh and fix upon the great, over-fed, shaggy-haired lion that rises unexpectedly from his normal spot below Hat-Shep-Sut's throne. Natee takes immediate notice of the stranger, rises to his feet and issues a low growl opening his gaping jaws and baring his monstrous fangs. Hipa-Giluk's hand goes up to her mouth trying to stifle an involuntarily shriek, but the hand is too late. Her scream echoes around Pharaoh's chambers. Natee takes Hipa-Giluk's scream as a challenge and roars back. Hipa-Giluk half stumbles, half backs away. Natee bares his fangs even wider his rumbling, deep chested growls coming in rapid succession. Normally, Natee is indolent and lies about, paying not the slightest attention to any of Pharaoh's visitors. Never has he behaved this way before. Even Awab, who is afraid of lions, on occasion, rubs Natee's shaggy mane. But the lion does not like Hipa-Giluk and lets her know it. Thut-Moses' wife slinks backwards. Natee follows her step for step. But when Natee reaches the end of his leather tether, he leaps at Hipa-Giluk issuing forth a bone-rattling roar. So strong is Natee's lunge that he almost topples Hat-Shep-Sut from her throne. Hipa-Giluk falls over backwards. But like a dancing contortionist, the Mitanni priestess leaps up, regains her balance and accomplishes the nearly impossible feat of running backwards in the direction of the double doors.

"Natee!" Hat-Shep-Sut shouts. "Why are you behaving this way?"

Natee turns and glances back at his mistress before returning his full attention back upon Hipa-Giluk who frantically paws at the doors of Hat-Shep-Sut's chambers. Once her escape route is open, the 'amazon' leaps out, races the hall and bursts down into the palace courtyard. Displaying amazing agility for one so tall, Hipa-Giluk then leaps into her litter and screams at her bearers *"Take me to my palace, immediately!*

Hipa-Giluk is disoriented and confused for the first time in her life.

Embarrassed by her undignified departure from Pharaoh's audience chamber, the high priestess of Niobe cowers in her own chambers. Buried in her personal chambers, she refuses even Neferu-Re's visits, terrified that somewhere Natee lies in wait.

Hipa-Giluk's own evil intentions haunt her and she now fears everyone and everything in this land that now has become both strange and savage to her.

"Get this message to my brother," Hipa-Giluk instructs her servants secretly dispatching them back to Mitanni with the assistance of the Mitanni spy network. "Tell him to send someone to rescue me. I'm afraid for my life!"

Hipa-Giluk's messengers slip through the Karnak's gates and make their way to the harbor where a small, cramped river launch secrets them down the Nile and out of Egypt. But her messengers do not escape detection. *Seeing Waters* keep them under the close scrutiny and report their movements back to Hapu-Seneb.

"Come with me!" Iby implores Senen-Mut. "It will be just like when we followed those Mitanni into Nubia for the first Thut-Moses, remember?"

"I remember," Senen-Mut says. "That was our first great adventure."

Thut-Moses sends Aron to Iunu. He wants Iby and a band of *watchers* to follow Hipa-Giluk's messengers into Palestine.

"Thut-Moses' *War Council* wants to know what she's telling Barattarna," Aron confides to Iby.

Senen-Mut is immersed in his latest research project. He is combing the temple's records of nilometer readings. The nilometer readings are annual records for the Nile's height going back centuries. So immersed is Senen-Mut in his research that he can hardly tear himself away from his scrolls long enough to even acknowledge Iby and his request.

"This will be another great adventure," Iby urges. "The co-Regent is convinced that his bride is sending information back to her brother, for an attack upon the Two-Lands. But Thut-Moses needs to know when and where."

"In the old days," Senen-Mut says momentarily looking up from his calculations, "we were both young and adventurous and I was in love."

"I know neither of us are young, any longer," Iby acknowledges, "but we can both enjoy this one last adventure. Come with me as far as Gaza. We can send people from there to learn what the Mitanni are planning. We won't have to travel all the way to

Megiddo. It'll be a short trip. It will do you good to get away from this musty old temple."

"Spying on the Mitanni is a young man's job," Senen-Mut sighs. "Young men take risks because the rewards are great and they have nothing to lose."

"They can lose *their lives*, " Iby retorts. "When did you become afraid?"

"My life," Senen-Mut says calmly, "has already been spent." He lays his hand on his friend's shoulder. "There is nothing left to lose."

Iby is torn. His time at Iunu has been wasted, but on his last trip to Palestine, Iby was afraid the entire time and he does not want to return to Palestine on this mission. But spying is all he knows. Besides, learning what Hipa-Giluk and Barattarna are planning is not a difficult a task. He doesn't need to visit Megiddo. Gaza is filled with wagging tongues. And Egyptian gold buys a lot of information. Iby only needs to contact those in Gaza who the information he seeks.

"We both have our final adventures," Iby smiles. "Yours is here, unlocking secrets; mine is as a stranger in strange lands."

Senen-Mut waves at the scrolls piled on the table in front of him. "These records contain the secrets that I can use to assure the eighteenth dynasty's future." Senen-Mut gives Iby a friendly pat on the arm. "Your must go to the land of the asiatics and assure the dynasty's present."

"War with the Mitanni is inevitable," Iby tells Senen-Mut. "Daily asiatics encroach upon our borders. Thut-Moses' marriage to the Barattarna's sister could not have put off the war, neither will Pharaoh's obstinacy. Everyone knows that the fate of the Two-Lands is in the hands of Thut-Moses. I know now that my duty, and the duty of everyone who follows the gods, is to serve him as best we can."

Senen-Mut nods in agreement. Iby starts to depart, but then he returns and gives his master a worried look. But Senen-Mut gives him a great hug and a smile.

"Don't worry," Senen-Mut says. "I will be here when you return."

"And if I do not return?" Iby asks.

"Then you will have fulfilled your destiny and can approach the *Scales of Djeheuty* with a heart as light as a feather of Maat."

Once again, Senen-Mut embraces his friend; this time he has tears in his eyes. Senen-Mut has not lost his power to dream,

Iby and several former *Eyes of Horus* follow Hipa-Giluk's handmaidens to Gaza, but the Mitanni do not tarry. They make their way up the coast of Palestine and cross over the Aruna Pass to Megiddo. Iby's party remains on their trail up the coast. But at the Aruna Pass, the watchers are surrounded and overwhelmed by a unit of Mitanni palace guard. Iby and his watchers are taken to Megiddo, tortured and then beheaded.

It's one of those rare days, in Lower Egypt, when it is cold and overcast. On this strange day, Senen-Mut learns of Iby's death. He, along with others throughout the Two-Lands, weeps.

CHAPTER TWENTY-EIGHT

It's the end of summer and it's the hottest in memory. A pestilence breaks out in the Nome of *Wast* south of Thebes. This pestilence is like none other. Especially hard hit is Senen-Mut's home of Armant. Though his parents are dead, his brothers and sisters still live on the family plantation, growing the flax that produces the finest linen in the Two-Lands. This latest pestilence has already claimed the lives of thirty of Armant's townspeople. Double that number die elsewhere throughout the *Nome of Wast*. These dead do not include the hundreds who have died in Thebes.

Normally, Seth's pestilence, a contagious disease created by the heat and the Nile's stagnant waters, spreads downstream infecting people further and further north. However, this pestilence claimed its first victims in Thebes and then spreads south, striking villagers and townspeople *upstream* from Thebes. User-Amen urges Hat-Shep-Sut to take a personal interest in this outbreak. "This year Seth's pestilence kills your people in epidemic proportions, Majesty," User-Amen pleads. However Pharaoh remains indifferent to her people's suffering.

"My councilors have the blessings of their Lord and know that my only thought is for the happiness and prosperity of my people," Hat-Shep-Sut responds. "Now you may go!" But her councilors refuse to leave Pharaoh's Seal Room.

"Great Lord, we seek your guidance," User-Amen says. "Seth has already struck down many of the people, here and in the south."

"Whenever *Hapi* does not run freely, stagnant water dwells in the canals and pools," Hat-Shep-Sut reminds them. "Then Set sends the pestilence that emerges from the dank, wastewater. This is the waste that has accumulated in Seth's bowels." Pharaoh is irritated at being bothered with such issues. "Must I tell you what to do? You should know what to do. Send out the healer priests."

"But Great Majesty," User-Amen counters, "there are not enough healer priests to handle this pestilence. We fear that it is spreading to a greater number of towns and villages, than ever before."

"This is not the first time the Two-Lands have suffered from Seth's pestilence," Hat-Shep-Sut snaps, "why can't you do what has been done for generations *before* you were here?"

"Great Lord," User-Amen explains to his mistress, "the pestilence has spread from Thebes *upstream* into nomes south of *Wast*. This disease is like no other."

"Am I a healer priest?" Hat-Shep-Sut asks. "Hapu-Seneb, you are the high priest of Amen. See to your responsibilities."

From the earliest days, the people turn to the priests in times of catastrophes. But the priests do not respond as they have in other times.

"I accompanied Senen-Mut to Armant," Pen-Nek-Heb explains to Pharaoh. "His entire family was stricken by Seth's pestilence."

"How are they?" User-Amen asks. He sees a look of concern register briefly upon Hat-Shep-Sut's face. He senses she would have her Grand Vizier inquire into the health of Senen-Mut's family's.

"All of them are in various stages of the disease." Pen-Nek-Heb shakes his head. "His two sisters seem so frail that I fear that they will be added to the list of Seth's victims." "Is he still in Armant?" Hat-Shep-Sut asks.

"No, Majesty," Pen-Nek-Heb replies. "He found conditions in Armant and elsewhere so appalling that he has come to Karnak to help us develop a plan to relieve the suffering."

"Well go," Hat-Shep-Sut tells them. "You have my permission to follow the guidance of *Pharaoh's Former Consort.*"

One by one her advisors depart the *Seal Room*. Hapu-Seneb and User-Amen shuffle out with their heads together. They're the least likely to develop anything together. User-Amen despises Hapu-Seneb as a crass opportunist who would do anything to remain in Pharaoh's favor. Pen-Nek-Heb catches up to them and tells them that Senen-Mut wants to meet at Amen's temple. Pharaoh's vizier and Amen's priest nod their assent.

"Does Pharaoh know what is happening out there?" Senen-Mut asks. The others confer with him in Amen's temple. "The people are panicking."

"The *Living* God has directed us to take care of it," User-Amen says giving Senen-Mut a weak shrug.

"What are your temples doing for those afflicted by Seth's pestilence?" Senen-Mut asks Hapu-Seneb.

"Too many are flocking to my temples," Hapu-Seneb complains. "My priests cannot treat them all. They're not even trained in the healing arts. What have we to do with Seth's victims?"

"In times like these, people expect their priests to care for them," Senen-Mut reminds Hapu-Seneb.

"The healing arts are taught in the temples of Sekhmet," Hapu-Seneb replies.

"Pharaoh wisely directs that all priests, including those of Amen, protect the people against Seth's pestilence," User-Amen reminds Hapu-Seneb. "She will be displeased to hear that Amen's priests have failed her people." This last remark gets Hapu-Seneb's attention.

"My priests are doing what they can," Hapu-Seneb whines, "but we need assistance."

"The people report that your priests shut their doors to the sick and dying," User-Amen retorts. "Instead of caring for the people, your priests are turning the sick away saying that the pestilence is a sign of Set's anger."

Shrugging his shoulders, Hapu-Seneb says nothing.

"Your priests," User-Amen continues, "even caused some villages to turn to sorcerers for assistance."

Hapu-Seneb raises his arms in mock innocence.

"Don't pretend that you don't know what's going on," User-Amen challenges Amen's priest.

"I have no notion of what you are saying," Hapu-Seneb protests.

"In almost every village infected by *Seth's Pestilence* that we visited," Pen-Nek-Heb says, "villagers pay sorcerers to use the blood of murdered children to protect their huts from Seth. "

"What?" User-Amen exclaims.

"Yes!" Senen-Mut declares. "The sorcerers are killing orphaned children and smearing their blood on entry posts of villagers who pay them to ward off Seth's pestilence."

"And that's not the worse," Pen-Nek-Heb interjects.

"What can be worse?" User-Amen asks.

"The village elders tell us that the sorcerers do not wield the "killing" knives," Pen-Nek-Heb replies. "The *priests* and *acolytes* are conducting the sacrificial rites upon orphan children in their temples." Pen-Nek-Heb stares at Hapu-Seneb; Amen's priest stares at the floor. "This is why the priests are keeping the people out of their temples."

"Fear is stalking the land and death is feasting in its wake," User-Amen declares. His face bears the solemn look of one preparing to meet Anubis.

"And Pharaoh does nothing," Senen-Mut mutters.

"This is not the normal summer fever," Hapu-Seneb again whines. He knows about the infancides. "There is terror in this pestilence. It is not the fault of the priests. None can face god's wrath."

"What's so different about this disease?" User-Amen asks.

"The bowel movements of Seth's victims are soaked with blood," Senen-Mut recounts. "It's as if the body is putrefying from within. Blue marks, resembling bruises, appear on the victim's stomach. I've seen many pestilences, but never anything like this."

User-Amen nods his understanding.

"This pestilence moves *up* the Nile, traveling backwards," the vizier ponders, "*as if it were following one of the asiatic rivers.*"

"I have sent scribes to consult the archives," User-Amen announces. "Thus far, none of the herbal formulas or magical rites taught by the ancients have any effect on this disease."

"Which is why the only thing we can do now is wait until the pestilence runs its course and fresh water flows down the Nile, once more," Hapu-Seneb blurts out.

"Thebes cannot wait for the pestilence to run its course," User-Amen states. His normally calm voice quivers. "Fear of the disease is almost as bad as the disease, itself. Nobles and their families are fleeing Thebes and the pestilence. Many are injured and even killed in accidents."

"What kind of accidents?" Senen-Mut asks.

"Injuries and drowning, boat collisions, mostly," User-Amen replies.

Panic seizes Thebes. The nobles are hoarding their yachts and heading down river. The harbor and canals interconnecting with the river are jammed, the waterways are choked and river traffic is paralyzed, everywhere. The larger boats challenge the smaller boats for maneuvering room. Yachts and barges challenge skiffs and fishing boats. Great transport vessels, crammed with nobles, their families and their possessions, attempt to force their way through the congestion invoking the nobles' privilege of right of way. Invoking the privileges of nobility avails no one. Pilots and captains panic and ram each other.

"Just yesterday, the harbor master and his entire family were lost," User-Amen narrates, "when a transport barge rammed their yacht, broadside."

"This is not Seth's pestilence," Senen-Mut says.

"What are you saying?" Hapu-Seneb asks.

"What looks like Seth's pestilence," Senen-Mut replies, "is really something else."

"What do you recommend?" User-Amen asks.

"For now, we need to worry less about causes and more about cures," Senen-Mut concludes. "We need to dispatch trained healers to every affected town and village. The healers are to be accompanied by soldiers. The soldiers will prevent the murder of any more orphan children." All eyes turn towards Hapu-Seneb.

"Even here in Thebes there are not enough healer priests," Hapu-Seneb says. "Each one is caring for hundreds of sick. More than a thousand here in Thebes receive no care at all."

"There are no healer priests available," User-Amen confirms.

"In villages outside of Thebes," Pen-Nek-Heb remarks, "the dead lie unburied in the streets. People stricken by the pestilence are abandoned by their families and left to die alone."

"And with the temples turning away everyone bearing Seth's mark," User-Amen adds, "all order in the Two-Lands will soon disappear."

"Yet," Senen-Mut says, "Pen-Nek-Heb and I have seen a courageous few ignore the danger to care for the sick and comfort the dying. If we don't have enough healer priests, I am certain there are many people like these."

"But where do we find people like these?" Hapu-Seneb asks.

"We find some of them at *Horus Nest*," Senen-Mut smiles. "We find them at *Neb-Heb Valley*. We find them in Thut-Moses' army."

"But its not the work of soldiers to nurse the sick," Hapu-Seneb says looking over to User-Amen for support. "Healing is a job for priests."

"Each nome, city and town must be told of the pestilence," Senen-Mut continues as if Hapu-Seneb had not spoken. "Each affected town must designate a building that is isolated from all others. This is where the sick will gather. In Thebes, designate many such buildings."

"Listen to Senen-Mut," Pen-Nek-Heb urges User-Amen. "He understands what must be done."

"I have already notified Thut-Moses and the Overseer of his *War Council* that we require his cooperation," Senen-Mut explains. "User-Amen, you will be responsible for selecting the *Houses of the*

Sick here in Thebes. Stock them from Pharaoh's warehouses as well as those of the temples." Hapu-Seneb stifles his urge to protest the seizures of temple supplies. "I want Amen's temples open to the sick. Your priests will take their instructions from healer priests *or whomever else I delegate*. Do you understand?"

Hapu-Seneb mutters to himself, but finally agrees.

"But where will we to get the healer priests?" User-Amen asks. They all look to Senen-Mut.

"I don't know, yet," Senen-Mut responds. "But send for scribes to copy and distribute my instructions until we can get them."

User-Amen copies and sends each nomarch in the Two-Lands the following instructions to be followed as they would the desires of the *Living* God:

Protect every source of water.

Use only wells certain to be clean. Put these wells under the control of an army officer and his soldiers. The officer is to allow no one other than a young girl, under twenty and born under a full moon, to draw water from the clean well. If the well is large and many people use it, increase the number of young girls drawing water.

The Drawers of the Water will purify themselves each day.

The Drawers of the Water must wash their hands and feet each morning and evening in raw wine. Each day they must wear a fresh tunic of white linen bleached for six hours in the sun. The Drawers of the Water may eat only well-baked bread, fresh fruit whose skin they, themselves, have peeled. They may drink only wine or water that they have drawn.

Keep the wells clean.

Only new water jars are allowed within thirty paces of clean wells. Neither are unclean persons or animals to be allowed within thirty paces of any clean water well.

Protect your food and water

Guard against allowing flies, mice and bats to contaminate food or water.

Each House of the Sick must be provisioned.

Houses of the Sick are to be provisioned with fruits, vegetables, milk and wine. Bales of coarse linen and ample quantities of clean straw are to be stocked as bedding for each of the sick. The bedding is to be burned once a sick person either dies or recovers. Sick persons are to have their own individual drinking vessels and eating bowls which are to be broken after each use.

Disposal of the Dead

Soldiers will collect the bodies of the dead. Anyone who dies of the pestilence must be burned before burial. Gather up wood in preparation.

This decree is to be posted by order of the Grand Vizier until further notice.

Senen-Mut sends out scribes to scour the Two-Lands, especially the northern nomes, for healer priests. He decides to increase their number by having each healer priest train as many assistants as possible. "Use priestesses, acolytes, anyone capable of following directions," he orders.

Soon healer priests have assistants who can mix herbal teas, wash and bandage bleeding sores and prepare meals. Others of Sekhmet's priests teach the healing rituals involved in the burning incense, invoking Sekhmet's image and chanting prayers. Once the newly trained assistants become adept at ministering to the sick, they train others. This army of healers spread out through Thebes and up to afflicted towns and villages bringing help and comfort to thousands. Yet despite this cohort of healers flung into battle against the disease, the pestilence continues to rage, respecting neither rank, nor sex nor age. All Seth's victims follow a cycle of fever, chills, the retching of black vomit and expelling of bloody excrement. Some victims become too weak to hold down nourishment and die. Others take in nourishment, fight to stay alive and recover. In the towns and villages where Senen-Mut's instructions are heeded, many lives are saved. But even where the instructions are not followed, Thut-Moses' soldiers maintain order and burn the bodies of the dead. Thut-Moses gives Senen-Mut his complete cooperation. Unlike Pharaoh, he is concerned that Seth's pestilence may have a foreign origin.

"Majesty! Come quick! It's Neferu-Re!" Tuua bursts into Hat-Shep-Sut's private chambers, screaming.

"Neferu-Re!" Hat-Shep-Sut responds more than a little irritated by the intrusion. "What is it that Neferu-Re wants now?" *My daughter takes too many liberties,* Hat-Shep-Sut bristles. *I must remind her who is lord in the Mansion of Millions of Years.*

"Come quick, Majesty," Tuua blurts out, "Your daughter has the mark of *Seth's pestilence!*"

"What?" Crying out, Hat-Shep-Sut grabs a gown and outraces Tuua back to her daughter's chambers where Neferu-Re lies shivering on her sleeping mat though covered by a wool cloak. Hat-Shep-Sut places her hand upon Neferu-Re's head. She burns with fever.

Already two healing priests are in attendance. "How long has she been like this?" Hat-Shep-Sut asks. "Why wasn't I informed *immediately?*"

"It happened just this evening, Majesty," Tuua responds. "The healing priests have just arrived."

Hat-Shep-Sut cradles Neferu-Re's head in her lap. One priest attempts to pour a medicinal concoction between her daughter's parched lips, but Neferu-Re gags and coughs out the tea along with splotches of blood and mucous. In all her life, Hat-Shep-Sut has never known such fear. Slowly it invades her body and clutches at her heart.

"Oh my daughter! My daughter!" Hat-Shep-Sut moans over and over. "What ails you?"

"Its Seth's pestilence," one of the priests says.

"How do you know this?" Pharaoh thunders. "She may only have a chill."

One of the healing priests reaches down and pulls back the linen sheet. A large black and blue bruise covers Neferu-Re's stomach.

"Send for her father!" Hat-Shep-Sut shouts. A palace guard races out the door. Then Hat-Shep-Sut hisses to the healing priests. "I order that you save my daughter or your heads will decorate pikes and your bodies will feed the jackals."

The priests merely gaze back serenely at the *Living God*.

Flickering lights from alabaster vases cast eerie shadows upon the linen drapes surrounding Neferu-Re bedchamber. Hat-Shep-Sut already imagines the forty-two judges peering down upon her daughter's sleeping mat.

I was indifferent to the harm Seth's pestilence had on my people, she moans, *now, as a punishment for my indifference, Seth claims my own sweet child, my most precious possession, my own first-born.* Hat-Shep-Sut is wracked by guilt.

Tuua hovers just beyond the dim lights. She feels the *judges'* presence as well. The nurse wrings her hands, shakes her head back and forth and cries out to Sekhmet, begging the goddess to spare Neferu-Re and take her life, instead.

Tuua has reason to bargain with the goddess for Neferu-Re's life. It was she who trusted Hipa-Giluk's words that her mistress would not be harmed. It was Sekhmet's only female priest who tells the high priestess of Niobe how to dispense her poisons. So Sekhmet ignores Tuua's prayers while Neferu-Re stubbornly refuses to *fight for her life.*

When Senen-Mut arrives, he says not a word, but takes his daughter in his arms. It's the first time that he has held Neferu-Re since she was a small child. Salty tears stream down his face repeating the scene just recently enacted in Armant where both of sisters and his youngest brother all lose their battle to Seth's pestilence.

Over the next three days, Neferu-Re passes in and out of consciousness, awakening only to cough up blood and bile or to pass bloody matter from her intestines. Both Hat-Shep-Sut and Senen-Mut remain by her side. They speak softly to her, but Neferu-Re says nothing. Towards the end of the third day, the dying princess recognizes her father. Rising up ever so slightly, she gives him a wan, enigmatic smile. Then she falls back down in a fit of coughing. On the fourth day, weakened by her lack of nourishment and failing to thrive, Neferu-Re returns to her *KA*.

Hat-Shep-Sut goes into shock. Torn between complete disbelief and unimaginable grief, she teeters back and forth between the reality of her sorrow and the madness of her guilt. The healing priests carry Pharaoh back to her own chambers and maintain a vigil over her for the remainder of the night. No one knows whether or not she will survive. But sometime early the next morning, after Ra has renews the eastern sky with his crimson glow, Hat-Shep-Sut abandons her grief and falls into a fitful sleep. Later in the afternoon, she awakens. For the next several days and nights, Hat-Shep-Sut alternates between incontrollable grief and unimaginable pain. For a while, she even raves as one possessed.

Why is it not possible that the Living God cannot command that Neferu-Re return to her? She shouts out in her Red Chapel where she has gone for solace.

Anger and helplessness battle ferociously for control of her mind. Servants, guards and priests alike believe Pharaoh has become permanently deranged. However after a week, a healing priest, seeking to ease the mother's pain, distracts Pharaoh from her grief by recounting the unusual circumstances surrounding Seth's pestilence.

"Normally, Seth's pestilence travels north down the Nile to the *north*," the priest explains. "But this year the pestilence began in Thebes and traveled south *up* the Nile."

Suddenly Hat-Shep-Sut's mind clears and she understands who and what was behind her daughter's death. Pharaoh now sets aside her grief long enough to summon her Captain of the Palace Guard.

"Bring me that Mitanni bitch's head," Hat-Shep-Sut orders. "The vultures can feed on whatever remains!"

Two new moons pass since Seth's pestilence first lays its deadly grip upon the Two-Lands. The myriad of healers, soldiers, drawers of water, helpers and assistants are exhausted. Eating little and sleeping less, they wage a heroic struggle against the contagion masquerading as Seth's pestilence, but in reality is an attack by an underhanded and sneaky enemy. For weeks now the disease begins claiming fewer victims. Then comes the long anticipated cry.

"Hapi rises! The river is rising!"

Indeed, the Nile rises and the inundation of new waters begins to freshen the air and wash away stagnation. The sick begin recuperating. Within a week of the inundation, after racking up a terrible toll of lives, noble as well as commoner, the epidemic of Seth's pestilence ends.

Eugene Stovall

CHAPTER TWENTY-NINE

It takes the entire seventy-day mourning period to prepare Nefe-ru-Re for her journey into the afterlife. Her organs are stored in four canopic jars under the watchful care of the goddesses *Neith, Selkis, Nephithys* and *Isis.* Each canopic jar bears one of Neferu-Re's likenesses. The four jars are stored in a canopic chest that will accompany Neferu-Re's coffin to her tomb across the Nile in the *Valley of the Dead.* Neferu-Re's heart, the seat of her *KA,* remains in her body. Anubis will weigh it against a feather of Maat upon the *Scale of Djeheuty.* Many in Karnak, including her mother, fear that Neferu-Re's heart, weighed down with wickedness, will feed Anubis' forty-two judges. The Royal Embalmer immerses Neferu-Re's body in a natron bath for thirty days. Then he carefully prepares Pharaoh's daughter for mummification. He attaches protective amulets to her body using thin layers of narrow-cut linen wrappings. Once the amulets are in place, the Royal Embalmer enshrouds Pharaoh's daughter in many layers of broad, thick, sweet-smelling linen wrappings that have been soaked in aromatic resins and perfumed oils.

Meanwhile, laborers and artisans assemble Neferu-Re's funerary necessities. A gang of workers digs her tomb into one of the rocky hills of the western desert. Masons cut and design her stone sarcophagus. Artists design the emblems, masks and scarabs required to decorate the sarcophagus. Wooden sculptors fashion four separate coffins for the princess. Each coffin represents one of Neferu-Re's titles, God's Wife, Daughter of Pharaoh, Consort of the co-Regent and Crown Prince and Princess of the Eighteenth

Dynasty. They all fit inside each other. Another corps of artists decorates the walls of Neferu-Re's tomb with carvings and paintings informing the gods of Neferu-Re's importance and explaining why she should be permitted to enjoy the afterlife.

When the mourning period ends, and all is in readiness, Neferu-Re's funeral procession snakes out from Pharaoh's *Mansion of Millions of Years* down to the royal dock where a fleet of royal barges carries the princess and the royal family across the Nile to the *Valley of the Dead*. On the other side, Neferu-Re's coffins are then loaded upon a sled pulled by white oxen. Neferu-Re's canopic jars follow on a second sled. Hat-Shep-Sut leads Neferu-Re's funeral procession on foot. Senen-Mut trudges by her side. User-Amen, Hapu-Seneb, Thut-Moses and Aron accompany the grieving parents at a discreet distance. Pen-Nek-Heb takes his place among the other priests.

Hat-Shep-Sut thinks how nice it would be if Iby were here. She misses the strange little man with the lop-sided smile. From behind are heard the hideous wailing of temple priestesses, screeching and screaming in the manner proscribed by ancient tradition. Pharaoh finds this ritual expression of grief inappropriate and disrespectful. But she knows that it is just one of those traditions that she must tolerate.

How can they sound so dreadful when it is I who actually suffers the loss? she cries out in the silence of her heart.

More priestesses follow. They strum bow-shaped harps, beat on tambourines and play an assortment of wind-flutes, reed pipes and sistras. Bald-headed priests walk alongside Neferu-Re's coffins, burning incense, pouring libations of oil and milk upon the ground and chanting prayers pleading for Neferu-Re's protection. Family, nobles and dignitaries follow behind the priests.

Neferu-Re's household servants carry all the personal possessions she might require for her journey ____ clothes, cosmetics and furniture. Neferu-Re's great white python, fully embalmed, is carried in a litter. Tuua walks in front of the snake, tears pour silently, yet unceasingly down her cheeks. Tuua look less like the fearsome hag responsible for her mistresses' death and more like the pathetic, old woman she had now become. The palace guard keeps a great crowd of distant relatives, dubious friends and court officials, scribes, administrators and army officers far in the rear. These also raise lamentations in competition with the wailing priestesses.

Only Hapu-Seneb, his acolytes and attendants, accompany Hat-Shep-Sut and Senen-Mut into Neferu-Re's tomb. Hapu-Seneb orders Neferu-Re's coffins opened and he performs the *Opening of the Mouth* ceremony. Mid-way through, Hat-Shep-Sut becomes weak. Her knees buckle. She falters. Senen-Mut catches her by the elbow and props her up. Hat-Shep-Sut looks into Senen-Mut's eyes, swollen red with tears. She experiences a not unpleasant emotion. Hapu-Seneb completes the *Opening of the Mouth* ceremony. The attendants reseal Neferu-Re's coffins and lay them in her sarcophagus. Once again, Hat-Shep-Sut weakens, her chest heaves and tears flow, unbidden, from her eyes down her cheeks.

No parent should be forced to bury a child, she mourns.

But her tears gradually cease, she forces herself to once again become Pharaoh, the Golden Horus and Ruler of the Two-Lands of Upper and Lower Egypt.

Outside her daughter's tomb Hat-Shep-Sut enters a great white pavilion flying the crimson pennants that bear her cartouches and emblems. Seating herself upon a golden throne, Pharaoh accepts the condolences of the mourners streaming through the gigantic white funeral tent. Hat-Shep-Sut must handle this ordeal, alone. None but the palace guard and her faithful Awab remain in the pavilion with her. When User-Amen appears, Hat-Shep-Sut beckons her Grand Vizier to her side and whispers a command in his ear.

Outside the white pavilion, family, friends and court dignitaries partake of a great funeral banquet. After all have offered their condolences, the palace guard escorts Pharaoh back across the

Nile to her *Mansion of Millions of Years*. Now Hat-Shep-Sut's grieving begins in earnest.

In the meantime, User-Amen delivers Pharaoh's message to Senen-Mut. "The Great God wishes for you to call upon her at the *Mansion of Millions of Years* at your earliest convenience," User-Amen whispers in Senen-Mut's ear.

Senen-Mut is not surprised by Pharaoh's summons.

CHAPTER THIRTY

B oil, boil, toil and troubles, witches brew and caldron bubbles.

    Two full moons pass since Barattarna demands that Thut-Moses marry his ten-year old daughter and Hat-Shep-Sut send him an exorbitant amount of gold. Hat-Shep-Sut refuses to respond to the crisis. She believes Barattarna's mention of Neferu-Re's health is an acknowledgement of his involvement in her death. It's an insult he will live to regret, she vows. But her failure to act forces User-Amen journey to *Horus Nest* in order to enlist the aid of Pharaoh's co-Regent.

"We disposed of as many of Hipa-Giluk's servants as we could find," User-Amen tells Thut-Moses, "but Barattarna still has spies everywhere. Undoubtedly, he knows exactly how his sister met her KA."

"The truth of Thoth is on your tongue," Thut-Moses replies. "An invasion from the Mitanni is inevitable, whether or not I marry this child."

"I agree with you," User-Amen sighs, "It's just a matter of time."

"I am curious," Thut-Moses confides to User-Amen. "Does my step-mother believe that bringing Senen-Mut back to Karnak will end her troubles?"

"I'm afraid so," User-Amen replies. "She talks as if he can do anything, restore her *Eyes of Horus*, negotiate a peace with Barattarna, keep you from taking the throne. She is not quite rational. The loss of Neferu-Re ___."

"She was like that before Neferu-Re's death," Thut-Moses snaps.

"Yes, I'm afraid you're right," User-Amen agrees," but if it means anything, Senen-Mut doesn't believe we gain by giving into Barattarna's demands, either. He continually urges Pharaoh to invite your majesty back to Karnak for discussions."

"I will consider your words," Thut-Moses tells User-Amen. "I imagine my step-mother is unaware of this meeting?"

"The *Living God* may not be aware of it, but Senen-Mut knows," User-Amen replies. "It was he who sent me to your majesty."

After Pharaoh's Grand Vizier departs, Aron warns his 'nephew' against going to Karnak.

"She's unstable," Aron says. "Hipa-Giluk's execution was unnecessary. Do you really know what she's planning?"

"When Pharaoh summons me to Karnak," Thut-Moses replies, "I must answer her summons."

Aron becomes more agitated. "How can you trust User-Amen or even Senen-Mut," he asks. "Who knows? She might even blame you for Neferu-Re's death. *They both might!*"

"The co-Regent must obey the will of the *Living God*," Thut-Moses repeats. "This is what I will expect when I become Pharaoh."

Once they arrive in Karnak and settle comfortably at Pharaoh's *Mansion of Millions of Years*, Thut-Moses and Aron receive Hat-Shep-Sut's messenger inviting them to join her for supper. Aron remains apprehensive but Thut-Moses feels quite secure as they are ushered into one of Hat-Shep-Sut's more intimate dining chambers.

In the center of the room is a marble table surrounded by high backed leather-bound chairs. Over to the side, seated on a low sofa, Senen-Mut and Pen-Nek-Heb are engaged in a quiet conversation. Hapu-Seneb paces slowly back and forth his leopard skin cloak flaps at his skinny legs. For some reason, Hapu-Seneb's cloak reminds Thut-Moses of Natee. Hat-Shep-Sut's great-hearted, though gentle pet. The lion had died so mysteriously at the beginning of Seth's pestilence. Natee's keeper believes Natee was poisoned, but decides not to share his suspicions fearing for his own life.

On a separate sofa, User-Amen chats with Amen-Hotep. The high priest of Anubis is new to Pharaoh's circle of advisors though, for years, he has served as Pharaoh's *Director of Works*. Amen-Hotep supervised the construction of Neferu-Re's tomb and all her funerary regalia. He was also the chief architect and builder of Hat-Shep-Sut's temple at Deir el-Bahri. Amen-Hotep is not quite as old as Pen-Nek-Heb or User-Amen but far older than Senen-Mut and Aron.

Seeing the co-Regent enter, User-Amen rises with all the others to bow to their knees. Thut-Moses nods for all to rise,

"Majesty, Ptah has blessed this gathering with your presence, I trust that your journey was pleasant." User-Amen says.

"Yes, thank you," Thut-Moses replies. "Shu favored the oarsmen by filling the sails with the fullness of his breath."

"But why is Senen-Mut so angry with the high priest of Anubis?" Aron asks. None in the room is oblivious to the obvious hostility Senen-Mut has with Amen-Hotep's presence. Every once in awhile, Senen-Mut darts jealous glances at Hat-Shep-Sut's *Director of Buildings* which even Thut-Moses finds hard to ignore,

"Have you not heard?" User-Amen asks. "Pharaoh has bestowed upon Amen-Hotep the title, *Pharaoh's Beloved Confidant*. He has become her new consort."

Aron reacts as if someone has slapped him in the face. Instantly he sympathizes with Senen-Mut. It's not as if Aron is still in love with Hat-Shep-Sut, that's been over long ago. But it's just that he didn't think that he would hear about her new lover like this. And besides Amen-Hotep is so old.

How could she? Aron fumes. Senen-Mut's jealousy is now his jealousy. But as he thinks about it, when Amen-Hotep worked on the *Grand Vizier's Palace,* Aron remembers, even then, rumors circulating on the *Street of Barbers* and the bazaars of Upper Thebes about Pharaoh and her *Director of Works*. At the time

Amen-Hotep told his many admirers at the *Palace of Ladies* that the *Grand Vizier's Palace* was really to be his.

"Now the gossip is really been flying," User-Amen confides. "Some say that she's about to evict Senen-Mut from the Grand Vizier's Palace for a second time."

"It's no wonder there's such hostility between them," Thut-Moses observes. "Neither man is happy. The one who occupies the *Grand Vizier's Palace* wants to share Pharaoh's sleeping mat and the one who shares Pharaoh's sleeping mat wants to occupy the *Grand Vizier's Palace*.

"How can two men make such fools of themselves?" Aron whispers to Thut-Moses, after User-Amen departs. "Especially when the *Street of Pleasures* has so many women and none of the heartache, eh?" Thut-Moses laughs.

But one look at Aron's face tells Thut-Moses that his friend's discovery of Pharaoh's new consort is painful.

Thut-Moses also notices that something else about this gathering is not right. None of Pharaoh's servants are present. User-Amen rushes about the banquet room to see to the needs of Pharaoh's guests.

The gathering all looks up at once. The curtains behind the marble table begin to rustle and the drapes separate. All conversation ceases as Hat-Shep-Sut, seeming a little smaller and a little more vulnerable, without Natee on his leash and without *God's Wife* at her side, enters. Hat-Shep-Sut wears no crown nor does she wear any jewels. In fact, she wears no ornamentation, at all. She is dressed in a simple sheath covered by a finely spun woolen cloak. No cosmetics other than the mandatory black eyeliner mark her face. Most surprising of all, Hat-Shep-Sut's head is shaved and she stands before her guests completely bald. As her guests stare at Pharaoh in astonishment, she strides over to the marble dining table, followed by the ever-watchful Awab and sits upon the high-backed chair at the center.

"Welcome *Friends of Pharaoh*," Hat-Shep-Sut says. "Please join me."

Aron needs no second invitation. Despite the grave wound to the love in his heart, a love that he refuses to recognize even exists, Pharaoh's former consort retains a healthy appetite. The big man immediately finds a place and falls upon a particularly delicious-looking breast of pigeon dripping with savory garlic sauce.

Thut-Moses accepts a seat immediately at Hat-Shep-Sut's right and User-Amen takes the one at her left. The others find their own seats. Not surprising, Senen-Mut and Amen-Hotep sit at opposite ends from each other. The atmosphere is strange and subdued without Pharaoh's bevy of waiters, servants and wine stewards, rustling guards and pigmy fan bearers present. The entire party, including Pharaoh, herself, must serve themselves. However despite the lack of help, all of Pharaoh's guests seem to manage quite nicely, especially Aron who attacks a whole rack of lamb once he has finished off the pigeons. Everyone enjoys the novel meal and the conversation around the table is light and unburdened by what the servants overhear. Once all have eaten and drank their fill, Hat-Shep-Sut speaks.

"Recently I received a letter from Barattarna, the King of the Mitanni and brother to my co-Regent's former wife who I confess that I had killed, needlessly." Pharaoh looks about. It still seems strange to see her head completely shorn. "I doubt not that Hipa-Giluk deserved to meet her *KA*, though User-Amen advises me that she might have served a better purpose than feeding the jackals in the western desert."

Searching the faces of her guests, Hat-Shep-Sut wonders whether they understand what she is trying to say. But none of her listeners react. She continues.

"Most of you already know the contents of Barattarna's letter." Her voice is clear and firm, tinged neither with guilt, sorrow nor remorse. "But so that you will have no doubt as to Barattarna's intentions, hear his words for yourselves." Hat-Shep-Sut nods to User-Amen who reads Barattarna's letter out loud. Afterwards Thut-Moses is the first react.

"How does Pharaoh propose that we deal with this *fool's* threats?" he spits out. "I doubt that you expect me to marry his Mitanni brat nor will you accede to his demand for gold."

Hat-Shep-Sut demurs. "Why would Barattarna make such a threat if he did not believe that we are ill-prepared for war?"

"His spies have misled him," Thut-Moses says.

"But listen to his words," Hat-Shep-Sut urges. "'*I must have more war equipment though I know I have more than Pharaoh has already*'."

"How does Barattarna know that he has more war equipment than we?" Thut-Moses asks. "Each day that *RA* passes through the sky, our army grows stronger. Our ranks are filled with battle-tested veterans trained to kill. My soldiers are armed with weapons that penetrate flesh and hack off limbs. Our bowmen slaughter Pharaoh's enemies at great distances. My chariots fly like the wind. We are not the weak army that the Hyksos, defeated centuries ago! Where does Barattarna get his information?"

"Spies! His sister's handmaidens! What does it matter?" Hat-Shep-Sut dismisses her co-Regent's concern. "From the time Hipa-Giluk arrived in Thebes, Hapu-Seneb's *Seeing Waters* continually intercepted a stream of messages from Hipa-Giluk to Barattarna. Who knows how many reached him?"

"Possibly, the information came from Iby," Senen-Mut interjects. "He knew nothing of the *War Council's* plans, but Barattarna might have thought he did." Looking over at Aron, Senen-Mut asks, "Exactly what was Iby instructed to accomplish on his last mission into Palestine?" Just as Aron is about to speak, Thut-Moses signals Aron to remain silent.

Just as I thought, Senen-Mut tells himself. *They sent my poor friend to spread disinformation.* Senen-Mut feels a wave of revulsion for Aron as well as for the co-Regent. Then he realizes his own role in the tragedy. We all were responsible for sending Iby to his death! Senen-Mut sighs.

"Your friend had gotten rusty and soft," Thut-Moses says. His gaze is like the hawk-headed god, Horus, eyeing his prey, without mercy or pity. "He made mistakes."

"We didn't force him to go," Aron adds. "He went of his own free will."

"Yes, that is true," Senen-Mut confirms, "though he had neither the guile nor the duplicity to understand what he was being asked to do."

User-Amen intervenes. "I believe that the co-Regent's point is that Barattarna overestimates his own strength while he underestimates ours. Is that correct Lord?"

"Yes," Thut-Moses replies with a smile upon his face.

"So it is untrue what Barattarna says about the state of the Two-Lands?" Hat-Shep-Sut asks.

"Majesty?" User-Amen asks.

"Does Seth, God of Chaos, rule my lands?" Hat-Shep-Sut asks. "Do my people disrespect me and disobey my commands?"

The room is silent. Pharaoh's advisors hold their collective breath. None wants to offend Pharaoh by telling her the truth. Even the co-Regent refrains from answering Hat-Shep-Sut directly. The entire room braces for one of Hat-Shep-Sut's tirades, but instead, she sits, looking into the distance, forlorn and alone.

"Great Lord!" User-Amen says. "The people have been cruelly afflicted by your tax collectors and the soldiers who enforce their will."

"Why do my nomarchs allow such to happen?" Hat-Shep-Sut asks. She keeps her voice calm.

"Majesty, your *War Council* now controls your army," User-Amen replies, glancing over at Thut-Moses who occupies himself with a slice of mutton and a mug of wine.

"If I may remind Pharaoh," Pen-Nek-Heb blurts out, "the *War On Pharaoh's Enemies in the North* was fought against these very same nomarchs. This is why Barattarna says that 'chaos rules your borders and disrespect rules your people'."

"But my people are prosperous! They are happy! I have given them festivals and I have given them victories! I have protected them from the asiatics and the Nubians! Why would they disrespect me?" Hat-Shep-Sut is genuinely incredulous at news that she is hearing.

"Perhaps, Great Lord," Senen-Mut says in a guarded voice from the far end of the table, "its because the people do not know you."

"And what do you mean by that, Lord Senen-Mut?" Pharaoh asks.

"Perhaps the time has come to announce Pharaoh's long postponed jubilee."

The afternoon shadows grow longer as Amen descends towards the western horizon. Thut-Moses and Aron recline in their chambers. Though they share a jug of wine, each man is lost in his own thoughts. Thut-Moses thinks about the inevitable war with the Mitanni. Aron sulks over being replaced as Pharaoh's consort by the elderly high priest of Anubis.

Finally Thut-Moses breaks the silence. "What do you think of my step-mother's performance?" he asks.

"Whatever she's planning," Aron replies, "you can be certain that Senen-Mut is behind it."

"I agree," Thut-Moses says, "but what is she up to?"

"Don't count out Pharaoh's *beloved* Director of Works either," Aron responds, ignoring Thut-Moses' question. "He's not just going to allow Senen-Mut to elbow him aside."

"Why do you say that?"

"Court gossip!"

"Which is?"

"Amen-Hotep is unhappy with Senen-Mut residing in the *Grand Vizier's Palace*."

"If that priest thought Hat-Shep-Sut was going to give him a palace," Thut-Moses laughs, "he doesn't know Pharaoh very well."

Aron also laughs but without much merriment.

"Whatever Senen-Mut and Hat-Shep-Sut are hatching, Amen-Hotep is not pleased," Aron observes. "I think we can use him."

"Use him how?" Thut-Moses asks.

"To learn Pharaoh's plans," Aron says. He gives his *nephew* a knowing look.

"She suspects that Barattarna knows who had Hipa-Giluk beheaded, right?"

"Yes, that's what she said."

"I think she's scared." Aron concludes.

"Scared!" Thut-Moses scoffs. "Scared of what?"

"Barattarna is not only threatening to invade the Two-Lands, but he's challenging Hat-Shep-Sut to personal combat!"

"You believe that?" Thut-Moses asks blinking with wonder. "You really believe that she brought Senen-Mut back to defend her in personal combat with Barattarna?" Thut-Moses starts to laugh and then he can't control himself. The image of the overly effeminate Barattarna and the assertive Hat-Shep-Sut facing each other on the battlefield somehow tickles his imagination and Thut-Moses enjoys a good long laugh.

"She certainly can't depend on that old priest to defend her," Aron points out. I'm going to see to that!

"That wasn't too difficult, was it?" Senen-Mut asks Hat-Shep-Sut. All her other guests, including Amen-Hotep, have departed, but as an added precaution, the two decide to speak in her *Seal Room.*

"I have little difficulty doing what must be done," Hat-Shep-Sut responds. Her double *entendre* drips with sarcasm. *Ptah give me wisdom,* she prays. *Again he's acting like he's Pharaoh and I'm his servant!*

"Your performance this evening was perfect," Senen-Mut smiles. As usual, he is completely unaware of Hat-Shep-Sut's growing irritation. "You are, in every way, the great Pharaoh that you've always wanted to be."

"You've accomplished all that, *have you?*" Hat-Shep-Sut sneers. "And in such a short time."

Hat-Shep-Sut may have loved him once, but she never liked him. The purpose for the *Student of Wast* as well as for the *Student of Jackal* was to serve her. As smart as Senen-Mut believes he is, he doesn't understand this simple fact. Instead he dreams of how things will be.

The next time, I will not be her Grand Vizier, Senen-Mut tells himself. *When she tires of the brick mason and I am occupying her bedchamber, User-Amen can remain Grand Vizier.*

Even Pen-Nek-Heb warns him.

"One cannot return to the past, my son," the high priest cautions his initiate, but Senen-Mut ever the dreamer, is blinded by his own arrogance. But, for the time being, each serves the other's purposes. Though Senen-Mut infuriates her, Hat-Shep-Sut heeds his advice and arranges for a jubilee.

"Of course you are right my dear friend," Hat-Shep-Sut tells Amen-Hotep when they are alone together. "After all if I had heeded his advice, earlier, things might have been different and Neferu-Re might still be alive."

"Now don't scold yourself," Amen-Hotep comforts her. "Don't think about Senen-Mut," he urges. "Think only about the outcome."

Hat-Shep-Sut accepts Senen-Mut's plan to declare a jubilee at the upcoming *Opet*-festival to energize and reinvigorate her rule. Once her jubilee ceremony affirms that the gods smile down on her, the people will rally and defend the Two-Lands against any invasion the Mitanni might launch. By declaring her jubilee, Hat-Shep-Sut puts herself completely into Amen-Hotep's hands. And the high priest of Anubis promises Pharaoh a successful future.

But Senen-Mut doesn't trust *Pharaoh's Beloved Confidant* any more than Aron.

"If you give him the opportunity," Senen-Mut warns Hat-Shep-Sut, "Amen-Hotep will betray you. He's addicted to the same vice as Barattarna, except he doesn't polish his nails or wear paint on his face."

"If I were to believe every vicious rumor circulating my court," Hat-Shep-Sut replies, "I would not know whom to trust. You should hear what they say about *you*."

Senen-Mut considers asking her, but feels it beneath him to inquire about court gossip. He remains silent.

"Amen-Hotep understands me," Hat-Shep-Sut continues. "He's considerate and sympathetic. He's not a warrior nor does he need *watchers*, but all my ladies agree that no other man understands women quite as well as Anubis' high priest. You could take a couple of lessons."

"Just remember what I told you," Senen-Mut huffs trying to hide the pain of her last remark.

"Amen-Hotep likes your idea of building two obelisks to memorialize my jubilee." Hat-Shep-Sut says switching the subject.

"Good," Senen-Mut replies, "I have already chosen the site where I'll build lodgings for the workers and their families."

"What?" Hat-Shep-Sut snaps. "Amen-Hotep has completed the designs and begun cutting my obelisks from a quarry of red granite."

"It was my understanding, Majesty," Senen-Mut mumbles, "that we were building the obelisks to win the hearts of the people. We should see to their needs, first."

"I will see to their needs, when this crisis has passed," Hat-Shep-Sut snaps. "For now make preparations for my jubilee. We have no time to build huts for workers. Let their families remain where they are."

"But, Majesty ____," Senen-Mut begins.

"I have spoken," Pharaoh shouts. "Now go!"

CHAPTER THIRTY-ONE

Senen-Mut has labored a great amount of time on a gift for Hat-Shep-Sut. He believes this will be the gift that will win her over. Senen-Mut fears that Hat-Shep-Sut will not appreciate his gift, but he knows that it will change life in the Two-Lands, forever.

From the beginning, time in the Two-Lands is kept on the lunar calendar maintained at the Temple of Iunu. Upon this lunar calendar are recorded all the religious holidays celebrated by the people of the Two-Lands during one year. But even when he first began his studies at the Temple of Iunu as an officer cadet, one problem has always baffled Senen-Mut. Iunu's lunar calendar is unable to predict the arrival of the Nile's inundation that marks Akhet, the first season of the year.

Iunu's lunar calendar has never been able to accurately predict the annual inundation. None know for certain when the Nile's new waters will wash the Two-Lands free of stagnation and deposit its bounty of silt. This problem has baffled the Two-Lands' wisest men for centuries.

"We know that when Hapi's new waters come late in the year," Senen-Mut tells Pen-Nek-Heb, "Seth's pestilence brings disease. But we never know the time of Hapi's inundation or when it will arrive late."

In most years, the new waters first appear in *Thoth*, the first month of the new year. Knowledge of the new waters is obtained from nilometer readings first taken at Khnum's temple on

Elephantine Island, just north of the first cataract. In a year that the Nile's waters arrive late in the season of planting, Seth's pestilence almost certainly brings decay to the land and sickness to its people. Neither Pen-Nek-Heb nor any of his scholars have the knowledge necessary to construct an accurate lunar calendar, one that can accurately predict the arrival of the new waters. Every year the priests of Iunu must revise their calendar and reset the dates of all the public festivals and celebrations as soon as the new waters arrive. Senen-Mut is determined to solve the mystery and make a gift of his *perfect* calendar to Hat-Shep-Sut.

Month in and month out, year in and year out, Senen-Mut studies nilometer readings taken at Elephantine, at Dendera and finally at Iunu. The scrolls he examines record nilometer readings taken over centuries. Each one records the height of the Nile on a certain day in a certain year. He studies scrolls that record normal readings; he studies scrolls that record unusual readings; he compares and contrasts. Senen-Mut finds no patterns, no clues and no answers. He merely confirms what everyone already knows. *When the inundation arrives late according to the lunar calendar, the Two-Lands will suffer Seth's pestilence, as well as a poor harvest.* Out of despair, Senen-Mut takes the problem to Pen-Nek-Heb.

"Search the sky for your answer," the old priest advises. "I have a young initiate; his name is Hemit. He reminds me of you. The two of you should get along quite well. Hemit may have a key to unlock the secrets you seek to know."

As Pen-Nek-Heb predicted Hemit supplies Senen-Mut with an amazing fact about the annual inundation of new waters.

"I have studied the stars since I passed into the inner temple ten years ago, Master," Hemit tells Senen-Mut.

"What do the stars tell you about the coming of the new waters?" Senen-Mut asks.

"Always the new waters arrive within days of *Sopdet*'s appearance," the initiate replies.

"How often do the new waters fail to accompany *Sopdet*?" Senen-Mut asks.

"*Never, Master!*"

"Never, Hemit?"

Senen-Mut cannot accept it. After four years of searching, the answer cannot be *that* simple.

"Never, Master." Hemit has been a stargazer from the time he was brought to Iunu, as a precocious fifteen-year old. His ability to identify the comings and goings of planets, moons and even vast constellations, has given Hemit quite a reputation among Iunu's most esteemed astronomers. The wisest of Iunu's astronomers affirm that if Hemit asserts that the inundation and *Sopdet* appear at the same time, every year, then it must be so.

However, now comes the tedious job of correlating nilometer readings for the past ten years with the recorded observances of the star named for a goddess, *a star that appears for only two-weeks each year.* But if what Hemit says is true, Senen-Mut can construct a calendar that will never miss predicting the exact time of new year's inundation by more than two weeks.

Senen-Mut and Hemit pore through stacks of records. This time they only want to know the date of the inundation and the date that *Sopdet*, known as the 'dog star', appears low in the eastern sky a few hours before sunrise. When the astronomers learn what Senen-Mut and Hemit are doing, they join the team, searching records that go back thousands of years. After awhile not only does the tension build, but the competition increases as well. Try as they may, none finds a year when the new waters of the Nile do not appear within two weeks of *Sopdet*'s appearance in the eastern sky. The thousand-year-old records are indisputable.

Senen-Mut requests Iunu's Council of Initiates for the Inner Temple to consider his findings and pass on judgment. Iunu's Inner Temple unanimously accepts Senen-Mut's findings. He receives a commission from the Inner Temple to draft Iunu's first *solar* calendar. The following new year, scholars from all over the Two-Lands join Senen-Mut, Hemit and Pen-Nek-Heb on the Elephantine Island at the temple of Khnum to see for themselves if *Sopdet*, indeed, heralds the coming of the new waters. And just as Hemit predicted, when *Sopdet* makes her first appearance in the eastern sky an hour before dawn, the nilometer readings confirm that the Nile rises and the inundation is beginning. Of all Senen-Mut's accomplishments, this discovery gives him the most satisfaction. Now he can prove to Hat-Shep-Sut how much he loves her. This discovery will make her known as the most important Pharaoh in the history of the Two-Lands and truly the foremost of distinguished women. Yet despite this truly remarkable achievement, not even Senen-Mut's *solar* calendar can prevent Hat-Shep-Sut from losing her throne.

CHAPTER THIRTY-TWO

At the end of each year Amen is weary. He has expended all of his energies to produce bounty that gives the people of the Two-Lands everything that is good and beneficial from the land, from the air and from the great Nile river. At the end of the year, the god is exhausted. During the *Opet*-festival, Amen renews himself by stepping outside the world of harmony and peace and tapping into the awesome chaos of the cosmos. Out of the pure energy Amen is born. So it is that in this seething miasma of molten fire, so pure that it is invisible, that Amen is renewed.

The mysterious rejuvenation of Amen takes place at Dendera in a sanctuary at Hathor's temple. Few even know of the sanctuary's existence. The people celebrate the *Opet*-festival at Luxor. In the inner sanctum at Hathor's temple, a priest opens a portal into the cosmos and unleashes the full potential of chaos and disorder. This is no simple operation. The priests who open the *Portal of Power* risk mortal danger. Only the most experienced priests are allowed to conduct the ceremony.

During normal *Opet*-festivals, Pharaoh is a mere spectator to Amen's awesome renewal. However, on the first day of *Akhet*, marked on Senen-Mut' newly created *solar* calendar, Pharaoh's jubilee has been declared and Hat-Shep-Sut will be far more than a mere spectator to the *Opening of the Portal of Power*; she will be an active participant, opening the portal with her own hands, rejuvenating herself as well as Amen.

Hat-Shep-Sut hasn't felt this happy since before Neferu-Re's death. Her handmaidens have spent several hours preparing her for her jubilee. Outside, in the courtyard, beginning promptly at midnight, white robed priests of Anubis begin reciting specially prepared prayers over and over. The prayers, composed by Amen-Hotep, are meant to give Hat-Shep-Sut confidence. Somehow they only add to the sense of dread. She uses, her happiness to banish her dread. She remembers that Senen-Mut has promised her a gift even more wondrous than the *solar* calendar, although Hat-Shep-Sut doesn't see why he makes so much fuss over another method of tracking time. After all, time is time. Senen-Mut refuses to tell her about his wondrous gift. Rumors abound that Senen-Mut's gift is a magical switch associated with *Sopdet* for opening the *Portal of Power*. Hap-Shep-Sut can barely control her excitement.

Her handmaidens make their final adjustments to her *pharaonic* regalia before she inspects herself in the full-length bronze '*see face*'. When Pharaoh marches outside, she feels uncomfortable without Natee. Her litter takes her to the royal dock for her progress down river to Hathor's Temple at Dendera.

Awaiting Hat-Shep-Sut at Hathor's temple is Amen-Hotep's gift, a pair of obelisks. *Pharaoh's Beloved Confidant* completed her second pair of obelisks in a mere seven months. The project takes a terrible toll upon the workers. Some workers fall to their deaths from the high granite cliffs; others are crushed when one of the obelisks breaks while being lifted onto its transport barge. With the Opet-festival less than three months away, the accident forces Amen-Hotep to rush the construction of a third obelisk. Amen-Hotep's overseers drive the workers, mercilessly. Somehow, he completes the construction and places the two red granite obelisks at Dendera in time for Pharaoh's jubilee. Amen-Hotep is certain his obelisks will give Hat-Shep-Sut the maximum protection, possible, against the *Portal of Power*. Amen-Hotep manages to have her obelisks in place and on time, but Hat-Shep-Sut might have had less confident in her '*beloved confidant*' had she known of his meeting with Aron one month earlier.

"I know that you love the *Living God* with your whole heart and KA," Aron assures the high priest of Anubis. "Thut-Moses is as concerned for his step-mother safety as you. He is especially concerned that something might happen to her should the Mitanni attack."

The muscular Captain of Captains dwarfs the priest. Yet, hiding his true feelings from the high priest of Anubis, Aron uses friendly smiles and gentle touches to put Amen-Hotep at his ease.

"There is nothing that I would not do for her majesty," Amen-Hotep replies. Amen-Hotep is gentle and speaks quietly and reverently. "I trust that you and your master believe that my only interest is serving the *Living God*. She faces so many dangers." Amen-Hotep earnestly tries to convince Aron of his loyalty.

Aron nods his head in a sympathetic gesture. "Which is why I was so careful in the constructing her obelisks. There is no doubt that they will perform exactly as intended."

Senen-Mut overlaid Hat-Shep-Sut's first obelisks, those standing at Karnak, entirely with gold. But Amen-Hotep gilds only the upper parts of the red granite obelisks at Dendera. Their power is greatly reduced.

"I have heard rumors that Senen-Mut has created a device making it safer for Pharaoh to renew her power." Aron confides by lowering his voice. Even so, Amen-Hotep winces noticeably at the mention of Senen-Mut's name.

"Not only are my obelisks less dangerous," Amen-Hotep continues, "but one is shorter than the other, giving an added measure of control."

"Indeed you were wise to use every precaution to protect the *Living God*," Aron smiles. "I have inspected them myself. They are worthy of your reputation." Then he pauses. "It is a shame that in your haste, so many laborers lost their lives. Only you can say whether this tragedy portends worse events in the future. Of course, my only concern is for the safety of my beloved, who I still love with all my heart."

I mustn't overdo it, Aron tells himself. *Despite his other shortcomings, this priest is no simpleton.*

"The Inner Council will support the co-Regent," User-Amen warned Aron, "just as long as you do not provoke a civil war."

"What worries me is the Mitanni threat," Aron continues, bringing Amen-Hotep into his confidence. "You must know that Barattarna vows to avenge the murder of his sister."

The priest pales and his eyes dart back and forth in fright at Aron words.

"What can I do?" Amen-Hotep wrings his hands. His whining voice pleads Aron for help. "Pharaoh believes this renewal will prepare her to meet Barattarna's armies."

"You don't believe that do you?" Aron stares at the older man with hard, unblinking eyes.

"No-o," Amen-Hotep stutters. "No, my beloved will not survive any battlefield encounter.

"Then," Aron says, "after causing the deaths of so many innocent workers, I would hate to think that you would take the chance of causing the death of the woman that we both love."

Amen-Hotep does not respond. Aron presses his attack.

"The ancients intended the *pharaonic jubilee* to replace the ritual murder of a pharaoh unfit to rule over the Two-Lands," Aron tells Amen-Hotep. "Do you believe Pharaoh is capable of leading her armies against Barattarna?"

Amen-Hotep visibly shakes. He cannot imagine *himself* on a battlefield, much less his beloved Hat-Shep-Sut. The idea of his gentle Hat-Shep-Sut leading the army of the Two-Lands against asiatic hordes *and being hacked to death* genuinely frightens *Pharaoh's Beloved Confidant.*

"You can't believe that she is capable of leading the army against the king of the Mitanni, can you?" Aron continues.

Amen-Hotep merely shakes his head.

"Neither can I," Aron agrees.

"We must save her! " the confused and befuddled priest blurts out.

"I am with you," Aron replies, his words comforting and soft. "Together we can stop the gossip that the *Living God* has taken a weak old man as her consort."

"What do you suggest that we do?" Amen-Hotep asks.

"I am certain when the time comes," Aron replies, giving the priest a reassuring pat on the arm, "you will know how to save the woman that we both love. But we must also think of saving the Two-Lands as well. The co-Regent wants to know that he can rely upon your support."

"You may assure the co-Regent that I will do whatever it takes.

Back at Horus Nest, Aron reports to Thut-Moses. "The old fool will do whatever we want," Aron gloats.

"You don't understand," Pen-Nek-Heb warns Senen-Mut, "the *Portal of Power* has enormous energy." Despite Senen-Mut's obvious genius in designing the *solar* calendar, Pen-Nek-Heb does not believe that Senen-Mut's device will open the *Portal of Power*. Nor does he believe that Senen-Mut's plan to get Hat-Shep-Sut safely through her jubilee is '*foolproof*'. Pen-Nek-Heb believes that Thut-Moses and his War Council intend to take Hat-Shep-Sut's life during her pharaonic jubilee ceremony.

"The source of power still will come from the obelisks that Amen-Hotep has just constructed," Senen-Mut counters. "They are small and weak ____ certainly weaker than Dendera's main source of power."

"That matters little," Pen-Nek-Heb retorts. "Those obelisks still have enough power to turn anyone unfortunate enough to make the slightest error into a ball of fire."

Senen-Mut and Pen-Nek-Heb are sitting at the top of Iunu's circular observation deck. The deck is built on the top of a three-story building. Even though Ra has slipped beneath the horizon, from their position on the observation deck, they can still see his purplish-red glow illuminating the western sky. Several of the benches around them are already occupied by several of Iunu's stargazers. The astronomers, astrologers as well as their acolytes and scribes adjust their instruments and prepare to make their nightly recordings of the great stellar expanse.

"It was you who introduced me to the stars," Senen-Mut remarks his master.

"Yes and I gave you the services of an excellent stargazer," Pen-Nek-Heb observes. The master of Iunu has never known anyone to pass initiation as quickly and as astutely as Senen-Mut. Nor has he known anyone to rise to the heights of political power and fall as quickly. But this latest stunt, trying to manipulate the *Portal of Power* by using some magical device might be too difficult for even the brilliant *Student of Wast*. And another misstep will not only bring Senen-Mut down but his supporters, at Iunu along with him. Pharaoh is not known for her forgiveness.

"How did you manage to get Pharaoh to locate the obelisks at Dendera?" Pen-Nek-Heb asks.

"I suggested that she would need her own light for the ceremony at Hathor's Temple," Senen-Mut replies.

"That she will," Pen-Nek-Heb confirms. "That she will!"

"Do not frown so," Senen-Mut laughs, "I used Hemit's knowledge to help create my device. It is guaranteed to remove all danger when Pharaoh's opens the *Portal of Power*."

"Is that so," Pen-Nek-Heb replies. Even in the gloom of night, Senen-Mut can see the dubious look on the priest's face. "Tell me about it."

"I have fashioned a golden statue in the image of *Sopdet*, complete with a golden star above her head and two dark green emeralds for eyes," Senen-Mut announces, proudly.

"When the first rays of the *dog star* reflects in *Sopdet*'s eyes, a beam will shoot out from the star on the head and open the *Portal of Power*."

"This I must see," Pen-Nek-Heb laughs.

"Have you ever witnessed the *Portal of Power*?" Pen-Nek-Heb snorts.

"Not the actual *Portal of Power*," Senen-Mut hedges.

"I have!" Pen-Nek-Heb says. "A priest must join two powerful wands together before the portal open. Light does not open the *Portal of Power*. Energy opens it, the energy of a thousand oxen. No, my young friend, moonbeams are not strong enough to open the portal, no matter how cleverly constructed."

"It is true that I have never seen the *Portal of Power*," Senen-Mut smiles, "yet I have been in many tombs and underground chambers where illumination for the paintings and carvings are provided by similar portals." Senen-Mut gazes steadily at Pen-Nek-Heb. "Don't scoff so," Senen-Mut smiles. "Have you not instructed me in your mysteries and the power of the Aten since my sojourn at Iunu? Have I not had access to the wisdom of the ages?"

Pen-Nek-Heb concedes Senen-Mut's point. Power can be controlled by its absence, or maybe in a moonbeam, he wisely concedes.

"Possibly you wish to see a demonstration?" Senen-Mut asks.

"Of course," Pen-Nek-Heb replies. Senen-Mut's device not only endangers Hat-Shep-Sut's life, it jeopardizes the Inner Council's plans to remove her from the throne and install Thut-Moses, *Pharaoh over the Two-Lands*. If this device works, the council might consider getting Senen-Mut out of the way, permanently.

"There must be no civil war," User-Amen once again warns Thut-Moses.

"I promise that the only war that you will witness," Thut-Moses replies, "is my war with Barattarna and the kingdom of Mitanni."

"Then we are agreed," User-Amen says, resigned to what must be done.

"Senen-Mut has a device that can open the *Portal of Power* without touching the wands," Pen-Nek-Heb confides to Thut-Moses and the other councilors.

"Whether or not the device opens the *Portal of Power*, my step-mother will be removed," Thut-Moses declares.

Eugene Stovall

"What is to be done with Senen-Mut?" Hapu-Seneb asks. Amen's high priest hopes to finish the job he began many years ago. The high priest longs for the news that someone has finally slit Senen-Mut's throat.

"Thut-Moses should allow him to remain at Iunu, for the time being," Pen-Nek-Heb suggests, "you will have access to a remarkable mind. After all, you might need him when you become Pharaoh."

"But he could interfere," Hapu-Seneb argues.

"The decision has been made," User-Amen states. "There will be bloodshed enough when the Mitanni invade. It shouldn't start, now, needlessly. Besides it's Amen-Hotep who worries me."

"Then rest assured that our plan will succeed," Thut-Moses says. "The priest of Anubis is concerned for Hat-Shep-Sut's life. He will do anything we say as long as we spare her KA.

"And his KA as well," Aron snorts.

So the plan is set. The council agrees. If Hat-Shep-Sut accepts their decision, she will remain at Karnak as Thut-Moses' co-Regent, if not, she will be banished to Amen's temple at Amada.

When she is with Amen-Hotep, Hat-Shep-Sut recalls those days when her father walked with her in his garden and taught her what she needed to know to be a good ruler. Now she and her 'beloved confidant' take quiet strolls in secluded parks or in Pharaoh's private garden the same way she and her father did. And today, as Hat-Shep-Sut stares at her lover, it seems that she is seeing her father once again and she feels happy, just like she did when she was a little girl. Hat-Shep-Sut and her priest share stories from the *Manual of Good and Polite Conduct*. It's their favorite book. It quotes the maxims of Ptah-Hotep, the Grand Vizier to Maat-Ka-Re Isesi, a fifth dynasty Pharaoh.

"After my jubilee," Hat-Shep-Sut promises Amen-Hotep, "the *Manual of Good and Polite Conduct* will inspire my rule. Then my people will have many reasons to love and obey me."

"You have much wisdom, Great Lord," Amen-Hotep says. "Your people will cherish your days as the *Living God.*"

His words caress Hat-Shep-Sut's *KA* and sooth away her cares. She never tires listening to her *Beloved Confidant.*

"Once your jubilee is completed, my Queen," Amen-Hotep continues, "I promise that all your concerns will be at an end."

"You came into my life when I needed you most," Hat-Shep-Sut sighs, clasping his hands in hers. "Thank you!"

Tears run down her cheeks.

On New Years eve, the eve of the *Opet*-festival, Amen-Hotep sails with Hat-Shep-Sut and Thut-Moses to Hathor's temple at Dendera. Along the journey, Amen-Hotep recites the following:

We offer this prayer to Amen in the sixteenth year of the reign of Female Horus of Fine Gold, Two Ladies Flourishing of Years, Divine of Diadems, Pharaoh of Upper and Lower Egypt, Maat-Ka-Re Hat-Shep-Sut Khenmet-Amen Foremost of Distinguished Women. May Amen rejuvenate the Living God and cause the people throughout the Two-Lands to celebrate her jubilee.

Senen-Mut arrived at Hathor's Temple early to install his golden statue of *Sopdet.* Three priests from Iunu, experienced with the *Portal of Power* join Hathor's priests and priestesses along with a few acolytes. Once his marvelous device is installed, Senen-Mut awaits the arrival of the Royal Barge outside the temple. The nobles, members of Pharaoh's Inner Council and masses of people are assembling at Thebes, awaiting the announcement from Dendera and preparing for the procession of priests, priestesses and dignitaries from Karnak to Luxor.

The early morning mist drifts up from the water creating an eerie view for those straining to catch sight of Pharaoh's flotilla. Apprehension subdues the knot of court officials and priests straining for a glimpse of *Living God's* approach for her appointment with Dendera's *Portal of Power.* Peering at the gloomy river off in the distance, Senen-Mut sees what appears to be the glitter upon the surface of the water illuminating the night as if from a shower of moonbeams. Then slowly the misty night begins to glow as the moonbeams resolve themselves into thousands of torches lighting Pharaoh's flotilla over the Nile's dark waters with their fiery glow. Then, out of the torch-lit night, comes Pharaoh's Royal Barge, escorted by boats containing her palace guard, serving maidens and household overseers. Once the Royal Barge docks, the palace guard escorts Hat-Shep-Sut, Thut-Moses and Amen-Hotep through the pre-dawn darkness into Hathor's Temple. A faint glow lights the visitor's path as temple priests escort them down a secret passageway leading to the sanctuary of the *Portal of Power*. Double doors swing open and Pharaoh, the co-Regent and the high priest of Anubis enter a circular sanctuary with a raised altar in the middle. Upon the altar stands Senen-Mut's creation, a green-eyed statue of *Sopdet*, facing an alcove on the far wall. Amen-Hotep leads Hat-Shep-Sut around the altar to the alcove. Here the priest of Anubis intones a prayer:

When thou crossest the sky, all faces behold thee, but when thou departest, thou are hidden from their faces. Great fashioner of what the soil produces, profiteer to gods and men, hear the chattering of your creation at thy rising, it is the only praise that the living can give you.

Follow the Living God, the King of Upper and Lower Egypt, Maat-Ka-Re Hat-Shep-Sut, the justified, may she live enduringly. Follow she who is your most perfect earthly representative as you follow yourself. Follow and refresh her as you follow and refresh yourself, So that she may endure forever and ever, as you are Amen.

And, as if activated by the priest's words, the green eyes of Sopdet's image begin to glow. Then, quite suddenly, a beam of light shoots out from the star on Sopdet's head to the open sky and the chamber is bathed in a soft golden light. Hat-Shep-Sut, Thut-Moses and Amen-Hotep are struck with amazement. Senen-Mut's device actually works! Two priests stand on either side of the Portal of Power. Their hands, completely covered with thick linen wrappings, hold great golden tools that resemble paddles. When the light shoots from Sopdet's eyes, the priests leap back in amazement. The Portal of Power begins to slide open *without their assistance*. And the sanctuary is filled with the flashes of lightening bolts until Sopdet's eyes cease to glow and the *Portal of Power* closes back on itself.

For several moments, none present utters a word. Thut-Moses is first to regain his composure. The co-Regent nudges Amen-Hotep.

"The god has spoken," Amen-Hotep announces in a solemn manner, "Pharaoh's rule has not been renewed. The god chooses, in her stead, the co-Regent. Henceforth he is to be known as *Horus Powerful of KA, Lasting is the Manifestation of Re, Master of Power, Beautiful of Shape, Speaker of Truth, Lord of the Cobra, Pharaoh of Upper and Lower Egypt, Menkh-Kheperu-Re Thut-Moses*."

Hat-Shep-Sut freezes at Amen-Hotep's announcement. She has always known this time might come. Now it is here! She gathers herself in serenity, secure that she remains the *foremost of distinguished women*. Hat-Shep-Sut is not even surprised that her own *'beloved confidante'* is the instrument of her betrayal, but turns to stare at the man that she has loved and trusted, before marching unrenewed, yet undaunted out the sanctuary, the eyes of all those men, priests, acolytes and guards, watching Maat-Ka-Re Hat-Shep-Sut, truly the foremost of distinguished women.

Eugene Stovall

BOOK FIVE

CHAPTER THIRTY-THREE

"**I** am absolutely blind," Thut-Moses complains.

"While Mitanni and Canaanites squat about the *Anubieon* watching and reporting everything back to Barattarna, I know nothing of his preparations against us."

Pharaoh and his co-Regent, Queen Hat-Shep-Sut, meet in the *Seal Room* with Pharaoh's advisors. Queen Hat-Shep-Sut, who is not only the co-Regent, but *God's Wife* as well, has vacated the *Mansion of Millions of Years* and has settled in her new home, the *Grand Vizier's Palace*.

"Neferu-Re loved it here," she tells her servants. "I feel her presence here with me."

Months have passed since Amen-Hotep declares Thut-Moses Pharaoh at the *Opet*-festival. Hat-Shep-Sut decides not to fight the Inner Council. But by losing her throne, Hat-Shep-Sut gains power. Thut-Moses values her both as his co-Regent and as *God's Wife*. Pharaoh's entire court, indeed the whole of Karnak, defers to Hat-Shep-Sut, as never before.

"Actually it's a relief," she confides in User-Amen. "I knew that I couldn't have faced Barattarna, in battle, but neither did I want to give up the throne. Praise Amen that it was taken from me. Thut-Moses is welcome to lead the army against any asiatic horde. There are some tasks only women can do like give birth and some tasks men enjoy doing like causing death."

Hat-Shep-Sut forgives everyone involved in her ouster *except* Amen-Hotep. She doesn't blame Pharaoh's Beloved Confidant for his role in ousting her from the throne; his betrayal accomplished what everyone knew was best, *even her*. Hat-Shep-Sut hates Amen-Hotep because he broke her heart. Not only that he gave Senen-Mut the satisfaction of saying, *"I told you so!"* When she and Senen-Mut are together, Hat-Shep-Sut can it in his eyes.

She had been so certain of Amen-Hotep's love, so certain that she had found the one man who understood her and loved her unconditionally that she forgot her own beliefs. So now that Thut-Moses is Pharaoh over the Two-Lands, she is alone. Hat-Shep-Sut never cried before but now she cries. She lost Neferu-Re, she lost Amen-Hotep. She is all alone and she cries. But after all her tears have fallen and there are no tears left, Hat-Shep-Sut feels that Neferu-Re is at peace and the love that Hat-Shep-Sut once had for Amen-Hotep turns to hate.

"How could you lie to me?" she screams when Amen-Hotep comes to beg her forgiveness. "How could you betray me?"

"I did it for you, Majesty," Amen-Hotep whimpers. "I did it for us. *I did it so that we could be together!*"

"Together with you!" Hat-Shep-Sut gives out a sarcastic laugh. "I wouldn't spit on you if you were dying of thirst in the middle of the western desert!"

Hat-Shep-Sut calls the officer of her guard.

"If this jackal ever comes here again, the only part of him I wish to see is his head on a pole. Is that clear?"

The officer bows and orders his soldiers to escort Amen-Hotep from the Grand Vizier's Palace and to execute him if he is ever seen again. Thut-Moses even issues a proclamation banning Amen-Hotep from Thebes and any other place in the Two-Lands where he might disturb the serenity of his co-Regent. Amen-Hotep confines himself to the temple of Anubis at Hardai in the *Anubieon*. Hat-Shep-Sut weathers her personal crisis by taking an even greater interest in the affairs of state. Just as her father and brother did before him, Thut-Moses invites Hat-Shep-Sut to the Seal Room, where she fully participates in Pharaoh's deliberations.

"My *War Council* urges me to attack the Mitanni," Thut-Moses continues, "but without intelligence, I'd be a fool to attack."

"I see you learned your lesson in the Nubian desert well," Hat-Shep-Sut smiles.

"My co-Regent is correct," Thut-Moses responds. "So if I don't know what Barattarna knows, how can I attack?"

"Great Lord," Hapu-Seneb offers, "the *Seeing Waters* are at your disposal. Let them be your eyes and ears."

"They cannot do what the *Living God* requires," Aron replies. "To attack the Mitanni, Pharaoh's army will not be able to travel by ships as we did when we entered the land of Punt. He must march fifteen thousand men along with horses, donkeys, oxen and thousands of attendants and supplies across the Sinai desert without being seen."

"The last time I crossed the Sinai," Thut-Moses says, expanding on Aron's point, "I had only fifty soldiers and Barattarna knew my every move from the time I left Gaza until I entered the temple of Niobe in Megiddo."

Thut-Moses glances over at Aron to see if he can catch his 'uncle' smiling. Aron maintains a straight face, but his eyes dance back and forth.

"Even if I get to Gaza before he learns of our presence, after such a march my soldiers will be exhausted and nowhere near the Mitanni kingdom. Barattarna could attack me anywhere in Palestine. And his fighters will not be like the Nubians. His soldiers are battletested, tougher than any the eighteenth dynasty has ever faced."

"Then why not wait for him to attack?" User-Amen asks. "You have many fortifications in the north. Your garrisons are alert and well trained. Barattarna will have the same problem if he attacks us. Our soldiers will be fresh and his exhausted."

"Possibly, the Grand Vizier did not hear what I said," Thut-Moses sneers. "WE HAVE NO EYES! WE ARE BLIND!" Thut-Moses explains the problem; he tries to control his anger "Barattarna will not attack our forts. He will not attack our strongholds. He will attack where we are weakest and I have not enough soldiers to defend every nome and town in Lower Egypt."

"We need information from *watchers* not Nubians!" Aron says. "Your Nubians cannot lead men across unfamiliar ground on a cloudy night, nor help us determine how many servants are needed to supply a Hundred for a battle after a five-day march, or how much food and water a donkey can carry from the fortress of Sileh to Gaza. And they certainly cannot slip into a Palestinian town, posing as asiatics to get the information that Pharaoh *requires*."

Thut-Moses nods in agreement. But neither does he want to needlessly antagonize the *Seeing Waters*. Thut-Moses needs the Seeing Waters. They played an important role in the eastern desert.

"I do thank Amen's high priest for his offer of *Seeing Waters*," Thut-Moses says. "We are well are well aware of how faithfully they have served Amen. And when the time comes they will serve me just as faithfully. "

"Will the Great God allow his co-Regent to speak?" Hat-Shep-Sut asks.

"I will always welcome the words of my co-Regent, Queen Hat-Shep-Sut, *foremost of distinguished women*."

"There is one who has always served me well even when I rejected his advice," Hat-Shep-Sut says. "If he would, Senen-Mut might offer a solution, don't you agree, Pen-Nek-Heb?"

"Your Majesty knows well that even now, the Lord Senen-Mut wants nothing more than to serve Pharaoh, *as well as Pharaoh's co-Regent*." Pen-Nek-Heb gives Hat-Shep-Sut a knowing look.

"Then I direct the Overseer of Pharaoh's *War Council*, the Lord Aron, to meet with the Lord Senen-Mut at the Temple of Iunu and bring back any plan that he recommends for attacking the Mitanni and their allies."

In the *Nome of Throne*, Lower Egypt's seventeenth nome, the *Bahr Yussef* canal carries the Nile's waters west to Lake Moeris, through the Faiyum depression. Lake Moeris is a natural reservoir and the main source of fresh water for the entire Nile delta. The *Anubieon* is the land on either side of the *Bahr Yussef* canal running between the Nile and Lake Moeris. It has been home to nomads from Canaan since the time of the Hyksos. Nomads living in the *Anubieon* own their own brick huts, tend flourishing gardens and raise herds of goats and sheep. While Hat-Shep-Sut and Thut-Moses have long considered the *Anubieon* a nest of Mitanni spies, its residents have enjoyed a good life.

The *Anubieon* is the home of the Temple of Anubis. Residents of the temple and the Canaanites get along quite well. The Canaanite tribes bring their offerings to the temple whenever Amen-Hotep calls them. Amen-Hotep considers the Canaanites his folk and associates of his temple. The priest believes that the Canaanites want nothing more than to raise their families and live peacefully with their Egyptian neighbors. Amen-Hotep always opposed Thut-Moses' *War Against Pharaoh's Enemies in the North* especially because it took the lives of so many of his Canaanite friends.

"They are undoubtedly loyal to the Canaanite federation organized by the Barattarna," Amen-Hotep once confided to Hat-Shep-Sut, "but not because they are loyal to the Mitanni empire. These people are loyal to Barattarna out of cultural and economic necessity. They have family still living in Palestine."

"Whatever the reason these squatters are loyal to their asiatic masters, they betray the gods and the people of the Two-Lands!" Hat-Shep-Sut retorts.

"What the *Living God* requests can be easily accomplished," Senen-Mut tells Aron. "The stars have already foretold the coming events."

Since constructing his *solar* calendar, Senen-Mut has become quite a *'stargazer'* although he is not at the level of Iunu's eminent astronomers, astrologers, or even his young assistant, Hemit.

"*Stargazing* seems to be your true calling," Aron replies.

"All must serve Pharaoh in their own ways," Senen-Mut says.

It's the first time that Aron can remember being around Senen-Mut without feeling the need to compete. Senen-Mut's smile even reminds Aron of Iby's lop-sided grin. Aron misses the spymaster as much as anyone, even as much as Senen-Mut.

Senen-Mut's plan for invading the Mitanni empire is simple. Thut-Moses should lead his army of fifteen thousand infantry and five thousand chariots ___ along with horses, supplies, food, water, pack animals and carts ____ into Palestine and capture the city of Megiddo.

"Is that his plan?" Thut-Moses scoffs. Then looking over at Hat-Shep-Sut, he says "Your priest does not seem to be able to come up with anything very brilliant for me."

"This is what Senen-Mut proposes," Aron shrugs.

"How am I going to cross the Sinai with fifteen thousand men," Thut-Moses breaks in, "without telling the world that we are coming and causing Barattarna to mobilize his Mitanni army and the entire Canaanite federation against me?"

"Perhaps Senen-Mut should be brought to Karnak," Hat-Shep-Sut suggests.

"The fact that you are blind does not matter," Senen-Mut explains. "You have no choice but to attack Barattarna before he attacks you."

"How can we attack without being seen?" Aron asks.

"You must hide the fact that your army is crossing the Sinai," Senen-Mut tells him.

"How can I conceal my army and its supplies, pack animals, food, water, everything?" Thut-Moses asks.

"You can disguise all of that and more," Senen-Mut winks, "inside a mass *exodus* of Canaanites from the Two-Lands."

Thut-Moses takes only a couple of minutes to consider Senen-Mut's plan before beaming at Hat-Shep-Sut. "You're right!" Thut-Moses declares. "*He is a genius.*"

"But how are we going to force all the squatters out of Lower Egypt?" Aron asks, still skeptical of a plan he doesn't fully understand. "Even after the *War Against Pharaoh's Enemies in the Northern Nomes* they remain in the *Anubieon*."

"Well you weren't forcing any squatters out of the *Anubieon* by attacking Egyptian soldiers were you?" Senen-Mut asks.

Aron glares at his one-time rival.

"He's got us on that one," Thut-Moses smiles. "But Aron has a point, too. How do you propose forcing the squatters out of the *Anubieon?*"

"The high priest of Anubis will lead the Canaanites out of Lower Egypt for us," Senen-Mut explains. "They trust him. They'll believe that he is trying to rescue them."

Senen-Mut explains his plan to Pharaoh's councilors and top administrators. All give their approval. For months they plan and prepare. Senen-Mut suggests sending *Seeing Waters* into key nomadic communities to mingle, befriend and interact with them.

"The *Seeing Waters* can give us important information about the chiefs of their tribes," Senen-Mut advises.

"They can eliminate anyone who learns what we are planning or appears too curious," Aron says.

"We don't want too much bloodshed, beforehand," User-Amen says. "That will only start a panic."

"I agree," Thut-Moses says.

"Then we should send the palace guard along with the *exodus*," Aron suggests. "I don't trust those Nubians. The guard can take care of Mitanni agents or anyone else attempting to warn Barattarna."

"Won't they suspect strangers in their midst," Thut-Moses reflects. "After all the asiatics living in *Anubieon* probably all know each other."

"We'll drive them out of Avaris and other towns, as well," Aron suggests, "that way there'll always be pockets of strangers, about."

"Better still," Hat-Shep-Sut suggests, "have Amen-Hotep divide them into tribes, each tribe led by one of Amen-Hotep's priests. Mingle Canaanites from the cities with those from the *Anubieon.*"

"I like that idea," Thut-Moses comments. "I don't want this rabble joining up to fight with Barattarna." Turning to Aron, he says, "I want you to make certain these Canaanites never get out of the Sinai desert."

Aron's face clouds up. "But I thought that I would be accompanying you, Great Lord," he protests, "commanding your chariots."

"If these nomads join Barattarna's army," Thut-Moses declares, "everything could be lost. I need you to make certain that doesn't happen. You must keep them wandering around in the desert."

"For how long?" Aron asks.

"At least until I can get the army out of Gaza and into Palestine. *This is important; I'm depending on you.*"

"I obey Pharaoh's command," Aron replies.

"You will need a great number of water carts to support a desert crossing," Senen-Mut observes. "Your *Seeing Waters* should be able to fill the water carts from Lake Moeris without causing Barattarna's spies to become suspicious."

"They should leave water carts every *iteru* along the route and food and fodder every two iteru."

"Won't Barattarna's spies suspect something is amiss?" Thut-Moses asks. "These asiatics are not as dumb as the Nubians."

"Possibly they will suspect something," Senen-Mut admits. "But with all the confusion, by the time Barattarna realizes what you are doing, you could be in Palestine before he can mobilize his army."

"Our goal being?"

"Megiddo!"

"*Megiddo!*" they all exclaim.

Turning to Senen-Mut, Thut-Moses says, "You have an excellent plan, except for one thing."

"What is that, Majesty?" Senen-Mut asks.

"Barattarna will still have spies even when we force this *exodus* on the Canaanites. As soon as my army marches, his spies will alert him," Thut-Moses says. "Then Barattarna will still have time to mobilize his armies, against us. How do you prevent that?"

"Trust me, Lord" Senen-Mut smiles, "All is being prepared.

Thut-Moses, his co-Regent and members of his Inner Council spend hours in his *Seal Room* planning the *exodus* of the Canaanites. Afterwards Aron and Senen-Mut travel to *Horus Nest* where they spend hours with Pharaoh's *War Council,* planning, organizing and training Pharaoh's army for the largest military invasion ever undertaken by an Egyptian pharaoh. And all this planning, organizing and training takes place in absolute secrecy. Once his plans are finalized and the army begins its mobilization, Senen-Mut returns to Iunu to enlist Hemit's aid in carrying out one of the most daring and blasphemous acts of Senen-Mut's daring invasion plans.

He enlists a gang of stonemasons and divides them into two groups. He take command of one group and Hemit the other. They lead the stonemasons on a clandestine mission to erase and deface as many of Hat-Shep-Sut's monuments and stele in the northern nomes as exist. They have little time to complete the task. Senen-Mut orders the stonemasons to deface Hat-Shep-Sut's monuments in a painstakingly precise manner. The masons chisel out Hat-Shep-Sut's images and cartouches with broad cuts slanted in one direction alternated with narrower cuts slanted in the opposite direction. One by one, Hat-Shep-Sut's images are defaced with such artistic precision, so caringly and even tenderly, that none with any imagination, at all, can doubt that this is the work of the *Consort* of the *Female Pharaoh.*

CHAPTER THIRTY-FOUR

"**M**aster!"

An acolyte bursts into Amen-Hotep's private chambers. It's the second hour of Ra's dawning. Amen-Hotep raises his eyes from the scrolls on his table.

"Yes," he replies to the intruder.

"There is a great disturbance in the *Anubieon*," the acolyte announces.

His announcement is unnecessary. For the past hour, Amen-Hotep has been hearing the muffled screams of terror and anguish.

"Yes," Amen-Hotep replies, "the disturbance has interfered with my morning rituals. What is this commotion?"

"Pharaoh's soldiers are slaying the people of the *Anubieon*," the acolyte replies.

Senen-Mut's plan begins with the slaughter of every first-born Canaanite male child. It is the shrieks of wailing mothers and the screams of dying children that alarm Amen-Hotep and cause his acolytes to race down to the *Anubieon* and witness the ghastly sights for themselves.

"Make haste, Master!" An acolyte urges Amen-Hotep. "You must put a stop to the slaughter."

Reluctantly, the priest agrees to accompany his assistants, although his naturally timid disposition is made more so by each heartrending cry. But even before Amen-Hotep settles inside his litter, a war chariot whirls through the temple pylons and blocks the high priest's exit. A muscular charioteer, wearing the bronze armor of a senior officer and carrying a bloody sword, disembarks.

Once the officer removes his helmet, Amen-Hotep recognizes Aron. Amen-Hotep dismounts his litter and bows low before the overseer of Pharaoh's *War Council.*

"My good friend and *Pharaoh's Personal Confidant,*" Amen-Hotep exclaims, "how fortunate you have arrived at this moment. Please accompany me to the *Anubieon* so that you may assist in ending this terrible disturbance. My acolytes tell me that first-born of the tribesmen are being slaughtered by Pharaoh's soldiers."

"What disturbance are you referring to, priest?" Aron replies, not offering the customary greeting.

"Certainly you heard the cries as you arrived," Amen-Hotep replies. "You can hear them even now."

"Whatever you hear, priest," Aron says, his words dripping with contempt, "it needn't concern you." Aron's face twists into a sneer. "I have come to take you before the justice of Pharaoh. The *Living God* awaits your arrival at *Horus Nest.*"

"You've come for me!" Amen-Hotep catches his breath and his eyes widen in bewilderment. "How have I offended Pharaoh's serenity?"

Ignoring the priest's question, Aron orders his guards to, "Seize him!"

Quickly, Aron's soldiers dismount their chariots and grab the old priest by his shoulders and they dump him, unceremoniously, into a donkey cart. As his acolytes look on, incredulously, Amen-Hotep is carted off to the *Bahr Yussef* where a military barge transports Aron and the high priest of Anubis back to *Horus Nest.* Upon arrival Amen-Hotep is bound and cast into a pen for animals awaiting slaughter. The priest remains in the pen, untended and unfed, for a week. At the end of the week, Amen-Hotep is brought, bound and smelling of animal manure, before Thut-Moses.

"How have I offended Pharaoh?" Amen-Hotep cries out from his knees. The Captain of the Guard places his sandal on the top of Amen-Hotep's head and mashes the priest's face into the marble floor. Thut-Moses sits upon a raised dais in the *War Council's* planning room attended by Aron, several captains of captains and a number of scribes. Pharaoh wears a slightly amused look upon his face as Aron conducts Amen-Hotep's interrogation.

"You are a lying priest, is that not so?" Aron begins, taking a menacing step towards Amen-Hotep's quivering body.

"No-o," Amen-Hotep quavers.

"You lied at the co-Regent's renewal ceremony, did you not?"

"Yes-s I did," Amen-Hotep stammers, "but you know why I did it."

"How would I know that?" Aron asks, daring Amen-Hotep to reveal their secret conversations.

"But-t it was you," Amen-Hotep says, "who convinced me that I was serving the interests of my beloved Queen."

"In any case we do not care why you did it, priest," Aron continues. "Now we only care about you daring to send your asiatic squatters to desecrate the monuments and stele of Pharaoh's co-Regent, *God's Wife* and the *foremost of distinguished women*. Did you think your impious acts would go unnoticed and unpunished?"

"What?" the priest protests. "Never have I held anything but the deepest love and adoration for her Majesty."

"You lying jackal!" Aron roars out. "Your name is reviled throughout the Two Lands for conspiring to dethrone Her Majesty. Now you seek to avenge yourself by plotting against her with those *Anubieon* squatters who spy for Barattarna. Is that not so?"

"I have ____," Amen-Hotep begins but Aron interrupts.

"Silence!" Aron roars. Pharaoh's confidant enjoys tormenting the effeminate priest who stole Hat-Shep-Sut's affections from him. Thut-Moses and his generals are enjoying the show. "Isn't it true that even while you professed to love and serve Queen Hat-Shep-Sut, during the *War Against Pharaoh's Enemies* you welcomed Pharaoh's enemies into the *Anubieon*?"

"Yes, but ____," the priest quavers.

"And isn't it true that the northern nomes remain a nest of traitors and spies for asiatics pouring over our borders?"

"Yes, I suppose so, but __."

"And isn't it true that these asiatics, these Canaanites who you call your friends, worship their own god under the guise of the Aten?"

"Yes it is true," Amen-Hotep replies. "They also pay their taxes to Pharaoh as well as to Amen."

"And to Anubis as well," Aron says.

"Yes and to Anubis," Amen-Hotep confirms.

"They secretly plotted against the co-Regent when she was Pharaoh and now they desecrate her memorials with your assistance." The charges stun Amen-Hotep into silence. With the accusations ringing in Amen-Hotep's ears, Aron continues his badgering.

"You have aided Canaanites in their treasons and treacheries, have you not?"

"No-o!" the priest of Anubis wails. "I have always served the Queen faithfully as I now serve the *Living God*."

"But you are aware that the asiatics, the Mitanni and Canaanites, even now are plotting against the peace and serenity of the Two-Lands, are you not?" Thut-Moses' voice is softer, less strident, even though it carries an unmistakable tone of authority.

"Great Lord," the priest pleads, "often did I make my views known in Pharaoh's Inner Council that the *War Upon Pharaoh's Enemies in the North* had unfortunate consequences. But my concern was for Pharaoh's welfare."

"Do you condone these asiatics unlawful behavior desecrating the monuments of the *foremost of distinguished women* now that she is no longer Pharaoh?"

"No Majesty, I do not condone their sacrileges against the serenity of *God's Wife* and the co-Regent of the Two-Lands."

"Ah!" Aron screams. "So you have been aware of what they are doing, but you have remained silent!"

"No!" Amen-Hotep cries, "I didn't mean that I was aware of their misdeeds. I only meant that I don't condone any offences against the co-Regent, of any kind."

"I wish that I could believe you," Thut-Moses says. He hesitates briefly, giving the desperate priest a reason for hope. "What can you do to restore peace among these unruly intruders?"

Before the priest can answer, Aron breaks in, "I say exterminate the rabble to the last man, woman and child! We should never have stopped the *War Against Pharaoh's Enemies*."

"Of course, that is one answer," Thut-Moses says, quietly. "We have already begun with the execution of their first born as a punishment for their affront to my co-Regent." Pharaoh gives Amen-Hotep a look of contempt masked as pity. "But is that sufficient to restore *Maat* to the northern nomes? What do *you* say, priest of Anubis?"

Amen-Hotep blurts out his response without delay. "I will serve the *Living* God in whatever way he sees fit."

"Good, priest," Thut-Moses says, nodding to Aron, "very good."

"What is it Master?" Hemit asks.

For months, Senen-Mut's helper has carried out every assignment given him without hesitation. Senen-Mut doesn't tell the initiate what he is doing or why he is doing it. Even so, Hemit obeys Senen-Mut even as he commits sacrilege upon the female Pharaoh's monuments. As an initiate of the outer temple, Hemit has taken vows. Senen-Mut has taught the initiate that there are occasions when certain behaviors, sacrilegious in themselves, are without blame when done in accordance with his vows as an initiate of the Outer Temple, especially his vow of obedience. Once Hemit and his master return to Iunu from their most unusual adventure, Hemit sees to his own projects. By keeping busy, he is relieved not to be needed for any other of Senen-Mut's strange projects. But Hemit also heard rumors that Pharaoh and God's Wife consulted the Lord Senen-Mut's counsel on yet another matter affecting the Two-Lands. Hemit had not seen his master in over two moons. But receiving a summons to Senen-Mut's chambers, he now finds himself sitting in front of a creation beyond anything he has ever seen or even imagined.

"It's the *Barque of the Aten*," Senen-Mut replies, proudly.

"Master, it's unlike any barque that I've ever seen," Hemit observes.

"I know," Senen-Mut replies. "It's like nothing I've ever seen, either."

Senen-Mut's *Barque of the Aten* is an amazing container. It's fashioned from the *shittah*-tree, known throughout the Two-Lands as the *Tree of Life*. The box contains a perfect space whose dimensions conform, in every particular, to the *golden ratio*. Overall the container measures one and a half cubits wide and high, and two and a half cubits long. Senen-Mut employs a master joiner to work the container so artfully according to a *plan* so ingenious that none without knowledge of *per-t* and its *neter* can undo it. Senen-Mut employs a master goldsmith to gild the container so that it would appear as an egg within itself. Senen-Mut has the container's secrets inscribed upon the upper lid. Only initiates of Iunu's inner temple know the keys to decoding the words and opening the lock. Senen-Mut has two golden rings installed on each side of the wondrous container.

"Here is where I need you to put two wooden poles," Senen-Mut instructs Hemit.

"Wooden poles?" Hemit asks.

"We need wooden poles sheathed in gold to transport the *Barque of the Aten*," Senen-Mut says. "The poles fit through these rings and bearers to transport the barque upon their shoulders."

"But Master," Hemit asks, "what are these?" Hemit refers to the twin winged statues facing each other on top of the golden lid.

"These are two faces of *Maat*," Senen-Mut whispers.

Senen-Mut presents his creation to Pen-Nek-Heb.

"This *Barque of the Aten*," Senen-Mut announces proudly. "It represents all that I have learned under your guidance here at the temple of the Aten."

Pen-Nek-Heb is speechless. Tears brim in his eyes and flow down his cheeks.

"It's a perfect expression of the *Golden Mean*," he declares, " and a symbol of the universal law of proportion."

"As you have taught me," Senen-Mut whispers, "it symbolizes *all* universal law."

"What's inside?" Pen-Nek-Heb asks.

"Inside I have laid the *Grid of the Master Builder*."

"You mean that you have actually enclosed *Unity?*" Pen-Nek-Heb gasps.

"It is the *Duality of Seth and Horus*," Senen-Mut says, "the *Builder of Reality* and *the Power of Existence*."

Pen-Nek-Heb can only stare at Senen-Mut's perfect representation of the *Golden Mean*.

"I will tell you the secret of its power," Senen-Mut smiles at his teacher. But then Senen-Mut hesitates, for a moment before saying, "Its power is triggered by *sound*."

Pen-Nek-Heb nods. He approves of Senen-Mut's discretion.

"What do you intend to do with this *Barque of the Aten?*" he asks.

"It is not what I intend to do with it," Senen-Mut smiles, "it is what Pharaoh intends to do with it."

On the twenty-eighth day of *Payni* during the third month of *Shemu*, while all over the Two-Lands, laborers gather in the harvest, *Seeing Waters*, and special units of Palace Guards begin gathering up asiatics from the *Anubieon* and the major towns in the northern nomes, driving their captives into the Sinai desert. A week later, at *Horus Nest*, a regiment of palace guard, in the garb of asiatic nomads, prepares to join the *exodus* of the Canaanite nomads. Thut-Moses reviews the groups of Hundreds as they depart.

"Everything is going well," Thut-Moses remarks. "This will be our best adventure ever."

"I wish I could remain by your side," Aron mutters.

"You'll be there soon enough," Thut-Moses replies.

Just watching his cadres' depart, Thut-Moses feels the exhilaration of a conqueror.

Once Aron's special guard units depart *Horus Nest*, Thut-Moses begins the general mobilization of his regular infantry and cavalry regiments.

"I still do not understand how you intend to disguise your fifteen thousand man army following after us," Aron says. He tarries at *Horus Nest* long after his palace guard has departed. A look of concern clouds his face.

Thut-Moses laughs at his 'uncle's' concern. "They won't be disguised," he says, "they'll be explained."

"Explained!" Aron's eyes express his cynicism. "Explained how?"

"With this!" Thut-Moses indicates a cart nearby, bearing Senen-Mut's *Barque of the Aten*. "Once you are well into the desert, you will discover my barque among the belongings of one of Amen-Hotep's acolytes."

"You want me to have this cart placed among the belongings of Anubis' temple staff?" Aron asks.

"Yes, that's it," Thut-Moses says. "Have this cart covered with baggage from the temple so that when it's discovered it looks as if someone from Anubis' temple took it.

"My guard is to discover it, when?"

"Three or four days into the exodus."

"Then what am I to do?" Aron asks.

"Have Amen-Hotep convene a *Court of Justice* to try the thief. And when he is found guilty have him publicly executed. In the meantime, send messengers back here to *Horus Nest* with the news that Amen-Hotep has recovered *Pharaoh's Barque of the Aten*. Broadcast throughout the entire asiatic rabble that I approach with my entire army to reclaim this sacred treasure. Before our friend, Barattarna, knows anything we should be in Gaza and on our way to Megiddo."

"You have the wisdom of Thoth, My Lord," Aron exclaims. "I will do as you command."

"Then you may proceed, my *Loyal Companion*," Thut-Moses smiles, "and may Amen guide your way and give you success."

Aron gives Pharaoh a military salute, wields his chariot and, escorted by his personal guard, leads the cart bearing the precious *Barque of the Aten* out of the gate.

Thut-Moses marches his army north through the "Sea of Reeds" the marshy region north of the Gulf of Suez. Then they pass over the "Bitter Lakes". Pharaoh's army follows several days behind the wake of the exiting Canaanites. Undetected and unopposed, Thut-Moses takes nine days to move his regiments the forty *iteru* across the Sinai desert from Memphis to Gaza. At Gaza, Aron turns the Canaanite tribes east, leading them further into the Sinai desert while Thut-Moses marches his army another nine days up the Palestinian coast to the treacherous Aruna Pass. But now, Thut-Moses has lost his surprise.

The Egyptians have invaded! The cry echoes throughout Palestine. Canaanite tribes assemble and begin massing to intercept the Egyptian invaders at two possible locations. The Canaanites believe that the Egyptians will march either up the coast of the Great Green Sea or through the Jezreel valley. These are the safest routes to Megiddo. Either route allows Thut-Moses to deploy his chariots and protect his infantry's flanks. However both routes dramatically increase the distance his army must travel compared to a third shorter and more direct route through the Aruna Pass. Pharaoh's *Seeing Waters* report that Canaanite tribes are assembling in force to intercept the Egyptians both along the coast as well as up through the valley, but are absent from the Aruna Pass.

"That's because they don't need an army to defend the Aruna Pass!" one of Thut-Moses' generals scoffs. "All they need to do is roll a few rocks down on us and less than a Unit of Ten will get to Megiddo."

The precipitous Aruna Pass is a narrow rocky corridor that at times has a sheer drop off the face of a cliff. If Thut-Moses takes this route, his whole army will be strung out in single file. His chariots must be disassembled and transported on supply wagons. If the Canaanites catch Egyptian army crossing the Aruna Pass, they will annihilate it. All Pharaoh's generals advise him against taking the route. After eighteen days of continuous marching Thut-Moses' soldiers are exhausted and their morale is low. When rumors circulate through the ranks that Pharaoh wants to cross through the Aruna Pass, the men grumble. Thut-Moses regrets not having Aron with him.

My generals are more timid than my co-Regent, Thut-Moses mutters to himself. *What kind of fight are they going to wage when we meet our enemies.*

Though Thut-Moses argues with his generals that the Aruna Pass offers their best opportunity to conquer Megiddo, his generals resist.

"Majesty, your army is tired," they complain. "You cannot ask your men to do the impossible. *They will desert you!*"

Finally, his patience exhausted, Thut-Moses decides to behead one of his generals. He would like to behead the general who denounced Thut-Moses' plans to his soldiers causing low morale and a loss of confidence in Pharaoh among the troops.

Thut-Moses sends informants out to discover which regiment's officers speak most openly against Pharaoh's war plans. Thut-Moses vows to decorate a pole with the head if the general who commands these officers. Once again, Pharaoh calls his generals together, as if to reconsider the plan of march upon Megiddo. However before identifying the wretch that he intends to punish, his *Seeing Waters* return from their mission scouting the Aruna Pass. These *Seeing Waters* are the same scouts who accompanied Thut-Moses on his adventure in Nubia's eastern desert and he trusts them.

"What have you learned?" Pharaoh asks. His voice ripples with the irritation he feels for his generals.

"Great Lord!" the leader says as they 'kiss the ground' before Thut-Moses. "We traveled from Aruna over the heights to the plains before Megiddo, as you instructed."

Thut-Moses' face brightens. "What did you find?" he asks.

"Nothing, Lord," one scout answers.

"You saw no tribesmen or Mitanni soldiers?"

"No Majesty," the scout replies. "The Aruna Pass is completely clear."

"Do you hear that?" Thut-Moses calls out to his generals. "The Aruna Pass is clear."

"But Great Lord," the commander of the Seth regiment whines, "just as you sent scouts to spy on this pass, so might the Canaanites have spies watching to see if we choose this route. If they see us crossing these heights, they can summon their forces from where they await us now."

The other generals agree. Thut-Moses, himself, must admit that the risk is great.

"Majesty," the leader of the *Seeing Waters* speaks out. "We serve the *Living God* in all ways."

"Speak!" Thut-Moses replies.

"If the *Living God* says the word, we will guarantee that Canaanite tribesmen will neither spy upon Pharaoh's host as it passes through Aruna," the *Seeing Waters* leader says, "nor live to report anything to Barattarna or his allies."

It is what Thut-Moses wants to hear. His mind is made up. He will ignore his *War Council* and drive his army through the Aruna Pass directly upon *Megiddo*.

"Majesty," one of his generals announces, "my men will be unable to accompany Pharaoh on this impossible march."

The other generals seem intent upon supporting their comrade.

"Guards," Thut-Moses shouts. "Arrest that man." Pharaoh points to the offending general. "Now," Thut-Moses asks his other regimental commanders, "is there anyone else who refuses my orders?"

All the other officers quickly fall to their knees.

"Good," Thut-Moses says, "very good."

Pharaoh's gamble pays off. As promised, the corps of *Seeing Waters* attached to the *War Council* scours the Aruna Pass and the surrounding heights for Canaanites. They capture and execute every tribesman they find. It takes Thut-Moses army two days to march single file through the pass. They leave the baggage train with supplies behind under the guard of the now disgraced *Seth* regiment with the head of their commanding general sitting on a pole outside his tent.

Not only do the generals of Pharaoh's other regiments give their complete support for the plan, but their men as well. Pharaoh takes ten thousand men on an amazing three-day feat of strength, endurance and courage. On the morning of the fourth day, sentries on the walls of Megiddo are surprised by the sight of an Egyptian host, three infantry regiments flanked by chariots, assembled on the broad plain in front of its gates.

Amidst the sounding of war trumpets, the beating of drums and the thunderous shouts of acclaim, the entire Egyptian army parades past Pharaoh, battle armor glittering, flags fluttering and the standards of each battle regiment held aloft in the morning sun. At the rear of the battle formation, chariot horses paw the ground, eager to begin racing towards their asiatic foes.

Standing in his chariot of dazzling gold and silver and wearing the blue war crown of Horus, Thut-Moses divides his army into three fighting groups. One positioned to the northwest of Megiddo, another located on a hill near the brook of Qina and the third, commanded by Thut-Moses, himself, at the center.

In a mighty charge, the army from the Two-Lands bursts across the plain and explodes upon the Canaanite tribesmen assembled to oppose them. The Egyptians slaughter the Canaanites with ease. Barattarna's allies are so overwhelmed that they flee the battlefield abandoning weapons and equipment. Once the battle is over, Thut-Moses sends his messengers back to Thebes with the news of his victory.

The muffled cries of celebration penetrate even the seclusion of Karnak where Hat-Shep-Sut sits in her palace, renamed *Truth Is The Soul Of The Sun.*

"Now you are truly the *Foremost of Distinguished Ladies.*" Senen-Mut says. He has come to congratulate the co-Regent.

"I understand that you had my monuments defaced," Hat-Shep-Sut replies. Her words carry neither rancor nor anger.

"I did many of them myself," Senen-Mut smiles.

"I suppose it gave you great satisfaction," Hat-Shep-Sut surmises watching the man she has both loved and hated for so many years. A coy smile to brightens her still lovely face.

"Well, I must admit," Senen-Mut replies, "that I felt as though I were stripping away the façade of your images like I was removing barnacles from the bottom of the royal barge."

"Hmm," Hat-Shep-Sut says, "I must return the favor one day."

"I hope you will." Senen-Mut replies.

It takes nine months before Megiddo finally falls. Afterwards, Thut-Moses takes the sons of princes of Megiddo and other major Palestinian cities back to the Two-Lands as hostages.

Pharaoh Menkh-Kheperu-Re Thut-Moses leads many more campaigns throughout Canaan and into Syria. Eight years after the battle of Megiddo, he captures Kadesh on the Orontes. For the remainder of his rule, the whole of Palestine remains an Egyptian province and all the tribes of Palestine pay Thut-Moses an annual tribute.

Following his conquest of Palestine, Thut-Moses expands his navy and builds massive troop ships capable of transporting his army up the Great Green Sea and down into the Tigris Valley. Soon he is able to reach into the heart of the Mitanni Empire. Over the next twenty years, Thut-Moses wages military campaigns throughout Persia exacting tribute from the Assyrian, Babylonian and Hittite kings. Despite twenty years of military success, Thut-Moses never defeats Barattarna or the Mitanni Empire.

While Thut-Moses III wages war against the asiatics for a twenty-year period, Queen Maat-Ka-Re Hat-Shep-Sut, the Foremost of Distinguished Women, rules the Two-Lands as the co-Regent. Her consort, Senen-Mut, a commoner, remains by her side.

My literary interest in ancient Egypt and the Eighteenth Dynasty began with Allen Drury's *A God Against Gods* and *Return To Thebes*. In her books, *Winged Pharaoh, Lord of the Horizon, Eyes of Horus* and *So Moses Was Born*, Joan Grant's "far memory" ____ recalling the lives of the Pharaohs, their courts and their people during the Eleventh, Twelfth and Nineteenth Egyptian Dynasties ____ brings Egypt out of the tombs and into the temple. Other novels specifically about Hat-Shep-Sut ____ including Paul Doherty's *The Mask of Ra*, Moyra Caldecott, *Hatshepsut: Daughter of Amun* and Maria Isabel Pita's *Truth Is The Soul Of The Sun* ____ are not quite as vivid.

My historical facts come from a variety of scholarly sources including *Black Athena* by Martin Bernal, History of Ancient Egypt by the German scholar, Erik Hornung, Temples of Ancient Egypt edited by Byron Slater, The Literature of Ancient Egypt by William Kelly Simpson and Barbara Watterson's Women in Ancient Egypt. I found intellectual whimsy in Joyce Tyldesley's book, Hatchepsut [sic]: The Female Pharaoh as well as Egypt: Revisited edited by Van Sertima. These scholarly works raised questions, riddles, enigmas and mysteries, but, for 'enlightenment', I had to search elsewhere. Isha Schwaller de Lubicz's Her-Bak: The Living Face of Ancient Egypt and Her-Bak: The Egyptian Initiate, unlocked the intellectual truths and eternal verities found in The Temple of Man, the major work by R.A. Schwaller de Lubicz. I still remained in complete darkness, however, until I gained some rudimentary understanding of hieroglyphics.

I began with E.A. Wallis Budge's **An Egyptian Hieroglyphic Reading Book for Beginners, The Gods of the Egyptians, The Egyptian Book of the Dead** and **An Egyptian Hieroglyphic Dictionary**. But as diligent as I was, Budge did not speak to me. It was not until I discovered **How To Read Egyptian Hieroglyphics: A Step-By-Step Guide To Teach Yourself**, co-authored by Mark Collier and Bill Manley _____ complemented by Mark Millmore's **Imagining Egypt** _____ that I achieved the rudimentary understanding of hieroglyphics that enabled to write this book.

Eugene Stovall